LADY OF THE NIGHT

"Invite me outside," she whispered.

Before anyone could interject a dance request, Nolan slid his arm around Laura's waist and shepherded her toward the terrace door. "I could use a breath of fresh air while we continue our conversation on Shakespeare," Nolan announced loudly to all within hearing distance. "I would certainly like to hear why you think England's greatest contribution to the literary world has a dark, unpublicized side to his personality—"

The discreet jab in the ribs sent Nolan's breath out in a *whoosh*. He made a mental note that the dainty, sophisticated lady was as good at hand-to-hand combat as she was with pistols and arrows. He would do well to remember that.

Once they were out of earshot of the other guests, Laura halted in front of Nolan, staring at him with pensive deliberation. "I have the inescapable feeling you are going to make a nuisance of yourself, Mr. Beecham."

"Odd, I find myself thinking the same thing about you, my lady," he countered. "And while we are on the subject of nuisances, I advise you to keep your distance from Geoffrey Spradlin. I have heard several nasty rumors about that oafish officer."

"And I advise you to mind your own business and leave me to mine. I'm quite capable of fending for myself . . ."

And to Nolan's stunned amazement, Laura slid her arms over his shoulders, pushed up on tiptoe and kissed him full on the mouth . . .

Pinnacle Books is proud to present this third book in a series of exciting romances where the hero takes center stage. Experience love through *his* eyes and rapture in *his* arms. Discover romance as you never have before . . . with the hero of your dreams. Let the Midnight Rider take you on a ride of mystery and adventure into the dark unknown where passion and desire rule the heart and the soul . . .

IF ROMANCE BE THE FRUIT OF LIFE—
READ ON—
BREATH-QUICKENING HISTORICALS FROM PINNACLE

WILDCAT   (772, $4.99)
by Rochelle Wayne
No man alive could break Diana Preston's fiery spirit . . . until seductive Vince Gannon galloped onto Diana's sprawling family ranch. Vince, a man with dark secrets, would sweep her into his world of danger and desire. And Diana couldn't deny the powerful yearnings that branded her as his own, for all time!

THE HIGHWAY MAN   (765, $4.50)
by Nadine Crenshaw
When a trumped-up murder charge forced beautiful Jane Fitzpatrick to flee her home, she was found and sheltered by the highwayman—a man as dark and dangerous as the secrets that haunted him. As their hiding place became a place of shared dreams—and soaring desires—Jane knew she'd found the love she'd been yearning for!

SILKEN SPURS   (756, $4.99)
by Jane Archer
Beautiful Harmony Harper, leader of a notorious outlaw gang, rode the desert plains of New Mexico in search of justice and vengeance. Now she has captured powerful and privileged Thor Clarke-Jargon, who is everything Harmony has ever hated—and all she will ever want. And after Harmony has taken the handsome adventurer hostage, she herself has become a captive—of her own desires!

WYOMING ECSTASY   (740, $4.50)
by Gina Robins
Feisty criminal investigator, July MacKenzie, solicits the partnership of the legendary half-breed gunslinger-detective Nacona Blue. After being turned down, July—never one to accept the meaning of the word no—finds a way to convince Nacona to be her partner . . . first in business—then in passion. Across the wilds of Wyoming, and always one step ahead of trouble, July surrenders to passion's searing demands!

Available wherever paperbacks are sold, or order direct from the Publisher. Send cover price plus 50¢ per copy for mailing and handling to Penguin USA, P.O. Box 999, c/o Dept. 17109, Bergenfield, NJ 07621. Residents of New York and Tennessee must include sales tax. DO NOT SEND CASH.

Midnight's Lady
Debra Falcon

PINNACLE BOOKS
WINDSOR PUBLISHING CORP.

PINNACLE BOOKS are published by

Windsor Publishing Corp.
850 Third Avenue
New York, NY 10022

First Printing: February, 1995

Printed in the United States of America

This book is dedicated to my husband Ed and our children Christie, Jill and Kurt, with much love.

One

Golden flames cartwheeled through the darkness as a glowing torch landed amid the six British soldiers who trotted their horses toward Boston's wharf. Horses whinnied, reared and darted sideways, defying their scowling riders.

Peter Forbes, lieutenant in His Majesty's Army, spat a string of curses when the darkly clad rider appeared out of nowhere. The daring rebel charged straight through the middle of the armed patrol and thundered away on his devil stallion.

"Bloody damned patriot," one of the soldiers muttered before he broke rank and gave chase.

Before Lieutenant Forbes could regroup his men, the whole lot of them lurched off in pursuit of the unidentified patriot who was turning the Crown's men into an army of blundering clowns. The £500 placed on the Midnight Rider's head by the Royal Commission of Inquiry was tempting lure, and the soldiers and sentries had been chasing this phantom dressed in black for months, without success.

The elusive horseman had come to be known by many names, none of them complimentary. Some of the British soldiers stationed along the colonial coast called him the Dark Phantom who inspired his flock of dissenting rebels. Others called him the Midnight Rider who materialized in the darkness and vanished as if he had never been there at all. But no matter what name the specter went by, he had become a nuisance and an embarrassment to the king's troops.

Still swearing profusely, Lieutenant Forbes raced after the Patriot Rider. 'Twas a merry chase—as usual. Peter watched the caped shadow hunker down on the midnight-colored stallion and dart between the trees, marveling at the man's impressive equestrian skills.

The lead soldier yelped in surprise when his horse cut sideways to avoid a tree. The sound of human flesh colliding with wood caused Peter to grimace. The unhorsed soldier had no sooner slumped to the ground when Peter heard another pained groan. The second soldier was scraped off his saddle by a low-hanging branch and landed spread-eagle on the grass.

While the fallen soldiers hauled themselves to their feet to round up their mounts, Peter forged ahead of the faltering posse. His gaze was transfixed on the fleeing silhouette ahead of him. Nothing would make Peter happier than tracking down this nuisance-of-a-rebel and tossing him in the dungeon at Castle William. Capturing the Patriot Rider would earn Peter a hefty reward, not to mention a prestigious promotion. 'Twould also go a long way in squelching the rebellious spirit of these cloddish colonials who defied the Crown's decrees every chance they got.

These independent-minded bumpkins had lost all respect for regal authority, Peter reminded himself as he gouged his steed into a faster pace. These rebels had come to the outrageous conclusion that they could— and should— have the right to govern themselves. The secretive Sons of Liberty, who had a stronghold in Boston, were inflaming the minds of citizens in other colonies with defiance and rebellion. The sooner the unruly lot of dissenters were rounded up and herded to jail the better Peter would like it . . .

Peter's resentful thoughts trailed off when the Midnight Rider raced through the wrought-iron gates of the cemetery situated on the outskirts of town. The wind died into eerie silence, broken only by the thud of hooves on mellow ground. Peter caught his breath and stared in amazement when the elusive shadow leaped over a granite headstone and darted between the monuments that stood cold and quiet against the night.

"Blast it," one of the soldiers grumbled as he reined up beside Lieutenant Forbes. "That devil has no fear of God or man. Just look at him! He's riding through a bloody graveyard— "

The soldier's voice trailed off when the peal of distant bells struck the midnight hour. To the disbelieving eyes of the soldiers who halted at the cemetery gate, the shapeless shadow and steed disappeared into a clump of trees, encircled by tombstones.

"Holy—" Peter swallowed his breath when the devil stallion emerged from the trees without its rider. The powerful steed cleared the iron fence on the far side of the graveyard in a single bound and disappeared down the hill.

The night grew silent. Peter heard nothing but his own accelerated pulse drumming in his ears, saw nothing but the silhouettes of tombstones in the moonlight. "We should investigate," he declared.

"Investigate a graveyard at midnight?" one of the underling soldiers croaked. "I'd rather not, if you don't mind, Lieutenant. It seems ill-advised to me. If that devilish rebel disturbed the spirits, I don't want to be the one who catches hell for it."

Peter Forbes inhaled a determined breath and nudged his mount forward. " 'Tis superstitious nonsense. We are going to finish what we began. That pesky patriot will be easier to chase down on foot than on horseback."

"I'm not altogether sure ghosts have feet," came the disgruntled comment from the left flank.

Reluctantly, the soldiers followed their commander along the dirt path and then positioned themselves around the clump of trees into which the mysterious rider had disappeared. All eyes lifted to scan the outreaching tree limbs, but there was nothing except for the usual leaves and twigs.

A lone raven took to its wings with a heckling

squawk. In silence, the British guards watched the bird soar off into the night.

"Upon my word, Lieutenant. I swear that Midnight Rider really *is* a phantom."

"Don't be ridiculous," Peter snorted, as much for his own benefit as for his men's. "The Midnight Rider is only a man and he doesn't practice sorcery."

"Couldn't prove it by me, sir. I think he just changed forms and flitted off in the wind."

Peter twisted on the saddle to fling his men a condescending glance. "That rebel has to be around here somewhere."

"Then where is he?"

Peter had no answer to that question. He took careful inventory of his surroundings. There was no coiled human form clinging to the branches overhead, no cloaked figure lurking behind the headstones. From all indication, Peter and his men were the only *living* souls in the burying ground.

Heaving a resigned sigh, Peter reined his steed back in the direction he had come. "We've wasted enough time on this wild-goose chase. Our orders were to patrol the wharf to intercept incoming revenue cutters that might be bringing contraband ashore at night to avoid paying tariffs."

"Aye, I'm for getting out of here as fast as possible," one of the men muttered uneasily. " 'Tis the last time I'll go chasing after that phantom. The King may as well have put a £3000 reward on that pesky patriot's head— "

"Or even £5000, for all the good 'twill bloody

well do any of us who try to collect it," came the disgruntled interruption. "You can't catch a man who isn't there."

Peter led the procession of baffled soldiers toward the docks, mulling over the unsettling events of the evening. The torch of liberty, which had become the mysterious rider's signature, seemed the only evidence that he existed. The rider had become a puzzling enigma who appeared at will and disappeared in the blink of an eye.

The colonists drew encouragement from the tales of the Midnight Rider's ability to elude patrols. That darkly clad patriot had become the symbol of the army's inability to suppress rebels who objected to strict enforcement of the Navigation Acts which levied taxes on imports, and the Quartering Act which decreed that Americans were to provide billeting for British soldiers. Worse, the Stamp Act— which was to go into effect within the next few months to pay the debts England incurred during the French and Indian Wars— had these belligerent colonials completely up in arms.

And of course, Peter reminded himself, the Writs of Assistance which allowed soldiers to search for smuggled cargo had these bumpkins in another uproar. They protested each time sentries inspected their warehouses. Led by the Midnight Rider, mobs threatened and intimidated stamp distributors into resigning their positions before the Stamp Act went into effect.

The colonies had become a keg of gunpowder set to fuse. Each time Parliament tried to clamp down on these rebellious misfits and keep them dependent on England, they loudly objected. Were it not for the standing army that monitored colonial activities, Peter shuddered to think how far out of line these bumpkins would have stepped by now.

Peter shrugged off his unsuccessful pursuit of the Rebel Rider and concentrated on scouting the harbor for incoming skiffs. He had received a tip that a revenue cutter was due in from the West Indies, planning to unload sugar and molasses without paying taxes to Customs agents.

If Peter could capture the ring of smugglers it would put a feather in his cap and boost him up another step on the military ladder. Then perhaps he would be in a position to ask for the hand of the stunning female who had stolen his heart without even trying . . .

The captivating vision of Laura Chandler overshadowed all previous thought. Even if Peter couldn't apprehend the Midnight Rider, he would be well satisfied to win that auburn-haired siren's affection. Just thinking of Laura made Peter's blood run hot. He had become the envy of all the Crown's men stationed in Boston when he had been quartered in the same house where the most sought-after beauty in town resided.

Peter smiled to himself as he moved toward the wharf. If he wasn't mistaken— and he preferred to think he *wasn't*— Laura Chandler had developed a fond attachment for him over the past few months. He had watched her beaus come and go, but Laura, who was reputed to be extremely particular about the company she kept, had not been charmed by any of the locals. She had reached the age of three and twenty without being lured into marriage.

Some rejected suitors claimed Laura was as fickle as the winds, or that she was too particular to settle for anything less than a crowned prince. Peter, however, had concluded that Laura had simply remained unwed so long that she had developed a strong mind of her own and wasn't easily swayed by the usual wiles men applied in courtship.

Laura resided with her wealthy, widowed aunt in a household that was without masculine influence. Since Laura had yet to take a husband, male attitudes and opinions had not been forced on her when she was young and impressionable. She had discovered her own identity and thrived on her sense of individuality. 'Twas part of her fascinating lure, Peter reminded himself. He enjoyed the challenge Laura presented, her quick wit and her intelligence.

But winning Laura's respect and affection could not be accomplished overnight, Peter had discovered. Laura was no empty-headed twit. She had a unique worldliness about her, a craving for excitement and adventure that captivated men.

Peter had made encouraging headway with Laura the past two months. And why shouldn't he? After all, he had been raised a gentleman in God's country— England. He possessed the kind of British pluck and confidence that cultured females appreciated and admired. In a few more months, after Peter had courted Laura with an English gentleman's sense of propriety, he would ask for her hand in marriage. When his tour of duty in the American outback ended, he would take Laura to England where a woman of her exceptional wit and beauty could flourish.

Peter rearranged his scarlet jacket and led his patrol down the dock. Aye, imagining himself strolling arm in arm with Laura Chandler was a far more pleasant pastime than rehashing his cross-country chase only to watch the Midnight Rider vanish into thin air. That rabble-rouser was a clever escape artist, to be sure, but he was no devil phantom, Peter assured himself. Even if the superstitious soldiers under his command preferred to spread fantastic rumors to explain their inability to apprehend the elusive patriot . . .

Peter's thoughts trailed off when he saw the torch of liberty still flickering on the wharf. In proud defiance, Peter walked his horse over the symbol of rebel spirit and continued on his way.

The waters of the bay glistened in the moonlight, but Peter saw no sign of skiffs coming ashore to unload their illegal cargo. After checking his timepiece, Peter dismissed his patrol and turned his horse toward the stately mansion on Beacon Hill. He would like nothing better than to spend the night in Laura's silky arms, rather than relieving his cravings with Mercy Reed, the indentured servant who made herself available to him.

Mercy Reed was aptly named, Peter decided as he trotted down the street. The plain-looking but accommodating housemaid provided *mercy* for a man who was unable to enjoy the charms of the woman he really wanted.

One day soon, Peter promised himself faithfully, he wouldn't have to settle for a substitute. He would lay claim to the lovely object of his affection. He simply had to be patient when dealing with the bewitching Laura Chandler. That fascinating female would be well worth the wait.

Two

Nolan Ryder lay flat on his back, his hands clasped on his belly. He stared up at the slab of stone concealing him from the British patrol he had lured away from the wharf. The sound of his own breath echoed around his rock sepulcher, assuring him that he was still very much alive, despite the soldiers' comments to the contrary.

Once the British guardsmen reversed direction and rode away, Nolan waited an extra quarter of an hour to ensure that the coast was clear. Although he didn't give a thought to dodging bullets during high-speed cross-country chases, he refused to emerge from his tomb to find unfriendly guests waiting to greet him— or capture him, as the case would be. Nolan had no intention of allowing the Brits to know he wasn't as dead as they presumed him to be. Furthermore, he had a considerable amount of business to attend to before he was well and truly buried six feet under.

Nolan braced his hands on the thin slab of granite above him and gently eased it down until he could sit erect. After rising to his feet, he slid the veneer of stone back into place. His gaze drifted to the headstone in front of him and he smiled wryly as he tugged the black hood from his head.

R.I.P.
NOLAN RYDER
Beloved son and brother
Born 1735   Died 1763

There were times when being presumed dead had distinct advantages, Nolan reminded himself. This was one of those times.

He unfastened his flowing cape and tucked it under his arm. Pivoting on his heels, he followed the skirting of trees to find the gray gelding that Spark McRae had left for him.

For a man who had ceased to exist a few years hence, Nolan had certainly led a busy life. From no identity at all to a double identity, Nolan mused as he effortlessly swung onto the saddle. Aye, his life had changed drastically over the past few years. But change was something Nolan appreciated, was familiar with— always had been.

Change, Nolan had determined, after becoming a wanderlust for the past two years, was a method of marking the passage of time, a way of measuring progress, of testing his abilities to their limits. He even felt the unexplained compulsion to rearrange his surroundings at irregular intervals, just to give life a new look. Spark McRae claimed Nolan's penchant for rearranging furniture— as well as his personal possessions— was peculiar. Nolan called it necessary, natural.

Everything changed, after all, Nolan had always contended. Perspectives, seasons, life's wants and needs were subject to alteration. Constant change quelled the restlessness that spurred Nolan, even when he had been no more than a child. His family claimed he had been born under a wandering star and that he was instinctively driven to follow it. Whatever the case, Nolan had never been satisfied to remain in the same place for extended periods of time. It seemed he was restless by nature and by habit.

Change also eased bitter memories of a past that refused to die— even if Nolan supposedly had. Constant change, new scenery, and noble purpose motivated Nolan Ryder. His troubled past clambered so closely on his heels that he was forever trying to outrun it— trying to forgive himself for what he had *not* been able to change . . .

Hearing the rustle in the underbrush, Nolan jerked up his head, his senses on full alert. In the batting of an eyelash, Nolan had his pistol in hand and he prepared himself to meet danger head-on.

Spark McRae emerged from the bushes, leading the coal-black stallion behind him. He tossed Nolan a sidelong glance and gave his gray head a resigning shake.

"You just can't keep from shavin' another layer off the cuttin' edge with those patrols, can you? I know you like to see how many consequences you can damn, all in the same night, but seems to me that if those redcoats could've gotten a clear shot, you would be a dead man right about now."

Nolan shrugged carelessly. "I *am* a dead man."

The crusty old frontiersman stared consideringly at his younger friend. "You know, there's times when I think ye'r tryin' to fulfill the prophesy engraved on yer headstone."

"Why not? 'Twas my own brother who buried me," Nolan replied as he led the way down the tree-lined path.

"Aye, and I've heard yer brother apologize all over himself for yer premature funeral," Spark tossed back.. "How was Ethan supposed to know the report Major Stewart sent to him was false?"

"The report was wishful thinking."

Nolan's silver gray eyes darkened at the unpleasant memories associated with the man he held personally responsible for his torment. Major Isaac Stewart had paved the pathway to his private niche in hell, Nolan mused resentfully. Too bad that pompous English bastard didn't have a conscience that would torment him until he reached his eternal destination— a place where the hottest of all possible climates prevailed.

"Whatever the case, I'd appreciate it if you'd put a bit more breathin' space between yerself and the British lobsterbacks while ye'r distractin' them. I'm gettin' too old to have ten years scared off my life every time you pull one of those death-defyin' stunts." Spark ran a meaty hand through his crop of unruly hair and stared meaningfully at Nolan. "Now that you've become the symbol of invincible rebel spirit, it wouldn't be good for morale to have you shot off yer devil stallion. As for myself, I've grown accustomed to havin' you around, and so has yer older brother. Ethan's become fanatic about keepin' you alive after he discovered you weren't as dead as the Brits thought you was."

"I'm deeply touched by your sentimentality, as well as my brother's," Nolan mocked as he ducked beneath a low-hanging limb.

"You know what yer problem is? You've forgotten what fear is. Ye'r too darin' for yer own good, boy."

"I had little choice tonight." Nolan defended himself. "If the patrol had reached the wharf, Ethan's shipment of smuggled goods from the Indies would have been confiscated and he would have landed in jail. I had to intervene and I had to do it quickly. Someone obviously tipped off the British."

Spark's thick chest rose and fell in an audible sigh. "The patrol's timin' was uncanny, wasn't it?"

Nolan snorted disdainfully. "Uncanny? I have the inescapable feeling that we have an informant in our midst, one who is selling juicy tidbits to the scarlet coats."

Spark stared incredulously at Nolan. "Ye'r jokin'. Surely you don't think any of the Loyal Nine or the Sons of Liberty would betray one of their own kind."

" 'Tis becoming alarmingly clear to me that we have a traitor in our rebel network. I'd bet my life on it."

"Which life? The one you supposedly lost a few years ago or the two ye'r leadin' now?"

Nolan gestured westward, ignoring the sarcastic

comment. "Take the stallion back to the cottage before a wandering patrol spots him. I'm going to make sure Ethan's cargo was rowed ashore without Customs officers breathing down his neck."

When Spark veered off, Nolan headed toward the marshes. He found his brother and the ship's crew loading smuggled imports into wagons to be distributed to Boston merchants.

"You saved our necks, little brother," Ethan murmured when he saw Nolan emerge from the shadows. "Things were getting a mite tense around here earlier. We saw the British patrol heading this way and we feared we would be caught red-handed."

While Captain Romby and the sailors loaded the last of the cargo in the wagons, Nolan carefully scanned the surroundings. After the wagons rolled away, Nolan glanced grimly at Ethan. "I have a hunch that someone tipped off the Brits," he confided. "The patrols are cracking down on colonial smuggling in every port along the coast. They have no intention of allowing you and the other merchants to escape paying their outrageous taxes."

Ethan shook his head and sighed. "You still believe there is a Tory spy among us, don't you?"

"Indeed, the want of a gold coin can make a man do practically anything," Nolan contended. "The patrol's appearance tonight was too timely to be coincidental."

Ethan studied his brother's shadowed face and powerful physique. It never failed to amaze him that he and Nolan shared the same bloodlines. Two years Ethan's junior, Nolan stood six feet two inches in his stocking feet and weighed a solid two hundred and twenty pounds. His eyes were the color of mercury and his hair was as black as coal. Ethan, on the other hand, stood five feet ten inches in his boots, was prone to sunburn if he went without a hat and coat, and his eyes were cedar-tree green. In short, never had two peas— shelled from the same pod— differed so much in appearance and behavior.

Nolan had been an adventuresome daredevil since the day he learned to crawl. Ethan had been born cautious, and took chances when he was left with no other choice. He functioned on forethought and logic while Nolan relied on instinct and hunches. As children they neutralized each other. As grown men, their differences divided them.

Of course, the ordeals Nolan had endured during the Seven Years War had noticeably affected him. He had become more cynical and mistrusting, hardened by untold experiences of battle, and he had grown as keenly alert as a stalking tiger and as daring as the devil himself. Ethan was also certain his brother couldn't remain in the same place, even if he was planted in it. Nolan possessed more restless energy than a man naturally ought to have. As for Nolan's suspicious streak it had been driven bone-deep these thirty years.

"Despite your hunch, I have the utmost confidence in the Sons of Liberty and Committee of Correspondence," Ethan insisted. "We are all devoted to preserving our rights, protesting unrepresented taxation and establishing a sovereign government."

"You were always too idealistic."

"And you have become even more cynical and skeptical since— "

"I have valid reason," Nolan cut in quickly. "I suspect one of our compatriots was paid handsomely to notify the Crown's sentries when incoming revenue cutters are due to arrive."

Ethan fell silent. As much as he hated to admit it, the British soldiers *had* been showing up at inconvenient times— and with alarming regularity. Ethan preferred to believe that the reason for tonight's near-discovery lay in the Crown's policy of clamping down on colonial trade with the French, Dutch and Spanish West Indies by increasing the number of roving patrols. Nolan obviously had his own theory.

Nolan had lived in a war zone beyond the Appalachians before he took to hunting and trapping and honing his skills of self-defense in the untamed wilderness. These days, when Nolan wasn't posing as a Tory dandy to acquire information, he was leading demonstrations and diverting attention away from the wharf to protect his brother and the other Boston merchants. Since Nolan was involved in espionage himself, he was understandably suspicious.

"Even if you have complete faith in the members of our supposedly loyal society, I intend to have a closer look at them when they meet at the

Green Dragon Tavern tomorrow night," Nolan announced.

"Oh, for God's sake, Nolan— "

"Nay," Nolan corrected, flinging Ethan a hard, unyielding stare. "For *liberty's* sake. As cautious as you have always been, I expected you to agree that it's become necessary to question the reason why the Crown's men arrive at the right places at just the right time."

Ethan expelled an exasperated breath. "Fine, keep surveillance on the members of our secret clan, but don't be surprised to discover every member of our society is devoted to the restoration of our provincial governments and protesting the latest round of stifling taxes. I've known our compatriots longer than you have, Nolan. While you were battling on the frontier and wandering around every uncivilized outpost in the backwoods, I have been dealing with the citizens of Boston and the surrounding communities. If you had more personal contact with our clan, you would realize there isn't a traitor in the bunch."

Nolan let the matter drop. While 'twas true that Ethan had associated with many Bostonians the past five years, Nolan still smelled a rat. For that reason, Nolan had purposely kept his distance from the other rebels. Ethan was his sole contact, his liaison.

Considering the kind of life-threatening business in which Nolan engaged, the fewer people who knew his true identity the better he liked it. Nolan had learned to rely upon no one but himself, a policy which had kept him alive for thirty years. He had become a loner by instinct and necessity, especially during those first few months after the wilderness battle had become a death trap— courtesy of Major Isaac Stewart. The bastard.

Nolan well remembered the night he had arrived in Boston to track down his brother. His first stop had been the cemetery. Nolan had gone to visit his parents' graves. To his shock and disbelief, he had found *himself* buried beside Frederick and Catherine Ryder.

Aye, 'twas true that Nolan had felt like the living dead the past few years, but 'twas still unsettling to discover he had been listed as a casualty of war. Again, compliments of Major Isaac Stewart.

Because of the grim state of affairs in the American colonies, Nolan had utilized his premature death to his advantage. He had come to the conclusion years earlier that the colonies had outgrown their parent country and could no longer subject themselves to oppressive regulations. The high-handed decrees sent down by Parliament— a flock of molting old owls who knew nothing of life in a land three thousand miles away— were crippling the American economy.

These days, Americans and their British cousins had nothing in common. Colonists were being restrained from developing the natural resources beyond the mountains. They were treated like second-class citizens.

Nolan had tolerated all the British snobbery he could endure while serving with the King's Army during the last French and Indian War. If he had his way, the standing army would be marched on board ship and blown home under the power of a fierce gale.

Although the Loyal Nine and Sons of Liberty shared Nolan's opinions and his driving need for independence, Nolan was not the kind of man who relied on blind faith. He had learned that such faith led to betrayal and death. Nolan intended to outlive the dates on his headstone and a British snitch was *not* going to lead him into doom.

"I'll be in touch," Ethan murmured, jostling Nolan from his pensive reverie.

"By carrier pigeon," Nolan instructed. "I don't trust your human chain of communication these days."

Ethan rolled his eyes at his brother and turned himself toward home.

A short while later, Nolan emerged from the marsh to survey the docks. All was reasonably quiet, with the exception of tittering feminine laughter and an answering masculine chuckle. Nolan immersed himself in shadows to watch a gaily-adorned woman glide her arms around a British officer's neck, tilting up her face for a kiss.

A fleeting shadow beside the wharf pilings caught Nolan's attention. He frowned curiously while he watched an urchin in homespun clothes slink toward Geoffrey and his conquest-for-the-moment. The little ragamuffin was likely to get an eyeful while watching Geoffrey in action, Nolan concluded.

Casting one last glance toward the dock, Nolan

crept back to fetch his horse and aimed himself toward the obscure cabin he shared with Spark McRae. He left the scrawny Peeping Tom to the education he was about to receive and Geoffrey Spradlin to what he loved best— notching his bedpost with another conquest.

Three

Nolan paced from wall to wall while rain pattered against the roof of the cabin. Since the day he had been flogged and tossed in the army stockade, he had never been comfortable with confinement. Freedom had become vital to Nolan. During the two years he had spent hunting and trapping in the wilderness, self-reliance had become his way of life, his philosophy—one that British regulations hampered and threatened.

The steady downpour drenching the wooded hills near Boston made Nolan even more restless than usual. To occupy his time, he had rearranged the furniture in the cottage and cleaned the homing pigeons' cages—twice. Yet he still had more restless energy than he knew what to do with.

While Spark was tossing several unidentifiable ingredients in the stew, Nolan read the pamphlets and handbills he was to deliver to the circuit riders who distributed information to the Sons of Liberty in other colonies. Nolan stared at the window, listening to raindrops thump like impatient fingers. The storm had gone on for hours. A full day of being cooped up in the cabin was making him stir-crazy . . .

A dull thud, followed by Spark's hissed curse roused Nolan from his musings. He glanced around to see the stout old frontiersman balancing bowls and silverware in one hand while he rubbed his bruised shin.

"Blast it, Nolan, I just got used to yer last furniture arrangement and you've moved everythin' around again," Spark grumbled as he set the bowls on the table— one that had been scooted from the north wall to the south wall. "In all my sixty years I never knew anybody who changed things around as often as you do. Even my three ex-fiancées weren't this bad!"

Nolan ambled over to the stove to hoist up the simmering pot of stew and carried it to the table. "After more than two years of sharing quarters with me, I thought you had grown accustomed to my habits."

"To yer idiosyncrasies," Spark corrected. "But not yer blessed furniture arrangements. 'Tis a wonder I have shins left after stumblin' over chairs that move around more often than migratin' birds."

While Spark poured the tankards of ale level full, Nolan stared dubiously at the steaming kettle. "What is in this stew?"

Spark levered his hefty body into his chair and scooped up the ladle. "A bit o' this and a bit o' that."

Nolan spooned up a chunk of unrecognizable

meat and stared quizzically at his gray-haired companion.

" 'Tis owl meat to make you wiser," Spark identified. "I also added a few chunks of hawk meat to make you see better and I tossed in a few morsels of crow— "

"Crow?" Nolan snorted. "Nobody likes to eat crow."

Spark shrugged his thick-bladed shoulders and slurped his soup. "Better to eat crow in yer stew than to have it served up to you some place else, I always say."

Nolan sighed in resignation and ate his dinner. He should have grown accustomed to Spark's odd concoctions by now— should have and hadn't.

In silence Nolan took to his meal and listened to Spark smack his lips. As adept as Spark was in the wilderness, his table manners left a lot to be desired. Nolan wondered if those faults contributed to Spark's inability to keep a fiancée on the hook for more than a few months. Probably. Women were picky about such things as polished table manners and courtly etiquette.

"Are you still plannin' to run interference for the revenue cutter due in tonight?" Spark asked between slurps. When Nolan nodded affirmatively, Spark shook his fuzzy gray head. "With all this rain, you'll have to be exceptionally careful. Yer tracks will be easy to follow."

"The British patrols aren't known for their impressive tracking skills," Nolan reminded him.

"Maybe not, but they might get better at it if

there's a chance of collectin' the reward on the Midnight Rider's head . . ."

Spark's voice dried up when the flutter and coo of an incoming pigeon interrupted him. Nolan bounded up from his chair and strode toward the storage room at the end of the hall. The winged courier landed on the windowsill and fluffed its feathers before hopping onto the perch outside its cage. Nolan unclamped the banded message and then shooed the pigeon into its straw-lined nest.

"Somethin' amiss?" Spark questioned from the doorway.

Nolan scanned the coded message from his brother. "One of Ethan's fellow merchants had three wagon loads of cargo confiscated this morning," Nolan reported. "William Hammel was marched off to jail."

"Yer brother was damned lucky you managed to set a smoke screen for him when his goods were rowed ashore." Spark turned back toward the table. "Those patrols have certainly learned the knack of spottin' revenue cutters and sniffin' out black-market cargo."

Nolan still wasn't convinced that the Crown's men had located the contraband by themselves. His instincts told him the Brits were buying information. Ethan, like many of the merchants in the colonies, had resorted to large-scale smuggling to sneak dry goods, hardware, and glass past Royal Customs. If His Majesty and Parliament had their way, the colonies would trade only with England. But despite restrictions, colonial merchants continued their illegal practices so as to provide a variety of goods for their fellow countrymen.

As a result, 'twas even more difficult for Nolan to run interference for merchants and shippers. British patrols were so thick along the eastern seaboard that you couldn't stir them with a fence post. Nolan often needed to be three places at once to divert soldiers' attention and lure them off on a wild-goose chase. 'Twas not helping matters one whit that some sneaky snitch was selling tips for gold coins. Nolan would sincerely like to know who that someone was so he could put the traitor permanently out of the colonists' way.

After Nolan had choked down the rest of his mystery soup, he changed into the Midnight Rider's black garments and cloak. When he emerged from the bedroom, Spark was poised beside the front door.

"Watch yer step tonight," Spark warned. "I don't want to have to serve my soup for yer last supper before ye'r marched to the gallows."

"Aye," Nolan said as he strode off into the wet night. "And I don't relish the thought of leaving this world with the taste of your stew on my lips."

Spark snorted at the teasing rejoinder. "You should be thankin' me for addin' deer meat to yer soup, so you'll be more sensitive to the sound of approachin' danger."

Nolan rolled his eyes and then pulled his cape around his neck to ward off the chill. He was fond of the old codger, but Spark was a superstitious sort. Hawk meat to improve eyesight? Deer meat to improve hearing? The next thing Nolan knew Spark would be feeding him one of their homing pigeons, in hopes the Midnight Rider could sprout wings and fly away at the first sign of trouble!

Nolan's attention was caught by the drone of voices and the sight— beneath a streetlamp— of men dressed in scarlet coats and buff-colored breeches. The skiffs carrying smuggled cargo were being rowed into the marshes and the patrol was heading straight toward them. Sure as hell the Brits had been tipped off again, Nolan concluded bitterly.

A fleeting shadow caught Nolan's eye, just as it had a few nights earlier. It looked like the same scruffy little waif scurrying for cover like a mouse scrambling toward safety. Before Nolan thundered off to waylay the approaching patrol, he cast one last suspicious glance at the urchin crouched on the wharf.

Nolan had the unshakable feeling that the scavenger was doing more than looking for a soft place to bed down on a cold and rainy night. He wondered if the beggar might be responsible for alerting British patrols, rather than one of the Sons of Liberty. Too bad Nolan didn't have the time to snatch up the rascal and scare the truth out of him. Unfortunately, Nolan had more pressing matters to attend to.

* * *

Captain Oran Milbourne muttered several salty oaths when the symbolic torch of liberty arched through the air, scattering the soldiers' mounts in all directions. Oran jerked his musket into position, prepared to drop the infuriating Midnight Rider in his tracks. To his dismay, one of his men charged forward with sword in hand, making it impossible for Oran to get off a clear shot.

The attempt at hand-to-hand combat met with swift and humiliating defeat. A pained grunt erupted from the corporal's lips when the Phantom Rider thundered past, toppling his challenger from his perch and leaving him sprawled in the mud. The patriot's billowing cape fanned out like bat wings as he raced off, practically daring the patrol to chase him.

Before Captain Milbourne could spout an order, his men clambered off with visions of collecting the reward dancing in their heads. Oran found himself impulsively giving chase . . . and he found himself unhorsed when the darkly dressed raider leaped a rain-swollen creek that the military mounts refused to cross. Oran howled furiously when his horse skidded in the mud and dumped him in the creek, soaking his uniform and his dignity.

Sputtering, Oran staggered to his feet to brandish his fist at the departing rebel. "I'll get you if it's the last bloody thing I do!"

Nolan smiled to himself when he recognized the gravelly voice of the officer he had encountered at a Tory ball the previous week. Captain Oran Milbourne would have a fit if he knew he had had occasion to shake hands and converse with the Midnight Rider. That thick-headed, incompetent English dolt was a prime example of British arrogance.

Nolan made a mental note to question Oran Milbourne about this incident when next they met. No doubt, Oran's rendition of the chase would differ greatly from Nolan's . . .

When a musket ball zinged past Nolan, he pressed himself against the side of his horse. Veering toward a row of trees and underbrush, he dropped to the ground, letting his steed race off with the black cloak strapped to the saddle.

The British brigade skidded to a halt when the elusive rider seemingly melted into the saddle. The stallion plunged into the dense foliage and vanished from sight, its hoofbeats evaporating into silence.

"Did you see that, Captain?"

Oran cursed himself mightily for even daring to believe what he thought he saw. Men did not vanish into a puff of fog . . . did they?

"He disappeared into thin air again," the corporal mused aloud. "I'm beginning to think the tales we've been hearing are fact rather than fiction. The Midnight Rider does possess supernatural qualities."

" 'Tis the second time that rascal has escaped us in two weeks," Oran grumbled as he slopped toward his horse. "I'd give my commission to know how he creates those phenomenal illusions."

"He's a phantom, no doubt about it," one of the soldiers confirmed.

Oran gnashed his teeth, spit out mud and reined his horse toward the wharf. That phantom theory was fast becoming the army's general consensus. All the King's men were having one devil of a time catching that crafty rebel.

But one day soon that dark-cloaked patriot would make a mistake, Oran promised himself. Then the mysterious Midnight Rider would be exposed for who he was and left hanging from the tallest tree on Boston Common. Once the rebel leader had met his deserving end the cloddish colonials would realize they were no match for the Crown's army of occupation and they would cease their cries for liberty and freedom.

On that consoling thought, Oran regrouped his patrol and trotted off to inspect the wharf.

Nolan was already tucked in his concealed niche outside the meeting room at Chase and Speakman's Distillery on Hanover Square when the Loyal Nine and members of the Sons of Liberty filed into the room. Nolan had been on hand at Green Dragon Tavern a few nights earlier when the rebels congregated, but no one's activities had struck him as suspicious. Whoever was feeding information to the Brits was cunning and clever, Nolan decided. To find the traitor had become his primary concern. And if none of these men were responsible for leaks in the rebel network, Nolan was going to have to track down that scrawny waif. He might be the culprit, after all.

Nolan had anticipated that tonight's meeting of patriotic activists would center around discussions of halting England's never-ending attempt to tax the colonies into dependence and poverty. Circular newsletters, dispatched to other communities, kept rebels informed of resistance tactics elsewhere. Nolan predicted that boycotting British goods and planning demonstrations to protest the Stamp Act would be the main topics of tonight's conversation, followed by the most recent list of complaints from Bostonians about the abuse inflicted by unruly soldiers who were prone to pillaging and raucous drinking sprees.

To accommodate the overflow of the King's men, tents had been pitched on Boston Common. Every night hostilities between disgruntled citizens and soldiers erupted. Brawls broke out at local taverns and ordinaries. Women were accosted, insulted and often raped, but His Majesty's officials did little more than verbally chastise the offenders. The army of occupation was making a nuisance of itself, drawing even more support to the patriot cause.

From Nolan's unnoticed position in the small adjoining room on the second floor of the distillery, he watched the men file inside. Ethan Ryder ambled in behind John Hancock and Thomas Chase. The forty-three-year-old, prematurely gray-haired Samuel Adams was a step behind. The stockily built Paul Revere arrived a few minutes later.

'Twas the usual crowd, Nolan mused as he propped himself against the wall and peered through the partially opened door. Nothing seemed out of the ordinary . . .

When a shabbily dressed waif, with head downcast, scuttled in behind the plump-faced John Adams, Nolan's gaze narrowed warily. The unexpected appearance of the ragamuffin put Nolan on alert. He had seen this lad on two other occasions the past week and his instincts had been niggling him ever since.

The instant the sooty-faced waif sank down in a shadowed corner, Nolan found his attention focusing on the lad. Nolan couldn't imagine why his half-grown pup in tatters had been allowed into the secret meeting, but the other men paid the lad no heed, as if his presence was accepted without question.

Nolan stared around the dimly lit room, appraising each man in attendance. Although Ethan was quick to defend this congregation of loyal supporters, Nolan was still plagued with suspicions. The only ones who knew about the time and location of the dispersal of contraband were the merchants involved, and the Sons of Liberty. Nolan could only draw one sensible conclusion: Someone was playing both sides against the middle— for profit. With plans being made to escalate protests and intimidate stamp agents into resigning their commissions before the Stamp Act went into effect, 'twas not a good time for informants to be selling patriots out to the army of occupation.

Again, Nolan's gimlet-eyed gaze settled on the waif tucked in the corner. While Samuel Adams conducted the meeting, Nolan appraised the lad, waiting for the youngster to raise his face to the light. 'Twas a half hour before the waif finally glanced up, and then for only a brief moment.

Nolan studied the luminous brown eyes embedded in the smudged face. Then the lad looked down at the toes of his scuffed boots. He looked malnourished in his oversized, homespun garb. He didn't appear to be more than sixteen years old if he was a day. Nolan couldn't fathom what role this urchin played in this secretive clan, unless he was a messenger for the Committee of Correspondence . . .

Or a devious spy . . .

Nolan would be damned if a mere boy would cause the downfall of this noble cause.

" 'Tis going to require unified action to denounce the Stamp Act," Samuel Adams was saying when Nolan got around to listening. "We will not receive Parliament's attention unless every stamp collector resigns his post before those cursed stamps reach the ports, to be attached to every deck of cards, newspaper and legal document in the colonies."

Samuel's soliloquy provoked the grumbling murmurs of the crowd, along with several suggestions as to where His Brittanick Majesty could stash his hated stamps. Tarring and feathering was also mentioned, and Nolan was in favor of extending the practice to informants who betrayed the cause.

"We have heard reports from express riders that our secret militias and arsenals are being established throughout every colony," John Hancock announced. "With the Midnight Rider as our inspiration, we are gathering more supporters by the day. If we join forces with our fellow countrymen, we can ensure that every stamp agent in every colony is forced to resign his commission. The raid our Rebel Rider led last week was effective. Lexington's stamp distributor was thoroughly convinced that the payment he would receive for issuing the King's stamps would not be worth the loss of his life."

While the committee discussed information that was to be included in the newsletters, Nolan eased away from the door and tiptoed toward the steps. He intended to be on the street, waiting to keep surveillance on the waif who had roused his suspicions. In Nolan's opinion the boy was up to no good, even if he was considered harmless by the other members of the Sons of Liberty.

A quarter of an hour later, the secret meeting adjourned and the patriots trooped from the distillery. Following at an inconspicuous distance, Nolan trailed the waif through the honeycomb of byways and alleys known mostly to tomcats and children.

Puzzled, Nolan watched the waif veer away from Boston proper to hike up the path leading to the cemetery. The urchin paused long enough to pluck

up a handful of wildflowers before venturing into
the very same graveyard where Nolan had supposedly been buried.

Nolan concealed himself in the clump of trees
near his burial plot and watched the waif kneel
down to place the bouquet beside a small headstone. And to Nolan's bemusement, the lad carried
on a one-sided conversation with whoever was resting in peace.

After several minutes, the waif ambled eastward
to hop the iron fence. After the boy disappeared
down the hill, Nolan stood indecisively in the shadows of the trees, debating whether to track the
mysterious lad or to learn the identity of the departed soul who had received the bouquet of wildflowers.

His gaze circled back to the small headstone and
his footsteps took him to the site that had been
decorated with flowers. A muddled frown plowed
his brows when the name of Martha Winfield
stared back at him from the tombstone. The
woman had only survived to celebrate her nine-
teenth birthday, but she had obviously not been
forgotten.

Nolan glanced in the direction the waif had
taken, wondering if it might have been the boy's
sister or mayhap a lost love. Heaving a perplexed
sigh, Nolan spun around and ambled off. He had
a task to perform before dawn—a good deed to
further the cause. Of course, the King's men
wouldn't appreciate his efforts, but that was too

bloody bad. They deserved what they were going to get.

The stockpile of food that raiding soldiers had swiped from local farmers was about to be returned to its rightful owners. According to Ethan, several drunken soldiers had helped themselves to the contents of vegetable gardens, smokehouses and storage sheds, under the pretense of searching for smuggled goods.

Citizens were openly objecting to the presence of soldiers who made it their policy to take whatever they wanted. As far as Nolan was concerned, the standing army stationed in the colonies could grow their own food supplies. They had little else to occupy them while off duty, besides drinking, cavorting and causing disturbances in the streets.

With determination, purpose, Nolan hiked off to fetch his stallion and give His Majesty's men a few more tales to add to their anthology of the legendary Midnight Rider.

Four

Nolan drew his rented landau to a halt and surveyed the palatial mansion on Beacon Hill where the evening ball was being held. He permitted himself a scowl of contempt as he took inventory of the lights blazing from every window, the row of carriages that lined the circular drive of the Georgian-style monstrosity, whose whitewashed brick, gambrel roof and terraced gardens denoted excessive wealth.

As Nolan heard it told, the eccentric Miriam Peabody, widow of Angus Peabody, had inherited a staggering shipping fortune. It annoyed Nolan that Mrs. Peabody was so obviously a Tory sympathizer. The party being held at her estate was indication enough that her loyalty was to the Crown. 'Twas a pity that Miriam Peabody's funds weren't supporting the patriot cause. No doubt, the old dowager insisted on living like a member of the British *ton*, clinging to regal protocol and supporting Parliament's decisions.

Nolan straightened his Steenkirk scarf and his powdered Ramillies wig, mentally preparing himself to portray the self-indulgent Tory fop who went by the name of Ezra Beecham. Each time Nolan was forced to mingle with loyalists he cursed himself for letting his brother persuade him to assume this double identity. It demanded considerable acting ability for Nolan to pretend indifference to the patriot cause. More than once he had had to bite his tongue to prevent blurting out comments that indicated his true colors.

According to Ethan, Nolan was the perfect candidate for this masquerade. Because the Ryders had relocated during Nolan's military service, he was not a familiar face in Boston and his presence aroused no suspicion. And since Nolan had been presumed dead, Ethan decided 'twould be a simple matter for his brother to pose as a loyalist and associate with British officers. So here he was, chumming about with the King's men and their devoted Tory supporters.

Nolan stepped down from the coach, vowing to keep his political views to himself. Garbed in the latest fashion of silk stockings, polished black shoes with shiny silver buckles and an elegant velvet waistcoat, Nolan swaggered up the steps like any self-respecting dandy. For the duration of the dull evening he would become Ezra Beecham and he would behave like a Tory . . .

"Ezra, good to see you again."

Glancing sideways, Nolan pasted on a nonchalant smile and greeted the stork-legged aristocrat who had befriended him a few months earlier.

"Haven't seen you at the pubs and clubs of late," William Fitzgerald commented before he dipped into his snuff box. "What have you been doing with yourself?"

Nolan struck an arrogant pose on the porch. "My ventures in the fur business have kept me busy," he explained.

"Finance is such a dreadful bore," William replied as he sauntered through the door. "My family has been nagging me to return home to manage our plantation in Virginia, but the social life in Boston is far more entertaining."

"Until your allowances dwindle?" Nolan managed to say without a sardonic smirk.

The subtle jibe flew over William's bewigged head. He was much too haughty and self-absorbed to realize he had been insulted. "My funds are quite inexhaustible," he boasted. "The coins and property I received from my grandfather's estate should keep me living in a fashionable manner for years to come . . ."

When William's voice trailed off, Nolan followed the younger man's gaze to see Miriam Peabody making her dramatic entrance via the spiral staircase. The plump matron of sixty was decked out in her finest feathers. With exaggerated flicks of her wrists and a self-important incline of her gray head, Miriam floated into the foyer amid yards of pink satin.

After the proper introductions were made, Nolan propped himself against the wall. He was already bored and the evening had only begun.

"Blister it, I wonder where Laura is," William muttered, jostling Nolan from his thoughts. William craned his neck to scan the crowded ballroom. "I had hoped that, by arriving early, I might have a better chance."

"Better chance at what?" Nolan questioned.

Willie flung Nolan a withering glance. "The chance to spend the evening with the love of my life, of course."

Nolan arched a thick brow. "I thought you had set your cap for Beatrice Hornsby."

" 'Twas ages ago," Willie said with a dismissing shrug.

" 'Twas only three weeks ago, as I recall," Nolan prompted.

"The woman is entirely too dull and has not a brain in her lovely head." Willie flicked an imaginary speck of lint from his sleeve and glanced around. "I informed Beatrice that she should turn her affection elsewhere."

William had only two things on his mind— wine and women, the latter being his first priority. As for Nolan, he had only the basic of uses for both. He had discovered— to his everlasting dismay— that women were fickle, deceptive and disloyal creatures who used their feminine wiles to their best advantage. As for wine, Nolan would take a tankard of colonial rum any time. Women and drink, he had decided, were vices that befuddled the male brain. And lately, he hadn't had time for drink or feminine diversion. He met himself coming and going too often while leading this double life.

A chorus of laughter wafted through the open

window and William scurried down the hall to investigate.

"Strike me blue, I should have known," Willie grumbled.

Nolan strolled up behind William and frowned curiously at the throng of elegantly dressed men and officers in scarlet uniforms. On the south side of the backyard was a vacated bowling green scattered with fallen pins. On the right side of the lawn was a target that had been nailed to a tree. Two arrows protruded from the target, indicating that an archery contest was in progress.

Nolan had never considered archery to be an amusing sport. Most of the arrows he had seen flying around had been aimed at him during battle and during his extensive travels in the wilderness. But then, there was no accounting for the eccentric habits and pastimes of the social elite.

With mild curiosity, Nolan watched another arrow sail away from the group of dandies. The quilled missile lodged in the middle of the distant target. Oohs and aahs drifted from the crowd of men. Another arrow arched through the air, missing the tree completely, provoking outright laughter.

Nolan failed to see the humor . . . until a dainty, auburn-haired female and a scarlet-coated officer strode forward to retrieve their arrows.

"I knew it," Willie grumbled. "I would have had to camp out on the lawn at dawn to beat my rivals for an audience with Laura Chandler."

"The female archer is the light of your life?" Nolan asked dubiously.

"Don't look so skeptical, Ezra," Willie chided. "I can assure you that Laura is every man's dream come to life, even if she does enjoy unconventional pastimes." He leaned close to add confidentially, "I'm told she is also a fair shot with a pistol."

Nolan tried to look properly surprised. "Do tell."

In fact, Nolan didn't give a flying fig if Laura Chandler, the darling of unconventionality, could hurl daggers with both hands—blindfolded. All that concerned Nolan was prying the redcoats away from Laura's skirttails long enough to wheedle useful information out of them. Willie and the throng of men sniffing around the auburn-haired chit were welcome to her. Tory ladies served only one function for Nolan—gathering information about the activities of British officers, as it pertained to the patriot cause . . .

Nolan found himself momentarily distracted when the chit in yellow satin plucked up the two arrows that had landed dead center, while her challenger retrieved his meager attempts. The lady was definitely an accomplished markswoman. Perhaps Willie hadn't exaggerated about pistols, either, Nolan mused. How odd that a woman with her obvious good breeding and lofty position in Boston society had become so adept with weapons that were usually handled by men . . .

Nolan's thoughts scattered when Willie grabbed his forearm and towed him out the back door.

"Ezra, do me a favor and let me introduce you to Laura. 'Twill give me an excuse to approach her."

Nolan half-heartedly allowed himself to be propelled toward the admirers who hovered around
Miss Chandler like bees buzzing around nectar. He
was not the least bit eager to become Willie's tool
of courtship . . . until the auburn-haired female
turned to face him.

When Nolan found twinkling brown eyes staring
back at him from beneath a fan of sooty black lashes,
recognition hit him like a doubled fist to the jaw.
For a moment, he could not believe what he was
seeing! But he knew there could be no mistake. He
would have recognized those black-diamond eyes
anywhere. They belonged to the scrawny waif he
had seen on the wharf and again at the Sons of
Liberty meeting!

'Twas excessively difficult for Nolan to smile politely while he was silently cursing the deceptive
chit who was obviously as adept at playing charades as he was. Curse her lovely hide! This female
was as cunning as she was captivating.

Nolan carefully concealed his stunned disbelief
and promised himself he would have his full measure of revenge on this crafty darling of Tory society. No doubt, she had perfected her talents with
weapons, so she could defend herself while she
sneaked around the streets, dressed like a lowly
urchin, passing information to the scarlet dragons
that sought to stifle rebel activities.

Just wait until Nolan got this sneaky snitch
alone. He would make her bloody damned sorry
she had betrayed the cause!

Five

"Good evening, Miss Chandler. You look stunning." William clutched Laura's free hand and bowed gallantly over it. "I have been counting the minutes until I could see you again."

Nolan was counting the minutes until he could expose this little witch for what she was— a thorn in the Sons of Liberty's sides!

With careful scrutiny, Nolan appraised the five-feet-three-inch package of shimmering beauty whose swanlike throat and delicate wrist were draped with matching diamonds and emeralds. Laura Chandler was indeed stunning and alluring, Nolan reluctantly admitted. Even though he despised her, the man in him reacted instinctively to her.

Duped and betrayed by a mere wisp of a woman, Nolan silently seethed. He shouldn't be the least bit surprised. Females were notorious for deception.

"I'm glad you could join us this evening, Mr. Fitzgerald," Laura courteously replied to William. "I trust you will enjoy yourself."

When Laura's gaze ran the full length of him

the second time, Nolan supposed he should be flattered by the attention he was receiving. 'Twas always nice to be noticed by a beautiful woman. However, he was too furious with this cunning female to think past his need for revenge.

When Willie finally regained his lovelost senses, he gestured toward his companion. "I don't believe you have chanced to meet my friend Ezra Beecham. He has made his fortune in furs."

Laura extended her hand and Nolan offered all the proper amenities. Although Nolan believed his duplicity served a noble cause, he considered Laura Chandler's deception to be anything but noble! She had charaded as a waif to attend secret conferences, so she could sell information to the British. 'Twas infinitely worse than Nolan portraying a dandy at loyalists' parties to scare up facts. And furthermore, Nolan wasn't receiving monetary compensation for *his* efforts. He was certain that wasn't the case with this perfidious female.

The greedy little chit was probably lining her already padded pocket for some selfish, frivolous purpose. A new gown perhaps? A plumed bonnet like the ones that were all the rage in England? Or was she saving her money for a voyage to Britain to captivate some unsuspecting earl or duke?

With Laura's exceptional good looks, bewitching face and voluptuous figure, she could pick and choose among the English gentry. With her peaches-and-cream complexion, her dimpled smile and those mesmerizing eyes that were so dark they appeared black, she was the shining example of treachery wrapped in a most entrancing package.

She was also danger in its deadliest form. Nolan vowed never to let himself forget that, even if Laura Chandler did appeal to everything masculine in him— and she did.

" 'Tis a pleasure to make your acquaintance, Miss Chandler," Nolan murmured, brushing his lips over the soft texture of her hand. He slowly rose to his full height, cursing himself when his betraying eyes lingered on the lush swells of her breasts that were encased in bright yellow satin.

Despite his irritation, Nolan found himself ridiculously flattered when Laura cast him another glance that indicated she found him appealing. He could understand why men fell head over heels for her, why men gravitated toward her. Not only was she a breathtaking sight to behold, but she had a remarkable way of looking at a man, as if he were special, unique. 'Twas in those entrancing eyes and those impish dimples that bracketed her beautifully-sculpted mouth. 'Twas in the curve of those lush lips that reminded Nolan of ripe, juicy cherries waiting to be tasted and savored. Her generous feminine curves were nothing to scoff at, either, Nolan found himself thinking. She was a perfect fit for male contours . . . and dangerous.

"I am honored to make your acquaintance, Mr. Beecham," Laura replied when Nolan finally released her hand. "I hope you will enjoy your evening at my aunt's home. Miriam has taken great pains to ensure that all her guests will be serenaded by the best musicians and stuffed full of the most succulent refreshments."

When Laura looked as if she were about to turn toward the tall, red-haired British officer who hovered behind her, Nolan blocked her retreat. "The only music I will need to hear is the sound of a siren's voice— "

Nolan's breath wobbled when Willie discreetly gouged him in the ribs. Obviously Willie wasn't taking kindly to having another male rival vying for the lady's attention. But that was just too bloody bad, Nolan decided. He wasn't through with Laura Chandler yet. Indeed, he was just getting warmed up. Nolan could be as charming and gallant as the next man when he felt like it. He had served with enough stuffy English officers during the war to mimic their accent and prance like a royal prince. And if he could charm this Tory spy out of her frilly petticoats then he would double his satisfaction. 'Twould be exactly what she deserved for her devious deception.

The sound of a cello, violin and flute filled the evening air and Nolan made certain no man beat his time with this crafty female. "I beg the first and last dance, Miss Chandler," he boldly requested, ignoring William's indignant gasp and the fallen faces around him. "You have bewitched me."

One perfectly arched brow elevated as Laura regarded the man before her. "Are you always so brash, Mr. Beecham? After all, we have just met."

"We have?" Nolan knew better.

"Haven't we?" she questioned his question.

Nolan graced her with his most disarming smile. "I feel as though I have known you forever, my lady, for you are the vision of my dreams."

Her delicately shaped brows arched even higher as she inclined her head to study him from a slightly different angle. "I should warn you that insincere flattery has never made much of an impression on me."

"Nay?" Nolan begrudgingly found himself amused by the chit's wit and her obvious spirit. 'Twas becoming increasingly apparent why this young lady was pursued by so many men. Laura Chandler had a bright mind and she obviously knew how to use it. No wonder she made such a clever spy.

"Very well then," Nolan conceded, "if you prefer to be spared flattery, so be it."

"I would appreciate it."

As Laura began to turn away, Nolan glanced at the bow in her hand and smiled wryly, saying, "Perhaps you would prefer to be challenged in an archery contest since you seem to be fond of the sport."

Laura swiveled her head around to meet his twinkling silver gaze. "And if I should win, Mr. Beecham?"

"You won't, but if the improbable happens, I will retract my dance requests and leave you to your endless rabble of admirers."

The comment drew several snickers from the all-male crowd, assuring Nolan that 'twas not the first time Laura had been challenged and had outshot masculine competition.

"Well, for heaven's sake!" Miriam Peabody's voice sliced through the air. She appeared on the back stoop, a disapproving frown puckering her aging features. "Have you gentlemen no sense of propriety? I have a ballroom full of crestfallen young ladies who would very much appreciate the company of the most eligible men in Boston. And here the lot of you are, camped out on my back lawn, challenging my niece with bows and arrows! Laura, come inside at once. We have guests to entertain."

The flock of men automatically migrated toward the house when their hostess waved them inside. 'Twas widely known that Miriam Peabody knew how to host a party and that she spared no expense in entertaining her guests. Not to be included in Miriam's social activities was worse than being demoted in the military ranks.

"Well, Miss Chandler?" Nolan prompted as the crowd dispersed. "Will you accept my challenge?"

Laura stared after the older woman before focusing her attention on Nolan. "I suppose I should do the proper thing and assist Aunt Miriam as hostess."

"Proper?" Nolan smiled devilishly. "My dear lady, you strike me as the kind of person who thrives on the unusual, the unexpected."

"Do I? And on what do you base your opinion?" she wanted to know.

Nolan couldn't help himself. He moved closer, only to become entrapped in the heady fragrance of roses. Damnation, what was the matter with him? He knew exactly how dangerous she was to his cause. And yet, he was fascinated with her wit and blinded by her beauty. She was a woman full of secrets and Nolan felt the impulsive urge to discover them all— before he pointed an accusing finger at her and exposed her for the spy she was, of course.

Those entrancing onyx eyes widened when Nolan boldly advanced, crowding her space, forcing her to look up to meet his penetrating gaze. "Am I making you uncomfortable, Miss Chandler?" he murmured as he stared at her parted lips, wondering why the need to taste this Tory spy suddenly seemed as essential as breathing.

Her lips twitched when his voice hit a noticeably husky pitch. "Am *I* making *you* uncomfortable, Mr. Beecham?" she retorted. "It has been my experience that men make women uncomfortable when they venture improperly close at improper moments, but men seem to become uncomfortable when they cannot get close enough.

"You men always remind me of tightly wound clocks. We women, however, are like sundials. We prefer to proceed at what seems a more natural pace, when it comes to liaisons with men. If you believe me to be a quick and easy conquest, you are very much mistaken."

Nolan chuckled and retreated a respectable distance. "I'm beginning to understand why you were holding court on the lawn, like a fair lady amid a cluster of gallant knights. I'm also beginning to understand why you have eluded marriage, while females younger than your years have succumbed to it. You are wise to the wiles of men. And you do have an answer for everything, don't you?"

"Nay," she contradicted as she walked back to the spot where another bow was propped against a tree. Glancing over her shoulder, she added, "I haven't yet determined the answer to why you have singled me out, when there are dozens of women inside who are more susceptible to your roguish charm. Have I somehow become your most recent challenge? Does it disturb you that I prefer to pick and choose my masculine companions, that I actually enjoy functioning without being dependent on a man for my amusements? Does it seem an uncommon quirk of nature that I have no desire to rush into a marriage which will undoubtedly restrict my adventurous spirit?"

Nolan reached around her to retrieve the bow, his arm brushing lightly against her shoulder, amazed at his instinctive need for even the slightest physical contact. He was quick to note that Laura gracefully sidestepped him to avoid his touch. For such a bold and self-assured female, she certainly appeared leery of him— physically speaking. Why was that? he wondered.

"You are definitely a challenge— in archery, too, I suspect." Nolan handed her a quiver of arrows. "And I do admire your notion of self-reliance and your desire for personal amusement. You are a woman after my own heart."

"I am not after your heart, Mr. Beecham," she

said with a breezy smile. "So do not presume to toy with mine. I am hardly a naive maid who falls for those age-old ploys men practice." Laura brought her bow into position and sighted down the arrow. "We shall get on grandly if you avoid making a bothersome nuisance of yourself, as most men do."

She let the arrow fly with experienced ease, striking the target so close to center that Nolan was granted only the smallest margin of error if he hoped to compete with her. Damn, she was remarkably skilled! He could imagine how awkward and humbled her male competitors felt when she got through with them. Nolan had no desire to be her victim of defeat.

Laura waited until Nolan had drawn his bow and took aim before mischievously adding, "I would never be interested in testing a man's skills in bed unless I'm assured he is a passable marksman. Men with inadequate aim don't make satisfactory lovers. Don't you agree, Mr. Beecham?"

Nolan had always been cool and steady under fire, but the provocative comment affected his disciplined control and his aim. That was not the type of remark he expected from a proper aristocrat. But then, he was vividly aware that a man should expect the unexpected from Laura Chandler. She was no ordinary woman, after all. She was a cunning spy who possessed unique skills of self-defense.

When Nolan's arrow quivered beside Laura's, he noticed her disgruntled frown. "Nice try, Miss Chandler," he said wryly. "Did you employ the same deceptive tactic on your last challenger?"

Laura plucked up her second arrow and tossed him a hasty glance. "I didn't have to."

"Why not?" Nolan waited until she was poised to release her arrow. "Did he have poor aim— in bed and out?"

With extreme amusement, Nolan monitored the trajectory of the misfired arrow. The missile flew wide to the right, barely hitting the tree. While Laura was muttering under her breath, Nolan drew down, took quick aim and hit the target— square and true.

"As for me, Miss Chandler, I hit what I aim at," he said with a scampish grin. "Only Cupid is a better marksman."

"And more modest, I expect," Laura sniffed sarcastically. "I owe you two dances, neither of which I will enjoy, but I am good to my word, nonetheless."

"Are you truly?" he asked with a smirk.

Laura regarded him for a long, pensive moment. "I have the feeling you are purposely antagonizing me. Why is that?"

Probably because he was peeved at himself for actually enjoying the company of this Tory snitch, Nolan thought sourly. 'Twas aggravating to be so compellingly attracted to a woman who would betray his identity and enjoy every minute, if she knew who he was. If Laura Chandler had the slightest notion she had come face-to-face with the Midnight Rider, she would have turned him over to the authorities for the reward the Crown's Army had placed on his head. Nolan intended to enjoy himself at this crafty chit's expense before he exposed her deception to his fellow patriots. That would put a dent in her feminine pride, he predicted.

"Laura!"

Laura and Nolan simultaneously pivoted to see Miriam Peabody's rounded figure filling the doorway.

"Aye, Aunt Miriam?"

The matron frowned disapprovingly at the tall, masculine figure beside Laura. " 'Tis almost dark and most improper for you to be without a chaperone. We have a room full of male guests who are straining their necks to determine when you are coming inside to favor them with a dance."

"I will be there directly," Laura assured Miriam.

"See that you are very direct, my dear," Miriam insisted before she disappeared from sight.

When Laura hiked up her skirts to scurry toward the house, Nolan clutched her elbow to detain her. "I prefer more than a dance with you, Miss Chandler," he said.

Brown eyes widened in disbelief. "Never think for a minute that I intend to offer you more than that, Mr. Beecham. Despite your elegant dress and polished airs, you are certainly no gentleman!"

"And you are no lady," Nolan countered. "Perhaps you have fooled those drooling dandies who hover around you, but you don't fool me."

"I don't have the foggiest notion what you're babbling about," she sniffed, nose in the air.

"I realize that. It gives me a certain advantage." And while Nolan had her attention he added, "Next time you deliver flowers to the cemetery, perhaps you should dress in a manner more befitting the lady you want everyone to *think* you are, Miss Chandler."

With immense satisfaction Nolan watched the color seep from her cheeks and her jaw drop open.

"There you are at last," Peter Forbes declared as he surged off the stoop. His gaze bounced back and forth between Nolan and Laura, noting her stricken expression. "Is something amiss, my dear?"

Nolan surveyed the lieutenant who had chased after him several nights earlier. From all indication the young officer was hopelessly enamored with Laura. Lieutenant Forbes appeared ready and willing to come to the lady's defense, if she felt the least bit offended.

Laura quickly composed herself, pasted on a smile and pivoted toward Peter. "The only thing amiss is my ability to hit the target," she explained, ignoring Nolan as if he were another tree in the row of oaks that lined the lawn.

"Did Mr. Beecham prove to be challenging competition?" Peter questioned as he took Laura's arm and escorted her inside.

"Indeed." She paused long enough to toss Nolan an I'll-get-even-with-you glance. "I will have to insist upon a rematch at a later date."

Nolan wasn't sure, but considering the glare she flung at him, before she and her lovesick lobster-back veered into the ballroom, she was silently promising to aim the next arrow directly at him.

A devilish smile pursed Nolan's lips as he ambled into the mansion. He had the unmistakable feeling that dealing with Laura Chandler would be nothing if not interesting and challenging. Judging from the expression in those luminous eyes, her only quandary was whether to go for his throat or his heart.

Six

Nolan had accomplished his ulterior purpose on the back lawn of Miriam Peabody's mansion. He had gained Laura Chandler's notice. Although Nolan kept his distance from her, chatting leisurely with the British officers he had met on previous occasions and dancing with a few eligible heiresses, he knew Laura was monitoring his activities. Nolan wasn't sure why he felt the need to draw her attention. Probably because he found himself unwillingly attracted to the enchanting but perfidious female.

There was more to Laura Chandler than met the eye, 'twas for sure and certain. She was an enigma, a woman whose depths of character and complex personality intrigued men— Nolan included. The woman, he noted, was never without a dance partner. The fact that she danced every Virginia Reel, every Roger de Coverly, and Contra Dance also indicated Laura was in exceptional physical condition. But of course, a woman who disguised herself as a waif and scuttled through the maze of Boston's cobbled streets at night to attend rebel rallies as a spy and then hiked off to cemeteries to deliver flowers got plenty of exercise . . .

Nolan was jostled from his thoughts when Peter Forbes strolled over beside him at the refreshment table. While Nolan watched Willie Fitzgerald high-stepping with Laura, Peter edged closer.

"Just in case you had hopes that your encounter on the back lawn was the beginning of a romantic liaison with Laura, I thought I should inform you that I have set my cap for the lady."

Nolan tossed the distinguished soldier a nonchalant glance and then watched a red-haired British officer replace Willie to whirl Laura around the ballroom. "You and half the eligible bachelors in attendance seem to share the same objectives." Nolan bit into a cherry tart and leaned negligently against the wall. "And furthermore, Lieutenant, I hardly see how you have time for courting with all the rebel activity around Boston. Many of my constituents are in a furor about the Stamp Act, as I'm sure you're aware."

Peter scowled sourly. "I'm definitely aware. The first two men who filled the position as stamp collectors in Boston have been threatened and their homes stoned. I suspect that before long General Gage will send up military reinforcements from New York. Boston has become the hub of dissension."

"Additional troops will only fuel more resentment," Nolan prophesied. "Before long, this town will become a keg of gun powder, on the verge of explosion."

Peter sniffed haughtily. "Surely you realize the Crown's men will have no difficulty controlling those pesky rebels."

"Do I?" Nolan arched a dark brow. "You must admit most of the King's enlisted men are undesirables who joined the military because they had difficulty finding employment in England. With their drinking and carousing while they're off duty, they cause more problems than they resolve."

Peter lifted his square chin to a challenging angle. "You sound as if you are siding with those rebel bumpkins, Mr. Beecham."

"I sound like a neutral observer who has no inclination to have my personal pursuits of leisure spoiled by the inconvenience of rebellion and outright battle," Nolan replied before sipping his sillabub. "Like my friend Willie Fitzgerald, I have no desire to dabble in politics. Life is too short to clutter it with strife and turmoil. I simply pay my taxes and go about my own business and pleasures, wishing everyone else would do the same."

"Would that your fellow Bostonians would follow that policy," Peter grumbled.

"They aren't my fellow chaps, actually. I'm from"— Nolan thought fast— "Charleston." 'Twas as good of a place to be from in his fictitious past. He hoped Peter had never been there. 'Twould make two of them. "Like my crony, I have traveled to Boston in pursuit of amusement. Had I known the city would be in an uproar I would have stayed home."

" 'Tis that rabble-rouser known as the Midnight

Rider who's causing all the problems. He's been flitting around town, leaving his torch of liberty, inspiring the commoners, and stirring up this whole bloody town like a witch's caldron."

"Midnight Rider?" Nolan prompted with just the right amount of curiosity.

"Some bumpkin in a mask and cloak has been prowling the darkness, taunting patrols and scattering pickets of military mounts that must be rounded up every morning." Peter flicked a glance toward Laura and frowned when Geoffrey Spradlin clutched her closer to him than necessary.

Nolan also made note of the amorous attention Laura was receiving from Geoffrey. He had no use whatsoever for that hard-drinking, womanizing soldier. Nolan was surprised Laura tolerated his obvious advances. He couldn't imagine what she saw in the man. But then he mentally shrugged and reminded himself there was no accounting for some people's tastes— especially a Tory spy's.

"Captain Milbourne urged the Commission of Inquiry to place a higher price on the Rebel Rider's head," Peter went on to say. "I received a dispatch this morning, indicating that I was to add another £100 to the reward for his capture."

My, Nolan thought to himself, his head was certainly worth a great deal more this week. Laura Chandler would make a killing— literally— if she delivered information to her flock of enamored suitors, wouldn't she?

"Now then," Peter declared, focusing full attention on his most recent male rival. "About Laura."

"She is the Midnight Rider?" Nolan questioned in feigned shock. "Good gad, I never would have thought it."

Peter flung him a withering glance, refusing to be amused by Nolan's dry wit. "Don't be absurd. I was referring to the comment I made earlier. If you are not aware, I am residing in this mansion with Laura and her aunt."

For some reason that annoyed Nolan to the extreme, but it certainly explained how easily information could be conveyed from Tory spy to British officer. "Protecting this household of females from the rebel menace, are you, Lieutenant?" Nolan mocked. "How noble . . . and convenient for you."

Peter's chest swelled like an inflated bagpipe. "I'll have you know, that I have been the perfect gentleman where Laura is concerned, Beecham. I happen to be in love with her and I intend to make her my wife."

That tidbit of news didn't set well with Nolan. And furthermore, he was not so gullible as to believe Peter had been the "perfect gentleman" or that Laura wanted him to be. She had certainly given Nolan the impression that she knew what she was about and picked her lovers when the mood struck.

"From the look of things, you'll have to stand in line to propose to her, much less dance with her, Lieutenant." Nolan indicated the string of men who surged forward when the music ended. "Your future bride appears very much in demand."

"I realize that," Peter muttered. "She is a rare

and lovely creature who attracts men without trying."

"Rest assured that I am not in the market for a wife," Nolan told Peter before draining his glass of sillabub. "According to a very dear friend of mine, women should always be taken lightly and enjoyed in a temporary capacity. I intend to dance with the young lady before the night is out, simply because it amuses me to do so. But I have no intention of a serious courtship."

His silver-gray eyes twinkled down at the fair-skinned lieutenant who was a good four inches shorter in height. "From the comments Miss Chandler made earlier, I doubt she will be an easy catch, even for a man of your obvious good breeding and refined manners. She has remained single too long to be manageable. Just exactly how old is she, by the way?"

"Twenty-three," Peter reported.

Nolan nodded consideringly. "Then she is far past the impressionable age for a husband to impose his ideas and opinions on her. And from my brief encounter with her, I would say she is an extremely independent woman who would not take kindly to being told how to behave and what to do."

"Your first impression is correct," Peter admitted.

"But you are determined to wed her, nonetheless," Nolan presumed.

"Aye, 'tis my intention."

"Lieutenant," Nolan said with a chuckle. "You will be taking on a difficult task if you try to tame that particular lady. The rebels you encounter in

Boston cannot possibly be as unmanageable as that female strikes me as being. It sounds like entirely too much work and dedication to me. I try to avoid such things when possible.''

When Nolan sauntered off to request a dance with a petite blonde, he intercepted Laura's pensive glance. She was back in Geoffrey Spradlin's arms— the worst of all possible choices, in Nolan's opinion.

In silent satisfaction, Nolan felt Laura's eyes on him as he moved in rhythm with the fast-tempoed folk melody. He rather liked knowing that crafty little witch was stewing in her own juice, wondering how he could possibly have known she was leading a double life.

To Nolan's surprise, Laura Chandler approached *him* an hour later, requesting a dance. Nolan was quick to note Peter Forbes's disappointment and Willie Fitzgerald's frown of dismay. Geoffrey Spradlin didn't look all that pleased that Laura had singled Nolan out, either. All three men appeared to be plagued with jealous streaks.

Nolan thanked God he had never suffered such wasted emotion. But then, he had seen women for what they were after his encounter with Phoebe Hart more than two years earlier. She had cured Nolan for life. The woman had been inappropriately named. She had no heart— a characteristic indicative of females.

"Mr. Beecham, I wish to speak with you," Laura murmured against his shoulder.

"I suspected as much." Nolan tamped down the arousing sensations of having her breath whispering against his neck. Damnation, he really had been too long between women.

"I wish to know your purpose," Laura quietly demanded.

"Why, only to dance with the fairest of the fair," Nolan declared with exaggerated gallantry and a debonair smile.

Laura set her back teeth. Clearly, she was irritated with him. Good, that made them even.

"I am many things, Mr. Beecham— "

"You may call me Ezra," Nolan generously allowed.

"I'd rather not," she shot back. "We will never be more than nodding acquaintances at best and antagonists at worst, I expect."

Nolan expected she was right. She annoyed him . . . aroused him . . . and he resented every second of it. Nolan hated to lose control of situations, of himself. This clever little sorceress was hard on both.

"Now then, in reference to your earlier comment about visiting cemeteries— "

"Don't insult my intelligence by denying it was you," Nolan warned as he spun her in a graceful circle. "I know things about you that you obviously prefer to conceal from this prestigious social circle."

Her sensuous lips thinned in noticeable restraint

and Nolan ignored the ridiculous impulse to steal a taste of her.

"I'm sure you must be mistaken," she insisted.

Nolan smiled wryly, silver eyes deflecting hypnotic brown. "I'm quite sure I'm not."

Her smile momentarily faltered. "What are you planning to do, Mr. Beecham? Concoct some wild tale in an attempt to blackmail me? Is it money you want? Or do you wish to soil my reputation with this ridiculous yarn, just for the amusing sport of it?"

If only her money and damaged reputation among the gentry would have pacified him, Nolan thought in self-contempt. He was unreasonably attracted to her. 'Twas as simple and infuriating as that.

"Are you planning to tell Peter this outrageous tale? Or have you already done so?"

Nolan gnashed his teeth. The question implied this unconventional female had a certain fondness for that lovestruck lieutenant. But what did Nolan care? He didn't, he tried to assure himself.

"I haven't— yet," Nolan baited as he stepped back apace.

The music ended, making it impossible for Laura to continue the conversation without being overheard. She glanced sideways, noting the three prospective dance partners who aimed themselves in her direction.

"Invite me outside," she whispered.

Before anyone could interject a dance request, Nolan slid his arm around Laura's waist and shepherded her toward the terrace door. "I could use a breath of fresh air while we continue our conversation on Shakespeare," Nolan announced loudly to all within hearing distance. "I would certainly like to hear why you think England's greatest contribution to the literary world has a dark, unpublicized side to his personality— "

The discreet jab in the ribs sent Nolan's breath out in a *whoosh*. He made a mental note that the dainty, sophisticated lady was as good at hand-to-hand combat as she was with pistols and arrows. He would do well to remember that.

Once they were out of earshot of the other guests, Laura halted in front of Nolan, staring at him with pensive deliberation. "I have the inescapable feeling you are going to make a nuisance of yourself, Mr. Beecham."

"Odd, I find myself thinking the same thing about you, my lady," he countered. "And while we are on the subject of nuisances, I advise you to keep your distance from Geoffrey Spradlin. I have heard several nasty rumors about that oafish officer."

"And I advise you to mind your own business and leave me to mine. I'm quite capable of fending for myself . . ."

To Nolan's stunned amazement, Laura slid her arms over his shoulders, pushed up on tiptoe and kissed him full on the mouth. While his lips were still tingling with pleasurable surprise, her right hand glided down his arm, lingering momentarily at his elbow before she stepped back into her own space.

Nolan's gaze narrowed. "What brought that on?" he asked in a voice that wasn't as steady as he would have preferred.

She smiled cryptically before she pirouetted around and began to move toward the entrance to the house. As expected Peter Forbes appeared, refusing to allow his ladylove out of his sight for more than a minute at a time.

"Laura, I don't think it wise for you to be seen alone on the terrace with Ezra after the two of you lingered on the lawn earlier this evening," Peter admonished. "It might invite uncomplimentary speculation. Reputations have been ruined with less than that—"

"My bracelet!" Laura wailed abruptly.

Her right hand folded around her left wrist and her stricken gaze lifted to Peter who had often made it known he would move heaven and earth to please her. Nolan scowled under his breath. He had the inescapable feeling he wasn't going to like whatever ruse this crafty witch had devised.

"Aunt Miriam entrusted the family emeralds and diamonds to my care and now my bracelet is gone!"

With a dramatic flair, Laura lurched around to search the dimly lit terrace for her missing jewels. Her breath hitched on a shocked gasp when she directed Peter's attention to the sparkling gems that protruded from Nolan's pocket. Nolan found himself thinking he had never been so skillfully ensnared in a trap.

"Mr. Beecham, what are you doing with my heirloom bracelet?" Laura demanded.

Nolan inwardly cursed his predicament. He didn't have the slightest notion how the bracelet had gotten into his pocket. A moment earlier Laura had unexpectedly kissed him and her hand had moved caressingly down his arm to his elbow . . .

Damn that wily witch! Under the pretense of a kiss, she must have picked his pocket— in reverse! He was definitely going to wring her lovely neck the first chance he got. He hadn't realized he had fallen into her carefully laid trap until he was already there. Hell and damnation!

"Explain yourself, Ezra," Peter demanded as he stalked toward Nolan. "Perhaps your fur trading business hasn't been as productive as you would have us believe. I need not remind you that thievery is a serious offense, punishable by imprisonment."

"I want him jailed immediately," Laura insisted, ignoring Nolan's murderous glower. "I should have known he was up to no good when he stole a kiss."

The comment put a snarl on Peter's lips and a dangerous glitter in his blue eyes. "You have gone too far, Ezra," he ground out.

"There is a perfectly reasonable explanation," Nolan said as calmly as possible.

"Aye." Laura smiled in wicked satisfaction. "You are a kissing bandit, Mr. Beecham. I should have known better than to have been beguiled by the like of you." She turned to direct Peter's attention to the steps leading off the south side of the gallery. "Take this wily thief out the back way. I will not have Aunt Miriam upset by this incident. You know how she thrives on entertaining her friends. If her party is ruined she will be extremely distressed."

Peter plucked up the missing bracelet from Nolan's pocket and returned it to Laura. "I'll take care of the matter, my dear, and you can rest assured this scoundrel will never have the opportunity to prey on you again."

"Thank you, Peter. Having you under our roof has proved invaluable more times than I can count."

Nolan swore Laura's syrupy tone could have drowned a stack of pancakes. The sticky-sweet smile she poured on her lovesick admirer gave Nolan an instant toothache. He considered voicing a protest on behalf of his innocence. Then he reminded himself of his encounters with the deceptive Miss Chandler. Nolan shuddered to think how much deeper she would dig the hole she had designed for him if he objected now.

With all the pomp and pageantry of military protocol, Lieutenant Forbes unsheathed the sword that hung on his hip and brandished it in Nolan's face. "In His Majesty's name, I place you under arrest for thievery and improper conduct."

Nolan presumed he was supposed to be intimidated and impressed by Peter's flashy display of swordsmanship. He wasn't. Considering the life-threatening ordeals Nolan had survived, while serving in the militia and in the wilderness, he was more amused than threatened. With casual nonchalance, Nolan pushed the gleaming sword out of his way with his forefinger and swaggered toward the terrace staircase. Peter fell into step behind him.

Nolan glanced back to see the dim shaft of lamplight glowing around Laura's auburn head like a shimmering halo. Nolan swore he had encountered a scheming witch, certainly not an angel. Her kiss was a curse and Nolan scowled at the lingering taste and alluring scent that still clung to him.

That shrewd female thought she'd had the last laugh, did she? Well, she thought wrong. Instead, she had issued a declaration of war that she would come to regret. Laura wasn't dealing with the frivolous dandy Nolan pretended to be. When he was finished with her, she would be on her knees, begging for mercy.

And *mercy,* Nolan vowed as Peter shoveled him into his carriage and clattered off, was the *last* thing Laura Chandler would receive from Nolan Ryder. She would have hell to pay— at his convenience— just as soon as Nolan devised a way to extricate himself from the predicament that infuriating female had left him in.

Seven

Ethan Ryder checked his timepiece for the fifth time as he paced the three-room cabin. Spark McRae sat in his rocker, puffing on his corncob pipe, as if Nolan's tardiness was of no concern.

"What the devil could be keeping him?" Ethan grumbled as he lurched around to pace in the opposite direction.

"He obviously got detained." Spark reached for his tankard of ale. After taking a hearty sip, he wiped the foam from his beard and mustache with the back of his hand. "He'll be here sooner or later."

"Nolan knows the Crown's men are hauling a wagonload of provisions to the barracks this evening. I passed the information to him by way of the carrier pigeons. He knows perfectly well that those supplies were the very ones the soldiers confiscated from the warehouses on the wharf using those cursed Writs of Assistance as their excuse."

"Calm down, Ethan. There's no sense workin' yerself into a frenzy, just because yer little brother is a few minutes late for his assignment."

"A few minutes?" Ethan howled, switching direction to wear a few more trenches in the floorboards.

"He's almost two hours overdue. What could possibly have gone wrong at that Tory party?"

Spark's bulky shoulders lifted in a noncommittal shrug. "Don't reckon I know what happened. Darin' and reckless as yer brother is, he gets himself into some tight scrapes. But he always manages to escape disaster— somehow or another."

"I wish I shared your confidence." Ethan sighed audibly and plopped down in the vacant chair in the corner. "Thinking him dead once was torment enough. I don't relish having to bury Nolan so soon after discovering he was alive and well."

"Yer fond of yer younger brother, aren't you, Ethan?" Spark asked between puffs on his pipe.

"Aye, I am, even though he's changed drastically after his years in battle and his treks through the wilderness. Nolan is all the family I have left."

"He's also the closest thing *I've* got to family." Spark blew a lopsided smoke ring in the air and settled back in his padded rocker. "Nolan has become an escape artist, with plenty of practice to his credit. Stop frettin', Ethan. Yer brother can take care of himself better than most folks I know. He'll be here, eventually."

Ethan slouched in his chair and inhaled a fortifying breath, trying to emulate Spark's unconcerned air. Together they waited . . . and waited some more . . .

Nolan expelled an exasperated breath and shifted restlessly on his prison cot. He despised confinement. It incited too many bitter memories from his nightmarish past. His fiery conflict with Major Isaac Stewart during the Seven Years War had left unsightly scars on his back, had landed him in the stockade and had cost his company of men their lives in battle . . .

The grim thought turned Nolan's soul wrong side out. He squeezed his eyes shut, forcefully ignoring the tormenting vision that hovered above him. The men he had commanded and called friends had been sent into battle and senselessly slaughtered because that arrogant English officer thought his European battle strategies could compete with the hit-and-run tactics employed by the French and their Indian allies.

Nolan would have thought the British might have learned their lesson after General Braddock marched his infantry into the valley of doom near Fort Duqesne. The general had insisted that his men would fight in close-ranked style, just as His Majesty's Army had done on open European battlefields. Sure enough, the general and his well-trained regiments had been ambushed and Braddock had perished with his men. It only served to prove what happened to men who resisted change.

Major Isaac Stewart had been very bit as obstinate about fighting like true English gentlemen. Stewart had lost his haughty temper with Nolan and confined him to the stockade for daring to object to a superior officer— and a blue-blooded Englishman to boot. Although Nolan had escaped confinement, leaving two unconscious guards in his wake, he had been unable to reach the wilderness battle site before his men were mowed down by snipers' bullets and hissing arrows. Not one of his men had survived the ambuscade, and Nolan hadn't learned until two years later that he had been presumed dead after he escaped the stockade to rejoin his company of men.

Distraught and burdened with excessive guilt, Nolan had ridden off to deliver the grim news to his best friend's wife in Pennsylvania. For three years Nolan had listened to Adam Hart describe and discuss his beloved wife— a true paragon, Adam had claimed. But Nolan had discovered that Phoebe Hart deserved not one shred of the affection her departed husband had heaped on her.

Nolan had conveyed the bleak news of Adam's death to Phoebe one day and found himself the object of her overt advances the next. 'Twas then that Nolan had discovered how fickle, treacherous and scheming the female of the species could be.

While Adam was singing Phoebe's praises she had been betraying her wedding vows. She had even propositioned the messenger who bore the news of her husband's death!

Shaking off the thought, Nolan unfolded himself from the cot and stared through the barred window. Although he had assured himself that he had come to grips with his tormented past, he could still feel simmering contempt when dealing with British officers and their holier-than-thou airs— now as then.

The distant sound of a creaking door and muffled voices cut through Nolan's bitter reflections.
Shadows slanted across the barred portal to his
cell. To Nolan's simmering fury and everlasting
surprise, a bewitching face appeared behind the
iron bars. Would that Nolan and Laura Chandler
could exchange places, he thought spitefully.

"You have a visitor, Mr. Beecham," the guard
announced.

Laura turned her head and smiled charmingly
at the wooly-faced guard. "I prefer to speak pri-
vately with Mr. Beecham."

The guard scratched his head and frowned. "I'm
not sure that's a good idea, Miss Chandler. The
lieutenant said this prisoner was to be left in soli-
tary confinement. I really shouldn't even let you
talk to him at all, especially after what he— "

"I will not come to the slightest harm," Laura
interrupted. "Mr. Beecham has no record of previous offenses, now does he?"

"Well— "

"And he has not shown himself to be violent or
belligerent since he arrived, now has he?"

"Nay, but— "

"You did say that he hasn't caused one shred of
trouble, didn't you?"

"Aye, I did, but— "

"Then there is no reason for you to fret about
my safety, is there?"

"Well, I— "

"I couldn't agree with you more, sir." Laura
plucked the key from the guard's pudgy hand, cast

him a dimpled smile and unlocked the door. "With you standing at the far end of the corridor, I have absolutely nothing to fear. 'Tis exactly the kind of security and protection I have come to expect from a noble servant of His Majesty." She pushed open the door and sailed inside. "I will call out to you when I'm ready to leave."

Nodding, the gaoler shut the door behind Laura and lumbered down the corridor.

When the enchanting vision of beauty appeared before him, Nolan propped himself against the wall. His scrutinizing gaze moved over her form-fitting gown and then lifted to meet those black-diamond brown eyes that he had vowed never to stare so deeply into again— at least not twice in the same night. If he did, he would probably find himself in a worse predicament than he was in now— if that were possible.

"And to what do I owe this late-night visit? Or do I dare ask?" Nolan smirked as he pushed away from the wall. He stalked deliberately toward the devious female, fighting the overwhelming urge to strangle her.

"I think we should talk."

Nolan expelled a disrespectful snort. "And what makes you think I have anything to say to a lying little witch?"

Her elegant face tilted to meet his menacing stare. "Because I hold the key that can unlock your prison cell," she reminded him.

"Believe me," Nolan sneered. "Strangling you for framing me holds more appeal at the moment than my freedom. Which, if you must know, is exceptionally near and dear to me."

Laura didn't even flinch when Nolan acquainted her with his most ferocious growl. She bravely stood her ground and flung threat for hissing threat. "If you lay a hand on me, you will find yourself on the gallows. You would be deprived of satisfaction, because we would be inevitably standing in line— side-by-side at the pearly gates."

Nolan's full lips curled and his eyes glittered like shards of steel. "You are deluding yourself if you think *you* are headed for higher ground. I firmly believe the devil has a special place for his own kind."

Laura shrugged off his attempt to intimidate her. "If that be true, you and I will be spending eternity together in an excessively hot climate, Mr. Beecham. You seem as much the devil's advocate as you believe me to be."

With the kind of self-assuredness that had Nolan grinding his teeth, Laura strolled over to the window to survey the view from behind bars. "Since we both seem to have a bit of the devil in us, I think we should both make a pact to live as long as we can, don't you?"

"Why bother prolonging my life, when I'll be left to mildew in prison for a crime I didn't commit," Nolan said after a moment. "Making a pact with the likes of you won't work to my advantage, not if tonight's fiasco is anything to go by."

"You prefer confinement to dealing with me?" she queried with an elfin grin. "You disappoint me, Mr. Beecham. I thought we had found a most entertaining challenge in one another."

"Nay, I told you I despise confinement, but I find you less amusing and entertaining by the second," he grumbled.

"Then consider me the lesser of two evils."

Nolan smirked impolitely. "My dear lady, I cannot even conjure up one evil that remotely compares to you."

She smiled as if he had paid her the highest compliment. "I'm glad you realize you aren't dealing with the village idiot. And if you are smart and have learned your lesson well, you will remember that threats and insults don't faze me, they challenge me."

Nolan moved a step closer, crowding Laura against the wall. When she tried to sidestep him, Nolan braced his hands on either side of her shoulders, effectively pinning her in place. To his surprise, he saw the flicker of alarm in those wide brown eyes, felt her stiffen apprehensively. It amazed him that she continued to hold her ground when she appeared to be leery of him at close range, intimidated by the potential threat of superior strength.

"If you force me to scream for help, you will bloody well rot in this jail," Laura muttered at him. "I came to effect your release, but unless you cooperate, I vow you will grow old keeping track of time in prison before you become the honored guest at your hanging."

Perhaps Laura was wary of their close contact,

but Nolan was unwillingly aroused by it. He had the insane urge to sample those soft lips again, to feel her delicious curves molded familiarly to his hard contours . . .

He needed his head examined for even thinking such things!

Frustrated at himself, Nolan retreated a step and watched Laura breathe a discreet but relieved sigh.

Inhaling a steadying breath he reined in his wandering thoughts. "Very well, my lady, what sort of cooperation do you have in mind for me?"

"What sort of blackmail did you have in mind for *me*?" she countered his question.

"I only sought to satisfy my curiosity about the reason a lady from your station would be tramping around a graveyard after midnight, masquerading as a lowly waif."

Laura eyed him suspiciously. "And how can you be so certain 'twas I who was supposedly garbed in homespun clothes— ?"

"I didn't say that, did I?" Nolan broke into a smile when Laura cursed under her breath.

"I only presumed— "

Nolan interrupted with a snort. "You may as well drop this facade of pretended innocence. It doesn't matter *how* I know that you aren't exactly what you seem, only that *I know*. You wouldn't have framed me for thievery if you didn't consider my knowledge of your late-night activities a threat."

Laura heaved a sigh and veered around Nolan to circumnavigate the cell. While she frowned, and paced, he found himself admiring and yet resenting the enigmatic female who cleverly landed him in jail.

"If you think I planned to use the information to extort money from you, you are mistaken," he said after a moment.

Laura paused and regarded him consideringly. "Why should I believe you?"

Nolan reminded himself that Laura believed him to be no more than a self-indulgent dandy whose greatest concern was his own amusements. She had no idea that he suspected her of being a spy who infiltrated the secret rebel society.

A wry smile pursed his lips as he ambled toward her. He slowly lifted his hand to cup her delicate chin, meeting her wary gaze. "You are a beautiful woman, Laura."

"What has that got to do with anything?"

"Hasn't it occurred to you that I might have wanted some kind of leverage over you, because I am attracted to you?" he asked reasonably. "When a man finds himself in fierce competition for the attention of an alluring woman, he often relies on any tactic at his disposal."

"Why am I having trouble believing that your only reason for mentioning this incident was to give yourself an edge over this supposed competition for my affection?"

"I haven't a clue," Nolan said smoothly. "Unless you have a highly suspicious mind. But with your fawning lieutenant hovering around you, as well as the infamous Geoffrey Spradlin, not to mention the herd of eager suitors you have collected, I had no choice but to use the knowledge to my advantage."

Laura sniffed caustically and stepped back apace. "The next thing I know, you will be pledging undying love or some such nonsense to lure me onto your cot. I thought I made it crystal clear that I am not in search of a husband."

"I wasn't proposing; I was propositioning," he corrected. "You claim you are not in the market for a husband and I am hardly in need of a wife."

Laura jerked up her head and glared at his teasing grin. "You are a most exasperating man, Mr. Beecham."

"And you are an authority on exasperation," he declared. "You have provided me with plenty of exasperation this evening. You still haven't told me whose grave site you were visiting in the cloak of darkness, dressed as an urchin. My curiosity is killing me."

"Would that it actually could," she muttered half under her breath.

Nolan ignored that. "I am also interested to know where you learned to pick a pocket with such amazing ease."

" 'Tis none of your business," she snapped. "I came here to free you from prison, but I must have your solemn promise that you will never mention the supposed incident again, not to me or anyone."

"And how do you intend to explain this misunderstanding about how your bracelet ended up in my pocket?" he wanted to know.

"I'll think of something."

" 'Tis no telling how you will twist the truth to your advantage."

Laura sighed impatiently. "Do we have a bargain or don't we? I will ensure your freedom if you give me your word as a gentleman that the incident will be forgotten."

Nolan inched closer, enjoying small consolation in the fact that Laura had to look up to him. "Shall we seal our bargain with a kiss? After all, 'twas what I was ultimately after."

"And nothing more?" Laura eyed him dubiously. "What of your claim that you had intended to proposition me into bed?"

" 'Twas *before* I discovered how adept you are with your hands," he murmured as his arm glided around her waist to pull her against him. "I cringe to think what you might steal from me if you had the chance. My manhood perhaps?"

'Twas with extreme satisfaction that Nolan watched her face flame with profuse color. His comment also caused his male body to harden at the sensual prospect of having those deft hands caressing him. He shouldn't have voiced that outrageous remark. It stimulated his vivid imagination and sent Laura's bewitching face up in flames.

Laura inhaled an audible breath and braced the heels of her hands on the wide expanse of his chest, ensuring that he didn't come any closer. "Very well then, a kiss to seal our bargain of confidentiality, Mr. Beecham."

"Ezra," he insisted as he drew her hands over his shoulders and pressed his lips to her.

Nolan forgot all about the mysterious waif he had seen at the Sons of Liberty meeting, the urchin who scampered through the honeycomb of Boston streets and wandered through cemeteries after midnight. He thought of nothing but the soft, alluring woman in his arms, the dewy taste of her kiss . . . and the hot throb of desire that set his male body aflame.

In less than a heartbeat Nolan had deepened their kiss, savoring every succulent taste of her. His questing tongue speared into the soft recesses of her mouth, exploring it as thoroughly as he yearned to possess all of her. His hands glided down her hips, bringing her into intimate contact with his arousal. He could feel her breasts meshed against his chest and he resented the fabric that separated them, resented his instantaneous loss of self-control, this obsessive attraction.

Nolan knew what a lethal threat this sorceress could be to him, and to his cause of liberty, but he couldn't stop himself from savoring her. Her reluctant but instinctive response fanned flames that seared every fiber of his being. 'Twas unnerving to be so lost in a woman he couldn't trust and didn't understand. Even now, Laura was tugging at his self-control, transforming him into a mindless creature of unruly passion. Holding her against him was nowhere near enough to appease the ravenous needs one kiss aroused. He wanted to feel her beneath him, surrounding him, moving with him in ageless rhythm.

'Twas absurd . . . 'twas dangerous . . . 'twas necessary . . .

Nolan called upon his floundering willpower and lifted his raven head. When his gaze dropped to her kiss-swollen lips, 'twas all he could do not to help himself to another addictive taste of her. Wanting her was becoming unbearable as well as illogical.

Ah, the kind of passion to die for, Nolan thought cynically. 'Twas exactly what would happen to him if he let himself surrender to this bewitching woman's dangerous lure. She would forsake him as quickly as she had stuffed her bracelet in his pocket and summoned her lovestruck lackey. If she knew Nolan's true identity, he would find his days numbered. He could enjoy her temporarily, but he could never allow himself to trust her.

"You have effectively sealed my lips," Nolan said huskily. "In fact, I don't recall anything that happened before this pleasurable moment."

In wicked amusement Nolan watched Laura wobble on unsteady legs and drag in several ragged breaths. At least he had been assured that he affected her as dramatically as she affected him.

"And you promise not to hold this alleged incident over my head?" she squeaked, her voice one octave higher than normal.

"What incident?" Nolan rasped. "Your kiss erased all memory. I remember nothing but the pleasure of holding you. Ah, that heaven itself could offer such bliss."

Laura frowned in disapproval. "I told you that I have an aversion to flattery," she reminded him.

Nolan smiled rakishly. "There, you see, your kiss did indeed erase every scrap of my memory."

When Nolan checked his pockets to ensure Laura hadn't planted other incriminating evidence on his person— while he was too enthralled in their kiss to notice— she grinned impishly. "Your memory must be returning, Mr. Beecham."

"Or perhaps 'tis only that I had hoped to find the key to your bedroom door and an invitation to take up where we left off."

His teasing remark drew another disgruntled frown. Laura rearranged her gown and ran a shaky hand through her hair to ensure she looked presentable before facing the guard. "Don't press your luck, Ezra Beecham. I have made it clear that I have no wish to take you as a lover or any man as a husband."

"Peter Forbes is going to be heartbroken when he hears the news."

One delicate brow arched. "And you don't approve of Peter?"

"The lieutenant isn't man enough to handle you, even if you deign to accept his forthcoming proposal," Nolan said with great confidence. "I'm not sure any man can handle you, truth be known."

"And that disturbs you, doesn't it? You, like so many men, seem to think a woman should not be entitled to her own opinion, to speak her own mind, to enjoy her own individuality."

"I didn't say that—"

"You were thinking it," she accused. "And you can think whatever you like, but I've no intention of changing the way I am for any man."

When Laura propelled herself toward the door to summon the guard, Nolan frowned quizzically. "Who was he?"

She pivoted to stare at him in puzzlement. "Who was *who*?"

"The one who has made you skittish when a man advances without gentlemanly restraint, the one who forces all other men to announce our intentions first, so as not to alarm you? Was it Geoffrey Spradlin?"

Obsidian eyes flared before she managed to conceal her surprise at his perception. Curiously, Nolan watched Laura compose herself before presenting her back to him.

"Good night, Mr. Beecham. If all goes well, you will be free within a few minutes. I will convince Judge Clover that the incident at the party was an unfortunate mistake. If you disagree, you will be staring at these gloomy walls much longer than you prefer."

"I hope this fictitious explanation you concoct for the magistrate isn't too farfetched to be believable," he grumbled.

"I will be convincing," she promised before she called to the gaoler.

Nolan didn't doubt that for a minute. He could see the cogs of her brain cranking. Laura Chandler had a fascinating flair for theatrics, and when she bestowed her blinding, dimpled smile on a man, he lost his train of thought. When Laura posed a few leading questions, she could make a man believe whatever she wanted him to believe.

Nolan wondered if he was the only man in Boston who knew Laura for what she was— a cunningly deceptive, impossibly enchanting Tory spy who would have to be stopped before she betrayed the patriot cause. She was a serious threat, Nolan reminded himself sensibly. No matter how much he desired that auburn-haired female— when she was soft and yielding in his arms— she was still dangerous. If she knew the truth of his identity, would she devise ways to spare his life or use the information to her profit and advantage?

When Laura exited, Nolan sank down on his cot and pondered those questions. He would be every kind of fool if he thought Laura wouldn't hand him over to British authorities in exchange for a pouch of gold coins. Nolan made a pact with himself, then and there. He would never allow Laura Chandler to discover his dual identity. She must never know that Ezra Beecham— a man who made it known to one and all that his sole ambition was the pursuit of his personal happiness— and the Midnight Rider were one and the same.

Now, Nolan asked himself, how could he remove the threat that alluring female posed to the cause of liberty without disposing of her— permanently?

Good question. Nolan wished he had a good answer to go with it.

Eight

Ethan Ryder leaped to his feet when Nolan, garbed in the fancy trappings of a gentleman and a lopsided wig, burst through the cabin door. "Where the blazes have you been? You should have been back hours ago. The British made off with more supplies to feed their soldiers and there was no one to stop them."

Nolan pulled off the periwig and unceremoniously dropped it on the table. Powder rose like a fog in the lanternlight. "I've been in jail," he announced in a sour tone.

"Jail!" Ethan and Spark erupted simultaneously.

"Jail," Nolan confirmed. "And you know what an aversion I have developed to confined spaces."

"Brings back bad memories, I'd guess," Spark murmured. "What landed you there this time? Another verbal battle with some haughty British officer?"

"Nay, a confrontation with a devious female whose hands are quicker than the eye. I was framed for thievery."

"What?" Ethan howled in disbelief.

Nolan poured himself a tankard of ale and

plopped into the chair his brother had vacated. " 'Tis a long story."

"I want to hear it, no matter how lengthy," Ethan declared as he pulled another chair up to the table.

Nolan formulated his thoughts and proceeded. "Do you remember who was present at the meeting at Chase and Speakman's Distillery last week?"

Ethan frowned thoughtfully. "Aye, all the charter members of our society, plus several new clansmen who've come to realize British tyranny is not going to go away without united opposition."

"Then you also recall the shabby waif who trailed in behind John Adams?" Nolan inquired.

Ethan went very still. "I remember."

"The waif is not a waif at all, but a woman," Nolan reported. He paused when Spark choked on his grog and sputtered for breath. When the old frontiersman had recovered, Nolan stared somberly at his brother. "The urchin aroused my curiosity that night and I followed him— her, as the case turned out to be. She made her way to the cemetery to deposit flowers by a grave. At the time, I thought perhaps the lad might have been paying his respects to a lost sister or sweetheart. But lo and behold, I met a young woman at the ball tonight who had the very same brown eyes and impish features I noticed on that would-be urchin's face."

"And?" Ethan prompted with an anticipatory grimace.

"And I have come to the conclusion that the lady in question, posing as a waif, has infiltrated our secret society and is passing information to the Brits."

"And that's how you landed in jail?" Spark asked, bemused.

Nolan shook his raven head, and then frowned when he noticed his brother's sudden interest with the lantern sitting on the table. The man was behaving rather oddly, Nolan thought.

"I made the mistake of mentioning the cemetery incident when the lady and I had a disagreement. Later, she summoned me to the terrace for a private chat. Before I knew it, she kissed me full on the mouth and dropped her family heirloom bracelet in my pocket. I was standing there dumbfounded when she called to the British lieutenant quartered in her home. She accused me of being a thief—"

Spark, who had taken another sip of ale, sucked in his breath and choked.

Nolan reached over to whack him between the shoulder blades.

"She's a spy and a pickpocket?" Spark wheezed, amber eyes bulging.

Nolan's attention fixed on his brother. Ethan had yet to react. He simply sat there with his blond head bowed, as if hypnotized by the dancing flames in the lantern globe.

"Are you listening, Ethan?" Nolan prompted irritably. "I discovered who the traitor is and she had me locked in jail."

"But how did you escape if the lieutenant did her biddin'?" Spark questioned, befuddled. "If those lobsterbacks are hot on yer heels, they'll find our hideout and that devil stallion tucked in the shed."

"There is no British patrol keeping surveillance on me. I made certain of it." Nolan never took his eyes off Ethan. "You're taking this amazingly well, big brother. Any reason why?"

"You have made a mistake."

Nolan expelled a gruff snort. "The mistake I made was allowing myself to believe I was dealing with an ordinary female rather than a shrewd, cunning witch. She came to the jail an hour ago to strike a bargain of silence with me. I haven't a clue how she convinced Judge Clover that she had made a mistake, but I was released."

"You should never have pressed the issue with her in the first place," Ethan muttered.

"She's a bloody informant!" Nolan blared at his brother.

"You should have confided your information to me first," Ethan shot back. " 'Tis no telling what kind of repercussions you might have caused the lady."

Nolan gaped at Ethan as if he had rhubarb growing out his ears. "The difficulty *I* caused *her*?" he repeated sarcastically. "I'm the one who landed in jail and missed my scheduled midnight ride. If I didn't know better, I would swear you are defending that little Tory spy."

Spark eyed Ethan suspiciously. "Why *are* you defendin' the chit? She obviously isn't one of us. If she freely offered to give billetin' facilities to an English officer she must be a Tory sympathizer. When did you change sides of the conflict, Ethan?"

"I haven't. My loyalties are the same as yours."

"Could have fooled me," Spark scoffed caustically.

Ethan slumped in his chair and raked his fingers through his straight blond hair. "I truly wish you could have kept your erroneous suspicions to yourself, Nolan. We don't need more complications than we already have, especially with a £500 price on your head."

"The army added another £100," Nolan amended.

"Damn," Ethan scowled. "If Sam Adams decides to proceed with the next protest rally he's planning against the Stamp Act, the Midnight Rider will probably shoulder the blame for inflaming more colonial tempers. Before we know it, there will be a £1000 reward on your head. And if your evening activities throw the slightest suspicion on Laura Chandler—"

"You know who she is?" Nolan choked out.

"Of course I know who she is," Ethan snapped. "You made a mistake," he repeated slowly and emphatically.

Spark threw up his hands when Nolan and Ethan glared each other down from across the table. "What the devil is goin' on? Nolan's conclusions sound perfectly logical to me."

"He doesn't know what I know, and neither do you, Spark," Ethan declared. With Spark hanging on the edge of his seat and Nolan leaning forward, elbows propped on the edge of the table, Ethan replied, "Laura Chandler is one of *us*, serving as a patriot spy who conveys information through channels about British army activities. She works for *me*."

Nolan nearly fell out of his chair. He could not imagine his brother being so gullible, unless he had been as bewitched as every other man who fell beneath that siren's spell.

"You honestly believe that shrewd female is a patriot sympathizer?" Nolan erupted in a snort. "She has hoodwinked you, too? You and every other man in town? I seem to be the only one who sees her for what she obviously is— a double agent at the very least and a clever Tory spy at the worst!"

Ethan heaved a gusty sigh. "You, my dear brother, have dashed off a tall cliff and leaped to ridiculous conclusions."

"I doubt it," Nolan grunted. "And do not take offense when time proves me right. I will take excessive pleasure in telling you I told you so."

"Laura isn't what you think," Ethan persisted.

Nolan's reply was another disdainful snort.

Ethan leaned back in his chair and drummed his fingers, trying to decide whether to reveal the truth to his cynical brother. It seemed he had no choice.

"The truth is that Laura's aunt is not really her aunt."

"What? Another deception?" Nolan mocked sardonically. "Why am I not surprised?"

Ethan flashed him a silencing frown and continued. "Miriam Peabody is a childless widow who took Laura off the streets almost six years ago and educated her with the finest tutors money could buy. Laura was an orphan. Her mother was sent to America after she had been ruined by some heartless earl who took his pleasures with her and then sent away the evidence of his indiscretion before his illegitimate child was born. Laura's mother died when she was a child and she lived in an orphanage for a few years before striking out on her own."

"And now the hoyden from the streets is intent on returning to her homeland to blackmail her natural father and live in grand style," Nolan cynically suggested.

Ethan shook his head in dismay. "You have become a hopeless skeptic."

"And you have gone from cautious to blindly stupid," Nolan accused. "Your street-wise pauper-turned-princess is playing you for a fool, Ethan. She would turn me over to her love-struck lieutenant faster than I could blink."

"Your identity is the best-kept secret in Boston and I will ensure it stays that way," Ethan assured him. "Laura's duplicity had been carefully kept under wraps until you forced me to admit her true purpose to you. She is considered one of the most sought-after aristocrats in town. She has spent a year establishing communications with British officers and loyalists. Miriam Peabody poses as a front to lure unsuspecting officers to social gatherings. But the truth is Miriam Peabody contributes to the patriot fund, just as John Hancock does."

"How can you be so certain of that?" Nolan demanded.

"Because Laura meets me each month to deliver the donations Miriam offers us."

Nolan seriously doubted Miriam Peabody was a financier for the rebel cause. More than likely, Laura was offering funds the British authorities presented to her to convince patriots that she and her supposed aunt shared rebel sentiments.

Things smelled a mite too fishy for Nolan's tastes.

"You seem to have forgotten about Malcolm Gridley, who proclaimed himself to be aligned with the patriot cause six weeks ago. He was caught meeting Captain Oran Milbourne in the alley behind the Royal Coffee House. Malcolm was promptly tarred and feathered for betraying the cause. The man had been living beyond his means for months, as I heard it told."

"Laura is nothing like Malcolm Gridley," Ethan said with perfect assurance.

"Nay, she is only a liar and pickpocket who brushes shoulders with Tories and British officials, and quarters an English lieutenant."

"You brush shoulders with Tories and British officials," Ethan didn't hesitate to point out.

" 'Tis different," Nolan insisted. "You know I'm on the side of freedom. But I'm not too sure about Laura Chandler's motives, even if you seem to be."

Ethan flung up his hands in frustration. "How am I to convince you that you are absolutely wrong about Laura?"

"Try explaining her visit to the cemetery," Nolan suggested.

"I can't."

"Did it occur to you that she may have been planted there by the Brits to determine how I disappeared into thin air? As you recall, the army tried to stash a young private there once or twice. 'Twas because of Spark's warning signals that I knew when not to use the cemetery to escape patrols."

"You are jumping to conclusions," Ethan grumbled.

"Am I? Then tell me why I saw the same waif at the docks the night I intercepted the patrol that came dangerously close to spotting the skiffs rowing away from your revenue cutter."

"I can't explain that, either," Ethan mumbled.

"I thought not."

Nolan chugged his ale and then peeled off his coat and cravat. " 'Tis been a long night. I suggest you make your way home and get some rest. If Sam Adams's upcoming rally turns out to be a repetition of the last one he organized, none of us will be allowed much sleep for a month. The whole town will be in an uproar."

"Aye, 'tis a fact." Ethan rose to his feet and scooped up his jacket. "I am leery of putting Ebenezer McIntosh in charge—"

"That blusterin' shoemaker and burly leader of the South End mob who engages in street fights with the North End gang?" Spark spoke up. "Dear Lord, the man has a reputation as a brawler. He caused too much trouble at the first demonstration.

I shudder to think what the next one will be like, now that the uncontrollable gangs and their infamous leader have gotten a taste of destruction."

"Aye, but Samuel claims organized protests of this nature will bring Parliament's attention to the complaints about the standing army and unfair taxes. And 'tis no doubt that men like McIntosh oppose British occupation as much as we do."

Nolan reluctantly agreed. "McIntosh and his friends have lost men to press gangs when sailors were needed to man British warships. Men like Adams, Hancock and my brother are protected against open affront, because of their distinguished rank and position in Boston society."

"Well, it sounds like trouble to me," Spark mumbled. "Mobs have a tendency to take on personalities all their own." He stared solemnly at Nolan. "You'll have yer hands full if you try to control a full-fledged riot. If I were the Midnight Rider, I wouldn't try to monitor that particular demonstration, because he'll shoulder the blame if things get out of hand— which I predict they will."

Nolan had lived with the wise old frontiersman long enough to know his prediction would probably prove accurate. Spark had a wealth of varied experiences. He had left the congested streets of Philadelphia to try his hand at hunting and trapping and served as a scout during the Seven Years War. Spark knew more tricks than a trained bear and he was usually an excellent judge of human nature. Except when it came to women, Nolan amended. Spark had three ex-fiancées to his humiliated credit.

After Ethan went on his way, Nolan crawled into bed. He concentrated on the difficulties that could erupt during the public demonstration rather than letting himself become distracted by lingering visions and uninvited memories of a woman whose kisses stirred sensations Nolan didn't want to feel.

Nolan didn't trust Laura Chandler. She was in position to sell the Sons of Liberty down the Charles River. And if Samuel Adams's *organized* mob blew the lid off Boston, every patriot leader might become a marked man. Nolan expected the Midnight Rider would become the focal point of British frustration if the protesting crowd degenerated into a violent mob.

Hell and damnation, Nolan thought as he tossed and turned on his bed. If Samuel's public demonstration did evolve into a devastating riot, the price on Nolan's head was likely to go right through the roof!

Ethan Ryder waited at the designated location beside the moonlit river. Within a few minutes he saw a shadow drifting along the row of trees. Ethan signaled with the call of an owl and the shadow responded in kind.

"Are the Brits anticipating trouble now that the Stamp Act has officially passed Parliament?" Ethan questioned when Laura strode up beside him.

Laura nodded affirmatively as she discreetly

dropped a pouch of coins in Ethan's pocket. "Officials are expecting the radical factions of the patriot movement to do more than threaten stamp distributors into resigning before the act goes into effect. They have seen the mob in action once, after all."

"Have they gotten wind of plans for another protest rally?"

"Aye," Laura murmured. "The military officials have beefed up patrols after receiving word of a possible demonstration and hearing rumors of protests and assaults against tax officials in other colonies."

"I'm not sure enlarged patrols can control the monster Samuel Adams is planning to unleash." Ethan glanced across the sparkling river and purposely changed the topic of conversation. "I received news that you were seen entering the jail recently. Was there a problem?"

Laura muttered under her breath. "Aye, and why I was moved to generosity over the incident, I cannot say. It must have been the fear of more complications arising from it."

Ethan was most anxious to hear her version of the encounter with his brother. "What happened, Laura?"

"I confronted a most exasperating man who appears to have discovered that I take to the streets in disguise. How he could have recognized me I can't fathom, but he did. I had no choice but to back him into a corner before I found myself in one."

"His name?" Ethan questioned, as if he didn't know.

"Ezra Beecham. Have you heard of him?"

Ethan nodded slightly. "He's an entrepreneur of the fur trade, a pleasure-seeker whose priorities revolve around his personal amusements."

"And why I find myself the least bit— " Laura swallowed her reckless comment and glanced quickly at Ethan. "I had to let Peter Forbes believe I had taken a fancy to Ezra in order to effect that scoundrel's release from jail."

Ethan's blond brow rose. "Taken a fancy to Beecham?"

"I would have preferred to take a whip to that scamp," Laura muttered resentfully.

"You are being exceptionally vague about the details," Ethan noted. "Any reason why?"

Laura shifted awkwardly beneath Ethan's probing stare. She was having enough trouble understanding her own feelings toward Ezra Beecham without trying to explain the unreasonable and unwanted attraction to someone else. "Suffice it to say that I countered Ezra's threat with my own. We have made a pact, he and I. After Ezra promised to forget he saw me in disguise, I promised not to use my influence with Peter Forbes."

"And you trust him to keep silent?"

Laura met Ethan's quizzical gaze with her usual amount of determination. "I trust my ability to see Ezra back in jail if he dares to make more trouble. But there is something about the man that worries me. I cannot pinpoint why, but I have been stung by the feeling that Ezra Beecham isn't exactly what he seems. And don't ask me to explain my intuitive hunch, for I cannot."

Ethan tensed, but he quickly masked his concern. Laura Chandler was wise beyond her years and extremely perceptive. Her unusual background enhanced her ability to read people with amazing clarity. Not that Ethan didn't trust her, but Nolan's suspicions had provoked him to be more cautious—just in case. If Nolan was right about Laura's divided loyalties, she could be playing both ends against the middle with Nolan's life hanging in the balance. Secrecy was of the utmost importance here.

"The less association you have with Ezra Beecham the better," Ethan advised. "Let Peter Forbes think your fascination for the rake subsided as quickly as it began."

"I had intended to," Laura assured him. "But Peter insisted on knowing why I retracted the charges of thievery. I had to humbly confess to Peter that my bracelet had come unfastened when Ezra and I embraced, and that it must have accidentally dropped into his pocket. I led Peter to believe that I was embarrassed and ashamed to admit I had been a willing participant of the kiss on the terrace. I told him that my nagging conscience got the better of me and I felt guilty about leaving an innocent man in jail. I also let it be known that Ezra Beecham possessed irresistible charm and I was bedeviled by it before I even realized it."

Ethan groaned aloud. "I'm surprised Peter hasn't

tried to call Beecham out for toying with your affection."

"He planned to do just that," Laura reported. "But I talked him out of it by insisting I was as much to blame as Ezra was. I assured Peter that 'twas simply my impulsive sense of adventure and reckless curiosity that got the better of me in a careless moment. Peter finally accepted my explanation and settled his ruffled feathers. Luckily, Beecham and I haven't crossed paths since. Henceforth, I intend to take great pains to avoid the man."

"A wise decision, I'm sure."

"So am I," Laura murmured.

"Have a care making your way home," Ethan warned as Laura turned away. "I passed two off-duty patrols who were making rounds at the taverns. I expect a few brawls will break out between patriots and redcoats."

"I will avoid the Brits' favorite haunts."

When the waif disappeared into the trees, Ethan reaffirmed his belief that Laura Chandler had not bamboozled him. Nolan was unnecessarily suspicious. If there was a traitor in their midst, 'twas not this female.

True, Laura had suffered difficult times that might prompt others to turn traitor for the want of gold coins. Greed was a dangerous flaw that could corrupt, but Ethan was reasonably certain Laura was not pretending to promote the rebel cause in order to line her pockets. Her motives were sincere, Ethan reassured himself. Nolan was skeptical because he simply didn't trust women—on general principle.

Ethan checked his timepiece. The Midnight Rider was going to be up to a good bit of mischief very soon. Nolan planned to raid the barracks to recover the confiscated supplies taken from the warehouses on the wharf the previous week. While Nolan lured the sentries away from the storeroom, Spark and Ethan were to reclaim the goods.

Ethan shared Nolan's opinion that the army could damned well pay for their supplies— just like everybody else. The high-handed lot of them were not going to swipe what they wanted from their colonial cousins, not if the Ryder brothers could help it!

On that determined note, Ethan tramped off to do his part in stealing the supplies the soldiers had stolen.

Nine

Spark surveyed the darkened barracks and the nearby storehouse where the confiscated colonial goods had been stashed. His gaze followed the two passing sentinels who stood watch during the night.

"I don't know about this, Nolan," Spark whispered in wary trepidation.

"I don't know about this, either," Ethan put in warily. "The storehouse is too close to the soldiers' sleeping quarters. Those redcoats will be all over us if we try to retake the stolen supplies."

Nolan calmly appraised the situation, then turned around and strode purposefully toward his stallion, adding as he walked away, "I'll distract the soldiers while you carry off the supplies."

"Distract the soldiers— *how?*" Spark questioned Nolan's back. Inhaling an exasperated breath, Spark spun toward Ethan. "I hate it when he does that. I never know what to expect and he usually scares the fool out of me— "

Spark didn't have time to punctuate his sentence before the devil stallion plunged from the thicket and thundered toward the barracks.

"Holy— " Ethan practically swallowed his tongue when the daring vigilante hurled his torch of liberty toward the sentries who had veered around the corner of the barracks.

To Ethan's shock and dismay, the guards whirled to fire at the approaching rider-in-black. Ethan was greatly relieved to note the sentries' shots went astray when blinded by torchlight. The Midnight Rider's tactic was clever, Ethan would give him that.

Ethan barely had time to recover from observing the first wild antic when the Midnight Rider dared to do the totally unexpected— again. Without concern for life or limb, he clattered onto the planked porch, reached down to open the door and *rode* his stallion into the soldiers' sleeping quarters!

Ethan nearly suffered heart seizure.

"I've seen him pull a lot of wild stunts before, but never one quite like *that*," Spark chirped, astounded.

"I better not see him do it again, either," Ethan croaked.

Shouts arose from inside the barracks, followed by yelps, curses and the crash of furniture. The sentries didn't dare fire their muskets, for fear their comrades would catch stray gunfire.

As bedlam broke out inside the barracks, Spark grabbed Ethan's rigid arm and steered him toward the storehouse. "I reckon that's our signal to make off with all the supplies we can get our hands on."

Ethan dashed madly toward the storeroom and slipped inside. Spark was two steps behind him.

Together they gathered all the goods they could carry, before reversing direction to load the wagon concealed in the thicket.

When Ethan pivoted around, his evergreen eyes bulged and he cursed colorfully. The Midnight Rider had emerged from the barracks, pursued by half-dressed soldiers. Pistols barked like rabid dogs and the flare of gunfire lit up the night. The soldiers gave barefoot chase, spitting salty curses at the Rebel Rider who performed a series of figure-eight maneuvers on the military drill field. Amid a barrage of fire, the cloaked rider personally saw to the waste of several rounds of British ammunition.

"Does that maniac know no fear?" Ethan asked the world at large.

"Nay," Spark replied, giving Ethan a nudge toward the storehouse. "He damns all consequences. Sometimes I swear that's what keeps him alive. That and the fact nobody believes his darin'. The patrols never know what he'll decide to do next until he does it."

While the Midnight Rider lured the soldiers to the far end of the square, Ethan and Spark scurried back to the storeroom. In a matter of minutes they had retrieved the last of the stolen supplies.

Spark and Ethan had just climbed onto the wagon seat to make their hasty departure when the Phantom Rider thundered straight through the congregation of soldiers. Again, the troops couldn't risk firing without dropping one of their own men.

And then, like a trail of black smoke drifting off in the wind, the rebel daredevil raced off into the night, leaving grumbling troops and wasted ammunition in his wake.

An hour later, mounted upon the gray gelding, Nolan reined up beside the wagon rolling down the dirt path. Ethan glared at his brother— good and hard. "I do not appreciate watching you defy death for the mere sport of it," he scolded gruffly.

Nolan shrugged a broad shoulder and led the way down the path. "Dead men have no fear of dying," was all he said in reply.

Ethan's breath came out in an exasperated rush. "I do wish you would stop saying things like that."

" 'Twas not that dangerous," Nolan said blandly. "Most of the military unit had been on another of their drinking sprees. They were too groggy to realize what was happening until I rode out the door. They were also too far into their cups to shoot straight."

"I don't care if the whole lot of them drank themselves blind and passed out on their cots! I expect you to employ more caution during future raids!"

"Aye, whatever you say, big brother. I'll try to remember that next time."

"You're patronizing me," Ethan grumbled.

"Am I?"

"Blast it, Nolan!"

"Sh-sh!" Spark elbowed Ethan in the ribs. "Keep yer voice down. There's no need to wake the whole bloody countryside. Yer lectures haven't affected that daredevil yet. I doubt they'll do any good now, either."

Ethan shook his head and clamped his mouth shut as the wagon rolled toward its destination. He swore he would *never* grow accustomed to these hair-raising shenanigans.

"I've gotten used to watchin' him ride the cuttin' edge," Spark added. "I don't like it, mind you, I've just learned to close my eyes and send a prayer heavenward. Luckily, yer brother appears to have as many lives as a cat."

"Not quite," Ethan mumbled. "As you recall, I've already buried him *once.*"

Nolan stifled a yawn while he stood beside Willie Fitzgerald. The previous evening's activities at the barracks had proved successful but time-consuming. By the time he, Ethan and Spark had distributed the goods the British had confiscated to their rightful owners, the first rays of dawn had spread across the horizon.

Tired though Nolan was, he hadn't wanted to miss this evening's opportunity to mingle with the congregation of Tories and soldiers who had ventured to Thomas Guntham's House of Fine Jewels to view the showing of the Microcosm.

The intriguing "World in Miniature" had arrived from Europe, and Boston's elite had turned out in full force to view a miniature city, and the mechanical planetarium which accurately depicted the movements of the sun, moon and planets.

While Willie craned his neck, hoping Laura Chandler would magically appear among the gaily adorned crowd, Nolan— in his role as Ezra Beecham— strolled over to the display of mechanical toys that had been imported from England. The miniature model of a port— much like Boston— boasted tiny ships in its harbor and coaches on the wharf with their minute wheels in motion. A miniature powder mill was at work at the opposite end of the table.

Although Nolan found the exhibit fascinating, Willie towed him toward the door before the curator had time to explain how the grove— where diminutive birds were batting their wings— worked.

"The evening needn't be a total waste," Willie declared as he propelled Nolan outside. "If I can't pursue my courtship with Laura Chandler, I may as well take my pleasures elsewhere."

"If your ultimate intent and purpose was to happen upon the unconventional Miss Chandler, you should consider yourself fortunate that she and her aunt didn't attend the exhibition," Nolan said as Willie herded him down the street. "I don't think that particular lady is quite right for you, Willie."

"Nay, I'm sure you don't since you seemed so taken with her yourself," Willie sniffed. "If I wasn't such a generous chap I wouldn't forgive you for trying to beat my time at Miriam Peabody's party." He frowned curiously. "Just where did you get off to that night, Ezra? I looked around and suddenly you were gone."

Nolan shrugged a velvet-clad shoulder and masked his irritation over the incident that had landed him in jail. "I called it an early evening."

When Willie veered toward the brothel near the wharf, Nolan declined to follow.

"You go ahead without me, Willie," he insisted. "I believe I'll return to the exhibit."

Willie chuckled mockingly. "You prefer to play with children's toys rather than satisfy a man's natural appetites? I say, Ezra, you are going to ruin your bad reputation if you aren't careful."

"I prefer to ease my masculine needs elsewhere, if you don't mind," Nolan replied.

He had used the imaginary mistress excuse the last two times Willie tried to drag him off to the bawdy house of his choice.

Willie nodded thoughtfully. "Aye, I remember your telling me you had a mistress you preferred to keep all to yourself. Very selfish and unsportsmanly of you, Ezra."

As Willie swaggered into the dimly lit parlor to amuse himself, Nolan returned to the exhibit. He had stumbled onto an interesting bit of information that he wanted to pursue. Lexington officials had appointed a new stamp distributor after the previous agent had resigned— prompted by a visit from the Midnight Rider. Nolan was inclined to pay his patriotic respects to the boastful Horace Muldoon, the new replacement . . .

Nolan stopped in his tracks when something

caught his eye. He could have sworn he saw a shadow darting around the corner of the bordello. There was something oddly familiar about . . .

A muffled curse tumbled from Nolan's lips when the shadow passed through the spray of light that poured from the window.

The waif again, Nolan muttered under his breath. He wondered if Laura Chandler ever stayed home. Apparently not. She was as busy as a bumblebee in a bucket of tar.

Now Nolan knew why Laura hadn't attended the exhibition. She was roaming the streets in disguise. What business she might possibly have at the brothel that was known to cater to British officers, Nolan could not imagine.

Unless she was on her way to deliver information, came the suspicious voice inside him.

When the urchin crept around the corner to ascend the outside staircase, Nolan dashed over to grab the hem of her shabby coat.

Laura bit back a startled gasp when she was pulled off balance. She glanced down to see Ezra Beecham decked out in his finery, smiling devilishly up at her.

"Go away," she hissed at him.

"Ah, our secret pact, right?" Nolan whispered conspiratorially. "I'm not to expose you for who you are, for fear I might find myself in jail again. For what crime this time, I shudder to imagine. But I'm sure you'll think of something— as you are so fond of saying."

Laura gnashed her teeth, glanced up at the lantern that had just flared to life in the room above her and then glowered at the pesky scoundrel who was making her life more complicated than it already was. She was on a personal crusade and the last thing she needed was this ornery dandy's interference.

"What are you doing, or dare I ask?" Nolan questioned as he watched Laura's gaze bounce back and forth between him and the overhead window.

"None of your business," Laura muttered impatiently. With a flick of her gloved hand, she shooed Nolan on his way. "Go pester someone else. I'm busy."

"Are you?"

"Of course, I am," Laura scowled at him. "You don't think I am skulking around this brothel for no reason at all, do you?"

"My lady, I have come to the conclusion that understanding the workings of your mind is beyond conception."

"Don't annoy me, Ezra," she threatened, baring her teeth for intimidating effect. "I will have Peter toss you back in jail on the flimsiest of excuses—"

Before Laura realized what he was about, Nolan gave the hem of her coat a hard yank, sending her tumbling off the landing and into his arms. When she wiggled and squirmed Nolan sat her to her feet and grabbed her by the nape of her grimy coat to ensure she didn't escape him.

"Since you seem insanely curious about the goings-on inside a den of ill repute, perhaps I should give you a grand tour."

Laura dug in her heels, only to be uprooted and dragged around the side of the building. To her outrage, she was escorted onto the stoop and shoveled through the door.

"You will pay dearly for this," she hissed furiously.

Nolan felt Laura tense and tuck herself against his shoulder when she recognized several of the redcoats who were snuggled up to half-dressed courtesans. 'Twas gratifying to see Laura's face flush beet red beneath the smudges of soot that disguised her feminine features.

Served her right, Nolan thought spitefully. No matter what her political preferences Laura had no business peering through the windows of a brothel. Standing in the parlor was education enough! Despite Laura's unusual background, visiting a bordello appeared to be a new experience for her.

"So you changed your mind, did you, Ezra?" Willie Fitzgerald stood at the head of the steps with his arm draped around a buxom brunette. He frowned when he noticed the waif who, with head downcast, was studying the toes of his scuffed boots. "Where did you find that little beggar?"

"He is one of my employees," Nolan lied smoothly. "I thought perhaps young *Lawrence* should be initiated into manhood."

"I will never forgive you for this as long as I live," Laura muttered. "You're fouling up everything— royally!"

That suited Nolan fine. If he prevented this cunning spy from relaying information— for even one night— he would be very pleased with himself.

"Come along, *Lawrence*. I'm sure we can find a place upstairs for you, and with just the right companion."

"Not without a bath," the harsh-featured madam snorted. She looked the scrawny urchin up and down and then turned up her hooked nose. "My girls are accustomed to the brass and polish of Brits, not common scruffs off the bloody streets."

"I'll see that *Lawrence* is squeaky clean," Nolan promised the dour-faced proprietor before he shepherded Laura toward the steps.

To Laura's infuriated dismay, Nolan hauled her upstairs. When the door closed behind Willie and his purring companion, Laura twisted sideways to break the hold Nolan had on the nape of her coat. She managed to land one sharp blow to Nolan's midsection before he clutched her arm and wrenched it up her back.

Laura swallowed a yelp and mustered every ounce of strength she possessed to escape. When she swung wildly with her free hand, her arm inadvertently collided with the lantern hanging on the coat rack.

The lamp crashed to the floor and whale oil instantly burst into flames.

Nolan muttered a string of curses when the explosive heat set the wall paper afire. True, Nolan was anxious to send the British soldiers back to England where they belonged, but he wasn't so vindictive as to ship their cremated ashes home in urns!

Smoke filled the hall like a black fog before Nolan could stamp out the fire. Intense heat consumed the upper story and there was naught else to do except shout a warning to the inhabitants.

"Willie!" Nolan roared. "Fire!"

Bare-chested, Willie appeared at the far end of the hall. When he saw the smoke and flames, he frantically beat his fist on the door beside him. Amid shouts and curses, the occupants grabbed sheets and quilts to cover themselves and scrambled toward the back steps.

Nolan clamped his hand over Laura's eyes when one of the soldiers darted into the hall, stark naked. Spinning Laura around, Nolan herded her toward the steps.

The brothel was blazing like liberty's torch by the time Nolan reached the ground floor. The parlor had been evacuated and a flurry of excited shouts rose up in the night. Nolan burst outside, towing Laura behind him. Inhaling a cleansing breath, he stared at the curls of smoke that seeped from the upper floor windows.

"Now see what you've done," Laura muttered, attempting to jerk loose from his grasp.

"What *I've* done?" Nolan echoed incredulously, watching patrons and paramours congregate a safe distance away from the crackling bonfire. "You're the one who—"

His voice trailed off when he noticed Laura's attention had abruptly shifted to the red-haired soldier who scurried away from flaming disaster. Nolan couldn't fathom Laura's fascination for Geoffrey Spradlin, but she was monitoring the man's every move. It made Nolan wonder if Geoffrey was one of her contacts, or if she had some foolish romantic interest in that scoundrel.

Well, she wasn't going near Geoffrey if Nolan had anything to do with it—and he did. While a crowd gathered to watch the brothel burn to the ground, Nolan shoveled Laura down the street.

"Let me go!" Laura snapped, squirming for release—to no avail.

"I'll let you go when I'm damned good and ready and I'm not ready yet," Nolan snapped back. "You are a disaster looking for a place to happen. I intend to advise your aunt to keep a closer watch on your activities—"

"You will leave my aunt out of this," Laura broke in.

Nolan stopped short, his silver eyes blazing with irritation. "I want to know what you were doing at the brothel and what your connection is with Geoffrey Spradlin."

Bewildered, Laura staggered back apace.

When she slammed her mouth shut, refusing to explain, Nolan gave her a sudden shake. "I want an answer and I want it *now*," he demanded.

"I told you, 'tis none of your bloody business!"

"Ouch!" Nolan instinctively recoiled when Laura gouged him with her elbow and stamped on his foot. Before he could recover, she launched herself away from him and took off like a speeding musketball.

Nolan watched her disappear into the dark alleys, as if she had never been there at all.

"Damned exasperating female," Nolan muttered as he stalked off to fetch his horse. "Hell if I know why I don't just shoot her and be done with it."

Thoughts of Laura Chandler had been hounding him for days, preoccupying him, distracting him. It had reached the point where he, like Willie, kept searching for his auburn-haired beauty in every crowd. Nolan told himself that his continued interest stemmed from his suspicions, but he knew there was more to it than that. This daring imp fascinated him, intrigued him. She was his curse, of course, but he couldn't seem to get her off his mind.

Nolan swung onto the saddle and delivered himself another scathing lecture about the folly of his obsessive interest in a woman who could turn out to be a threat to his cause. *Forget her,* Nolan told himself sternly. Laura Chandler would inevitably invite more trouble than Nolan had time to handle.

Indeed, if tonight was any indication, this mysterious female was in the habit of doing more than burning bridges behind her. She might set the whole world aflame— and Nolan right along with it!

If Nolan had a smidgen of sense, he wouldn't let himself forget that. But he was beginning to wonder if he did have any sense left, for even now, he was rehashing his encounter with Laura— behind and inside the brothel. He caught himself smiling in amusement— twice.

Ah, what an ironic twist of fate that 'twas this

deceptive Tory spy whose feminine companionship he enjoyed. Dear God, Nolan must have met himself coming and going so often that it had finally driven him mad!

Ten

Horace Muldoon stirred on his feather bed when an unidentified object nudged his shoulder. Groggily, he eased away, but the faint prick on his skin brought him to a higher level of consciousness. Groaning drowsily, Horace flopped onto his back and pried one eye open.

The fuzzy haze that fogged his brain evaporated in less than a heartbeat. Horace gasped in shock when he spied the foreboding phantom of darkness looming over him. To Horace's terror, he realized the prickly sensations that had roused him from sleep came from the point of a dagger.

"My God!" Horace croaked on a strangled breath.

"Nay," the Midnight Rider growled menacingly at him. "But you will meet Him soon enough if you insist upon keeping your position as stamp agent."

Horace's body clenched with paralyzing fear when he stared at the dark hood and swirling cloak that concealed his late-night visitor's identity. "Who are you?" he wheezed.

"The better part of your conscience," came the

hushed snarl. "Resign your commission or meet your maker—now."

Horace forgot to breathe when the gleaming dagger swooped across his line of vision and cold steel settled against the pulsating vein in his neck. For the life of him, Horace didn't know how this ominous phantom had learned he had accepted the vacant post of stamp distributor. The information had yet to become common knowledge.

Sweet mercy! This dark avenger of liberty seemed as omnipotent and all-knowing as God himself, and as terrifying as the devil!

"Your word of honor, Muldoon," came the muffled growl, accompanied by the prick of the blade against vulnerable flesh. "Resign and survive. Refuse and die where you lie . . ."

Horace wasn't sure he had enough breath left in his collapsed lungs to speak. "I—" Sure enough, he was scared speechless.

"You *what*, Muldoon?" The Midnight Rider snarled venomously. "You wish to resign and live to see another sunrise?"

Horace nodded his frizzy gray head—very carefully.

The dark phantom lifted the blade from Horace's throat. The weapon disappeared into the swirl of his black cloak. "Do not think to deceive me, Muldoon. If I do not hear of your resignation by morning, you can expect another visit, but when you are least prepared for it. 'Twill be the *last* call anyone will ever pay on you. On that you may depend . . ."

With that lethal promise hanging in the unnerving silence, the ominous specter floated across the bedchamber and swirled through the open window like evaporating smoke.

Horace sucked in a ragged breath and tried to swallow the lump that clogged his throat. He had come to the quick conclusion that the salary he was to receive for filling the vacated post of stamp agent wasn't worth the price of his life. And he had no intention whatsoever of provoking the Midnight Rider's return visit. Horace was positively certain he wouldn't survive the dark angel's prophesy. One house call had been more than plenty for him.

Peter Forbes eased down in bed beside Mercy Reed. The indentured servant who kept house for Miriam and Laura had sneaked into his room to await his return from patrol duty. While Peter practiced his policy of tumbling one female while dreaming of another, Mercy usually offered no complaints about the arrangement. In fact, she had been more than accommodating. Or at least she had been until recently. Mercy had taken to voicing snide remarks about Laura Chandler's fickle charms in an attempt to discourage Peter's pursuit.

Much to Peter's dismay, Mercy began harping on what was fast becoming a monotonous subject.

"I cannot fathom why you and your friends treat Laura like some regal princess," Mercy groused as she eased off the edge of the bed to scoop up her clothes. "Her ladyship's encounter with that dandy at Miriam's party is proof that she isn't interested in your attentions. She charms men for the mere sport of it."

"I thought I made it clear that I do not want to hear you cast aspersions about Laura," Peter muttered.

Mercy tossed her head, sending a tangle of sandy red hair over her shoulder. "And I have made it clear that my affection for you forces me to speak my mind," she declared as she tugged on her gown. "I have your best interests at heart. Laura doesn't."

"Leave off, Mercy. You and I have a satisfactory arrangement."

Mercy cursed at his obstinacy. "One day you will realize I am the one you need, not *her*. She knows nothing about pleasing a man and she doesn't care to learn. You will wear out your heart on Laura Chandler, just like every other man in Boston."

"I believe I said this conversation was over—"

The rap at the door had Peter scowling sourly. He groped for his discarded clothes while Mercy scurried toward the window to conceal herself in the bulky velvet drapes.

"Who is it?"

"Private Simpson, sir," came the quiet voice. "Mrs. Peabody said I should come up and deliver the message from headquarters in person."

Peter sensed trouble. The arrival of late-night couriers usually indicated that the Patriot Rider was up to his infuriating antics— again. The man was obviously part vampire bat, Peter decided. When the moon was on the rise, the masked vigilante materialized from the darkness to raid, taunt and intimidate.

Peter pulled on his shirt and breeches and strode toward the door. His hand stalled on the knob long enough to ensure that Mercy was hidden from view. Then he swung open the portal to accept the dispatch that affirmed the Midnight Rider had been on the prowl.

"Bring my horse around from the stables," Peter requested.

"I already took care of the matter, sir. Your patrol is waiting in the street."

"Where did that elusive rebel leave his torch of liberty this time?" Peter questioned on his way down the hall.

"On the newly appointed stamp agent's porch," Simpson reported. "Horace Muldoon accepted the position two days ago. How the Midnight Rider got wind of the distributor's replacement so quickly I cannot say."

Peter cursed all the way down the steps. The Midnight Rider was making Peter's life miserable. Lately he was unable to enjoy even one night of uninterrupted sleep. Ah, if only he could find himself nestled in Laura Chandler's bed for just one night, while that pesky patriot was hanging from the Liberty Tree on Boston Common! Now *that* would be a dream come true.

* * *

Nolan bit back an ornery grin as he trotted his stallion toward Boston. Frightening the newly appointed stamp collector had been a relatively simple matter. Nolan had only to expel a few fierce snarls and lay his dagger against Horace's jugular. The scare tactics had been one-hundred percent effective. The former-future stamp distributor had promised to resign his commission first thing in the morning, and Nolan was certain Horace would. Although Horace was especially fond of coins, he treasured his life more.

Having accomplished his mission, Nolan had hurled his torch of liberty on the porch and rode away. However, he had taken the precaution of dumping a pail of water on the stoop so the house wouldn't go up in flames. He wondered if Horace Muldoon appreciated the courtesy. Probably not. The man had probably been too terrified to notice . . .

The sound of a buggy bouncing along the path beside the river jostled Nolan from his pensive musings. When he heard a masculine snarl and a feminine shriek Nolan spurred his stallion into its fastest clip. Another feminine scream and furious protest pierced the air. Nolan's heart skipped several vital beats. He would have recognized that voice anywhere. It belonged to Laura Chandler.

Whenever disaster was about to strike, Laura always seemed to be in the vicinity. Nolan had come to the conclusion that 'twas no coincidence. The woman could attract more trouble than she knew what to do with.

Hell and damnation, what was that misfit up to now? She had framed Nolan for thievery and had him tossed in jail *last* week. She had already burned down a brothel *this* week. Wasn't that enough to appease her destructive tendencies? Apparently not . . .

Nolan's thoughts scattered when he spotted the coach. The team of horses had veered off the beaten path, causing the vehicle to bobble and careen more wildly than ever. The horses were racing unrestrained along the rocky bluff and Nolan cringed, knowing what would happen if the carriage lost a wheel. Laura and her male companion would be launched through the air, and there was no telling where they would end up— or in how many pieces.

With fiend-ridden haste Nolan chased after the runaway carriage. Before he could bring the team of horses under control, calamity struck. One of the wheels shattered when it collided with some protruding rocks. Spokes cracked and flew in all directions. The carriage whirled sideways, and a bloodcurdling feminine scream mingled with a masculine curse.

Nolan grimaced when the terrified horses switched directions, sending the skidding coach toward the edge of the bluff.

With a resounding crash the coach toppled onto its side, balanced half on and half off the cliff. The team of horses whinnied, reared, and tried to gallop away, but they were anchored to the overturned carriage that had snagged on the stony precipice.

By the time Nolan reached the bluff, the horses had snapped the broken whiffletree loose from the harnesses. The team thundered off, leaving the carriage rocking on its precarious perch.

Nolan reined his stallion close to see Laura hanging onto the seat by her fingernails. Geoffrey Spradlin was dangling off the side of the carriage, clinging to the hem of Laura's torn gown. Nolan doubted that Laura could last much longer, not when she had to support both their weight.

For a split-second, while Nolan stared down at Laura's haunted expression, he wondered if he might not save himself considerable trouble by choosing to do nothing except watch calamity strike its final blow. Even if Nolan tried to help, 'twas going to be difficult to save both of the hapless victims, because the carriage was delicately balanced on a protruding boulder. The laws of gravity would go into effect the instant Nolan reached out to hoist Laura up.

'Twas physically impossible for Nolan to lean out at an unbalanced angle and lift both Laura and Geoffrey to safety, while sitting atop his stallion. If he took time to dismount and use his cape as a rope, the struggling victims could upset the coach and send it plummeting over the edge.

When Geoffrey's wild flailing teetered the coach, Nolan instinctively reached toward Laura. The carriage wobbled again when Geoffrey tried to crawl over Laura, as if she were his human lifeline. Nolan retracted his hand when his stallion danced sideways to avoid the shifting carriage.

When Geoffrey grabbed hold of Laura's torn bodice to lever himself upward, Laura's wild shriek filled the night air. The sound of rending cloth was followed by Geoffrey's horrified howl. He dropped a quick four feet, clutching desperately at the ripped fabric that was knotted in his fist. His backward momentum caused Laura to lose her grasp on the edge of the seat and she clawed air in an effort to regain her handhold.

Nolan didn't even remember swooping down to grab her wrist, but his fingers contracted the same instant that the waist seam of her gown gave way. A terrified scream split the night as Geoffrey plunged downward, still holding Laura's shredded gown in his fist.

An echoing thud drifted up from the wild tumble of rocks . . . and deathly silence followed.

Moonlight streamed over Laura's heaving breasts while she hung in Nolan's grasp. He peered down at the chemise-clad female whose life he held in his hand— literally— and felt the jolt of awareness rivet him.

Despite the tragic circumstances, Nolan doubted he would forget the vivid memory of Laura's barely clad body awash with moonbeams. Forgetting himself for a moment, he allowed his imagination to run wild.

Nolan was still savoring the enticing scenery in

his forbidden fantasy when Laura hooked a leg over the side of the upturned carriage to secure herself against a deadly fall.

"Make up your bloody mind," she muttered when the Midnight Rider continued to stare at her through the holes of his black hood. "Do you intend to haul me up or let me drop? I would like to say my last prayers if I am to go the same way as Geoffrey."

The comment prompted Nolan to drag Laura over the side of the carriage and hoist her onto his lap. When he did, he upset the perilous balance of the coach and it cartwheeled down the cliff, landing with a splintering crash.

Nolan swore his arm had become exceptionally sensitive when he clutched Laura protectively against him. He could feel the weight of her full breasts resting in the bend of his elbow, not to mention the profound effect of the rounded curve of her backside meshed against his thighs. Holding her felt natural, right . . .

And forbidden . . .

Bloody hell, 'tis no time to be assailed by these erotic fantasies, Nolan told himself disgustedly.

Damnation, Nolan thought irritably. And why wasn't she crying her eyes out after her beau tumbled to his death? Didn't the woman have a sentimental bone in that curvaceous body of hers?

"Thank you. I owe you my life," Laura murmured as she self-consciously covered her chest with her arms.

Nolan lowered his voice one octave and dropped

the exaggerated English accent he employed while posing as Ezra Beecham. "You're welcome. Shall I check the condition of your . . . husband, my lady?"

"He was not my husband," Laura quietly informed him.

"Your intended then?"

Laura stared toward the spot where Geoffrey Spradlin had fallen to his death. "Nay, he was only a man who got exactly what he deserved, even if that wasn't what I originally planned for him."

Nolan frowned at the cryptic remark. He remembered seeing Laura's torn gown and he wondered if Geoffrey had tired to molest her. The team of horses could have run away with the carriage while Geoffrey was in ardent pursuit and Laura was fending off his amorous assault. Judging by the tone of Laura's voice, she felt little regret in watching Geoffrey meet his bad end. Unfortunately, Nolan was in no position to ask prying questions that might arouse her suspicions and threaten his duel identity.

It very well could be that Laura had been passing along information and Geoffrey decided to enjoy a few fringe benefits, when opportunity presented itself. 'Twas the most logical explanation, Nolan decided.

Nolan reined his stallion in the opposite direction and trotted toward town. If he tarried too long, he might find himself surrounded by roving patrols, and he didn't relish a wild ride with Laura clamped in one arm. She had come dangerously close to taking a fatal fall already. Nolan needed to deposit her in a safe place and return to the cottage before he was spotted.

"I suppose I should consider myself fortunate to be rescued by the legendary Midnight Rider," Laura murmured.

Nolan made a gravelly sound that could have meant anything. He wasn't going to press his luck. If this intelligent female recognized his voice he could be a dead man.

"You don't feel like the disembodied spirit the reports have made you out to be," Laura noted as she settled more comfortably on his lap. "You feel like flesh and bone to me."

No answer. Nolan had said all he dared to say. And he sincerely wished Laura would sit still! While she was cuddled so closely against him, he was entirely too sensitive to her every movement.

"I understand your need for secrecy," Laura said when Nolan made no comment.

Of course she did. Any self-respecting spy would.

"Rest assured that I have no intention of mentioning this incident to anyone."

Nolan wouldn't want to bet the fortune he had made in fur trading on that!

"You can leave me on the edge of town," Laura instructed a half mile later. "I can make my way home from there."

Nolan didn't doubt that. This unusual female probably knew her way around the dark alleys and byways of Boston better than he did.

When Nolan drew the stallion to a halt, he leaned

over to set Laura on her feet. The steed threw its broad head and pranced sideways, impatient for a run. Nolan stared down at the beguiling beauty in her revealing chemise and pantaloons and inwardly groaned. At the moment, he wished he were blind in both eyes so he wouldn't notice what a tempting package of femininity she was. He had the agonizing feeling that the memory of Laura standing before him in her unmentionables, with her auburn hair cascading over her like a cloak, was going to haunt his sleep— for several nights to come.

The realization that he wanted this woman as he had wanted no other woman in all his life came as a sizzling jolt to all five senses and a tormenting shock to what had once been his well-disciplined mind. Holding Laura had intensified the forbidden longings. The kisses they had shared in the past had become an obsessive craving that demanded feeding. Nolan hadn't known desire could become such a frustrating addiction . . . or such a dangerous threat to his existence.

When Laura turned away, Nolan jerked himself back to attention and untied his cape. "Here, cover yourself," he ordered gruffly. "You might find yourself attacked more than once in the same evening."

Hell's bells, he was considering pouncing on her *himself*. Scowling at his inability to control his traitorous thoughts and unruly desires, Nolan gouged his stallion and galloped away. It seemed that fate was conspiring against him, tossing this tempting beauty in his path. He should avoid Laura Chan-

dler at all cost. If not, Nolan could face his most
humiliating defeat. If he let this woman matter too
much to him, he would find himself on a collision
course with disaster.

He would *not* see her again, Nolan told himself
determinedly. If perchance he did, he would simply turn around and walk the other way.

The thought echoed hollowly through his mind.

Nolan wondered if this was what famous last
words sounded like . . .

Eleven

When the coast was clear, Mercy Reed emerged from the drapery and padded barefoot across the room. Her resentment was playing havoc with her temper. She couldn't understand why Peter fancied himself in love with a woman like Laura Chandler. All Laura had to do was flash one of her dimpled smiles and Peter trailed after her like a puppy on a damned leash. Men were so foolish and gullible, Mercy muttered to herself.

Mercy plucked up her shoes and snuck out the bedroom door, cursing her lowly position and envying the luxury Laura Chandler had at her disposal. If Peter would come to his senses, he would realize Mercy was more woman than Laura would ever be.

If she could convince Peter to abandon his futile pursuit, she might have the chance to better herself by marrying a British officer. When Peter returned to England she could accompany him. Surely Mrs. Peabody would agree to release Mercy from her indentureship. 'Twas not as if the dowager didn't have scads of money.

If not, Mercy would be stuck here for another

three years, watching Peter become even more obsessed with Laura . . .

Mercy's bitter thoughts evaporated when she heard a door creak open at the far end of the hall. Quickly, Mercy slipped into the storage closet to prevent herself from being seen. A curious frown knitted her brows as she watched Laura scurry past in her undergarments, clutching a wad of dark fabric against her chest.

A wry smile pursed Mercy's lips as Laura disappeared into her room. Perhaps the high and mighty Laura Chandler really had taken up with the handsome dandy she had met at the party. And maybe she had gone out to meet him while Peter was unaware.

Nothing could have pleased Mercy more than to see her female rival disgraced by scandal. Then maybe Peter wouldn't look upon Laura as if she were some bloody paragon and he would turn his full attention to Mercy.

On that optimistic thought Mercy crept to her room in the servants' quarters. In the future she would keep close surveillance on Laura's evening activities. If Laura was indeed slipping off to meet Ezra Beecham or some other panting suitor, Peter would realize he had been played for a fool . . . and Mercy would be there to console him . . .

Captain Oran Milbourne slammed his fist down on his desk and spewed several oaths to the Midnight Rider's name. "Blister it, that rascal has got to be stopped before he makes a laughingstock of His Majesty's entire army!"

Peter Forbes sighed tiredly. "We are doing our best, sir, but the man is proving to be as elusive as a wraith."

"I prefer that you use another analogy." Oran scowled as he bolted from his chair. He swiped his hand over the bald spot on the crown of his head and dropped his arm in a gesture of exasperation. "I have heard one too many tales about the Phantom Rider disappearing into nothingness when he races away from patrols."

Peter shook his blond head. "I cannot fathom how he accomplishes his feat of vanishing in the underbrush or into the trees or evaporates at the cemetery. I have checked every clump of trees, every headstone large enough to hide behind and I still have no reasonable explanation for it. The Midnight Rider is simply there one minute and gone the next."

"I suggest we plant one of our men at the cemetery to keep surveillance."

"I already tried that," Peter informed Oran. "When I send Private Simpson to keep watch, the vigilante avoids the cemetery. His unpredictability is wreaking havoc with our strategy. I'm beginning to think the Rebel Rider has an accomplice watching the area for him."

"Well, he *must* be captured, somehow or another," Oran blustered. "Our informants are able to provide reports about incoming revenue cutters and possible raids. They have even identified a few men within the underground network those rebels call the Sons of Liberty. So why can't we discover the identity of this evasive Midnight Rider? How difficult can it be, for God's sake? Someone has to know who he is. I do not wish to be demoted because I can't apprehend that pesky rascal!"

"Neither do I, sir," Peter put in quickly.

Oran plopped back into his chair to survey the handsome blond lieutenant. "We are going to have to purchase supplies for our men after the raid on the storehouse at the barracks. I want you to see to the matter for me. And we will need to name a replacement for Horace Muldoon who officially resigned his position as stamp agent. See to that also, Lieutenant."

Oran added, "I have the unpleasant duty of composing a letter to Captain Geoffrey Spradlin's family, informing them of his untimely death. I suppose we will never know what spooked the team of horses and caused Geoffrey to plummet over the bluff."

When Major Milbourne motioned him on his way, Peter offered his superior officer a snappy salute and executed an about-face. Once he stepped outside, however, he permitted himself a curse and a scowl. He had entirely too much on his mind these days. The Midnight Rider had become a household word and the army had no idea who the culprit or his accomplice was. Furthermore, Peter was pining away for the affection of a woman who had been charmed by the nonchalant rake she had only just met.

Perhaps Peter should take lessons in courtship from Ezra Beecham. The man had managed to steal a kiss, full on the mouth, while Peter had been limited to respectful pecks on the cheek. Maybe a spirited woman like Laura preferred the bold approach. She had openly admitted that Beecham had swept her off her feet in a reckless moment, even if she had been ashamed of herself later.

Aye, Peter decided. He would make his intentions more obvious. Heaven forbid that he, an Englishman raised in a well-respected family from London, could be upstaged by a colonial fur entrepreneur!

Spark McRae blinked in disbelief when Nolan emerged from his room at the cabin, garbed in the elegant trappings Ezra Beecham was noted for. "Why are you dressed like that? Are you goin' to the rally?"

"Wouldn't miss it." Nolan adjusted his periwig and straightened his ruffled cuffs.

"Yer leavin' the Patriot Rider at home? Good, I'm glad you took my advice, for once."

"Ethan sent word that the army is determined to have my head on a silver platter," Nolan declared. "The raid on the barrack storehouse, and Horace Muldoon's resignation have the Brits all abuzz. But I still intend to observe the rally."

Spark stroked his gray beard and nodded consideringly. "You would indeed be takin' a risk by attendin' the demonstration dressed in black. The lobsterbacks would probably single you out rather than takin' on the mob."

"That's the way Ethan and I have it figured," Nolan murmured as he scooped up his waistcoat. "I've decided to spoil their fun this evening by *not* showing my masked face."

Spark's amber-eyed gaze riveted on Nolan for a moment. "You aren't, by any chance, thinkin' of contactin' that Chandler woman again, are you?"

Nolan turned toward the door, avoiding Spark's probing stare. It had occurred to Nolan that he could approach Laura if he wasn't attired in his black cape and mask. For safety's sake, the Midnight Rider had to keep his distance from Laura, but Ezra Beecham could . . .

"Nolan?" Spark prompted.

"Aye?" Nolan mumbled, distracted.

"Despite yer suspicions, the chit has intrigued you, hasn't she?"

"Of course not," Nolan lied, not very convincingly.

Spark gave a loud snort of contradiction. "Don't try to deceive me. I know you too well. And I also know women, havin' been engaged thrice. They're nothin' but trouble waitin' to happen."

"I know what I'm doing," Nolan insisted as he turned to meet Spark's narrowed gaze. "Someone has to keep surveillance on Laura Chandler. My brother refuses to believe she might be acting as a double agent, waiting to betray us when the opportunity is ripe."

"I'd like to get a look at this spell-castin' sorceress," Spark grumbled. "She's pretty, I expect."

"Disturbingly so," Nolan reluctantly acknowledged.

"And witty, I s'pose."

"Exceptionally," Nolan confirmed.

Spark nodded sagely. "Those are the worst kind of females to get tangled up with. Sounds like my second fiancée. I was still in my prime when I met her. She was the worst mistake I ever made."

Nolan frowned. "I thought you said your third fiancée was your worst mistake."

"She was." Spark grinned. "All three fiancées were my worst mistake."

"Rest assured that my interest in Laura Chandler is strictly— "

Spark flung up his hand to forestall Nolan. "Don't be tossin' out declarations you have to retract," he warned. "The chit fascinates you, so don't humiliate yerself by denyin' it. Just don't get so attached to her that 'twill turn you wrong side out if she proves to be a traitor to our cause. I don't relish watchin' His Majesty's men hang you from the Liberty Tree just because you let the need of a woman do yer thinkin' for you."

Nolan accepted the good advice in the spirit it was given and strode outside. He told himself that his main objective was monitoring the rally as a bystander. He told himself his interest in Laura Chandler wasn't serious or personal, because if it was, she could become a perilous threat to his life. He had told himself all those things a dozen times, wanting to take them to heart . . . and still wanting her in the worst possible way.

When the door clicked shut, Spark levered out of his chair to pour himself a drink. "Ye'r too darin' for yer own good, boy," he muttered aloud.

Spark had come to know Nolan Ryder extremely well these past two years. They had practically lived in each other's pockets while they hunted, trapped and eluded Indian war parties in the wilderness west of the Appalachians. Nolan had never been— and would never be— a man content with the mundane and ordinary. He thrived on challenge, invited change. Nolan would become his own worst enemy if he didn't watch his step.

Grumbling, Spark chugged his drink and pocketed his pipe. His gaze strayed to the closed door and he frowned thoughtfully. Perhaps 'twould be wise to keep an eye on Nolan, just in case he did encounter Laura Chandler again. Besides, Spark wanted to view this protest rally firsthand. 'Twas his sincere hope that Samuel Adams could handle the mob better than he did the first time the opposing gangs of brawlers united and took to the streets. The Sons of Liberty might employ public protests to gain Parliament's attention, but destructive riots would draw military reinforcements into Boston. In Spark's opinion, there were enough lobsterbacks crawling around the streets already!

* * *

Miriam Peabody wrung her hands as Laura stuffed the curly mass of auburn hair beneath her cap and then shrugged on the brown homespun jacket that concealed her feminine curves. "I'm not at all sure 'tis wise for you to be on the streets tonight, my dear."

"Don't fret, Aunt Miriam." Laura swiped her hand inside the lantern globe and smeared soot across her cheeks. "You know perfectly well that I'm familiar with life on the streets. But for your generosity, I would still be there today."

"But *this* is a different matter entirely," Miriam argued. "Emotions are running high because of the political and social problems in Boston. The North End and South End mobs are bad enough with their brawling when they celebrate Pope's Day every November. But now that the two rowdy gangs of hooligans have banned together to protest the Crown's regulations and taxes, trouble is just waiting to happen."

Laura nodded grimly. She had been on hand the night the mobs had joined forces and swarmed toward Andrew Oliver's home, breaking windows and surging inside to swipe his stock of wine. Sir Francis Bernard, the royal governor, had been too cowardly to challenge the mob and had fled to Castle Island to save his own neck. It had been Lieutenant Governor Hutchinson who had attempted to control the surly crowd. Hutchinson had been pelted with stones for his efforts.

"Trouble or no, I plan to attend the rally in disguise," Laura announced. "Though I am thankful to have gotten rid of Geoffrey Spradlin once and for all, I cannot be satisfied until every soldier has been shipped back to England and our provincial representatives have been reinstated. We cannot be content until we are allowed to deal with our own set of problems in our own way, without Parliament trying to dictate unreasonable policy."

Miriam fell silent. She knew why Laura harbored a strong distaste for the standing army, knew why freedom and personal rights had come to mean so much to her. This lovely lass had suffered a great deal of tragedy and torment in her twenty-three years. Laura had developed a fierce desire to free the oppressed and right the wrongs she had witnessed on the streets.

A rueful smile pursed Miriam's lips when she reflected on the first time she had seen Laura scrounging in the gutters, performing menial tasks to support herself. When Laura had been accosted by a half-drunken soldier, Miriam had come to the poor child's rescue, took her into her mansion on Beacon Hill and granted Laura all the luxuries that wealth could provide. Miriam had been so taken with the girl's spirit and spunk that she had come to love Laura as if she were her own child.

In truth, Miriam envied Laura's bold daring, her ability to handle herself so adeptly in every crisis. And secretly, Miriam would have enjoyed garbing herself like an urchin and strolling through the streets to observe the demonstration. Instead, she would have to wait for Laura's report. Miriam had to keep up pretenses while Laura actively participated in the ever-growing movement to liberate the colonies from English oppression.

"Just have a care tonight," Miriam requested. "I expect to hear a full account of the goings-on when you return."

Laura grinned impishly, for she knew Miriam would have preferred to scuttle through the streets, just for the adventure of it. The spirited widow had grown even more independent over the years, Laura had noticed. Miriam Peabody didn't enjoy being told what to do or how to behave any more than Laura did. They may have been a mismatched pair in the beginning, but they were kindred spirits now.

"If Peter is curious about my absence at supper, tell him I retired to my room with a blinding headache," Laura suggested.

Miriam sniffed in objection. "The man is beginning to think you are plagued with that particular affliction. Of late, you've had a considerable number of headaches. I believe I will take it upon myself to be more original."

Miriam frowned in thought and then smiled conspiratorially. "A churning stomach should do the trick." She rose from the edge of the alcove bed to pull the tattered brown cap lower on Laura's forehead. "Be careful. I have grown immensely fond of you the past few years, you know."

Laura gave Miriam a fond hug and then turned toward the door. Before she could step into the hall, Miriam surged past to ensure the coast was clear.

"You know how Mercy hovers around when she thinks Peter will be returning from headquarters.

She is jealous enough of you as it is, and she would like nothing better than to discredit you in Peter's eyes."

When Miriam was certain no one was lurking about, she motioned for Laura to proceed toward the back steps. Like a darting mouse, Laura made her way down the stairs and scampered toward the concealment of the trees. These evening jaunts reminded Laura of her youth. Aye, there had been poverty and danger, but there had been a certain sense of freedom.

Each day had been rife with difficult challenges and unexpected change. Although Laura was eternally grateful for what Miriam had done for her, she missed living by no one's rules other than her own. The expectations of society limited Laura's natural sense of independence. She felt as if she were playing a constant charade for the benefit of men like Peter Forbes and the other British officers who hovered around her. Laura needed her own space, the chance to simply be herself.

A faint smile skimmed her lips when she recalled her encounters with Ezra Beecham. For some unexplainable reason, she felt more like her old self when she was with that rascal. Aye, he was bold and ornery and he knew more about her than she preferred, but she secretly delighted in the challenge Ezra represented.

Ezra could have given her game away several times, but he hadn't. Laura wondered why he had been generous with her, why she was attracted to a man who seemed indifferent to the conflict and suffering going on around him.

She wondered if Ezra enjoyed her company half as much as she enjoyed his, even if she didn't dare admit it to him. 'Twas all that self-assured dandy needed, she thought to herself. If Ezra knew she had developed a fascination for him, he would probably never let her hear the end of it and attempt to coerce her into bed . . .

Laura backed against the brick wall of the nearest building when she heard pelting footsteps approach. She muttered under her breath when she saw silhouettes darting hither and yon like a colony of bats swarming from a cave. The night was alive with flurries of activity. She could feel the excitement buzzing around her. Not the same fissions of excitement, however, that she had experienced the night Ezra Beecham . . .

Laura dismissed the arousing memories and surged onto the street. She really could not keep harboring these forbidden sensations, because she couldn't afford to become captivated by a Tory like Ezra Beecham. The complications could be dangerous. And yet, he was the only man who . . .

"Don't be ridiculous," Laura chastised herself. "Ezra Beecham is only a passing fancy. You never needed a man in your life before and you certainly don't have time for one now."

Laura was committed to a noble cause— one that Ezra Beecham could destroy. Ezra was a tempting threat and she couldn't allow herself to forget that, no matter how much she delighted in matching wits with him, no matter how the memories of forbidden sensations of his embrace tempted her to . . .

"Psst!"

Laura stopped short when she saw the scraggily dressed young man leaning negligently against a street lamp. The seventeen-year-old Daniel Goreman had been very much a part of Laura's past—the younger brother she never had. He and Laura and Martha Winfield had been a family, living their hand-to-mouth existence together and defending each other when necessity demanded.

In fact, Daniel was the one who had taught Laura to pick pockets with such deft ease after she and Martha had escaped the orphanage and its cruel, abusive master. Now Martha was gone, but Laura had never allowed the childhood memories to fade. The flowers Laura faithfully delivered to Martha's grave were her attempt to relieve the guilt of being unable to come to the younger woman's rescue in time.

"Thought I might see ya out on the streets tonight," Daniel said as he fell into step beside Laura. "The crowds are gatherin' like flocks o' sheep. I heard the beat of clubs and clomp of boots before I circled back to see if ya wanted to go to the rally. Some of the boys and Negroes built a bonfire in front of the State House where Sam Adams was givin' his speech. The mob had just crossed Mill Creek, headed for North Boston, when I switched direction to look for ya."

Laura paused to prick her ears, hearing the distant chants, seeing the smoke billowing up into the starlit sky. "I have a bad feeling about this, Danny. Ebenezer McIntosh has been taking on arrogant airs since he commandeered the last rally."

"Aren't we talkin' fancy these days, muffin," Daniel mocked playfully. "You've been livin' in that Peabody mansion so long you've forgotten where ya hail from."

Laura slanted the lanky waif a disparaging glance. "I haven't forgotten a single day of our life together. Nor have I forgotten how and why Martha died. And I haven't forgotten you, either," she went on to say. "I've also seen to it that you have earned a respectable sum for your efforts to the cause." She paused to stare carefully at Daniel. "Nay, Danny, I remember exactly where I hail from, what we've been through together."

Daniel looked the other way, remembering— too much. "And I appreciate the coins, muffin, I really do. Makes it easier for a poor beggar like me, what with the lobsterbacks takin' wages for jobs that me and the other streeters could've had. But them rich Tories always give the jobs to off-duty soldiers to keep on the King's good side."

Laura rounded the corner and halted in her tracks when she saw the throng of people surging toward Judge Story's house like a tidal wave. "Dear Lord!"

In disbelief, she watched the home ransacked in only a matter of minutes. Bottles of wine were carried from the cellar and passed through the unruly crowd. Loud guffaws and chants to liberty and no stamps resounded through the street.

Laura was thoroughly appalled by the destruction of property, but Daniel merely shrugged his thin-bladed shoulders and insisted the British sympathizers were getting what they deserved.

"Local protests and peaceful demonstrations calling Parliament's attention to the problems are one thing," Laura muttered. "But McIntosh goes too far! This kind of devastation will cause an influx of soldiers into Boston. 'Tis the last thing we need."

Grimacing, Laura watched, as the raucous crowd, half drunk on Judge Story's liquor, swooped toward one of the Customs commissioner's houses. Benjamin Hallowell's home suffered the same fate as Judge Story's. Fences were beaten to splinters with clubs and window shutters were smashed to smithereens. The residence was looted and the stock of imported wine quickly consumed. Outraged, Laura watched the mob make off with Hallowell's public and private papers and tote the furniture from his home.

Laura gasped in alarm when she heard the shouts that ordered Lieutenant Governor Hutchinson's house accosted. "We've got to stop them, Danny," she insisted. "We can't demand respect for our personal rights and property if we resort to British policies of breaking and entering at will."

When Laura surged forward, Daniel grabbed her jacket and hauled her back beside him. "Are ya mad, muffin? The whole lot o' demonstrators are already as drunk as lords. They won't listen to no sooty-faced waif." He flung his arm in an all-encompassing gesture. "Look around ya, muffin. Even the redcoats are layin' low. They know they can't control this mob in its dangerous state."

Laura wormed from his grasp. "I have to try to reason with McIntosh. Somebody has to try!"

Daniel scowled when his childhood friend darted down the darkened byway to reach Hutchinson's home before the mob converged on it. "You've forgotten the code o' the streets, muffin," he called after her. " 'Tis every man for hisself. If ya don't have a care for yer own hide nobody else will fret over it."

Laura refused to heed the warning. She sensed disaster in the making. If the Sons of Liberty received a black eye because of this disgraceful display, the patriots would defeat their purpose and draw unproductive attention to themselves. 'Twas not the sensible way to register a protest with Parliament. Intimidating every stamp agent into resigning his position would gain Parliament's notice without destroying personal and public property. This kind of violent destruction would only invite trouble and Laura knew it had to be stopped!

She predicted redcoats would swarm into Boston and curfews would be placed on citizens, further limiting their freedom. His Majesty's men would well and truly become the army of occupation and public resentment.

Curse it, Laura grumbled as she took another

shortcut through the alleys. When King George got wind of the attack, well-armed troops would be marching up from New York in droves, and patriots would feel the full measure of the Crown's wrath.

As of yet, the colonies were not completely unified or prepared to defend themselves. If opposition to unjust taxes and restrictive dependency upon England evolved into a full-blown revolution, the colonists would be crushed beneath superior fire power. Thousands of innocent lives could be lost.

On that unsettling thought, Laura scampered around another darkened corner and scaled a brick fence. She had to make McIntosh see the error of his ways before he reduced the lieutenant governor's home to shambles!

Twelve

Nolan expelled a dozen foul oaths when he saw the besotted mob descend on Hutchinson's home. Garbed in his blue and gold uniform, Ebenezer McIntosh was leading the crowd and wielding his cane like a baton. Barking orders through his speaking trumpet, McIntosh demanded the lieutenant governor to show himself and prove that he wasn't stockpiling the cursed stamps that had been shipped to the colonies.

After receiving news of the destruction of Benjamin Hallowell's and Judge Story's homes, Hutchinson had barricaded himself in his house. The lieutenant governor's family had been sent to a neighbor's home for safekeeping, but Hutchinson and his two oldest sons had remained behind. They were no match for the mob that had picked up axes and clubs along their route, prepared to destroy the symbol of tyrannical British authority in Boston.

When McIntosh demanded that Hutchinson step outside or risk having his house pulled down around him, Nolan cursed himself soundly. Perhaps if he *had* appeared in hood and cloak— despite the risk of capture— he might have been able to exert some measure of influence over this misguided mob. As it was, Nolan looked like a mere bystander. Hell and damnation . . .

Nolan groaned aloud when a now-familiar figure scampered across Hutchinson's lawn to reason with the pillagers. The daring waif might as well have tried to hold back the storm-tossed sea.

When one of the hooligans standing beside McIntosh gave the outspoken urchin a fierce shove, Nolan impulsively rushed forward. Unfortunately, shouldering his way through the surly crowd was like swimming upstream against a river in flood stage. Nolan heard the thud of a club connecting with human flesh, followed by a pained wail.

The crowd surged toward Hutchinson's home, trampling the waif who had unsuccessfully but valiantly tried to halt the destruction. The sound of axes splitting window frames mingled with drunken shouts. Nolan stumbled forward, colliding with members of the mob who sneered and looked down their noses at his elegant attire.

"Bloody damned Tory. You can go the same way as your friend Hutchin— "

Nolan didn't wait for the burly brute to complete his sentence or deliver the oncoming punch. He doubled his fist and slammed the man's belly into his backbone. The man stumbled backward, knocking his cohorts sideways. Before a brawl— which Nolan didn't have time to fight— broke out among the ranks of the surly mob, he plowed toward the spot where the waif was last seen. Nolan nearly stepped on her crumpled form before he realized it.

With a muted curse, Nolan swooped down to scoop Laura's limp body off the ground. While the mob forged ahead, intent on mass destruction, Nolan carried Laura toward the nearest tree and propped her upright.

If Nolan had any doubt where Laura's loyalties lay before, he had none now. This unconventional female was a British sympathizer. Why else would she have defied the crowd? She had obviously been trying to protect the symbol of royal authority in Boston. Either that, Nolan mused, or Laura Chandler had more courage and audacity than the other decent sort of patriots who disapproved of what was happening, yet refused to risk their necks to halt the devastation. Even Nolan hadn't dared to intervene, especially dressed as he was. He would have been seized and pounded flat before he could explain that he was a rebel at heart. And if he had dared to reveal his true loyalties, his charade would have been ruined forever.

When Laura moaned groggily and keeled over on the ground, Nolan propped her against his shoulder. " 'Twas a foolish thing to do," he admonished. "You nearly got yourself killed."

Heavily lidded brown eyes, rimmed with thick lashes, lifted to him before swerving toward Hutchinson's house. To Nolan's disbelief, Laura tried to gather her wobbly legs beneath her and dash off to stop the injustice.

"Sit still," Nolan demanded.

"Someone has to stop them," she answered.

"There's no controlling them now. The mob has become a living, breathing monster, hell-bent on destruction. 'Twould take an act of God to stop them."

Dismayed, Nolan saw the angry crowd bash in the front door and pour into the house. Shadows darted around the side of the house, assuring Nolan that Hutchinson and his sons had fled to safety. In grim resignation, Nolan watched looters carry portraits, furniture and china from the house. Hutchinson's historical papers were torn to shreds and the wainscoting was ripped off the walls before the interior of the home was battered by axes. Even several of the trees in the yard were chopped down and thousands of pounds in cash and personal items were stolen. The mob then invaded the wine cellar and drank toasts to their victory over British tyranny.

Nolan would have liked to wring Samuel Adams's neck for turning the mob loose in the name of liberty and personal freedom. This demonstration had wrought nothing but disaster. Even the most dedicated lovers of liberty would be appalled by the wrath the drunken populace brought down on the lieutenant governor. Nolan shuddered to think of the repercussions that would follow.

Heaving an angry sigh, Nolan hoisted Laura to her feet, but her left leg folded at the knee. When Nolan tried to pull her close, she instantly protested.

"I am perfectly fine, thank you very much."

"Truly, my lady? Perhaps you should tell that to your injured leg. It doesn't appear to be functioning as well as you think it is."

Despite Laura's objections— and she had several— Nolan carried her down the street toward his mount. Nolan lifted her onto the gray gelding and quickly swung up behind her.

"Your aunt truly should insist on confining you to parlors and drawing rooms for less strenuous activities that are befitting dignified ladies. A riot is no place for a woman, even in disguise," he didn't hesitate to lecture her.

"Kindly put me down," Laura demanded, squirming in his lap.

"I intend to, but in due time."

Nolan gnashed his teeth when her shapely derrière brushed against his upper thigh. Blast it, he was still so vividly aware of this female that his body instantaneously reacted to her.

She's a Tory, for God's sake, Nolan reminded himself fiercely. And furthermore, she was a traitor in the patriots' midst. He should despise her. So why was he pitying the beating she had taken and why he was still so desperately desiring her? Why did he feel the insane urge to veer down a darkened alley and help himself to kisses more tantalizing than illegally imported wine?

This ridiculous fascination had to stop, here and now, Nolan told himself sensibly. All he was doing was escorting this impossible misfit home— where she should have stayed in the first place.

"Halt!"

Nolan scowled when a red-coated young soldier, his musket clamped across his chest, leaped from the shadows. The British were guarding the alleyways rather than defending Hutchinson's home? Brave lot, weren't they?

When Laura squirmed to prevent her face from being recognized, Nolan clamped his arm around her, blocking the soldier's view, and stared at the other man. "If you are expecting trouble, private, you are looking on the wrong side of town."

At the sound of Nolan's heavy British accent, the soldier relaxed noticeably. "What have you got there, sir? One of the beggars who participated in the riot?"

Nolan felt Laura tense in his arms. No doubt, she expected him to turn her over to the soldier. He really should. This female ought to spend some time behind bars so she would fully appreciate the frustration Nolan had endured because of her.

"Actually," Nolan said calmly, "young *Lawrence* works for me. He was injured trying to stop the destruction. He deserves a medal, not punishment. The question I put to you is: where were you and the rest of your company when trouble broke out? Guarding the trash cans in the alley?"

The private shifted self-consciously from one polished black boot to the other. "I was only following orders and keeping a low profile on the streets."

"You certainly accomplished your mission." Nolan sent the solider a condescending glance. "I suggest you follow in the wake of the mob and see what can be salvaged from Hutchinson's home rather than skulking along the byways, waylaying Tory sympathizers."

On that parting shot Nolan nudged his heels against his mount's flank and trotted off.

"Now we're even," Laura murmured.

Nolan chuckled at her peculiar sense of fair play. "Do you think so? I rather thought we had called it even that night at the jail. Since then I have rescued you from a brothel fire— "

"Which would not have been necessary at all, if you hadn't been so bloody mischievous," Laura put in tartly.

"You never did tell me what you were doing slinking around the Brit's favorite fleshpot."

"Because 'tis still none of your business," Laura insisted, raising a bruised but stubborn chin.

"You are being exceptionally difficult for a woman who is eternally indebted to me, not only for saving you from considerable public scandal but also for protecting you from bodily harm tonight."

"Thank you."

"A mere 'thank you' will hardly suffice."

"And what is it you expect in return, Ezra?" she grumbled in question.

Nolan smiled wryly. "I should think you know me well enough by now to puzzle that out for yourself."

She snapped up her head and her dark eyes flashed in the scant light. "You are beneath contempt. If the only way you can coerce a woman into your bed is to bribe her, then I pity you."

"Is that what you think I want from you? A tumble in bed?"

"Isn't that what you want, what all men want?"

Nolan stared into her smudged face, assured that his masquerade as a self-indulgent aristocrat had been effective. Why shouldn't Nolan enjoy compensation for the trouble she constantly caused him?

"Where are we going?" Laura demanded when Nolan suddenly veered off in the opposite direction of Beacon Hill.

"To the inn, so I can treat your injuries," he informed her.

"I can treat my own injuries at home. I was taking care of myself long before you interfered in my life, you know."

"Be that as it may," Nolan replied belatedly. "I am feeling exceptionally kind-hearted and generous tonight."

"An exceptional occurrence, no doubt," she sniffed caustically.

"Aye, I'm not always so tender-hearted, so humor me. Perhaps you can claim credit for transforming me into a do-gooder who places the needs of others above his own."

"I doubt that will happen, not in this lifetime," she snipped.

Nolan couldn't resist grinning. He always enjoyed fencing words with this vibrant misfit. His association with Laura was unlike any previous encounters with females. She was unpredictable and spirited—a kaleidoscope of constant change. And if there was one thing Nolan appreciated, 'twas change.

When Nolan reached the wayside inn, he quickly dismounted. Although he courteously attempted to assist Laura down, she slapped his hand away as if it were a pesky gnat.

"Gentlemen do not cater to urchins," she reminded him before she slid off the saddle and balanced on her good leg. "Walk on ahead and I will skulk behind, like every submissive lackey should."

"Considering your temperament, I imagine that will require tremendous acting ability on your part," Nolan taunted playfully.

To his everlasting surprise, a small dagger appeared from beneath her coat, the blade glistening in her hand.

"Considering my temperament, I advise you to guard your tongue, Ezra Beecham. I am not in the best of moods at the moment, so behave yourself."

Nolan wasn't the least bit intimidated by the appearance of her knife. He could have wrested it from her hand with minimal effort, but he didn't even bother trying. He simply shook his head at the woman's unusual talents.

Spinning on his heels, Nolan swaggered toward the door. "Come along, lad. Let's tend your injury."

"Aye, yer lordship," she replied with a thick cockney accent. "Whatever ya say."

The proprietor's fuzzy brows flattened over his close-set eyes when he spied the waif limping along behind the elegantly dressed dandy. "I don't rent rooms to *his* kind, your lordship."

"The boy is with me." Nolan lifted several shiny coins as temptation. "Rest assured that I will prevent young *Lawrence* from stealing you blind. The boy may look a mite scruffy, but he is an invaluable and faithful servant. He injured his leg tonight protecting me."

The proprietor blinked in surprise as he stared at the urchin whose downcast head concealed his face. "Did he now?"

"Indeed he did," Nolan proclaimed, tossing the coins to the rotund man. "Have one of your servants send up water for a bath, a supper tray and bandages."

With Laura hobbling behind him, Nolan ascended the steps. Out of the corner of his eye, Nolan saw Laura stumble on her gimpy leg. He snaked out a hand to steady her before she tumbled down the stairs and sprained more than her knee.

"Thank ya kindly, yer lordship."

"You're welcome, *Lawrence.*"

Nolan assisted Laura up the remainder of the steps and veered toward his rented room. He paused before the closed door, knowing he should have taken Laura straight home, but unable to deny any longer his desire to have her all to himself. He was about to cross the threshold that would lead to the kind of forbidden temptation he knew he should avoid. But then, Nolan reminded himself as he reached for the doorknob, he had made a habit of living dangerously.

And there was nothing more dangerous than

craving a woman who could threaten his very existence. The hell of it was that, at this moment, nothing else seemed to matter.

Appeasing this forbidden temptation was all that did . . .

Thirteen

Nolan watched in wicked amusement as Laura plunked down on the foot of the bed and fidgeted nervously. "Relax, imp. I hardly have time to seduce you before the bath water, medical supplies and supper tray arrive."

"Seduce?" Laura sniffed sarcastically. "Never doubt that you will have a battle on your hands, if you dare make advances. I will gladly repay you for coming to my rescue tonight, but *only* with gold coins," she said in no uncertain terms.

Nolan towered over her, matching her stare for stare. "I think you'd better give me the dagger."

"Where would ya like it, yer lordly lordship?" she sassed him. "In the belly or the back—"

An indignant gasp burst from Laura's lips when the heel of Nolan's hand pressed against her shoulder, forcing her off balance. To her shocked amazement, his hand slipped inside her jacket with the swiftness of a striking cobra. He retrieved her dagger before she had time to blink. When his hand accidentally— or was it on purpose?— brushed against the swell of her breast, Laura froze like a slab of ice.

"Thank you so much for your cooperation," Nolan purred pretentiously, stepping back apace.

"You have quick hands," Laura muttered resentfully, watching him tuck her knife in his belt.

"Not as quick as yours." Nolan well remembered how she had stashed her bracelet in his pocket while he was oblivious to her unexpected kiss. "But because of the company I have been keeping of late, I have learned to be more cautious and move swiftly."

Her dark-eyed gaze drifted down his muscular torso in reluctant admiration— and wary consternation. "Why do I have the feeling there is more to you than you would have me believe, Ezra Beecham?"

Nolan shrugged a broad shoulder before planting himself in a chair. "Probably because you are a suspicious sort yourself." He pulled off his periwig and tossed it on the table beside him. "And while we are on the subject of *you*— "

"We weren't," she quickly corrected as she surveyed his jet-black hair.

Nolan ignored her rejoinder, but he was very aware of her perusal. If he wasn't mistaken, Laura Chandler approved of what she saw. Nolan shifted position and forced himself to concentrate on his casual interrogation.

"I would dearly like to know why a lady from your prestigious position in society takes such pleasure in masquerading as a scruffy urchin."

He waited, wondering if she would divulge the truth or ply him with lies. This was a test. If Laura would confide in him, Nolan might be persuaded to believe his brother's firm convictions about Lady Chandler. Nolan *wanted* to believe she was a fellow libertarian, not a devious spy, but he kept suspecting that Laura had Tory inclinations.

"I can think of no reason why I should divulge my purpose to you," she said, tilting her sooty chin to a defiant angle.

Nolan braced his elbows on the arms of the chair and steepled his fingers. He stared at the disguised female for a moment and decided he was going to have to be more direct if he wanted to wrest information from her. "You portray the street-wise ragamuffin far too well. You have not always lived in the lap of luxury, have you?"

Laura winced at the perceptive question. "Nay," she said honestly. "But I prefer Peter Forbes doesn't get wind of that."

Before Nolan could press Laura for details about her previous life in the streets, a rap resounded on the door. He strode over to admit two servant boys who filled the small copper tub with steaming water. A large-framed coarse-featured female filed inside to set the tray of mincemeat and cheese on the table. Her gleaming eyes slid over Nolan's fashionable attire and she smiled invitingly.

"Would ya be needin' any other services tonight, luv?" she questioned in a provocative purr.

Nolan stifled a grin when he intercepted Laura's condemning glower. "Nay, a bath and nourishment is all I require."

Visibly disappointed, the wide-hipped wench

trooped out behind the bath-water brigade. She paused to strike her most seductive pose against the doorjamb. "In case ya change yer mind, luv, I'll be downstairs in the tavern."

With a wink and a smile, the wench sashayed away.

When the door creaked shut, Laura peeled off her grimy cap and shook out the long tresses of curly hair. "A pity you didn't accept the offer. The wench was obviously ready and willing to pleasure you."

Nolan loosened his cravat and shrugged off his jacket. "Let's just say that, these days, I have a fascination for unconventional females. And despite what you probably think, I happen to be very selective."

Laura eyed him for a ponderous moment, apparently admiring the wide expanse of his chest and the muscular columns of his thighs that were accentuated by his form-fitting gray breeches. "I am still left to wonder if perhaps you are a libertine who delights in counting his worth by the number of females he conquers."

Nolan scowled at the comment. In the first place, he shouldn't even be entertaining thoughts of stripping this sassy female down to her luscious skin and taking his pleasures. There were scores of other women who could appease him without the kind of complications this imp invited. In the second place . . .

Irritated by the riptide of thoughts floating across

his mind, Nolan shoved the tray of food at Laura. "Eat your meal before you soak in the tub."

One delicate brow arched. "The proverbial last supper before the human sacrifice is to be made? How noble you are, Ezra," she added with blatant sarcasm.

"I doubt you're the sacrificial virgin, not with a constant string of lovers sniffing at your heels," he muttered.

An odd smile pursed her lips before she bit into a slice of cheese. Nolan frowned, wishing he could read her complex mind. He didn't like the expression that settled on her sooty features. It made him more suspicious of her than he already was.

In silence they took their meal. When Laura had eaten her fill, she hobbled over to drag the dressing screen in front of the tub. While she was preoccupied, Nolan unclasped the gold chain he wore around his neck. If she noticed the Sons of Liberty medallion, Nolan could braid the rope for his own hanging. Sure as hell, Laura would use the information against him.

On that unsettling thought, Nolan tried to decide what to do with his secret medallion. He didn't dare tuck it in his pocket, for fear his pocket would be picked. With this unusual female, a man couldn't be too cautious.

Damn, now he was sounding like his brother.

Nolan dropped the chain inside his shoe for safekeeping.

A splash of water, succeeded by a contented sigh, drew Nolan's attention to the hand-painted dressing screen. He could well imagine how Laura would look, her naked flesh glowing in the lamplight, a waterfall of auburn curls tumbling over her creamy shoulders . . .

A hard knot of desire coiled beneath his belt buckle. Nolan squirmed uncomfortably in his chair. His betraying gaze slid toward the bed— and his imagination went toward wild fantasies.

"Um . . . Ezra . . . ?"

Nolan jerked himself to attention "Aye?"

"Could you . . . um . . . hand me the towel? I forgot to fetch it off the end of the bed."

Nolan surged out of his chair to pluck up the towel. One bare feminine arm, glistening with water droplets, protruded over the top of the screen. Nolan forgot everything except the sight of her silky skin. His height gave him the kind of advantage that could easily become his doom. His traitorous gaze drifted over the curly mass of auburn hair that tumbled downward, concealing just enough of the swells of her breasts to present the most tantalizing vision ever to whet a male appetite. Her enchanting face was devoid of soot, except for the smudge on the tip of her pert nose. Nolan reflexively reached over the screen to wipe away the soot.

"You missed a spot." His voice cracked, despite his attempt at iron-clad self-control.

She dodged his lingering hand and wrapped the towel around her. "Thank you," she murmured awkwardly.

"Let me have a look at your leg," Nolan insisted,

even though he preferred to look at all of her, damn his lusty hide.

When those dark, hypnotic eyes narrowed on him, Nolan jerked himself to his senses. He doffed his shirt and tossed it to her from over the top of the dressing screen. "For your modesty, my lady."

Laura quickly shrugged on the garment and emerged from behind the screen. "How gallant of you to offer me the shirt off your back—" Her voice trickled off when her gaze settled on the rippling planes of his muscular chest and then drifted down the dark furring of hair that disappeared into the band of his breeches. "You are quite large, aren't you?" she said stupidly.

A grin captured Nolan's bronzed features. He was instantly reminded of the saucy remark Laura had made the evening he had challenged her to an archery contest. "And my aim is straight, as you recall," he prompted with a suggestive waggle of his eyebrows.

Laura blushed redcoat-red. Mustering her dignity, she cleared her throat and hobbled across the room to retrieve the bandages.

The long hem of the shirt descended to her thighs and Nolan felt another jolt of awareness hit him below the belt. He sorely envied his shirt. It lay against creamy flesh that he ached to explore— every luscious inch of it.

All eyes, Nolan watched Laura ease down on the edge of the bed to scoop up the bandages. Nolan gave himself a mental slap for gawking. He strode over to inspect the purple bruise on her chin and the discolored swelling on her knee.

The instant Nolan laid his hand on her thigh, Laura flinched and scooted away.

"Does that hurt?" he questioned. His husky voice betrayed the calm facade he tried to project.

"Aye." Laura stared at the air over his left shoulder. "I think I must have been stepped on once or twice after I was knocked down. I was too dazed at the time to know for sure."

Nolan sank down on his haunches in front of her, reaching out with his index finger to trace the bluish swell that rimmed her knee cap. "How will you explain the limp you're going to have for the next few days to your lovesick lieutenant?"

"I'll think of something," she said with great confidence.

"I don't doubt it. Lies tumble from your lips as easily as the truth."

"You appear to be an accomplished liar yourself," Laura didn't hesitate to point out. "You didn't even bat an eyelash when you told that soldier and the innkeeper I sustained injury while trying to protect you from harm— "

Her breath evaporated when his hand glided over her thigh to check for further injury. "Don't do that," she gasped.

Nolan couldn't drag his eyes— or his hands— away from the satiny texture of her flesh. Touching her was pleasure in itself, a reminder of the forbidden dreams that had haunted him since the first time he had lost himself in the dewy taste of her kiss. Nolan was fooling himself if he thought he could leave this room without testing his most intimate reactions to this mysterious beauty.

Laura Chandler was a woman of the world, after all. She had endured the hazards of Boston's streets, just as Nolan had battled a treacherous enemy on the frontier before testing his survival skills in the wilderness. He and Laura both knew what passion entailed. He had no intention of taking anything from her that she hadn't given to other men.

His hand moved up the sensitive flesh of her thigh and Nolan gave in to the need to end this sensual suspense and appease his curiosity. He knew Laura found him attractive. Her appreciative glances told him as much, and he could feel her flesh tremble beneath his roaming hand, hear her breath catch with each caress. Despite her tormenting games of hard-to-get, she wanted this as much as he did.

Nolan eased his hip onto the bed. His raven head went dipping down to trace the soft column of her throat with moist kisses. He heard her quiet moan, felt the aroused tingles ripple across her skin, making her shift restlessly beneath his wandering hand.

"You're a bona fide devil, Ezra Beecham," Laura breathed unevenly.

"And only a devil would dare tangle with such a dangerous little witch. I suppose we deserve each other . . ."

His mouth came down on hers, savoring the honeyed taste of her, remembering the mindless haze that engulfed him when they had sealed their bargain of silence. Nolan forgot every semblance of sanity when Laura responded to him.

He nearly groaned aloud when he glided his hand beneath the hem of the shirt to discover the warm heat he had summoned from her. He traced her feminine secrets with thumb and fingertips, hearing her breath tear out on a wobbly sigh, feeling her body quiver like an arrow.

Laura was as wildly passionate as she was adventurous. He was afraid that would be the case . . . and he instinctively responded.

Nolan was in the worst trouble he had ever encountered . . . and the most pleasure any man could ever hope to experience . . .

"Ezra, stop . . ." Laura gasped as his roving hand scaled her ribs to encircle the velvet peaks of her breasts. "I— " Her voice shattered when he brushed his lips over the aching crests. His hands flooded over her like a gentle tide, eroding the last of her resistance. Another betraying sigh of pleasure escaped her lips as he treated her to the kind of gentle seductive persuasion that knew no defense, only hopeless surrender.

Nolan could no more resist discovering every silky inch of her body than he could have sprouted wings and flown to the moon. She beguiled him, enchanted him. She made each sensuous contact feel as if it were the first intimate encounter either of them had ever experienced.

No wonder Peter Forbes was so bedazzled by her. She could make a man feel as if his amorous techniques were special, unique. She was truly a cunning sorceress, a skilled seductress who used her wiles to bewitch and conquer.

But Laura Chandler would never conquer him, Nolan confidently assured himself. He knew of Laura's deceptive secrets. And soon, he would discover all the erotic intimacies that her other lovers had enjoyed . . .

Nolan forgot to breathe, to think, when her fingertips drifted from one male nipple to the other, pausing to toy with the dark mat of hair that covered his chest. He hadn't expected to be so devastated by this woman's caress. But then, he had never taken quite so much time in the pursuit of his needs before, never allowed a woman the privileges his body was suddenly begging to experience. Nolan was discovering a new dimension of passion, a slow, unhurried encounter that prolonged and intensified desire until he was absorbed in it.

With hands shaking, he drew the shirt from her shoulders. His glittering silver gaze swept from the tangle of auburn hair that billowed around her delicate face like a cloud and dropped to linger on the creamy swells of her breasts. His hungry eyes feasted on the sweet delights of her body.

The dim candlelight flickered and sensuous shadows shifted, concealing and revealing Laura's soft angles and lush curves. Nolan dipped his head downward. His tongue flicked at the mauve beads that captured his fascination. With a surrendering moan Laura arched to him, and Nolan suckled the taut peaks with delicate care. He drew each roseate bud into his mouth, tasting her, caressing her until the pleasure of exploring her delicious textures riddled his own body with a barrage of bulletlike sensations.

Nolan was certain that in the future, when he closed his eyes and let his mind drift, his thoughts would circle back to this night. He would remember every overwhelming sensation that assaulted him. He would be able to taste her again, feel her seductive responses . . . and he would burn then as he was burning now . . .

While Nolan feasted on the beaded crests, he coasted his hand over the flat plane of her belly to fully discover her feminine secrets. With a gentle nudge of his elbow, he parted her thighs. When he settled his hand between her legs, he felt the honeyeyed heat of her response bathing his fingertip.

Desire coiled so tightly inside him that he moaned aloud. He had never known that giving pleasure offered such stimulating reward.

With more patience than he realized he possessed, he traced her, aroused her by deliberate degrees. His gentleness was rewarded tenfold, when she all but came apart in his arms, in his hands. Nolan experienced a sense of power and control that he had never known . . . and wanted to savor . . .

When Laura gasped at the onslaught of shock waves that riveted through her, Nolan smiled against the soft swell of her breast. His penetrating fingertip glided, teased and stroked, inciting her raspy groan of pleasure— and his answering growl of burgeoning need.

"You are truly and surely the devil himself," Laura said raggedly. "You possess the devil's tempting touch, but there's something I must tell you . . . Oh, God . . ."

Nolan shuddered when he felt her caress his fingertip in the most sensual, intimate way imaginable. The fervent need he had summoned from her echoed through him, and he experienced her shimmering pleasure as if it were his own.

Nolan was utterly intrigued by Laura's uninhibited responses. He yearned to draw another, and yet another helpless tremor from her, until she was begging for him to appease the compelling obsession that thoroughly consumed them both.

"My Lord!" Laura gasped in breathless disbelief, when yet another wildly devastating sensation swept through her.

Wide, thick-lashed ebony eyes lifted as Nolan unfastened his breeches and eased himself between her thighs. He could see the dramatic effects of passion capturing her enchanting features, and he ached to glide into that honeyed fire he had kindled in her.

When Nolan lifted Laura to him and penetrated her softest flesh, a hot chill snaked down his spine. He sheathed himself fully within her . . .

And suddenly encountered an unfamiliar barrier beyond his previous experiences with passion.

She couldn't be, he tried to tell himself.

She was, the voice of undeniable truth assured him.

Hell and damnation, Nolan thought in frustration— and satisfaction— he wasn't sure which. Who would have thought Laura Chandler was such an unbelievable contradiction of worldliness and innocence? She was teeming with startling surprises.

And what a pity that Nolan was the kind of man who thoroughly appreciated the element of surprise. He had made it his business . . . and now his greatest pleasure . . .

Fourteen

When Nolan heard Laura's whimper of pain and felt her tense against his intimate invasion, he battled for self-restraint. She was holding him so tightly inside her that 'twas as if they were forged into the same flesh.

"I tried to tell you, blast it," Laura said through clenched teeth. "Now let me up. You got what you wanted."

Nolan felt like cursing— or laughing, maybe both at once. If she thought he had everything he wanted, she was greatly misinformed. The best was yet to come. And by damned, Nolan vowed as he went perfectly still, Laura Chandler was going to discover that truth for herself, right down to the splendorous moment when she was willing to die once or twice in the ecstasy of it all . . .

"Don't move," Nolan instructed when she tried to escape intimate captivity.

" 'Tis easy enough for you to say," she muttered against his sturdy shoulder. "You're not the one being tortured."

Tortured? A lot she knew! Nolan readily accepted the challenge of correcting Laura's misconceptions of what intimacy entailed. Aye, she *was* going to enjoy this, even if it killed him. And considering the barely restrained need that hammered at him, Nolan wondered if it might. Primal instinct whipped him like a merciless rider, urging him to do what came naturally. Having and not having was the ultimate in torture, despite what this innocent female thought.

"If you let me take command, imp, if you will follow my lead, we will both enjoy this," Nolan assured her huskily.

Luminous obsidian eyes peeked up at him from beneath a fan of long lashes. "You mean we aren't finished yet? Dear Lord, I thought . . . Ezra— ?"

The residue of pain and wariness Nolan detected in her features vanished as he moved against her with the most exquisite care. He felt her untried body melt beneath him, around him, and another explosion of pleasure rumbled through him. When she whispered his name again, Nolan whimsically wished he could hear his given name tumble from her lips. He also wished for things that could never be when she yielded so completely, so generously to him.

Even if they were destined to be political enemies— and they undoubtedly were— Nolan was discovering the kind of passion that exceeded previous realms of pleasure. He wondered if he would always crave the forbidden, wondered if he would ever forget this wild, reckless night, the glorious rapture of this moment . . .

His thought processes broke down when he felt

her fingernails flex into his shoulders like cat claws anchoring against tidal waves of turbulent sensations. He drove into her— more impatiently than he intended. Unleashed desire had taken such a fierce, uncontrollable hold on him that he could do nothing but surrender to the fervent needs that took him to the brink and left him falling into infinity.

Nolan held onto her so tightly that he couldn't even breathe without inhaling the scent of her, couldn't move without absorbing the very essence of her. And still, Nolan felt intolerably far away from this enthralling siren. 'Twas as if taking intimate possession wasn't quite enough to satisfy him, as if he needed— demanded— something more from her, from himself.

Before Nolan could puzzle out what that elusive sensation might be, the physical demands of unrivaled desire gave way to shudder after helpless shudder of effusive pleasure. Male strength abandoned him in the wake of all-consuming splendor. Nolan couldn't muster the energy to raise his head from the soft curve of Laura's neck. Mere breathing took conscious effort. Nolan could not remember experiencing total physical and emotional devastation. What in the name of heaven had overcome him?

"How very strange," Laura murmured a few minutes later. "I don't understand why— "

Nolan brushed his forefinger across her lips to shush her. He had no inclination to discuss the strange, unprecedented sensations that claimed him. Knowing that he had succumbed to tender feelings for a woman— who might eventually betray him— was plenty of food for thought.

His consolation was knowing that he alone had conquered and claimed this vibrant beauty. *That* was most important, Nolan told himself. Now her bewitching lure would subside. Now he could focus on his objectives and forget this destructive obsession . . .

Or so he thought . . .

When Laura stirred beneath him, Nolan's confident belief that he had become immune to her mystical powers shattered like stained glass windows. He should have been completely satisfied after the immeasurable pleasure she had given him.

He wasn't.

He wondered if he ever would be, not when making love to her intensified rather than satisfied this overwhelming addiction. Damnation, this wasn't normal . . .

Nolan could feel her sensuous curves molded intimately to him, feel his body reacting instantaneously. And where, he would dearly like to know, had he even found the energy to meet the phenomenal demands of his own body when he swore he had just depleted every ounce of strength only minutes before?

This lovely misfit was indeed a spell-casting witch, Nolan concluded. The naturally erotic movements of her body were a silent incantation and he found himself sensually entranced.

His lips slanted over hers, his tongue invading

the moist recesses of her mouth as he took full and complete possession for the second time in only a matter of minutes. He heard Laura's muffled moan as she accepted his passion, matched him thrust for penetrating thrust. They were moving together as one living, breathing essence, seeking those storm-tossed waves in yet another sea of immeasurable rapture.

And later, when the tide of passion had ebbed, Nolan asked himself if he would be content to walk away after discovering a multitude of sensations he never realized existed. But he really had no choice. If Laura didn't return home until dawn, Miriam Peabody would ask too many questions. And there was Peter Forbes to consider, even though Nolan didn't give a damn what Peter thought.

Reluctantly, Nolan eased away and then silently cursed the fact that he was still wearing his breeches. Even a deceptive imp like Laura deserved more consideration and courtesy than to have her innocence stolen by a man who was so starved for her that he hadn't bothered to doff all his clothes. The deed made him appear to be the pleasure-seeking rake he pretended to be.

It shouldn't have bothered him in the least.

It did.

Nolan winced when he noticed the evidence of Laura's lost virginity clinging to him. He turned away to fasten his breeches and retrieve Laura's shabby disguise. When he strode toward the window to stare out into the night, he heard her quiet gasp behind him.

"Ezra?"

"Aye?" he murmured awkwardly.

Laura modestly covered herself with the sheet and gingerly sat up. Her gaze was fixed on the scars that marred the rippling muscles on his back. "Who whipped you?"

Nolan cursed under his breath. Earlier, he had been careful not to present his back to her, in hopes of avoiding the question she had just asked. "It isn't something I want to discuss," he said with a hint of finality.

"And tonight isn't something *I* want to discuss or have bandied about," she insisted. "I prefer this encounter becomes another one of our private secrets. 'Twould not bode well if Peter—"

"Hang Peter!" Nolan scowled as he wheeled around to snatch up his shirt.

Laura was curiously amused by the unexpected explosiveness of his voice and the puckered expression that claimed his rugged features. "Knowing what you know and he doesn't, I hardly see the point of hanging *Peter.*"

Was this jealous possession spurting through his veins provoked by the mere mention of that handsome lieutenant's name? Surely not. Nolan had never been the jealous type, but he had developed a resentment for Peter Forbes.

Nolan was aware that Peter had the kind of dashing good looks, polished manners and regal deportment that attracted those of the female persuasion. In comparison, Nolan had a more weather-beaten, less refined appearance. Living in military camps on the frontier and enduring the elements in the wilderness left definite marks on a man. Peter Forbes had the look of fine English breeding while Nolan hailed from sturdy colonial stock.

Laura studied Nolan pensively as he handed her the scruffy urchin's garb. "You can't possibly be jealous," she said with a chortle.

"Of course not," he scoffed. "Why should I be?"

"Why indeed?" Laura self-consciously slipped into the cream-colored shirt, taking care to shield herself as much as possible with the sheet. She still could not believe the reckless abandon that consumed her earlier— or the awkwardness that claimed her now.

Laura was impossibly confused. What she had previously believed to be a man's degrading domination over a woman was not necessarily so. After her near mauling at Geoffrey Spradlin's hands, after what she had seen and heard . . .

Well, it didn't matter now, Laura told herself, disregarding the unpleasant memories. Nor did it matter that she had lost her innocence. She had vowed to marry no man, so there was no reason to save herself for an event that wouldn't take place.

Laura had come to cherish her freedom, especially after years of being a slave to poverty and struggling through a life in the streets that had been nothing but an endless test of survival. She welcomed change and challenge, because she had grown accustomed to that way of life. She wasn't going to whimper and cry that she had been ruined like some of those silly aristocratic females— who supposedly valued their innocence above all else— were prone to do. No doubt, those same females were partially responsible, weaving cunningly deceptive webs to secure marriage proposals.

There were, however, exceptions, Laura grimly reminded herself. There were situations in which a woman was given no choice but to accept the lusty demands of overpowering men. When Geoffrey Spradlin tried to attack her in the carriage, she had discovered that first-hand. As adept as she had become in self-defense, the ogre had nearly gotten the best of her. She had discovered the difference between forceful molestation and skillful seduction when she fell beneath Ezra Beecham's impossible spell. This ruggedly handsome wizard had crumbled her resistance with his gentle touch.

Ah, if only Martha Winfield had been allowed to experience what Laura had discovered. If only Martha could have . . .

Laura willfully set aside the tormenting memories. It hurt too much to remember what she had spent almost a year trying to forget . . .

When Nolan's hand grazed her thigh, Laura's thoughts instantly focused on him and her body quickly responded. When he knelt down to wrap a bandage around her swollen knee, her gaze flooded over his virile form. A strange sensation squeezed around her heart, even while she warned herself that 'twas folly to become sentimentally attached to this beguiling rogue.

"Wear this for support," Nolan instructed as he pulled the bandage snugly around her leg. "You suffered a severe bruise and strain. 'Twill be tender for a few days, I expect."

Her lashes fluttered down, fighting the memory of his heart-stopping caresses, remembering where those irresistible caresses had led. Laura knew she should have been ashamed of her uninhibited responses. Yet, no other man had remotely tempted or intrigued her the way Ezra Beecham had. For all his faults and obvious lack of interest in the political upheaval transpiring around him, he was still the only man who intrigued her. To be sure, there was no logical explanation for this mismatched attraction. 'Twas only the reality of it, no matter how brief or temporary their liaison would have to be.

When a woman grew up living one day at a time, as Laura had, she learned not to depend on consistency. Laura had discovered that life was a procession of unpredictable change. She had learned to adapt. What she and Ezra shared would become a private but very precious memory. Yet, she could not permit herself to harbor whimsical expectations. Indeed, Ezra could create more complications for her than he already had. And he had created plenty already!

"Laura, about what happened tonight . . ." Nolan began hesitantly.

She had anticipated this, of course, had mentally prepared herself for what she predicted to be the standard speech Ezra offered his female conquests.

'Twas fun while it lasted, he would say. *But the moment has come and gone and so must I.*

Laura had too much pride to allow Ezra to end their reckless tryst. No man, she had fiercely vowed over a year ago, would ever get the better of her. She would not allow herself to make more of this moment than Ezra obviously intended to.

"Enough said," she insisted with a careless shrug. "I accept partial responsibility for what happened." She twisted her long tresses around her hand and tucked them under her cap, casting him a seemingly unconcerned glance. "You satisfied my curiosity and I appeased your needs. We struck another bargain, is all."

For some reason, Laura's noble attempt to reduce their encounter to a simple experiment in passion annoyed Nolan beyond words. Damned if he knew why. He had no intention of further muddling what was already a difficult situation. But still, she didn't have to take this so bloody well, did she?

"Curiosity, imp?" he repeated, watching her wriggle into her oversize breeches.

Black-diamond eyes glinted with mischief. "Very well then, I take *full* credit for compromising you. Does that make you feel better?"

Nolan couldn't contain the chuckle that exploded from his lips. This vibrant female's irrepressible wit and resilient spirit were part of the reason he found her so captivating. Laura Chandler was no clinging vine, but rather a steel-willed rose who had learned to roll with life's punches and land on her feet—bruised knee and all.

"What I was trying to say, before you nobly accepted the burden of responsibility, is that if, by chance, we created a—"

That brought her head up in a hurry. "Dear Lord!" Laura hadn't considered that!

"In the event—"

"I'll handle everything," Laura cut in quickly. "You need not—"

"I wish you would let me finish at least one sentence," Nolan growled at her.

"Fine, speak your piece, Ezra, but be quick about it. The hour is late and I have no wish to encounter Peter in the upstairs hall."

Peter again. Nolan was getting damned tired of hearing that British officer's name bandied about. "I have a right to know if we made a child together."

She stared incredulously at him. "Why would you care?"

Nolan gaped at her. "Why?"

"That is what I asked," she prompted as she fastened her breeches. "I know perfectly well that a man like you is more interested in *conquests*, not *consequences*. I should think you would be relieved to hear I won't be pointing an accusing finger at you, should complications arise." Her chin tilted to a proud angle. "I do not wish to find myself burdened with a husband any more than you want to be tied to a wife's apron strings. I will take care of everything."

Nolan muttered under his breath when Laura surged onto her good leg to test the supporting brace. He was getting bloody tired of hearing this independent female claim she would take command of every situation. Nolan wasn't accustomed to dealing with a strong-willed woman who had a mind of her own and relished using it. Indeed, he limited infrequent encounters with females to physical appeasement and walked away without looking back.

Laura Chandler had launched Nolan's previous theories and cynical generalizations about men's dealings with women into orbit— and kept them there. He rarely felt in control when Laura was underfoot. The woman was definitely more than a handful.

An unstoppable whirlwind was more like it, Nolan amended.

Maybe his suspicions about Laura were ill-founded. Maybe she had tried to stop the destructive riot for the same reason Nolan disapproved of it. Perhaps he had become too cynical by habit, as Ethan contended.

Nolan found himself wavering between Laura's guilt and innocence as he followed her out the door. He hoped Ethan was right about her. The thought of finding himself bewitched by a traitor to his cause would be a tormenting blow. Somehow or another, he was going to have to determine if Laura Chandler was friend or foe. Wanting her while suspecting the worst about her was sure to drive him crazy. He had to resolve the matter once and for all if he had any hope of retaining his sanity!

Miriam Peabody sat in Laura's room, glancing at the mantel clock at regular intervals. What was keeping Laura? she wondered. Had the girl met with trouble? And if she had, how was Miriam to get word to Laura's contacts when the names were kept confidential? This not knowing what difficulties Laura might have encountered was tying Miriam in nervous knots.

Her head swiveled around when she heard the quiet creak of the door. "Thank God you're home!" Miriam said with an enormous sigh of relief. "Are you all right?"

Laura nodded mutely and hobbled into the room.

"You are not all right," Miriam fussed when she noticed Laura's limp. "What happened to your leg? How did you get that nasty bruise on your cheek? What on earth happened?"

Laura gave a brief, concise report while Miriam gasped and groaned in dismay. The incident with Ezra Beecham was omitted. If complications developed because of her recklessness, Laura would deal with the situation. Miriam was too overset by the destructive riot and Laura's injuries to bring up the encounter with Ezra Beecham.

"I shudder to think what repercussions we'll face after royal officials were harassed and their personal property was destroyed." Miriam ran a hand through her fuzzy gray hair and paced the room.

" 'Tis getting too dangerous for you to be roaming the streets."

"I'm perfectly fine," Laura insisted.

"You are not fine at all," Miriam was quick to point out. "You were injured in a demonstration that degenerated into a devastating riot." When Laura placed her index finger to her lips in silent warning to lower her voice, Miriam continued in a quieter tone. "Peter is still at Castle Island, thank goodness, so we needn't fear his overhearing us. But we are going to have a devil of a time explaining your bruises and limp."

"I simply tripped on the hem of my gown and stumbled down the steps," Laura prefabricated.

"Well, we better get our story perfectly straight," Miriam grumbled. "Neither of us needs to be caught in a trap. Thus far, that lovesick lieutenant suspects nothing. I prefer to keep it that way. He will undoubtedly explode in towering fury if he discovers how often he has been deceived."

While Laura and Miriam were inventing a believable explanation for Laura's injuries, the darkly dressed figure lurking in the hall inched down the back steps to escape without being detected. By the time Miriam padded barefoot to her room, neither she nor Laura knew that the scruffy ragamuffin had been under surveillance when she returned home.

Spark McRae lit his pipe and leaned back against the rough-hewn wall of the cabin. He was not a happy man. Shadowing Nolan had revealed several interesting facts, none of which pleased Spark.

Nolan should have had more sense than to detour to a wayside inn with that mysterious chit in tow. But then, Spark reminded himself grimly, a man's urges often did his thinking for him the first half of his life. Men only became the masters of their own minds the second half of their lives— if they should be so lucky to live that long.

From all indication, Nolan had ignored the good sense he had spent thirty years cultivating. Too bad Nolan had gotten into the habit of living so dangerously, Spark thought, disgusted. That daring rascal was definitely asking for trouble.

The sound of muffled hoofbeats signaled Nolan's return. Spark tapped the ashes from his pipe and tucked it in his pocket. " 'Bout time," he grumbled irritably.

" 'Tis been a hectic night," Nolan replied as he dismounted.

"Is that a fact?"

Nolan frowned at Spark's sarcastic tone. "Did something happen that I don't know about?"

Spark snorted disgustedly, turned on his heels and stalked inside the cottage, slamming the door behind him.

"What the devil is eating you?" Nolan demanded when he returned from tending his horse. Ordinarily, Spark wandered down to the shed with him, bending his ear with conversation. Tonight, Spark had tramped off and sulked in his chair.

"I thought you had more sense," Spark blurted out.

The mutinous glance Nolan received had him frowning warily. "Spit it out, Spark. You're not the kind of man who beats around bushes."

Spark's wrinkled face puckered in a scowl. "Since when have you become so taken in by bits of fluff?"

Nolan's hand stalled in midair while he was reaching for the bottle of rum on the table. "Meaning?" he asked neutrally.

"You know bloody damned well what I mean. I know where you went after you left Hutchinson's house and I know who you were with, so don't play innocent with me, boy!"

"You followed me?" Nolan stared incredulously at the crusty old frontiersman who was glaring flaming arrows at him.

"I hope you gathered valuable information when you were waylaid, not the other way around," he muttered. "Is she one of us or isn't she?"

Nolan uncorked the bottle and poured himself a drink. "I'm not sure."

Spark sniffed disdainfully. "Of all the things you probably know about the chit by now, discoverin' where her loyalty lies should've been yer first priority."

"Spark . . ." Nolan said warningly.

"Don't Spark me. You swore you learned yer lesson after yer dealin's with Adam Hart's fickle widow. Apparently you've forgotten. I hope this Chandler chit was worth all the trouble she'll probably bring down on you."

"I do not want to continue this conversation," Nolan growled, his eyes narrowing into glinting silver slits.

"Well, that appears to be the *only* thing you aren't wantin'— "

"I said that's enough!" Nolan snapped.

"Was it? One tumble in bed will satisfy you?" Spark dared to ask. "If not, you might find yerself permanently planted in that empty plot in the buryin' ground. And if you ask me— "

"— Nobody did— "

"— 'tis not the question of that chit's deception, yer fightin' right now, 'tis the truth!" Spark declared.

"And what, pray tell, is that supposed to mean?" Nolan muttered in question.

"I think you know. Problem is you think you can escape it the way you've escaped every British patrol that chases yer heels. But not this time, Nolan."

Wearing a grim, disapproving frown, Spark levered out of his chair and stalked toward his bedchamber. "I spent two years huntin' and trappin' with you, watchin' you learn to depend on yer instincts. You should've known better when it comes to women— especially that Chandler woman. There's more females than you can shake a stick at around here, who could've pacified you without causin' the kind of trouble you don't need. But you had to do more than flirt with danger, didn't you?"

Spark was still muttering and scowling when Nolan snuffed the lantern and eased into bed. Maybe

he deserved the harsh reprimand for his recklessness, but 'twas impossible to regret a night of such
unexpected pleasure.

And what did it matter? Nolan rationalized.
Laura Chandler didn't have a clue that he was
leading a double life. As long as that secret was
kept under wraps he was reasonably safe. No harm
had been done, as long as Nolan didn't make a
habit of visiting with Laura Chandler.

On that thought, Nolan drifted off to sleep, only
to have his dreams take up where splendorous reality had left off a few hours earlier . . .

Fifteen

Several nights later Nolan tucked his black shirt into his breeches and tied the cape— one that had become the Midnight Rider's trademark— around his neck. When footfalls resounded on the planked porch of the cabin Nolan inched around the corner into his room.

"I'll take care of it," Spark insisted, snapping his rifle into ready position.

Two slow raps rattled the door and the password seeped through the cracks. Spark lowered the barrel of his rifle and stepped aside.

Ethan Ryder strode into the cabin and his cedar green gaze immediately swung to the darkly clad figure looming in the hall. "I did as you asked," he grumbled begrudgingly.

Spark's gray brows rose sharply as he glanced from one brother to the other. "And what did you ask Ethan to do for you?"

"He wants to test Laura Chandler's loyalties," Ethan spoke up. "Nolan asked me to make the arrangements through her before he delivers the newspapers and pamphlets for the Sons of Liberty to the express riders."

"Well, at least yer reckless brother has a little sense left," Spark snorted as he retrieved his pipe from his pocket.

Ethan frowned, befuddled. "What are you implying?"

Sparked hitched his thumb toward Nolan. "The bull moose couldn't control his—"

"Spark!" Nolan's baritone voice boomed like a cannon and ricocheted off the walls. "Don't let your tongue run away with itself."

Ethan's inquisitive gaze landed on his scowling brother. "Control what, Nolan?"

"Nothing," he muttered, staring murderously at Spark. " 'Twas a personal matter that has nothing to do with the rebel cause."

Ethan was puzzled by Nolan's sour mood and Spark's condemning glances. But 'twas obvious Ethan wasn't to be privy to whatever incident had put the outspoken old frontiersman and Nolan at odds.

"Have a care tonight, little brother," Ethan cautioned. "After the destructive riot, His Majesty's men are patrolling the streets, refusing to allow more than a handful of citizens to gather in the same place, for fear of mobs forming again. Lieutenant Governor Hutchinson went before the Admiralty Court to protest the injustice leveled on him by the mob. Our informants warn that more troops might be marched up from their stronghold in New York to clamp down on unruly Bostonians."

Nolan had predicted as much. Express riders who were distributing handbills and pamphlets through the secretive networks in the other colonies were destined to meet with difficulty while trying to deliver information. The British hadn't taken kindly to the riots that left royal officers fleeing for safety and left their homes in shambles. Objections to the Stamp Act had become a living, breathing beast that the Crown was desperately trying to bring under control.

Nolan pulled his silk hood over his head and grabbed his saddlebags. "Spark, meet me, and leave the gray gelding at the cemetery. If all goes well, I will deliver the pamphlets to the circuit riders and linger long enough to run interference for the other men, in case any of them were followed."

Spark nodded curtly as Nolan strode toward the door. "Hope you strapped on a full set of armor under yer garb. Those lobsterbacks have been swarmin' like hornets since the riots. And if there's a traitor in our midst, you're the one who'll catch hell, what with such a steep price on yer head." He glanced at Nolan's departing back. "I also hope the incident that took place a few nights past was worth the trouble that might come from it."

Nolan broke stride and gnashed his teeth, but he refused to cast Spark a glance. It was glaringly apparent that Spark disapproved of Nolan's mixing pleasure with secretive business. Spark didn't trust females any more than Nolan did. The old backwoodsman was of the opinion that women were a vice.

Nolan had heartily agreed with that philosophy until he'd stumbled onto Laura Chandler and found himself bewitched. He hoped he was dead wrong about her, but tonight would be the telling truth of her loyalty. She had been fed the information about the Midnight Rider carrying correspondence to the expressmen. If trouble arose, Nolan would know exactly where to lay the blame.

In determined strides, Nolan aimed himself toward the shed to fetch his black stallion. Fleeting clouds scudded past the moon, alternately flinging shadows and silvery beams across the countryside. The stallion pricked up its ears when Nolan swung onto the saddle and reined down the tree-lined path. Nolan could feel the powerful creature's muscles bunching in anticipation, eager to stretch his long legs and chase the wind.

As promised, the bundles of pamphlets from the Sons of Liberty were stashed in the underbrush beside the creek. After Nolan crammed two stacks of handbills in his saddlebags, he tucked two more bundles beneath his cloak. Then he trotted toward the secluded spot where the express riders waited.

The stallion danced skittishly beneath him, and Nolan was quick to recognize the creature's uneasiness. Nolan had lived in the wilderness long enough to detect trouble by an animal's behavior. His own keen senses went on full alert as he emerged from the canopy of trees to cross the clearing ahead of him.

Nolan was halfway across the meadow when the crackle of twigs caused the spirited stallion to gather himself behind and lunge into a gallop.

The clatter of a dozen horses resounded around Nolan and he cursed foully. He had been set up!

With thundering troops behind him, Nolan flattened himself on his mount and gave the stallion its head. A vision of treacherous beauty rose above Nolan as he raced across the clearing, his cloak billowing wildly around him. A musket ball thudded beside him, causing his steed to break stride the instant before Nolan braced himself for the flying leap over the split rail fence.

The second whining musket ball caught Nolan in the shoulder as he and the stallion left the ground and sailed over the fence. Pain seared Nolan's arm and he clenched his teeth in fierce determination. He had been in worse scrapes while battling the French and Indians in the wilderness. He had also found himself afoot once or twice when he disturbed a den of bears while setting beaver traps. One measly musket ball wasn't going to slow him down, not when he vowed to live long enough to repay Laura Chandler for her betrayal.

Damn her! Nolan seethed as he zigzagged through the trees, the King's men hot on his heels. 'Twas one thing to pick and choose when and where to let the redcoats take pot shots at him. 'Twas another matter to let a cunning traitor decide for him!

No wonder she had surrendered to Ezra Beecham, Nolan thought mutinously. She obviously thought she had succumbed to a Tory sympathizer.

Cursing furiously, Nolan spared a glance over his shoulder to estimate the size of the patrol that followed him. Fourteen scarlet dragons, with their swords slapping at their sides and muskets in hands, fanned out in a semi-circle behind him. Nolan swiveled back around to stare at the secluded cove beside the river. If his luck held, he could toss the pamphlets in the brush and veer away before the waiting express riders were detected and apprehended.

Nolan tried to move his injured arm, but it refused to cooperate. He took the reins in his teeth and grabbed the pamphlets beneath his cloak. Swerving toward the cove, Nolan flung the bundles aside and scooped up the saddlebags. With the correspondence delivered, Nolan veered left, reining the laboring stallion in a sweeping circle.

Another muted oath tumbled from Nolan's lips when the moonlight slanted across Peter Forbes's blond features. Nolan expected as much. Was it little wonder Peter's name was constantly on Laura's tongue? Despite her insistence that she had no wish to marry, she and the refined lieutenant were as thick as thieves. Curse that little traitor. She was going to discover what all nine kinds of hells were like before Nolan got through with her.

"He's trying to ford the river!" Peter yelled to his men. "If we can surround him, that patriot menace will be swinging high by noon tomorrow!"

Water splattered when Nolan plunged into the river. The troops had divided in thirds, trying to confine him to the river bank that was bounded by a steep cliff and thick vegetation. But Nolan was familiar with this area and he knew exactly where to locate the Indian footpath that angled up the steep incline. As soon as the troops had ridden into the water, slowing their progress, Nolan came ashore. He dug his heels into the winded stallion, demanding all the powerful creature had to give. In a series of graceful lunges, the devil stallion reached the narrow trail and scrabbled up the slope.

"Where the blazes did he go?" Private Simpson questioned incredulously.

"There! On the ridge above us!"

Nolan watched the soggy troops wade ashore to follow the winding riverbank. He granted the King's men time to close ranks before he thundered across the crest of the hill, remaining just out of musket range.

While the Midnight Rider led the Crown's soldiers on a merry chase, the express riders tugged their mounts from the concealment of the underbrush to collect the pamphlets. The expressmen veered off to make their appointed rounds, relaying news from Boston to the widespread network of riders at way stations along the King's Highway. Within days, news of the overthrow of Customs officers and stamp distributors in Boston would reach every colony, and more protests against British tyranny would be staged.

As the riders dispersed, avoiding the English troops, Nolan crossed the narrow neck of the river and retraced his route toward the cemetery. He didn't bother to wait for the soldiers to narrow the distance since they could see him clearly as he raced across the meadow, his cape waving like a banner.

Nolan predicted Peter Forbes had a pretty good idea where the Midnight Rider was headed, having given futile chase several times before. Nolan was in no condition to take unnecessary risks by leaping into the underbrush and racing off on foot. Blood had saturated his sleeve and trickled into the palm of his left hand. The initial numbness had worn off and pain throbbed in rhythm with his accelerated heartbeat. He needed extra time to disappear into the tress in the graveyard and ensure he didn't leave a trail of blood for the Brits to follow.

Gritting his teeth against the pain, Nolan urged his steed over the wrought-iron fence rather than wasting precious time following the dirt path through the burying ground. He intended to be in his stone niche long before the troops arrived. And later, when the coast was clear, Nolan was going to make a beeline for Miriam Peabody's grand mansion on Beacon Hill and drag Laura Chandler out of her bed by the hair on her head. And despite his wounded arm, he would tar and feather that traitorous snitch all by himself. By God, just see if he didn't!

Laura Chandler flattened herself on the ground beside Martha Winfield's headstone when she heard the rapid pelting of hooves. In awed amazement she watched the Midnight Rider clear the fence in a single bound and thunder toward a grove of trees. The coal black stallion, slick with sweat, emerged without its mysterious rider and galloped toward the east end of the cemetery. Laura heard the devil stallion leave the ground to soar over the distant fence, but she kept her gaze trained on the clump of trees into which the Ghost Rider had vanished.

She had heard several versions of the phenomenal tales circulating among British officers, but she knew for a fact that the Phantom Rider was flesh and blood, not a wraith. No one knew who the fabled centaur was, but he had been evading British patrols and collecting a high price on his head. The symbol of colonial liberty was a clever, fearless vigilante of justice . . .

Her thoughts trailed off when a shadow darted from the trees. To Laura's disbelieving eyes, she saw the caped silhouette virtually melt into the ground. And then, in the time it took to blink, the shadow disappeared entirely— like a water puddle evaporating in the summer sun.

Her curious gaze darted toward the row of headstones that lay beyond the grove of trees. Before she could gain her feet to investigate the odd phenomenon, the thunder of more hooves brought down the night.

Laura cursed under her breath when she recognized Peter Forbes leading the pack of redcoats. If Peter spotted her, while she was in disguise, she would be grilled with questions that would demand the most inventive answers Laura could devise.

With her heart pounding in apprehension, Laura slithered across the ground, placing as much distance between herself and the approaching troops as possible. She buried herself in the tall grass and lay there like a misplaced corpse while the mounted patrol clattered down the path and halted beside the trees.

"Blister it, I'm bloody tired of having that Midnight Rider vanish into thin air. He's got to be hiding out here somewhere," Peter growled as he swung from his snorting mount.

The other soldiers followed their commander's lead. They fanned out in all directions, jabbing their bayonets into the grass. They covered every inch of ground within fifty yards of the trees before striding south to survey the entire cemetery.

Laura held her breath and prayed for all she was worth. If she bolted and ran, she would be pursued. If she remained where she was, she could anticipate having a bayonet lodged in her spine. Neither prospect was appealing. She was doomed if the patrol searched every square inch of the cemetery with the same meticulous care they were displaying now!

Heavy footsteps approached and Laura wished herself as invisible as the elusive Midnight Rider. Her time of reckoning had come. She wondered if the King's men would give a second thought to hanging a woman. Nay, probably not, she told herself grimly. She could anticipate having her head chopped off like all the wives of King Henry the Eighth.

Laura grimaced when the thrashing sounds were amplified by the stillness of the night. Wouldn't Ezra Beecham be shocked out of his silk stockings when he learned she had been arrested as the Midnight Rider? At least one good deed would come from Laura's arrest, she consoled herself. The phantom's true identity would remain a carefully guarded secret. Laura would be hanged— or beheaded— in his stead and he could reappear like the specter he was reported to be.

Indeed, the incident might generate a legion of Midnight Riders who inspired rebels throughout the colonies, Laura mused as the soldier drew another step closer to her hiding place. Her death would become the ultimate contribution to the cause of freedom . . .

"Close ranks!" Peter's voice echoed in the night.

The thrashing sounds three yards away from where Laura was nestled in tall grass came to a halt. When the galumphing footsteps receded, Laura heaved a gusty sigh of relief.

When the thud of hooves evaporated into silence, Laura lifted her head to survey the cemetery. With no more than a slight limp to impede her progress, she made her way toward the row of headstones that had drawn her attention earlier.

Moonlight slanted over the markers and Laura's eyes bulged. Two headstones marked the eternal resting places of Frederick and Catherine Ryder, the beloved parents of Ethan and Nolan Ryder.

Laura frowned curiously when her gaze drifted to the slab of granite to the north. According to the engraving on the headstone, Ethan Ryder's younger brother had perished almost three years earlier, while serving with His Majesty's troops in the Seven Years War.

Strange that Ethan had never mentioned that he had a brother. But then, Laura's association with Ethan had been limited to the transfer of money and information passed through the network of patriots. 'Twas not uncommon for secret agents to have minimal contact with each other, she reminded herself. Most of Ethan's messages were delivered in code or invisible ink that magically appeared when held up to the heat of a lantern. Ethan was her superior and they only crossed paths once a month when Laura delivered funds from Miriam to finance the pamphlets and the purchase of weapons for the secret militias.

A muddled frown knitted Laura's brow as she stared at Nolan Ryder's grave. It couldn't possibly have been a ghost that rode for the cause of liberty. She had met the Midnight Rider— in person. He had felt and sounded real enough to her.

Midnight . . . From the dark side . . . of the grave perhaps? she wondered. *Rider . . . Ryder.* Laura frowned ponderously. Could it be that Ethan's younger brother wasn't quite as dead as his tombstone proclaimed him to be?

Laura carefully surveyed her surroundings. She

could have sworn she had seen the caped figure crouch down somewhere near these grave sites. But how was it possible . . . ?

Paralyzing panic riveted Laura to her spot when she heard the granite stone give a grating hiss. To her dumbfounded amazement, a shadowed form arose from the opening below Nolan Ryder's headstone. Owl-eyed, Laura stared down at the black hood and the broad shoulders that turned in her direction.

Dear God, she thought wildly. Was this Phantom Rider really rising from the dead or was he as human as she thought he was?

Starlight spun furiously around Laura when shock reached overwhelming proportions. She stumbled back, struggling to make sense of the eerie scene that unfolded before her. Was it Ethan Ryder's dead brother who carried the torch of liberty or wasn't it?

Laura inhaled a fortifying breath and struggled for composure. She was about to meet the Midnight Rider again. She wondered if he would recognize her in her urchin's garb. She wondered if he would choke the life out of her to protect his identity before she could assure him that his secret was safe with her . . .

Sixteen

Nolan swore profusely when he emerged from his grave to find the woman who had betrayed him standing over him. The pain in his arm was a throbbing reminder of how treacherous Laura could be.

Snarling, Nolan swiveled his head around to determine if Laura had summoned the patrol. Obviously she had not had the chance— yet. Nor would she be granted the opportunity to collect the reward on his head. Damn her, Nolan had come dangerously close to becoming a victim of her fatal charm!

A vicious growl exploded from Nolan's lips as he surged up to grab hold of Laura's tattered sleeve. His abrupt attack spurred her into action. She reflexively hurled herself away from him, desperate to voice the scream that froze in her throat.

Nolan leaped on her, sending her stumbling forward. When Nolan snaked out his good arm to grab her, she vaulted to her feet and dashed toward the fence that surrounded the cemetery. Nolan bounded up and charged after her, refusing to let her escape.

Just as Laura flung a leg over the top railing, Nolan latched onto the nape of her coat and roughly hauled her backward. As she tumbled to the ground Nolan noticed the horrified expression in her eyes. When she looked as if she were about to scream bloody murder, Nolan dropped on top of her, forcing the air from her lungs, clamping his gloved hand over the lower portion of her face.

Sheer terror pulsated through Laura's veins when she heard the animalistic snarl, felt the crushing pressure of the hurtful hand that sealed her nose and mouth. She couldn't breathe; she couldn't scream; she couldn't do anything.

The icy dread of panic washed over her as she fought wildly for escape, but the oppressive weight bearing down on her made it impossible. He was going to smother her where she lay! she thought wildly.

"You bloodthirsty little witch," Nolan sneered. "If I had a rope I would hang you— here and now."

Laura froze at the haunting sound of the voice that rumbled inside the black silk hood. Her astonished gaze transfixed on the holes in the mask. For a moment Laura stared up at the hooded face, noticing what she had not been permitted to see the first time she and the Midnight Rider crossed paths. Holy Mother of God, the Midnight Rider had silver-gray eyes!

This couldn't possibly be the nonchalant rake who had lured her against her will and seduced her with tender caresses. Surely not, Laura tried to tell herself. She must be mistaken.

This growling beast's eyes were the same remarkable shade of silver, but the vicious sparks glinting down on her were more reminiscent of a wild animal. And furthermore, the menacing strength and ominous aura he exuded were nothing like the soothing gentleness and nonchalance she had come to expect from Ezra Beecham.

"I'll remove my hand from your mouth if you promise to keep silent," Nolan snarled at her. "But I swear to God, if you scream for help I'll wring your damned neck."

Laura went limp beneath him. Although she had sensed potential vitality in Ezra Beecham and had been stung by the niggling feeling that there was more to him than met the eye, she never once suspected he might be the Midnight Rider. But 'twas him! It *had* to be him . . .

That startling realization left another baffling question floating across her mind. Why on earth was Ezra Beecham hiding in Nolan Ryder's grave? And where, she wondered, were Nolan's last remains?

When Nolan removed his hand, Laura stared into the silvery slits that reflected in the moonlight. "Ezra? Is that you?" she asked softly.

Nolan gnashed his teeth when Laura burst into tears of relief. She thought she was safe from harm, did she? She didn't know Nolan was as close as he ever wanted to come to poisoning, stabbing and strangling a female.

None too gently, Nolan hoisted Laura to her feet. He didn't care that he might have scared twenty years off her life when he rose from the dead and chased her down. He didn't care if she cried those beautiful black-diamond eyes out, either. Sympathy was not the emotion roiling through him, cold fury was.

Without another word, Nolan propelled Laura along the dirt path and hopped the fence to reach the spot where Spark had tethered the gray gelding. When Nolan set Laura on the saddle and tried to pull himself up, his wounded arm fell limply to his side. Gritting his teeth, Nolan dragged himself up behind Laura and reined toward the remote cabin in the tree-clad hills.

Laura half-twisted when she felt the sticky wetness against her neck and caught the scent of blood. "You've been shot!"

Aye, Nolan thought bitterly, and Laura had his blood on her hands—literally. The last thing he wanted or needed was her pretentious concern. All he really meant to her was the gold coins she could collect when she revealed his identity.

"Ezra, I don't understand what you were doing in Nolan Ryder's grave. Are you truly the Midnight Rider? I thought your loyalties lay with the Crown, if anywhere at all. What is happening here?"

Laura received nothing for her efforts of interrogation. Nolan simply growled at her through his black hood.

"Where are we going?" she questioned when he

veered off the beaten path and forged through the underbrush.

Again, Nolan refused to dignify the traitor's question with an answer. He was too busy trying to decide what to do next. For sure and certain, Laura Chandler would have to disappear. She was too great a threat. If Nolan allowed her to run loose, the Midnight Rider would find a patrol of redcoats standing over his grave when he emerged from beneath the veneer of stone after the next breakneck chase. Peter Forbes would be ready and waiting to fit him for a hangman's noose, which would entitle the Brit to the promotion he coveted.

The dim glow from Spark's corncob pipe indicated that the old frontiersman had already locked the stallion in its stall and was waiting Nolan's return on the front porch. Spark stepped down to grab the gelding's reins, his hand stalling in midair when he spied the urchin held captive in Nolan's arms.

"Trouble." 'Twas not a question, 'twas Spark's grim statement of fact.

"Aye, plenty of it." Nolan handed Laura down to Spark. "Keep a tight grip on this little traitor. She has become even more dangerous to us than before."

Spark didn't like the sound of that. He clamped hold of Laura and shepherded her up the steps.

"Leave the gelding," Spark insisted. "I'll care for it later."

With pained effort, Nolan slid from the saddle. His arm burned like fire and the loss of blood left him as weak as a newborn lamb. Sheer will and smoldering fury provided the strength to reach the cabin without collapsing.

The instant Nolan stepped into the light, Spark noticed the wet crimson stains on the cloak. His angry gaze swung to the sooty-faced urchin beside him. "What did you do to him?" he growled in question.

Laura blinked in surprise when the bewhiskered old man in buckskins glowered murderously at her. "I did nothing."

Nolan expelled a derisive snort and doffed his cape, revealing the bloody stains that soaked the left side of his shirt. "The musket ball was compliments of her lovesick lieutenant. Forbes and his patrol were waiting in ambush when I crossed the meadow."

"Peter did this?" Laura stared at the concealing hood, her expression frozen in disbelief. "How could he have known the pamphlets were to be delivered— "

"Because *you* knew," Nolan sneered.

"I'll fetch some water and bandages," Spark offered while Nolan glared daggers at Laura. He scuttled off, but not before he flung Laura a malicious glower for good measure.

When Nolan slumped into the chair beside the table and shed his mask, Laura rushed forward to inspect the wound. Nolan knocked her hands away as if her touch was poison.

"You have done quite enough for one night."

Grimly, Nolan shrugged off his shirt to examine his wound. The musket ball had grazed his upper arm, peeling away the flesh. His scathing gaze darted to Laura, noting she didn't so much as flinch at the sight of his blood.

Why should she? he asked himself bitterly. She had no fond attachment to the Midnight Rider, and obviously no real affection for Ezra Beecham, either. As she had annoyingly declared, their tryst had simply happened in a reckless moment. 'Twas simply an experiment.

Spark came to an abrupt halt when he spied the serrated wound. His venomous amber gaze swung to the urchin who stood quietly to the side.

"Hope you're proud of yerself, witch," Spark muttered as he stalked toward the table. "I told him to expect no less from yer kind. Pickin' his pocket in reverse and havin' him toted off to jail was one thing, but havin' yer British beau bush-whack him is somethin' else again. Leave it to a female to stab a man in the back or bring him down with a musket ball, every chance she gets."

Spark dipped the cloth in water and glanced bleakly at his patient. "Get a good grip on yerself, Nolan— "

"Nolan?" Wide onyx eyes met glittering silver. "Nolan Ryder? So you *are* Ethan's dead brother."

"Not as dead as you would have preferred." Nolan braced himself before Spark dribbled water on the wound. He hissed in pain when another wave of fire rippled down his arm, numbing his fingers.

"Now just one blessed minute," Laura huffed. "I don't know where you got the idea that I had anything to do with the ambush, but—"

"Save yer guiltless speeches for someone gullible enough to believe them," Spark snapped. "You set the Midnight Rider up for a trap while he was deliverin' pamphlets for the Sons of Liberty and we all know it."

"I did nothing of the kind!" Laura loudly objected.

Nolan was expecting her to say something to that effect. Too bad no one around here was stupid enough to believe her. "In case you haven't figured it out, you have been permanently dismissed from your duties as a so-called rebel agent— ouch!"

Sickening pain pelted Nolan when Spark sloshed whiskey on the sensitive wound.

Laura instinctively moved forward when Ezra— or Nolan Ryder, she hurriedly corrected herself— turned as pale as the phantom he was reported to be. Before she could offer consolation, Spark waved her away.

"I'll tend to him. You've had yer turn at him—"

When Laura pivoted away, Spark snaked out his hand to drag her back, just in case she considered making a run for it. "Sit down or I'll tie you down, wench. And if you expect preferential treatment from me ye'r doomed to disappointment. I have very little respect for women and no sympathy whatsoever for traitors."

Reluctantly, Laura parked herself in the vacant chair. 'Twas obvious she was to be held prisoner for the crime Spark and Nolan assumed she had committed. They refused to do her the courtesy of letting her speak in her own defense. And if Spark McRae had his way, she predicted she would be stretched out on a torture rack and left for the buzzards.

In dismal resignation, Laura held her seat while Spark applied an amber-colored poultice to Nolan's wound. And all the while, Nolan Ryder's smoldering glowers condemned her to the farthest reaches of hell.

When Spark completed his ministrations, he disappeared into the storeroom at the end of the hall and reappeared a few minutes later, holding a pigeon with a band tied around its leg. Without a word, he opened the door and sent the winged courier on its way.

"His brother will be here shortly to see the truth for himself." Spark flashed Laura another resentful glare. "You may have fooled Ethan for a time, but he won't take kindly to the news that you left a bullet hole in his younger brother. Ethan thought he had lost Nolan once before in battle and he prematurely laid him to rest. And believe you me, Ethan has no intention of losin' his younger brother again. If ye'r expectin' Ethan to come to ye'r defense, he won't do it."

Laura winced at the mutinous glowers Nolan and Spark hurled in her direction. Although she needed Miriam Peabody to verify that Laura's loyalties were tied to the patriot cause, neither man intended to let her out of his sight long enough to summon a character witness.

When Laura lapsed into resigned silence, Nolan studied her profile. Any tender affection he might have felt for her evaporated as if it never existed. There would be no more illusions for either of them, Nolan mused bleakly.

Now he had to decide what the blazes he was going to do with this devious witch. He should sentence her to instant death. 'Twas what she deserved . . . But the prospect of her execution tied his emotions in knots. And damn her, she was probably counting on him to be lenient with her because of the intimacies they had shared.

What the devil was he going to do about Laura Chandler? Nolan asked himself.

Nolan still hadn't puzzled out a solution to the problem by the time Ethan barged through the door a good while later.

"Nolan, thank God! Are you all right?"

Nolan swallowed down the ale Spark handed him. "I'm in splendid shape, considering your traitorous informant set her British hounds on me." Nolan lifted his mug in mocking salute. "To treachery, my lady, you are exceptionally good at it."

Laura winced when Ethan rounded on her, his eyes flaring like evergreen flames.

"How could you have betrayed my trust?" Ethan muttered in disappointment.

"I didn't, despite what they think." Laura lifted her gaze in silent appeal to Ethan. "I swear it—"

"Just as you swore you lost your heirloom bracelet, which conveniently landed in my pocket?" Nolan smirked sardonically. "And I cannot wait to hear you explain how you happened to be at the cemetery at the same time the patrol arrived. Were you trailing behind them to ensure the ambush met with success? Or were you hiding at the burying ground to determine what actually became of the Midnight Rider after he supposedly vanished into nothingness?"

"I had nothing to do with any of that!" Laura angrily defended.

One thick black brow rose in taunting challenge. "Oh, really? Then how do you explain the fact that you weren't discovered when the patrol started thrashing around the graveyard?"

"I was hiding in the grass."

Nolan downed another sip of ale. "Of course you were."

Laura bolted to her feet, fists clenched at her sides. "I was very nearly discovered. In fact, I was lying there trying to decide how to explain my way out of my predicament when Peter called a halt to the search—"

Three pairs of condemning eyes riveted on her.

"Scheming again?" Nolan smirked. "How like you, my lady. You always have an answer for everything, don't you? And if by chance you don't, you are confident that you will think of something eventually. Ah, how often have I heard that optimistic comment? More times than I care to count."

Laura threw up her hands in frustration. The court had reached its verdict. She had been found guilty as charged. She could appeal to a brick wall, for all the good 'twould do her. These three men were prepared to believe the worst, and she couldn't convincingly explain how the British had gotten wind of the Midnight Rider's evening activities unless . . .

A tormenting thought flared in Laura's mind. Nay, it couldn't have been. It simply was not possible! She had left the coded message in her room when she went to inform Miriam of her plans. Laura had then garbed herself in her homespun clothes and crept out the back door. She had heard faint sounds before she scurried off, but she had presumed . . . Curse it, she should have presumed nothing!

"Spark, show Lady Chandler to my room," Nolan requested. "And make certain she has no opportunity to escape. I don't relish tracking her down tonight, only to find another patrol ready to lodge a musket ball in my good arm."

Nodding curtly, Spark clamped hold of Laura's elbow and towed her to the bedroom.

"I hope you'll be comfortable, Lady Chandler," Spark said in a tone that indicated he hoped nothing of the kind. He scooped up the leather strips from the dresser drawer and then gave her a nudge toward the bed. "Not that I'll lose much sleep over it, of course."

"Spark, I tell you true, I did not reveal the Midnight Rider's destination—"

Spark interrupted her with a loud snort. With quick efficiency, he lashed her hands together and secured them to the headboard. "I told Nolan women weren't to be trusted. For the most part, he believed me . . . until you cast yer devious spell on him. But don't think you can deceive him again. He never repeats his mistakes."

When the door clanked shut, Laura choked on a sob. Her hopes had soared when she discovered Ezra Beecham was the Midnight Rider and that he supported the cause of liberty. But then her spirits plunged to rock bottom, knowing the only man who had touched the tender emotion she had buried deep inside her believed she had betrayed him.

The menacing glitter in those silver eyes could have frozen stone. What little affection Nolan had felt for her was gone, she realized. He held her personally responsible for the ambush. He was irrevocably convinced she had leaked information to the British, all for the love of gold coins, no doubt. Nolan believed her to be a heartless mercenary.

Laura slumped defeatedly, squeezing her eyes shut against the onrush of tears. Perhaps being captured by the British patrol would have been the lesser of two evils. Suffering Peter's condemnation couldn't be as dispiriting as knowing Nolan Ryder hated the very sight of her . . . and would never trust her again . . .

Seventeen

Ethan half collapsed in his chair and raked his fingers through the tuft of sandy blond hair. "I still can't believe it," he mused aloud. "If we had a leak of information, I was positively certain it wasn't Laura. She has provided useful information in the past—"

"To both sides of this political conflict, no doubt," Nolan broke in. He stared at the contents of his mug for a long moment before adding bleakly, "We have to dispose of Laura. Her knowledge makes her too great a threat."

Ethan jerked up his head. "Dear God, Nolan, she's a woman!"

"She is a *spy*," Nolan corrected in a rumbling voice. "With a British officer quartered in her home, no less. We can't risk sending her back to Beacon Hill. She knows entirely too much and she can't be trusted."

"What would you have me do? Hand her over to the mob to be lynched?"

"Sounds like fair punishment to me," Spark put in, striding into the room. "Either that or I could lead her out into the wilderness and let nature take its course."

Ethan looked horrified by the suggestion.

Nolan frowned.

"For sure and certain we can't turn the chit loose." Spark grabbed his glass and helped himself to the grog. "She knows who the Midnight Rider is and how he escapes from patrols. And Nolan isn't in any condition to take unnecessary risks now."

While Ethan and Spark debated the complicated issue, Nolan nursed his drink. As he saw it, there was only one solution to the problem— other than a quick hanging. As much as he despised what the devious woman had done, he simply didn't have the heart to sentence her to death, because he . . .

Scowling, he tossed back his drink and immediately refilled his mug.

"Ethan, you'll have to invent a plausible excuse for Lady Chandler's departure from Boston," Nolan abruptly announced.

Ethan peered at his brother for a grim moment. "You can live with her death on your conscience?"

A haunted expression settled on Nolan's craggy features and clouded his silver-gray eyes. Since the tragic ambuscade in the wilderness, Nolan had carried the deaths of an entire company of colonial militiamen on his conscience. Although he despised Laura's treachery, he didn't want her blood on his hands, too.

"Spark made a valid point," Nolan replied belatedly. "The Midnight Rider will have to go into hiding for a time, until his wound has healed. We have no recourse but to remove Lady Chandler from the network of secret agents who convey information."

Ethan frowned, perplexed. "What are you suggesting?"

"A less strenuous assignment that will enable me to keep Laura under constant observation and conveniently remove her from the Sons of Liberty's operations," he replied.

"What? Are you mad?" Spark crowed incredulously. "The chit will bury a hatchet in yer back, first chance she gets— "

Nolan flung up his good arm to forestall the old frontiersman's objections and then focused on his brother. "Tell me what news you have received from your sources, Ethan. There must be some useful purpose I can serve while I'm mending."

"You won't be mendin' for long, if that witch is underfoot," Spark grumbled sourly. "You'll wind up in worse shape than ye'r in now."

Ethan fished into his pocket for the dispatch he had received that morning and held it up to the lantern globe. In between the sentences scrawled in bold handwriting, another message appeared.

"According to the information delivered by the express riders, several of the colonies have engineered their own protests, following Boston's lead. The Rhode Island Patriots dragged three effigies of stamp distributors through the streets on ropes and then hung them from the gallows at the courthouse in Newport. The mock lynching sent the

Crown's stamp collectors into hiding and their homes were ransacked by raiders.

"In Connecticut, pageants that featured mock trials for newly appointed tax agents were held. Straw-filled dummies were towed through the streets and delivered to an actor who was impersonating the devil. The effigies were tossed into a bonfire in warning."

"Now there's an idea," Spark piped up. "Burn that witch. 'Twould cremate her traitorous tendencies."

Nolan ignored the drastic suggestion and gestured to his brother to continue the report.

"In New York, the Sons of Liberty placed an effigy of their lieutenant governor in a carriage and wheeled it under the cannon at Fort George. Then the patriots descended on a British officer's mansion and reduced it to ruin," Ethan went on to say. "According to our sources, the Crown blames Boston's patriots for setting off this series of protests in the other colonies. We have been labeled as a nest of vipers that must be contained. Regiments of soldiers have been mobilized and reassigned to the duty of keeping a tight clamp on Boston."

Nolan lifted his tousled raven head and stared at Ethan over the rim of his mug. "By what means will the troops be deployed?"

"By both land and sea. There is even talk of sealing off Boston Harbor with ships from His Majesty's Navy and halting all trade and smuggling operations. Until those arrangements can be made, the army will be bringing in more soldiers and military provisions cross-country."

Nolan smiled wryly as an idea hatched in his mind. "And of course, the redcoats will have to be ferried across rivers along the way to Boston."

"Naturally, but— "

"And 'twould be a pity if the incoming weapons and supplies disappeared or were damaged en route, wouldn't it?"

"Certainly, but— "

"And 'twould be ironic if British weapons and ammunition made their way to the secret store-houses our colonial militias have been stockpiling, in case we are forced to take up arms to defend ourselves against the army of occupation, wouldn't it?"

A grin caught the corners of Ethan's mouth. His cedar green eyes twinkled in devilish amusement. "I don't suppose you have a volunteer in mind for the assignment of managing the ferry and catering to His Britannick Majesty's incoming troops."

Nolan took another sip of his drink and then nodded affirmatively. "I should think a seasoned frontiersman, placed at a strategic trading post and ferry station between Boston and New York, would prove invaluable to the cause."

"What about Laura?" Ethan and Spark questioned in unison.

"She will be the serving maid at the ferry station. I will keep her under constant surveillance to ensure she doesn't make contact with the soldiers."

"Ye'r a glutton for punishment," Spark muttered. "That chit will find a way to betray you again."

"She will be miles from Boston," Nolan reminded him.

"And in contact with every redcoat between here and New York," Spark sputtered in objection.

"Not if I can help it."

Spark expelled a caustic snort. "She'll tuck a message in one of those lobsterback's pockets, the same way she stashed her bracelet in yer pocket."

Ethan pondered the plan for a long moment. "It might work."

"And it might get Nolan killed—for good, this time." Spark gave his bushy gray head an adamant shake. "That girl is trouble personified. Burn her at the stake and be done with it. That sure solved the problem with the Salem witches. Cured them for life, it did."

Spark sighed heavily, knowing Nolan wasn't paying him any heed. He could talk until his face turned purple, but Nolan was thinking with his foolish heart instead of his head. 'Twas when men always ended up in the worst disasters.

Ignoring Spark's incessant objections, Nolan glanced at his brother. "You'll have to send a note to Willie Fitzgerald, informing him that Ezra Beecham has left town to consult with his solicitor and agent and cannot attend the scheduled fox hunt next week. Miriam Peabody will also have to be contacted so we can fetch some of Laura's belongings. You'll need to concoct a believable explanation for Laura's absence—without alarming Miriam."

"Hell, why not let the chit dream up her own excuse?" Spark suggested flippantly. "She seems to be an accomplished liar."

Nolan glared Spark into silence. "We will leave at dawn. Tall Oaks Ferry will serve our purpose exceptionally well. Coon Ashburn is managing the inn and his loyalties are in the right place. The express riders have been using his ordinary as a relay station for the past few months."

"Coon Ashburn?" Spark chuckled for the first time in hours, and his amber eyes regained their customary sparkle. "That old coot is a few logs short of a rick and he's always kept some peculiar pets, if memory serves."

When Ethan frowned, Nolan prompted his memory. "Coon is the man Spark and I hunted and trapped with one winter, before he established his trading post beside the river. Coon is reliable—"

"And a little crazy," Spark didn't hesitate to reiterate. "The only reason he still has his scalp is because the Indians thought he was possessed. I'm not so sure they were wrong about him, either."

Nolan smiled faintly. "As I recall, 'twas a spirited debate over who had more bats in his belfry, you or Coon."

Spark finally relented and abandoned his protests. "I suppose Tall Oaks Ferry wouldn't be such a bad spot to recuperate, just as long as you don't let yer guard down. Coon can help you keep an eye on that Tory snitch."

Ethan surged out of his chair, headed toward the door. "I'll speak with Miriam while you get some rest, Nolan."

Nolan intended to do exactly that. If he were to deal with Laura Chandler, as well as the unforeseen hazards of forging through the backwoods to reach their destination, he would have to be wide-eyed and alert. At least Nolan wouldn't have to fret about Laura escaping and returning to Boston to issue a warrant for his arrest. That clever female may have known her way around the alleys and streets of Boston, but she would be hopelessly disoriented and completely out of her element in the rugged terrain between civilization and Tall Oaks Trading Post.

The only pockets she could pick along the way would belong to possums. It should be amusing entertainment to watch Laura cope with unfamiliar surroundings. She would have to depend on Nolan to survive. That would be a pleasant switch, he decided.

Nolan drifted off to sleep, anxious to return to the wilderness that had been his home for more than two years. 'Twas there that he had truly come to appreciate being the master of his own fate. He had lived by his own rules, honed his survival skills and tested his abilities to their limits. 'Twas in the backwoods that Nolan had experienced the height of personal freedom and made himself a fortune in furs in record time. Spark called it phenomenal, Nolan called it hard, relentless work. He also called the wilderness paradise a heaven on earth, teeming with natural resources the British had now declared off limits to colonists.

Of course, Laura Chandler might not appreciate life in the wilds as Nolan did. There would be no luxurious mansions and gay parties for Laura to attend, no starry-eyed beaus following at her heels. The rigorous journey would force that independent-minded female to become totally dependent on Nolan. For once, he thought with a tired sigh, he would have complete control over Laura. 'Twould be consolation for her treachery—and punishment for her. And all the while they were forging through the wilderness, Nolan would use her for his own purpose and his lusty pleasure . . . but he would never trust that woman again. And that, Nolan reaffirmed before he faded off to sleep, was one promise he would keep.

Miriam Peabody awoke with a start for the second time in two hours. A gloved hand covered her face before she could make a peep. Her alarmed gaze fixed on the unidentified man who loomed over her.

"I intend no harm, madam," Ethan assured the frightened dowager. He sincerely hoped Miriam was of stout constitution. He had no time for a fainting spell. "I need your assistance."

Miriam's wide hazel eyes darted around the room before refocusing on the shadowed figure that loomed beside her alcove bed. She clutched her chest and forced herself to breathe normally.

When Ethan removed his gloved hand, Miriam propped up on her elbows. "What's wrong?" she questioned anxiously.

"Laura Chandler has been sent on an assignment that will take her away from Boston. She requires a few garments for her journey. She also requests your cooperation in explaining the reason for her absence," Ethan murmured.

"Where is she going?" Miriam demanded.

"I cannot say, madam."

"When will she return?"

"I cannot tell you that, either."

Miriam frowned, disconcerted. "But it is for the cause? You're sure?"

"Absolutely," Ethan confirmed.

"Well then, what excuse would you have me give Lieutenant Forbes to explain her absence?"

"Do you have any kinfolk who might possibly be in need of her assistance?"

Miriam contemplated the question for a moment. "I have a stepsister in Philadelphia. She and her husband manage a print shop."

Ethan nodded in satisfaction. "Then you can tell the lieutenant that your sister has suddenly been taken ill and Laura has volunteered to replace her aunt in the print shop until your sister has recuperated."

Miriam gestured toward the tuft chair. "If you will kindly hand me my robe I'll see to packing Laura's belongings."

Ethan did as requested. He politely turned his back while Miriam modestly covered herself. When she reached for the candle on the nightstand, Ethan's hand folded over hers.

"For your own protection, and mine, 'tis best that we remain strangers bound by a mission of secrecy."

"You expect me to pack Laura's belongings in the dark?" Miriam sniffed.

"I'm afraid so, madam. Laura will require only the simplest of gowns for this assignment. After all, she will supposedly be tending the sick and setting type at the printers, not entertaining Philadelphia society."

Miriam led the way to Laura's chamber. She cast a cautious glance toward Lieutenant Forbes's room, hoping he had collapsed in exhaustion after returning home two hours earlier. Miriam had heard Peter clomping down the hall, making enough racket to startle her awake when his saber clanked against the wall.

Silently, Miriam groped around Laura's room to retrieve the satchels. In the darkness, 'twas difficult to tell what she was packing. She hoped she had gathered enough unmentionables to see Laura through, but there was no way of knowing for certain. As for the simple muslin gowns, Miriam was reasonably sure she had collected enough of them from the wardrobe.

"I'm not certain I have packed all she'll need," she murmured as she handed the satchels to Ethan.

Despite Miriam's concern, Ethan tucked the bulging pouches under his arms. "Whatever else Laura needs will be provided," he assured her. "Your most important task is to be certain Lieutenant Forbes believes your explanation. You must be convincing, madam, or you will invite suspicion."

When Ethan turned away, Miriam tapped him on the shoulder. "She will be all right, won't she?"

"She will be in most competent hands," was all Ethan said before he slipped into the hall.

Miriam heaved a sigh and tiptoed back to her room. Laura's assignment appeared to be of utmost secrecy. Hopefully, 'twould not be equally dangerous. Laura was the closest thing to family Miriam had left. She couldn't tolerate the thought of that vibrant, spirited beauty coming to harm.

Easing into bed, Miriam peered up at the ceiling, mentally rehearsing her excuses. Peter Forbes was going to be full of questions, Miriam predicted, and she must be prepared to offer reasonable answers. Of course, this unexpected absence would please Mercy Reed to no end, Miriam mused. The maid fell all over herself trying to cater to Peter's every whim. In fact, Mercy went out of her way to gain Peter's notice.

Miriam tucked the sheet around her and dozed off, only to hear a quiet thud in the hall. She presumed her mysterious late-night visitor had stumbled down the unfamiliar steps while trying to make his exit.

Thankfully, he hadn't made as much noise as Peter Forbes usually did. The man was reminiscent of an elephant tramping down the darkened hall, when he returned from midnight patrol duty.

* * *

Laura groaned uncomfortably when she tried to roll over in bed and found herself tethered to the bedpost. Ordinarily, she awoke eager to tackle the challenges of the day. This particular morning offered little anticipated pleasure. She was reminded of the days she had spent on the streets, fretting over where to find the funds to purchase food, to provide for the two younger children who shared the back-street shack with her . . .

The whine of the door brought Laura's head around. Spark McRae greeted her with a scowl. After tossing her satchels on the foot of the bed, Spark tramped over to untie the leather straps.

"Time to rise, yer ladyship," he said disrespectfully. "I'll fetch you some fresh water so you can make yerself presentable."

"Thank you, I would appreciate that."

Spark snorted an inarticulate reply and stalked out the same way he stalked in.

Laura worked the kinks from her back and scooped up her satchels. To her dismay, she found wads of her clothing crammed in the pouches. Three gowns had been rolled and stuffed atop an oversupply of pantaloons. There was no chemise to be found.

When Spark returned to fill the basin with water, Laura peered questioningly at him. "There seems to be a few items missing. Is there another satchel?"

"What you've got is what you get, yer ladyship," Spark declared. "You aren't goin' to no fancy social gatherin', after all."

"Where exactly *am* I going?" she wanted to know.

"If I had my way, you would be headed straight to— "

"Spark . . ." Nolan's low, threatening voice rumbled across the room.

Spark jerked upright and tilted his chin a notch higher. "You'll find out all you need to know at breakfast," he told Laura. "And don't think you can sneak out the window. I'll be standin' guard outside while ye'r dressin'."

On that sour note, Spark spun on his heels and sailed out the door. Without so much as a glance in Laura's direction, Nolan followed Spark into the hall.

Laura stared at the contents of her satchels, smiling ruefully at the mismatched shoes and wrinkled yellow gown that had been hastily packed. The tippet which modestly concealed the plunging neckline of her dress had been left behind, along with the necessary undergarments she customarily wore beneath it. She was again reminded of those days in the streets when she garbed herself in whatever garments she could find to ward off a chill. Fashion had never been a concern then and 'twould not be much of a concern now.

It made little difference what she wore to her execution, Laura reminded herself. How ironic that she should exit this world the same way she came in— like the humble pauper, not the wealthy princess Miriam Peabody had tried to make of her.

While Laura refreshed herself with the basin of

water, she pondered her fate, curious who would be her executioner. Spark McRae most likely, she decided. The crusty old frontiersman could barely abide the sight of her.

Laura plucked up her sunflower-yellow gown, bleakly reminding herself that, all too often, 'twas the innocent who usually suffered first. Martha Winfield was a prime example of injustice.

Laura expected she was about to become another . . .

Eighteen

Nolan grumbled under his breath when Laura emerged from his bedroom, looking beautiful in her fitted yellow gown. The scooped neckline accentuated the generous swells of her breasts, revealing entirely too much creamy skin to tempt and torment a man. Her face had been scrubbed clean of soot and her auburn hair cascaded to her trim waist like a waterfall that glimmered in the sunlight.

And he thought to torment her by toting her through the howling wilderness? Nolan asked himself sourly. No doubt about it, he was the one who would suffer most. 'Twould be difficult for Nolan to remind himself of her deception, when looking at her made him want her in the worst way. She was purposely tormenting him with that revealing gown, he thought resentfully.

"Put on something more modest," Nolan muttered at her.

Laura met his thunderous scowl. " 'Tis the best of the lot," she informed him. "As it happens, several necessities were missing from my satchels." She tugged up the hem of her skirt to reveal one black shoe and one indigo blue one. "If I were to guess, I would say whoever packed for me did so in the dark."

Spark barged through the front door and stumbled to a halt when a vision of innocent beauty and radiant sunshine captured his attention. Thus far, he had seen Laura garbed in nothing but her urchin's disguise, with her delicate features camouflaged by soot and grime. Spark, who was rarely at a loss of words, promptly swallowed his tongue— and his breath. Owl-eyed, he appraised the young woman whose auburn hair shimmered like a halo in the morning light.

For a moment Spark couldn't quite seem to make the connection between the straggly ragamuffin and this enchanting siren. She reminded him of an angel who had floated down from the pearly gates. Only Laura's dark, luminous eyes assured Spark that the alluring goddess and the scrawny-looking waif were one and the same.

"Sweet mercy," he chirped. His incredulous gaze shifted to Nolan. "No wonder you—"

"Sit down, Spark," Nolan cut in gruffly. "Breakfast is getting cold and we have a long journey ahead of us."

Laura blinked. "We do? How far is it to Perdition from here?"

Laura was always ready with the clever rejoinder, Nolan noted as he gestured for her to take a seat. "Far enough to necessitate a hearty last meal."

Laura flung Spark a curious glance as she approached the table. The grumpy old backwoodsman was still gaping at her with his mouth hanging open wide enough for a pigeon to roost there.

Despite Laura's attempt to dismiss Nolan Ryder, she found her eyes unwillingly drawn to the powerful, fascinating man across the table. Nolan was garbed in fringed buckskin, much like Spark. 'Twas amazing how natural Nolan looked in those garments— every bit as natural as he had appeared in the fancy trappings of a gentleman, and the dark, flowing cape that had become the Midnight Rider's trademark.

It occurred to Laura that she really didn't know this man at all. He was a chameleon who changed appearance and disposition to suit whatever role he chose to play. Which man was the real Nolan Ryder? she wondered.

Despite the sling that immobilized Nolan's left arm, he seemed only slightly discomforted by his wound. If he were in pain it didn't show on the chiseled features of his face, or in the glistening depths of his mercury-colored eyes. Of course, Laura quickly reminded herself, Nolan Ryder was an expert at concealing his emotions and his motives . . .

"Doesn't the meal suit you?"

Jostled from her speculative musings, Laura glanced up from her plate to find Nolan staring at her. "The meal is fine, thank you," she said with exaggerated politeness.

"Then why aren't you eating it?"

Laura picked up a chunk of bread and stuffed it in her mouth, just to appease him. Food was the least of her concerns. 'Twas her future—or the lack thereof—that worried her most.

"Exactly where are we going?" she asked.

"You'll find out when we get there."

Laura resigned herself to eating in silence. 'Twas obvious that she wasn't to be privy to Nolan's plans.

When she finished her meal, Nolan instructed her to gather her satchels and meet him outside. Spark was still gaping at her when she disappeared into the bedroom to collect her belongings.

"I still can't believe that's the same chit," Spark murmured as he followed Nolan onto the stoop. "I can see why yer juices have been hissin' like a tea pot. I'm old enough to know better than to be distracted by wily females, but that woman is the devil's own temptation."

Spark certainly had that right. However, Nolan had vowed to amuse himself at Laura's expense and appease himself with her when lust got the better of him. He would look upon her as no more than a convenient release for his physical urges, feeling not the slightest guilt. 'Twas to be her comeuppance for her perfidious deception. Nolan intended to be well—and often—compensated for the wound sustained during the ambush, compliments of Laura Chandler.

By the time Laura appeared on the porch, Spark and Nolan had retrieved both horses. Laura stared bewilderedly at the saddlebags strapped to the mounts.

"We obviously aren't traveling far, considering

the meager supplies we're taking with us," she speculated.

"On the contrary," Nolan said as he swung onto the saddle. "We will be covering a great many miles."

"We are stopping at wayside inns then?" she asked in surprise. "I didn't think you trusted me not to beg assistance in making an escape if the opportunity presented itself."

"There're no inns where ye'r goin'." Spark grabbed Laura's hand and assisted her onto the gray gelding. He stepped back apace and glanced meaningfully at Nolan. "Take care of yerself, boy."

Nolan reined away, leading Laura's mount behind him. "I fully intend to."

With raffish glee, Nolan headed toward the thick timbers, taking Laura Chandler completely out of her element. This should prove to be an unnerving ordeal for a woman who had never been anywhere except the streets of Boston and the sprawling mansion on Beacon Hill.

Ah, sweet revenge, Nolan mused with a scampish grin. There would be nowhere for this female to run without getting herself hopelessly lost. Now, Laura Chandler would have to stick to the very same man she had sent her love-struck beau to ambush.

Nolan wondered if Laura appreciated the irony as much as he did.

"Gone? When did she leave?" Peter Forbes stared incredulously at the gray-haired dowager who lounged at the opposite end of the table, stirring her steaming cup of tea. "Where did she go?"

Miriam sipped her drink and carefully formulated her words. Wearing an expression of grave concern, she met Peter's astounded gaze. "A letter from my sister in Philadelphia arrived in yesterday's post."

"Clarice has been taken ill and requested my presence. Naturally, I couldn't leave Boston while I have the distinct honor of quartering one of His Majesty's most prestigious officers. And 'twould have been most improper for me to leave you and Laura in the same house without a dependable chaperone."

"You sent Laura to tend her aunt in your stead?" he repeated, and then added, *"Unchaperoned?"* He looked utterly horrified. "If I had known, I would have requested a leave of absence to escort Laura on her journey."

" 'Tis kind of you to offer, but, with all due respect, Lieutenant, you would not have been a proper chaperone for my niece. Besides, Laura is hardly a child, and she is perfectly capable of fending for herself. I'm sure Laura will manage just fine, traveling over well-protected roads with an experienced driver and guard manning the coach."

"But a woman like Laura all alone? There are stretches of wilderness between here and Philadelphia where highwaymen could attack." Peter heaved an audible sigh. "I fear for her safety, madam."

So did Miriam, but not for the reasons Peter stated. 'Twas no telling what dangers Laura's secret mission entailed.

"I'm sure my niece will be fine," she reassured him, and herself. "Laura left quite early this morning, requesting that I convey this information to you. And furthermore, she would never dream of taking you away from your military duties. Laura had no wish to impose on you, what with all your responsibilities here in Boston."

Miriam quickly switched the topic of discussion before Peter could pose more objections to Laura's sudden trip. "You came trooping in quite late last night. Have those pesky rebels been up to no good again?"

Peter muttered at the reminder of his futile attempt to capture the patriot's legendary horseman. He had been certain his patrol could apprehend that elusive phantom after receiving an accurate tip.

"I spent most of the night chasing a man who has the infuriating knack of disappearing into nothingness like a disembodied spirit," he grumbled.

Miriam raised her gray brows and took another sip of tea. "I presume you are referring to the Phantom Rider, or whatever the patriots call their fearless leader. I suppose he was up to his usual mischief last night. Gad, he didn't lead those low-class heathens in another raid and ransack the home of another one of the Crown's officers, I hope?"

"Nay, and I would imagine things will simmer

down in Boston as soon as reinforcements arrive," Peter predicted.

"More soldiers?" Miriam quickly concealed her dismay. "Where will we quarter all of them? Boston homes are already bulging at the seams."

"We have sequestered one of the warehouses beside the wharf to house enlisted men," Peter reported. "Those rebellious vultures who have swooped down on British Customs officers will find their wings clipped. As for the Sons of Liberty and their auspicious leaders, they will become marked men who will not be allowed to walk the streets without surveillance. Captain Milbourne has ordered us to crack down on the malcontents."

Miriam wondered if Laura had received— and conveyed— that information before she was sent on this mysterious assignment. Probably. Her knowledge of the back streets and alleyways allowed her to obtain and relay valuable information quickly.

"When will Laura be returning to Boston?" Peter inquired.

"That depends on how quickly Clarice recuperates," Miriam hedged. "Laura will keep me posted on my sister's condition."

"It could very well be that Laura will require a pass to reenter Boston," Peter declared. "There is talk of sealing the city off as punishment for the riots."

"Seal off Boston?" Miriam chirped, her hazel eyes wide with disbelief. "Dear heaven, isn't that a mite drastic? I should think such tactics would incite more resentment and unrest among the rebels."

"They will dance to His Majesty's tune. You have nothing to worry about, madam. Loyalists will be protected." Peter rose from his chair and bowed gallantly. "Now, if you will excuse me, my superior officers have scheduled a morning conference to discuss the outbreak of protests in neighboring colonies. We must design an effective strategy to deal with these unruly demonstrators."

When Peter ambled through the foyer, Mercy Reed poked her head around the corner and motioned him into the parlor. Before Peter could pose a question, Mercy sidled provocatively against him and wound her arms around his neck.

Peter glanced cautiously over his shoulder as he untangled himself from her amorous embrace. "Someone might see us," he hissed.

Mercy tossed him a saucy smile. "Who? Your precious Laura? She's gone." That delighted Mercy to no end. Now Peter would devote his time and attention to her. "And I'll tell you something else, Peter, there is something strange going on around here."

Peter frowned at the baiting comment and grabbed Mercy's roaming hand. "What is that supposed to mean?"

Mercy stepped away, tossing Peter a breezy smile. She sauntered across the parlor to dust off the mantel. "If I'm not mistaken, and I'm sure I'm not, your beloved Laura has been playing you and Miriam for fools. I've seen her slipping in and out of the house at the oddest hours of the night while

I'm returning to my room. And I can tell you for certain that she wasn't dressed like a proper lady while she was doing it, either."

Peter cast a discreet glance toward the hall and strode up behind Mercy. "How was she dressed?"

The maid pirouetted and smiled cattily. "I thought the Crown paid handsomely for information about suspicious activities. What I know could be very valuable."

"What is it that you think you know?" Peter demanded impatiently. "What is this nonsense about Laura?"

Mercy gnashed her teeth. If she never heard that woman's name mentioned or saw her again, 'twould be all too soon. Peter couldn't even get through one night without chanting Laura's name. She felt no obligation to conceal what she knew about Laura's peculiar activities. Once Peter knew the truth he would forget his ill-fated obsession with Laura.

"Lady Chandler has been seen skulking into the house in the scruffy garments of an urchin," she confided. "After the last rebel riot she didn't return home until almost dawn. I have the sneaking suspicion that her bumps and bruises didn't come from falling down the steps, despite what she claimed. She has been deceiving you, Peter, and you have been too blind to recognize the truth."

" 'Tis ridiculous," Peter said in Laura's defense. "She told me herself that she took a spill and twisted her knee right here in this very house."

"And you were absent at the time of this supposed tumble," Mercy reminded him. "You seem to forget that I work here. Doesn't it stand to reason that I would have heard the commotion if she had fallen? 'Tis unlikely that your dear Laura fell while everyone was away from the house."

Peter wheeled away. " 'Tis utter nonsense."

Before Peter walked off, Mercy latched onto his arm, determined to plant and nurture the seed of suspicion. "She also came home late one night, wearing nothing but her unmentionables. I don't think her ladyship is as pure and innocent as she wants you to believe. If she was dallying with that rake at Miriam's party—"

"Ezra Beecham," Peter muttered furiously. "That lecherous libertine. 'Tis enough that he bedeviled Laura into lying for him to effect his release from jail. But now this! He must have convinced her to disguise herself so she could sneak off with him. And he repaid her by mauling her. Perhaps he was the one who caused her bruises and she was too afraid to admit the truth, for fear of what he might do to her."

Mercy scowled to herself. Peter was quick to lay the blame on everyone except his precious Laura. Well, Mercy would not permit it!

"I doubt that Ezra Beecham is the only man she has been dallying with. Last night I saw a cloaked figure sneaking up the back steps. I think Laura must have been entertaining a man in her room while you were on patrol. I could hear whispering behind the closed door.

"And I also believe Laura concocted this tale about Miriam's sick sister so she could sneak away with one of her lovers. There's no telling how many men she is keeping on a string. But for certain, she hoodwinked you into believing she's a proper lady," Mercy took great satisfaction in saying this to Peter.

"In fact, 'twould seem you are the only man hereabout who hasn't been in her bed. I wouldn't be surprised to discover those famous headaches Laura claims to have once or twice a week are nothing but excuses to slip off to meet her lovers."

"That's enough, Mercy," Peter snapped in outrage.

"You don't believe me?" She raised her chin in challenge. "Why don't you have a look around Laura's room before you trot off to your conference at headquarters. You might find it highly suspicious that she left without her combs, brushes, proper undergarments and fashionable gowns. I suspect Laura intends to let her secret lover purchase trinkets and new dresses for her."

When Peter's face contorted in a scowl, Mercy hastened to drive the spike of suspicion even deeper. "I can almost hear Laura gushing one of her long-winded explanations. She probably flashed one of her dimpled smiles and then informed her star-struck lover that she was so anxious for their tryst that she failed to pack the necessities. After she bats those big brown eyes of hers a few times, her hapless admirer will scuttle off to purchase whatever that scheming female wants and needs."

Peter lurched around and stalked off. He wasn't swallowing those jealous lies Mercy was trying to spoon-feed him. Laura had no lovers . . . except perhaps the insolent, pleasure-seeking Ezra Beecham . . .

The tormenting thought caused Peter's lips to curl in a snarl. He hadn't wanted to believe Laura had succumbed to that rake's devilish charm, but she had admitted it herself, much to Peter's chagrin. But surely Laura wouldn't let herself be completely taken in by that reckless dandy. Of course not, Peter thought. Laura had more common sense than that.

Mercy's wild tale was a crock of lies, Peter reassured himself as he marched upstairs. Laura hadn't tried to deceive her aunt so she could rendezvous with her lover . . .

His footsteps halted before Laura's bedchamber. To his own disgust, Peter found himself questioning the incident involving Laura's supposed tumble down the steps, as well as her scandalous encounter with Ezra Beecham at the ball. Peter turned the doorknob and surveyed the room. Just as Mercy proclaimed, the wardrobe closet was still teeming with Laura's elegant gowns. It looked as though few garments were missing— certainly none of the clothes Peter remembered seeing Laura wearing. When Peter spied the two mismatched shoes on the bottom shelf, he frowned curiously.

Further inspection indicated Laura's ivory combs and brushes were in their usual place on the bureau . . . But the tattered garments stashed in the bottom dresser drawer were by far the most baffling and incriminating evidence Peter stumbled upon. It seemed Laura Chandler was indeed leading a double life, and her motives could be even more deceptive than Mercy suspected . . .

When Peter scooped up the set of homespun garments, his heart slammed against his ribs. Beneath the urchin's garb was a long black cape, identical to the one the Midnight Rider wore.

Everything in Peter rebelled against the damning implications, but the evidence left him with no choice but to accept the truth. Laura Chandler was not what she seemed.

Suspicion clouded Peter's mind like a dense fog as he strode toward his room. If Laura had been seen skulking in and out of the mansion at all hours of the night, dressed like an urchin, it could very well be that she had disguised herself in order to feed information about military operations to the patriots!

Peter scowled in outrage, remembering all the times Laura had casually inquired about the goings-on at headquarters. Fool that he was, Peter had revealed several tidbits of information that should have remained confidential and classified. But he had been overly eager to share Laura's captivating company, to discuss any topic with her, never once realizing she intended to convey facts to those arrogant patriots!

Peter missed a step when he remembered what Mercy had said about seeing a caped figure exiting the house the previous night. Good Gad! Could Laura be in a league with the Midnight Rider? Was that why the black cape had been stashed beneath her urchin's garments? Was she somehow responsible for the Phantom Rider's phenomenal ability to disappear at will? Was she his accomplice, providing information that kept him from being captured?

Swearing profusely, Peter tramped from the house and aimed himself toward headquarters. He had the inescapable feeling that Laura Chandler could make a positive identification of the Midnight Rider. And she *would* reveal the man's identity to military authorities, Peter vowed fiercely. If not, she would find herself hauled to jail for withholding information— and worse, for treason against the Crown!

Peter swore, right there and then, that he would capture the legendary Midnight Rider and break these colonial rebels' spirit, if it was the last bloody thing he ever did! As for the devious Laura Chandler, she would be begging for his mercy and receive not one ounce of it. She had played Peter for a babbling idiot one too many times.

As for Ezra Beecham, Peter thought spitefully, he wouldn't be boasting of his conquest for long— if indeed there truly was one. The man had probably been humbugged, just as Peter had been. The moment Ezra learned that Laura was a traitor to the Crown, Ezra would be as outraged as Peter was. Laura had undoubtedly used Ezra for one of her crafty purposes as well. It served that self-absorbed dandy right . . . !

Unless Ezra Beecham was also a rebel spy . . .

Peter considered the possibility for a moment

and then discarded the absurdity. Ezra was a friend of Willie Fitzgerald. Both men were known to be loyal only to their personal pursuits of pleasure. Ezra had not the slightest concern for politics.

Dismissing the thought as highly unlikely, given what he knew about Ezra, Peter stalked off. He had every intention of seeing Laura Chandler pay for manipulating him, for deceiving him, for humiliating him. He had been prepared to lay the world at her feet. But no more, Peter silently seethed. He wanted revenge!

Nineteen

With extreme satisfaction Nolan led Laura through the untamed frontier. Since Nolan had left civilization behind, Laura had been flinching at every unidentified sound, appraising her surroundings with wide, curious eyes. Nolan had set as grueling a pace as his injured arm would permit, forcing Laura to remain on the saddle for hours on end. He had expected her to complain, like most females, but she had yet to voice one objection.

"Ezra . . . er . . . Nolan?"

Nolan swiveled around to glance at his companion.

"Don't you think this jaunt has lasted long enough?" Laura peered up at the towering trees that shielded the fading afternoon sunlight. "I doubt anyone who happens across my remains will take time to troop all the way back to Boston to determine my identity. No one is going to connect you with my demise, especially since you have been dead for almost three years yourself."

Nolan paused his steed, frowning at her from beneath flattened brows. "What makes you think

I plan to dispose of you? Because you're as guilty as sin?" he added with a sardonic smirk.

Laura heaved a weary sigh and shifted on the saddle, hoping to find a more comfortable position. There wasn't one. She had squired a dozen different ways, only to rub saddle sores in new places.

"I have done nothing to betray you or the patriot cause, despite what you think. But I've given up trying to convince you that I'm as devoted to colonial liberty as you are."

Nolan's disdainful snort showed that he didn't believe her.

"My point exactly," she continued. "So why not do your worst, here and now? Or is this part of my planned torture?"

Nolan dismounted, muttering under his breath. The reason he couldn't do his worst to this devious female had hounded him every step of the way. Despite everything, he wanted Laura Chandler, deceitful actress and accomplished liar though she was. 'Twas the infuriating truth, and Nolan knew he was every kind of fool for craving a woman who would forsake him.

"We'll camp here for the night," he announced abruptly.

Laura surveyed the tree-covered hills. "Camp where?"

Nolan indicated to the spot where he was standing. "Here."

"You must be joking. 'Tis no telling what kind

of wild creatures are lurking under rocks and looming in the shadows.''

Nolan swallowed a spiteful grin. "You have been telling me since the day we met that you can handle everything all by yourself. Yet you are certainly squeamish about camping in the wide open spaces.''

Once Nolan helped Laura out of the saddle, she squirmed loose from his encircling arms, and he let her go without objection. She would come to him of her own free will soon enough, he prophesied. When the unfamiliar sounds of night closed in around her, she would be anxious to share his pallet, if only for the warmth and protection he could provide. And then he would take his pleasure in her luscious body, giving nothing of himself in return.

"I'll see what I can do about hunting game for supper while you build a campfire.''

In disbelief, Laura watched Nolan drag his rifle from its sling on the saddle. "You're leaving me here? Alone? Aren't you afraid I'll escape and spoil your fun of killing me with your own hands?''

"Nay,'' he said moving away without a backward glance.

"Nay what? You aren't afraid I'll escape? Or nay, you don't care whose hands finish the deed?'' she demanded before he walked out of earshot.

Laura stamped her foot when Nolan continued on his way. "Blast it! Ez— Nolan, even if you despise me, you could at least do me the simple courtesy of answering my questions!''

Very slowly, deliberately, Nolan pivoted to face

her, his rifle braced over his good shoulder. "I seriously doubt you will attempt escape, because there is nowhere for you to go, my lady. I am the only hope of survival you have in the wilderness, and I think you are intelligent enough to know that."

"You don't know me at all, Nolan Ryder," she flashed, tilting her chin to a challenging angle. "I was prepared to meet my undeserved fate, if only to end my tormenting association with you. Every hour with you is an exercise in patience. And furthermore, if you think I intend to play your whore while you drag me all over creation, you have made a serious miscalculation. Why don't you just take my measure over your rifle barrel and be done with it?"

If she thought she could provoke him into anger, she thought wrong. Nolan wasn't rising to her bait.

"Watching your various phases of torture is half my fun." Nolan swallowed a grin when Laura pulled a face at him. "And by the way, you don't know me at all, either— "

"That's the truth," she broke in bitterly.

"You're interrupting me again," he pointed out.

Laura raised her chin another notch and stared daringly at him. "So shoot me."

Nolan strangled a chuckle. The woman had enough sass to fill a keg. "A quick and painless death? I already told you that it won't come that easy for you. 'Tis my opinion that traitors deserve to suffer slow, agonizing torture. It provides them with time to repent for their sins."

"I've spent a full day with you," she snarled nastily. "No torture is worse than that. I find Peter Forbes far more entertaining and interesting company. So was the recently departed Geoffrey Spradlin. But then, a stone fence post has more personality than you do."

"You might be correct," Nolan acknowledged. "And since you find me to be such a tedious bore, I'm sure you'll enjoy your solitude in the forest. You will discover the wilds are the ultimate in freedom, the epitome of personal liberty. You are free to do whatever you choose, at your own risk and your own pace. Out here, you can test your self-reliance and challenge your own abilities. The Crown can't tax this kind of liberty, and our British cousins three thousand miles away certainly don't understand it. 'Tis a whole other country, an entity unto itself. The wilderness makes you appreciate your unlimited freedom."

"Are you trying to convince me to turn patriot?" Laura called after him. "If you are, you're wasting your breath. I'm as rebellious as you are, so there!"

A deep resonant chuckle wafted through the dense trees before evaporating, leaving Laura completely alone with her thoughts, alone with the unidentified beasts that lurked in the shadows, waiting to eat her alive.

For an apprehensive moment, Laura assessed her surroundings. The forest was almost overwhelming in its enormity. Odd, wasn't it, that she never even flinched when she roamed the streets where most conscientious aristocrats wouldn't dare go alone after dark? But here in the vast wilderness she felt insecure and incompetent. And worse, she felt an intuitive need to rely upon a man she knew despised her, a man who believed she was a treacherous Tory spy who had sold him into ambush for the want of British coins.

Laura muttered an unladylike oath and kicked at the fallen leaves with her indigo blue shoe, which was now as dusty brown as the black one. Build a campfire? Well, fine. How hard could that be? She could adapt to the backwoods if she put her mind to it. She would simply pretend the trees were the buildings of Boston, crammed together to form narrow byways. The scenery might be different, but the survival skills were essentially the same— give or take a few bears, snakes and panthers. After all, Laura had dealt with her share of the two-legged varieties of predators in the streets. She could cope.

If Nolan Ryder expected her to dissolve into blubbering tears, because she found herself out of her element, he didn't know her very well. By damn, she would show him that she needed no man for protection, not even the man who had begun to matter to her more than he should have . . .

A strange hoot echoed in the descending darkness, followed by what sounded like a gargantuan, man-eating frog. Laura instinctively flinched. A wild, piercing cry— unlike anything she had ever heard— was proceeded by a thrashing in the underbrush. Laura glanced every which way, expecting to be attacked from all directions at once.

When a dangerous affront didn't come, she mustered her bravado and tramped off to gather kindling for the campfire.

Nolan Ryder wanted her to build a fire, did he? she mused spitefully as she plucked up a broken branch. Aye, he would have a fire all right, one large enough to hold the night beasts at bay— him included!

On that determined thought, Laura collected enough twigs and limbs for a huge bonfire and then went in search of the tinderbox.

Nolan heard the wild shriek echo in the night. The haunting sound went through him like a flaming arrow. His heartbeat leaped into triple time as he wheeled toward camp. With the rabbits he had snared dangling from the butt of his rifle, Nolan raced up the hill, dodging tangles of thick underbrush.

True, he was convinced Laura deserved to be frightened within an inch of her devious life. But he hadn't expected her fear to be so contagious. He felt as frightened as she sounded!

Nolan skidded to a halt when he heard gurgles and sputters rising from the creek. When he crept closer he spied a bare-chested Indian brave— most likely a stray warrior from the Wampanoag tribe, from the looks of his skimpy breechcloth and partially shaved head— shoving Laura underwater. From all indication Laura couldn't swim a lick. She was practically clawing her way up the warrior's naked chest like a cat headed for drier ground.

Nolan was familiar with the customs and rites of bathing new captives to cleanse them from their previous life before they were adopted into the tribe. Since the bronzed warrior looked to be in his late twenties, Nolan predicted the Wampanoag brave had it in mind to acquire a new bride.

If Laura was whisked off to the Wampanoag village, never to be seen or heard from again, 'twould simplify Nolan's problems of what to do with her. 'Twould also serve her right. Her initiation into frontier life would be complete. What a shame Nolan had made a pact with himself to use this lovely but cunning witch for his own selfish pleasures until he had tired of her, to personally torment the hell out of her every chance he got.

Trouble was, with one arm in a sling, Nolan was at a distinct disadvantage in recapturing his captive. Firing the rifle could alert other warriors to his whereabouts. Long ago, Spark had taught Nolan that cleverness, silence and stealth were the best methods of wilderness warfare. And now, when he could have found a practical use for a bow and arrow—far more practical than Laura's target practice on the back lawn of Beacon Hill—Nolan was without the weapon. The dagger in his boot was an alternative, but he preferred to save it as his last resort.

Setting his rifle aside, Nolan inched closer to the creek. Laura was being held underwater for her proper christening into Indian society. Nolan glanced down at the enormous stack of wood beside the tree and selected a sturdy club from the pile Laura collected before she had been attacked. Nolan had in mind to knock the brave senseless rather than leave a dead man on his trail.

The Indian tribes and colonists were in constant conflict on the frontier. 'Twould take very little provocation to incite more trouble. Nolan's attempt to rescue Laura before she drowned could result in retaliation against nearby white settlements.

While the distracted warrior was hunkered over his flailing victim, Nolan launched himself through the air. His improvised club landed on the back of the brave's shaved head with a loud *thunk*. The warrior pitched forward on Laura, forcing her deeper into the water. Nolan grabbed the warrior by his leg and dragged him ashore. He waded into the shallows to retrieve Laura the instant she clawed her way to the surface.

Moonlight reflected off the rounded whites of her eyes and spotlighted the horrified expression on her blanched face. She flounded in her soggy gown, practically crawling toward Nolan as if he were her salvation.

Nolan braced himself before she flung her arms around his neck and squeezed the stuffing out of him. Her tears mingled with the rivulets of water that dripped from her hair and saturated his buckskin shirt.

"Dear God in heaven!" she cried hoarsely. "He was going to kill me!"

"Nay," Nolan calmly contradicted. "He was planning to marry you— Indian style."

She lifted her head from his shoulder, her mouth open. "Indians drown their wives?"

"It prevents them from becoming contrary," Nolan said, straight-faced.

"The man tried to kill me and you are making jokes?" she fumed as she pushed away from his chest.

"What are you complaining about? An hour ago you were prepared to meet a quick end." Nolan grinned at the bedraggled beauty. "Drowning wasn't sudden enough for you?"

Obsidian eyes glittered furiously. "Damn you, Nolan Ryder."

"I have been already," he assured her, towing her up the slippery slope. "I got myself tangled up with the likes of you, didn't I? 'Tis damnation enough, the way I see it."

When Laura set her feet, refusing to budge from the spot, Nolan glanced down at her. "Now what?"

She stared at his swarthy profile, angry enough to spit tacks and yet awed by his unruffled composure. It occurred to her, just then, that the wilderness was the place where Nolan Ryder seemed most at home, most content. 'Twas where he thrived, the place he loved best.

Nolan could portray the frivolous dandy, as if he had been born to it. He could dodge bullets and outrun British patrols astride his devil stallion, for the mere sport of it. But 'twas here on the frontier, garbed in buckskins, that he displayed his powerful physique to its best advantage. Nolan Ryder became the true individualist he was. He appreciated the dome of stars that was his roof. He relished having his own space— and then some. He was impressively self-reliant, remarkably competent and utterly fearless. This natural-born predator was a part of the wilderness.

"Something wrong, my lady?" Nolan prodded when she stood there staring at him with an indiscernible expression.

Laura shook herself loose from the trance, refusing to let herself become too emotionally involved with a man who didn't trust her, would never care as deeply for her as she could have cared for him if he would simply give her a chance . . .

The warrior's muffled groan prompted Laura to wheel about. She scooped up Nolan's discarded club and gave the groggy brave another whack on the back of the head for good measure.

"And that," she said huffily, "is what I think of your courtship practices! I have no use whatsoever for such marriage rituals."

Nolan bit back a chuckle as he strode off to retrieve his rifle. With the exception of the incident with the warrior, Nolan was actually enjoying himself. Laura provided amusing companionship— when she wasn't inventing ways to betray him . . .

The thought was a grim reminder of why his arm was in a sling, as useless to him in the wilderness as Laura was. Bearing that in mind, Nolan walked over to fetch his stallion.

"I thought we were bedding down for the night," Laura reminded him.

"Aye, but not here, not now. The Wampanoag brave likely has friends hereabout. I didn't snare enough rabbits to invite them all to supper."

Laura stared at the gray gelding. "I'm not sure I can climb back on that horse," she mumbled, unconsciously rubbing her tender backside. "I appreciated being separated from that great brute the past hour."

"Your choice, my lady." Nolan swung onto the saddle and reined southwest. "You can stay here and tie the matrimonial knot with your most recent beau or come with me."

"One of these days, Nolan Ryder—"

He halted abruptly and stared down at the soggy beauty. "One of these days, Laura Chandler, you will be as free of me as I will be of you. Until then, we are stuck with each other. Either mount up or prepare yourself for your wedding night. I really don't care what you choose to do."

Nolan steeled himself against the sparkle of tears in her onyx eyes. The wave of sympathy that threatened to engulf him was a waste of perfectly good emotion. Laura Chandler had asked for this. 'Twas the punishment for her deception and he wasn't going to coddle and pamper her the way most men did.

Allowing herself one sniff, Laura piled onto the horse. She wanted to lie down and cry like a baby, but that would have pleased Nolan no end. He wanted her to crumble, wanted her to reduce herself to begging and pleading for his mercy.

She wouldn't do it, if only just to spite him.

Laura inhaled a reinforcing breath and reminded herself of the years she had spent scratching and clawing for survival. Nolan was right on one count. She was a survivor. Self-preservation had been deeply ingrained since those days of hand-to-mouth existence. She would meet every obstacle Nolan flung in her path. She would follow him until she dropped in sheer exhaustion, and then she would pull herself up by her mismatched shoes and trail after him until they reached civilization. He might never trust her, but he would admire her perseverance, so help her he would!

Nolan glanced sideways when he heard the thud of approaching hooves. Despite the bitter resentment that hounded him, he felt a strange sense of pride while watching Laura defy his cold-shoulder treatment. She was exhausted; 'twas obvious. She was in unfamiliar surroundings, but she forged bravely ahead, if only to prove that while she might occasionally give out, she was not about to give up. 'Twas a shame that he and Laura . . .

Don't even think about that, Nolan lectured himself sternly. He had mentally listed his objectives for this journey and he was sticking to them. Feeling sorry for Laura was not on the list.

As Spark had preached time and again, women had their customary place and use in this man's world. Nolan wasn't idiotic enough to think Laura wouldn't escape if she had somewhere else to go.

He would have to watch her like a hawk when they reached Tall Oaks Ferry. He predicted she would try to slip off with the first man who fell beneath her bewitching spell. Her only loyalty was to herself, and Nolan had better not forget that if he knew what was good for him.

The muffled thud behind him indicated Laura had gone as far as it was humanly possible for her to go. She had dozed off and toppled from her mount, too weary to rise, perfectly content to sleep where she landed. Nolan dismounted to tend the horses. Once they were staked out to graze on the meadow beyond the timbers, Nolan shook out the bedrolls and plunked down to munch on the cornmeal hoecakes Spark had packed with the supplies.

Pensively, Nolan stared at Laura's sprawled form, his gaze flowing over the wild tangle of curls that were draped over her back like a cloak. A pity she opposed such a noble, necessary cause for the colonies. She would have made a most respectable rebel.

This trek through the wilderness served to reinforce Nolan's belief that freedom was essential and precious enough to fight for— even die for, if need be. 'Twas more valuable than all the gold coins in the British treasury.

Protests and demonstrations against the economically crippling Stamp Act were just the beginning of a long battle for liberty, Nolan prophesied. The sturdy individualists who had built their cities and settlements were Americans, not second-class British subjects who were born to depend on the Crown for their existence. The colonists had learned to govern themselves, to levy fair taxes that didn't crush the economy and provoke hardship. America was a world apart from England. Tax rebellion and colonial independence were as necessary as they were inevitable.

On that philosophical thought, Nolan scooped Laura up in his good arm and tucked her beneath the quilt. Perhaps he had toted Laura through the wilderness in hopes of converting her to his way of thinking, to enlist her support to the cause she had betrayed. Or perhaps the underlying truth was that he only wanted to . . .

Nolan smothered the dangerous thought and stretched out on his pallet. Setting his rifle within easy reach, he forced himself to relax. He was here to recuperate, to remove Laura from the network of rebel agents she had so thoroughly hoodwinked. Nolan was on a reconnaissance mission to estimate the number of redcoats and how much weaponry was being transported to strengthen British fortifications in Boston.

And that, Nolan reminded himself as he closed his eyes and drifted off to sleep, was his primary objective. He was committed to his cause, even if he had to drag this lovely Tory spy around with him like an albatross to ensure she didn't betray him again.

Twenty

Captain Oran Milbourne slumped back in his chair at military headquarters and stared incredulously at Lieutenant Forbes. "Are you sure about this? I hope you realize you are leveling very serious charges against Laura Chandler. I should not have to remind you that treason is punishable by death."

Peter nodded grimly. "Believe me, sir, I am fully aware of the severity of the crime and its punishment. But the evidence is incriminating. I have a credible witness who is prepared to testify that Laura was seen sneaking from her home in disguise on several occasions. A cloaked intruder was also seen exiting from the house. From all indication, Laura is in league with the Midnight Rider."

"It seems too incredible to be believed." Oran swiped a beefy hand over his head. "Laura Chandler? She seemed so loyal to the Crown's policies, so interested in our attempt to curtail rebel activity . . ." His voice dried up when he realized what he had said. "Bloody hell!"

"My sentiments exactly," Peter muttered. " 'Tis

almost too convenient that I am quartered in her home."

Oran frowned pensively. "Do you think Miriam Peabody is involved in this espionage ring?"

Peter chuckled at the absurdity. " 'Tis my belief that Miriam has been played as falsely as I have. She is concerned about her sister in Philadelphia, but I have the niggling feeling 'twas Laura herself who had the message delivered as an excuse to make her hasty departure. The rebels must be planning another protest. Either that, or they have decided to send their cunning spy to Philadelphia to lure other unsuspecting British officers into her confidences."

Oran rose from his chair. With hands clasped behind him, he paced the confines of his office. "Have you questioned Miriam about the unusual garments found in Laura's room?"

Peter nodded his blond head. "Miriam was duly shocked, almost to the point of hysterics. Naturally, she insisted there must be some mistake, some other explanation for the tattered garments. Miriam is exceptionally fond of her niece and refuses to believe the worst, unless she is left with no other choice."

Oran paused, sighed audibly and peered at the lieutenant. "This certainly explains why the Midnight Rider and Sons of Liberty know what we're planning before we carry out our orders."

"Aye, Captain. 'Tis an explanation of why Laura allowed herself to be courted by several British officers and insisted she isn't ready to settle into marriage. She has obviously been using her eligibility and feminine wiles to elicit as much information from as many unsuspecting sources as possible."

Oran wore ruts in the floorboards, silently pondering the problem. "We will have a likeness of Laura sketched and posted throughout Boston. There will be a warrant issued for her arrest and a sizable reward offered to anyone who can help us apprehend our fugitive. I should hate to make an example of a woman, but a rebel spy is a rebel spy. Her actions against the Crown are nothing but blasphemous. If we decide to make an example of her, perhaps her fellow patriots will realize we will make no exceptions in matters of treason."

"The rebels have certainly made their distaste of informants who aid Customs officers known by public tarring and feathering," Peter put in.

Oran grimaced. He had seen the results when the mob tarred and feathered one of the town's stamp distributors. The poor man had been boiled alive and patches of his skin had peeled off when his clothes were removed. Needless to say, the stamp agent resigned his commission. Several other tax distributors followed suit before they suffered the same fate.

"When Laura Chandler is apprehended, I will request that she be shipped to England to stand trial and endure her punishment. A public display in the colonies might incite the radical factions of rebels into revolution."

"But she will pay dearly for luring me and other unsuspecting officers into her treachery," Peter muttered determinedly. "She must become an example to other rebel spies. Our leniency would set an unfavorable precedence."

On that ominous note, Peter stalked off to begin work on the wanted poster. Wherever that crafty chit was, she wouldn't remain at large for long. Peter intended to inform every loyalist in Boston of her duplicity and deceit. By God, he would have the full measure of revenge for being played the naive fool. Laura Chandler would be very sorry indeed that she manipulated Peter Forbes.

Nolan came awake to the orchestral serenade of birds. He lifted his gaze to the canopy of trees that filtered the first rays of dawn. The comforting warmth beside him drew his immediate and complete attention. He felt a smile tugging at his lips when he realized that Laura was cuddled against him. A tangle of flaming auburn curls trailed over his shoulder and her arm was draped familiarly over his belly.

It seemed natural to have her nestled against him, as if that was where they both belonged— for a space out of time, at least.

Nolan refused to allow himself to think past the next few weeks. He still didn't know what the devil he was going to do about this crafty female when he ventured back to Boston. If he couldn't make her see the error of her ways, she would forever be a threat to him, to the patriot cause. Even then, he could never be sure where her loyalties lay. She was a problem Nolan wasn't sure he could satisfactorily resolve.

Laura groaned as she fought her way up from the depths of sleep. Nolan grinned and impulsively dropped a kiss to her forehead when she inched closer to the warmth of his body. When she nuzzled her face against the side of his neck, with her breath like an inviting caress, Nolan felt himself burning from inside out. Need coiled within him, causing his pulse to leap like a jackrabbit. He wanted her with a hunger that had been gnawing at him since the moment they left the cabin.

And there was no reason why he shouldn't indulge himself.

Nolan succumbed to the temptation of caressing the generous feminine curves and swells beneath the quilt. His languid explorations evoked Laura's soft sighs. Gently, he kissed her eyelids, her cheeks, the sensitive hollow he had once discovered at the apex of her throat and shoulder. She arched instinctively toward his seeking hand and lips, responding with the kind of reckless abandon he fully appreciated and had known only with her.

In passion, they were a perfect match, Nolan mused as his hand glided beneath the hem of her skirt. He and Laura triggered overpowering sensations in each other. Contrasting political views and personal conflict burned away in the sensual fire they awakened in each other— with just one touch, one kiss.

And that was what Nolan needed now— a kiss that spun the world into oblivion. He wanted to savor the honeyed taste of her as dawn spilled its majestic pastel hues over the countryside. He wanted to share her every breath, absorb her alluring scent. He ached to mold her to his aroused contours and feel her yielding to him as she had that splendorous night when he had claimed her as his private possession.

What Laura knew of desire Nolan had taught her. He had become the tutor of passion and yet he had learned things from her that he hadn't discovered in his previous experiences with women. Although spiteful revenge prompted Nolan to view their lovemaking as shallow and impersonal, it had not been the simple appeasement of basic needs, not that first time, that only time. The encounter had exceeded Nolan's definition of intimacy, affecting him on an emotional and physical level. He hadn't wanted to admit it, but he couldn't deny it, and he sure as hell couldn't ignore it . . .

When Laura's inarticulate mumblings of want and need hovered between them, Nolan abandoned any hope of treating this enchanting beauty as if she were no more than a morsel to feed his male appetite. Pleasing her had somehow become his pleasure. He longed to rediscover each place she liked to be touched, to feel the ripples of desire vibrating through her, reverberating through him. Arousing her aroused him— more than it should. Having Laura desire him until her need was almost tangible had somehow become vital to him.

With tender care, Nolan spread a row of moist kisses along the column of her neck, gently pushing the gown out of his way to flick his tongue against the beaded peaks of her breasts. Her soft moan encouraged him to summon another response, and yet another.

Nolan felt her flesh quiver as his hand skimmed her belly to trail along the band of her pantaloons. With dedicated care, he eased the hampering garment out of his way to trace the silky slope of her hips, to set every inch of her flesh aflame with his seductive touch.

The first time they made love Nolan had been so overcome by ravenous need that he hadn't thought to doff his breeches before mindless passion consumed him. But this time, Nolan promised himself, they would be flesh to flesh, heartbeat to heartbeat.

He yearned to explore her so thoroughly that he knew her better than he understood himself. He would climb inside her very soul if he could. He would be absorbed by her, and she by him. He would know all her secrets, and make them his own.

Nolan sighed aloud when he had bared her luscious body to the golden sunlight. She was such an incredible feast for masculine eyes— his eyes only. And here, in the wildness, with dewdrops sparkling like diamonds on the leaves and waving blades of grass, Nolan savored a vision so beguiling that he swore he was gazing upon an angel in his own private paradise.

His sensual caresses and kisses had Laura melting in his arms, beneath his lips and fingertips.

When he cupped her in his hand and glided his fingers across the satiny curve of her thighs he felt the secret rain of desire he had called from her. He shuddered in need so profound it stole his very breath.

The slow penetration of his fingertips brought her to shivering heights of rapture and sent Nolan's senses reeling. But he vowed to pleasurably torment her every way imaginable before he buried himself in the welcoming heat of her passion . . . and lost all touch with reality.

"Nolan . . ." Laura gasped when another lightning bolt of sensations riveted her. "Please . . ."

"You please me very well," he murmured against the velvet textures and flat plane of her belly.

When his whispering kisses trailed across her inner thigh, she lifted her hand to shield herself from the shocking intimacy. Nolan folded his hand over hers. "I crave the taste of you. Don't deny my obsession. Open for me, Laura . . ."

Her wild gasp echoed in the stillness of dawn as he eased her legs further apart to trace the dewy petals of femininity. When his mouth moved delicately over her, he felt her shimmering around his lips and fingertips. She was the hottest, sweetest kind of fire he had ever known, and he wanted to burn alive in the depths of molten desire— now . . .

Nolan doffed the encumbering sling that cradled his injured arm and pulled off his shirt. Laura's passion-drugged eyes fluttered up, focused on the broad expanse of his chest and the washboarded contours of his belly. Before he could strip off his breeches, she assumed the task of removing his buckskin trousers with such deft and languid ease that every inch of flesh she touched tingled in helpless response.

Nolan's breath caught somewhere between his chest and throat when her gliding caresses freed him from the confines of his clothing. Sweet mercy, he thought shakily. How could he have forgotten how skillful this female was with her hands. Her touch was feather-light— and as scalding as liquid flames!

When her fingertips grazed his most sensitive flesh and folded around the throbbing length of him, Nolan gritted his teeth against the tormenting pleasure that bombarded him.

Self-control, he repeatedly reminded himself. A man was nothing without his self-control . . .

Suddenly Nolan was nothing . . .

When Laura urged him to his back, Nolan went down without so much as a skirmish. The gliding stroke of her hand on his aroused flesh was like a velvet fire scorching him. His entire body clenched when her head dipped toward him and the curly mane of her long auburn hair drifted over his thighs like a bolt of silk.

Every sensible thought Nolan had accumulated in thirty years of existence scattered like a defeated army in retreat. He couldn't think; he could only feel her warm breath skimming his potent flesh, her moist lips tasting him as intimately as he had tasted her.

"You feel like satin steel," she murmured against

his pulsating length. "I like the feel of you, the taste of you . . ."

He fleetingly wondered if there was a more pleasurable way to die . . . and doubted there was . . .

'Twas definitely not what Nolan intended. 'Twas to be her downfall in mindless passion, not his! But Nolan could no more halt the erotic sway of her hands and lips than he could capture wispy clouds and fling them into the sea. He could only drift and sway with the soft, tortuous flow of pleasure that engulfed and consumed . . .

Nolan forgot why it was necessary to draw breath when her tongue trailed over his rigid flesh, measuring him, teasing him, arousing him. She was making a sensual study of his body, triggering bone-melting sensations that converged like pinpoints of living fire. He couldn't endure such sweet, excruciating torment, not when the sensations were more intense than any pain he had ever suffered.

"Nay, don't . . . !" Nolan rasped, clamping down on her wandering hand.

"Ah, but I do," she playfully whispered against his throbbing length. "I have discovered a far more pleasurable skill than picking pockets. And 'twas you who said I should learn to appreciate and explore this new frontier, was it not?"

Nolan would have chuckled at her teasing question, if he could have trusted his lungs not to collapse. There was barely enough air to sustain him as it was. " 'Twas not what I meant," he managed to get out.

"You have spoken of unrestrained freedoms." Her petal-soft lips glided to and fro, riveting his body with a dozen more indescribable sensations. "And now I swear I can never be content with anything less than uninhibited liberties . . ."

"Stop!" Nolan groaned when desire— white-hot and overwhelming— coursed through him.

"I will stop . . . eventually . . ."

"Eventually will be too late. Now is almost too late— "

Nolan hissed through clenched teeth when her thumb brushed the betraying evidence of his desire for her. She tasted his passion and scalding chills rippled down his spine, taking the last remnants of willpower with them.

Nolan was overwhelmed by the wildest kind of desperation he had ever known. With a tormented groan, he clutched at Laura's arm, gliding her supple body over his.

He needed her now— 'twas almost too late. And yet, 'twas too soon. He was to have been the commander at the helm during this slow, erotic voyage into ecstasy. But Laura had pushed him so far past the point of no return with her brazen caresses that Nolan couldn't have charted a course to anywhere without getting himself impossibly lost.

When her lips came down on his, sharing the taste of his own need, Nolan knew without question that he wasn't going to survive another second. His hands glided over her hips as he arched upward, becoming both the possessor and the possession. He felt her nails scoring his shoulders as he set the frantic cadence ungovernable passion demanded of him. Nolan squeezed his eyes shut and felt the heat of blazing passion inflame his very core and channel outward, leaving no part of him untouched.

And just as before, Nolan was vividly aware that he hadn't really experienced the full dimension of passion until he and Laura were sailing through a universe of inexpressible sensations. But this time, Nolan captured that which had once been beyond his grasp, by simply letting go of the last vestige of control.

There, beyond the leaping flames, was the quintessence of fulfillment— complete and utter contentment. Now he knew that mystical, once-elusive sensation by name . . .

This sometimes infuriating but thoroughly captivating witch, who cast impossible spells, was more than just the medium who put Nolan in poignant touch with himself, with life's deepest, unalterable truth.

Laura Chandler was the other half of his soul, for better . . . and worse . . .

And because Nolan could not resist Laura's forbidden lure, he had condemned himself to the fiery pits of hell . . .

In the debilitating aftermath of passion, Nolan opened his eyes and stared at the overhanging tree branches. Laura's cheek rested against his laboring chest, her hand stroking his good arm in a languid caress.

Nolan thumbed through the memories of his life

before this impossible female intruded. Bad or good, each day had been a new experience, a different challenge. Nolan had savored changes, thrived on testing himself. But now, like a fool, he whimsically wished for the world to stop spinning on its axis. He wanted his life to remain exactly as it was. He wanted to savor this contentment with Laura, to depend on it, to expect it . . .

You wish for dangerous impossibilities when you wish for illusions, came the cynical voice inside him.

Nolan gnashed his teeth and fought the self-betraying feelings that thrummed through him. It could very well be that Laura had surrendered to him, hoping to soften his resentment, scheming to bend him to her will—just as she manipulated the countless other men she bewitched. Once she had Nolan at her beck and call, once he let his guard down, she would forsake him—or escape him at the very least.

His only recourse was to accept the fact that the other half of his soul had devilish intent. He could make love to this enchanting siren, but he could never allow himself to love her. She was his Achilles heel, a weakness he could ill afford . . .

His heaven that promised hell . . .

The only way to save himself was to ignore the whispers of his foolish heart and employ seductive charm to win her affection. Nolan wondered if 'twas even possible to win the love of a woman whose strong will and fierce determination rivaled—and oftentimes seemed to surpass—his own. Did this dark-eyed beauty even have a heart to win?

"Nolan?"

"Aye?"

"I'm not really what you think I am," Laura murmured against the padded muscles of his chest.

Nolan's expression never altered. "Nay? It has certainly proved to be the case— twice."

'Twas what he expected, Nolan reminded himself. In the aftermath of passion, while he was still exceptionally vulnerable, Laura sought to practice her cunning wiles on him.

Laura lifted her head to stare into his craggy features. Tender emotion avalanched upon her, putting words to tongue that she knew Nolan would refuse to accept as truth. But for all the times Laura knew she did not love, she now knew when she did. She had never uttered the heartfelt phrase to another man, because no other man drew her admiration, respect and affection the way this raven-haired vigilante of liberty did.

"I think I'm falling in love with you . . ." The words sounded foreign, but they felt right in her heart. Obviously, they didn't sound right to Nolan's ears. He merely stared at her as if she were some curious creature that had dropped down from the trees. Her heart shattered in a thousand disappointed fragments.

"Do you really?" he asked, his silvery gaze probing into hers.

"Aye, I believe so," she murmured self-consciously.

"Well, be sure to let me know when you have decided for certain."

Nolan eased away before he fell victim to another perilous trance. If he stared overly long into those dark, hypnotic eyes, he would see what he wanted to see, rather than the deceptive pretenses of a carefully laid trap. He could not allow himself to be outwitted, lest he find himself planted in the empty grave site in Boston— permanently.

"We have another long day ahead of us. We're wasting daylight."

After Nolan had gathered his discarded clothes, he strode to the creek to bathe, giving himself time to reconstruct his broken defenses. He had heard too many lies tumble from those honeyed lips to believe Laura Chandler might actually have fallen in love with him.

Words were easy to come by, Nolan reminded himself. Deeds were solid proof. Only when Laura was forced to make a critical choice between him and her Tory philosophies would Nolan know for certain that he could trust her. Until then, he would take advantage of this supposed affection and sparingly offer cautious trust.

Ethan would be proud of him, Nolan decided as he walked into the stream to cool the fires that never completely burned themselves out while Laura was underfoot. Ethan had always preached caution. Now Nolan was practicing it, as he never had in his life— to *preserve* his life . . .

Twenty-one

Miriam Peabody was as nervous as a caged cat, a state in which she had been since Peter Forbes had interrogated her the previous day. True, Laura had always claimed Miriam could never be incriminated for secret activities concerning the Sons of Liberty. Indeed, Laura had been adamant about distancing Miriam from patriot contacts. However, Miriam wasn't concerned about her safety. She was fretting over Laura's whereabouts and the accusations of conspiracy leveled against her. Miriam didn't know how to convey a warning to Laura. If the girl reappeared in Boston she could be apprehended and interrogated without prior knowledge of the devastating turn of events. What could she do?

Restless, Miriam circumnavigated the parlor, her mind abuzz. The members of the Ladies Literary Club were due to arrive in a half hour. The last thing Miriam wanted to discuss was the symbolism in English poetry.

"A problem, madam?" Mercy Reed asked, propping herself leisurely against the doorjamb— an annoying habit that indicated she was inclined to hold up walls rather than expend energy working.

"Cook says the refreshments are ready and waiting. Is there something we've overlooked?"

Miriam absently waved her off. "Everything is fine."

"Then it must be your niece who's putting you to pacing."

Miriam's satin-clad shoulders slumped and she heaved an enormous sigh. "I simply cannot believe these alleged accusations. There has obviously been a mistake."

Mercy tilted her sandy-red head to meet the older woman's troubled frown. " 'Tis no mistake, madam. I saw your niece skulking in and out of the house, dressed like an urchin."

Miriam blinked. "You did? And what were you doing while she was supposedly prowling the night, doing whatever it is that Peter presumes she was doing?"

Mercy shifted awkwardly beneath Miriam's probing stare. "I was . . . um . . ."

'Twas apparent that Mercy's greatest commodity wasn't quick wit. Laura could dream up plausible excuses to conceal her clandestine activities in the bat of an eyelash and the flash of a dimpled smile. Mercy, however, stuttered like a tongue-tied idiot and glanced in every direction except Miriam's.

"You must have been doing some cavorting of your own," Miriam accused. "Either that or you have concocted this nonsense to cause Laura trouble."

"I didn't concoct a bloody thing!" Mercy snapped disrespectfully. "I was on my way back from Peter's room when—" She slammed her mouth shut and cursed under her breath.

Miriam's hazel eyes narrowed. "So that's how the wind blows, is it?"

Mercy stuck out her pointed chin. "I happen to be in love with Peter and he would love me back, if not for Laura. She doesn't give a fig about Peter or the other men who flock to her. She was using all of them to get information—just as she used you as her protective cover. If I were you, I would disown her!"

Miriam knew Mercy was goggle-eyed over Peter, but never in her worst nightmare had she dreamed this slothful chit had actually been tramping off to the lieutenant's bed! This female had to go, Miriam decided on the spot, and she would see to the matter immediately after she endured Mrs. Appleton's droning literary lecture.

"Until I have concrete evidence to support these preposterous accusations about my niece, I intend to uphold my belief in Laura's innocence. I'm sure Laura is tending my sister and I shall write to confirm that, first chance I get."

With a dismissing flick of her bejeweled hand, Miriam sent the servant on her way. Blast and be damned! A member of the household staff had betrayed Laura, and all because of female rivalry? What a dismal twist of fate!

Miriam was outraged to learn there was a traitor in her own camp. That jealous Jezebel had sold Laura out, in hopes of luring in the man she had set her cap for! Mercy Reed was going to be sorry indeed! Miriam fumed.

Nolan smiled in satisfaction when he stared down the hill to survey Coon Ashburn's spacious log cabin and wayside inn that was situated in a grove of trees beside the river. A large raft, equipped with towering sails, was moored by the planked wharf. Heavy cables, stretched between opposite shores, were secured to stout trees. Sun or storm, the ferry would be in operation.

Coon Ashburn was the kind of man who prided himself as being prepared for anything. If inclement weather, high water or strong wind hampered progress across the river, Coon could resort to his blocks, tackles and cables. One way or another, Coon intended to navigate across the river to accommodate travelers.

This inn had been a favorite way station for express riders headed south to communicate with the Sons of Liberty in other colonies. 'Twould soon become a favorite haunt for scarlet dragons marching north to put a lid on the belligerent rebel activities in Boston. Nolan intended to be nearby to monitor the migration of redcoats.

Nolan glanced sideways to see Laura absorbing the panoramic view that sprawled before her. After those first few hours of adjusting to life in the wilds, Laura had settled into the routine with amazing speed. From the streets of Boston to the aristocratic mansion on Beacon Hill and then into the backwoods, Laura Chandler had quickly adapted. She was a resilient survivalist, Nolan thought to himself. He admired that about her. Too bad he couldn't trust this enchanting female with his heart or his life.

"Is this our destination?" Laura questioned, appraising the rustic wayside inn.

"Aye. You will be cleaning the rented rooms and cooking for travelers while Coon Ashburn and I work the ferry and care for the stock."

"Cook and clean?" Laura repeated.

" 'Tis beneath your dignity, I'm sure, Lady Chandler," Nolan mocked as he reined his stallion down the hill. "But this is the wilderness. Everyone pulls his own weight out here."

If Nolan expected her to grouse about her designated chores she would prove she could handle any task he demanded of her. 'Twas a relief to know she wouldn't be confined like a condemned prisoner for the crimes this stubborn, muleheaded man believed she committed.

"Don't think you can poison my food and escape, either," Nolan added in afterthought. "Coon will track you down on my behalf."

"Not if I poison him, too," she flung back.

Nolan halted abruptly. He hadn't considered that.

Smiling impishly, her dark eyes dancing, Laura trotted past him. "I advise you to be especially nice to me, Mr. Ryder, if you know what's good for you."

Nolan snaked out a hand to grab her reins. "We

will both have to be especially nice to each other while Coon and incoming travelers are underfoot, *Mrs. Ryder*— or rather, Mr. and Mrs. *Ives.*"

Laura stared owlishly at him. Her mouth opened and closed, but no words passed her lips. 'Twas only the second time Nolan remembered seeing Laura struck speechless. The first, of course, had been the night Nolan emerged from his grave, nowhere near as dead as his headstone portrayed him to be.

"Ives?" she repeated.

"Aye," Nolan confirmed. "Until the furor dies down in Boston, you and I will pose as man and wife and assist Coon with his chores. According to reports— "

"The British are calling in reinforcements to control the rebels," Laura finished for him.

"And if you attempt to make contact with any of the troops ferried across the river— "

"I will be shot, bayonetted and hanged. Does that about cover it?"

"You forgot to mention tarred and feathered," Nolan grumbled. "And I do wish you would stop interrupting me. I am perfectly capable of issuing my own threats without your help. They lose their zing when you cut in to complete them for me."

The elfish smile evaporated from her lips as she met Nolan's suspicious silver gaze. "I did not betray you then and I will not betray you now."

Nolan steeled himself against the wave of tender sentiment that rippled through him. "That, my lady, still remains to be seen."

"I will expect a proper apology when you realize *I* was the one set up for treason," Laura declared. "Nothing less than having you down on both knees in humble regret will do, either."

When Laura trotted off, Nolan stared at her retreating back. Maybe she wasn't as guilty as he thought. Maybe . . .

Nolan inhaled a fortifying breath and cautioned himself against wavering in indecision. He wanted to believe Laura was innocent, but trust didn't come easily, especially when he was still nursing the wound she may have caused. Damnation, he wished he could make up his mind about Laura Chandler. As it was, the beguiling beauty was rubbing his emotions raw and leaving him adrift in a crosscurrent of conflicting beliefs.

Innocent . . .

Guilty . . .

Nolan wished the hell he knew for sure . . .

"As I live and breathe!" Coon Ashburn chuckled in astonishment when he recognized the midnight-haired man in doeskin. "Last time I saw you, you were headed back to civilization with that old codger on your heels . . ."

Coon's voice dried up when he caught sight of the second rider who was partially blocked by Nolan's massive frame. Sunlight gleamed in the long auburn tendrils like an encircling halo. "Who might this be? Yer guardian angel?"

"My wife," Nolan announced. "Laura, I want

you to meet Coon Ashburn. We crossed paths several times while I hunted and trapped beyond the mountains."

Laura gave the stout backwoodsman a sparkling smile. "My pleasure, sir."

"Nay, mine," Coon contradicted as he dragged his cap off his fuzzy red head and dropped into an exaggerated bow. His twinkling green eyes drifted to Nolan. "Prettier than a sunrise, she is. You've done well for yourself, son."

Nolan didn't respond, he merely swung from the saddle to assist Laura from her mount. "I've come to ask a favor, Coon."

"Name it. I still have my scalp, thanks to you and that blustering old codger you used to travel with."

Nolan cast Laura a quick glance before he shepherded Coon out of earshot. He still didn't trust Laura enough to let her be privy to this conversation.

"The Crown is mobilizing troops to curtail rebel activities in Boston," Nolan reported as he peered across the river.

"The first wave already passed here a few days ago," Coon confided. "The scarlet dragons marched through and nearly ate me out of house and home. Said 'twas my patriotic duty to His Brittanick Majesty to provide food and transport—for my countrymen."

Coon gave a disgusted snort. "You should've seen that high and mighty major who came prancin' in here on his pure white geldin'. Thought he was

God, or His brother at the very least. Major la-de-dah Stewart is likely to drown himself if it rains, what with his crooked nose stuck up so far up in the sky.''

Nolan felt every emotion inside him freeze like ice when memories assailed him. Isaac Stewart had whipped Nolan's back raw and tossed him in the stockade, when Nolan refused to lead his colonial militia into a death trap. Major Stewart had used the colonials as bait before sending in his company of regulars.

'Twas also Stewart who sent news to Ethan Ryder that his brother had perished on the battlefield. He had also taken excessive pleasure in reporting that Nolan had escaped the stockade where he awaited court-martial. Wouldn't that arrogant bastard be shocked out of his decorative uniform to see that Nolan had returned from the grave?

And wouldn't Nolan be in one hell of a fix if Stewart spotted him and had him arrested for breaking loose from the stockade almost three years earlier? Nolan could find himself in captivity, long after the French and Indian War ended. Stewart was the kind of man who held grudges, when his decisions were challenged and his orders defied. He was also a maniacal bigot who had no use for colonials, except as guinea pigs for battle.

Boston was going to be jumping alive with danger, Nolan predicted. 'Twas a stroke of luck that Ezra Beecham had left town before Major Stewart strutted in like the pompous peacock he was.

"Laura and I would like to pose as your assistants while monitoring the incoming troops and estimating the amount of weapons being hauled to Boston," Nolan said after a moment. "We will be using the assumed names of Nolan and Laura Ives."

"Request granted. I'm damned short-handed already. Havin' them lobsterbacks trouncin' through here is keepin' me busy and spoilin' my good disposition."

Nolan glanced across the river when he heard the clatter on the opposite bank. "Damnation, the Crown didn't waste much time sending up troops after the Stamp Act riots."

"Nay, and talk from passin' travelers has been buzzin' like a beehive," Coon replied. "More folks are sidin' with the Sons of Liberty by the day, joinin' in public protest. Does my heart good to see Americans speakin' up for themselves and standin' up for their rights. Those of us on the outposts of civilization have gotten partial to our freedom. We don't take kindly to havin' to ask His Royal Highness for permission to breathe."

When Coon strode off to ferry the waiting troops to the tavern, Nolan led the horses to the barn. Laura had already disappeared into the inn to appraise her new surroundings, but Nolan had no intention of leaving her to her own devices for extended periods of time. He stabled the horses in record time and made a beeline toward the inn.

When Nolan burst inside, he found Laura rummaging through the cupboards for ingredients to cook the evening meal. Nolan walked up behind her, startling her when he looped his arm around her waist. He pulled her back against him to drop a kiss to her bare shoulder.

"Your timing is terrible, my *beloved* husband," she murmured, her voice cracking in response to his amorous embrace.

"Is it?" His lips drifted up the swanlike column of her throat as his hand sketched the full swell of her breasts.

"Aye," she warbled.

"I came to warn you, my cherished bride, that you are to keep a respectable distance from the redcoats." Nolan shifted sideways to gauge her reaction to the command. "I should hate to call out one of His Majesty's finest for flirting with my new wife, not to mention what I would be inclined to do to my betraying wife."

"I don't know why you continue to doubt my loyalty when I only have eyes for you," she murmured, holding him captive with her hypnotic gaze.

Nolan would have sincerely liked to believe that she spoke the truth, but he knew Laura was simply playing the charade he had designed for her. He also had witnessed— on several occasions— the devastating effects this vibrant female had on those of the male persuasion. She radiated beauty and spirit like summer sunshine and men naturally gravitated toward her. Nolan couldn't risk letting his guard down for even a second. Laura might send word to Boston through one of her new admirers and Nolan would find himself forsaken all over again. 'Twas not a good time for Nolan to be dragged back to Boston in chains, not with Stewart ruling the military roost.

"Can you handle the cooking duties?" Nolan asked as he stepped away from tormenting temptation.

"Leave everything to me," Laura insisted with her customary confidence.

On that unsettling thought Nolan ventured outside to play his role as innkeeper. All the while he planned to tabulate the amount of provisions, ammunition and weapons being hauled north to curtail rioting in Boston. This influx of troops was going to cause even more animosity and conflict among the citizens, Nolan predicted. He wondered if the Crown realized that every attempt they made to crush rebel resistance was leading them one step closer to outright rebellion.

Twenty-two

Coon Ashburn stroked his salt-and-cayenne-pepper-colored whiskers and grinned in amusement as he watched Nolan hover around Laura while she served the hungry troops. Each time one of the soldiers stared overly long at the bewitching female, Nolan materialized at her side, looming over her captivated admirer like a threatening thundercloud.

When Nolan finally stopped prowling around the tavern long enough to prop himself against the wall, Coon was snickering wryly at him. "What do you find so entertaining?" Nolan demanded gruffly.

"You." Coon sipped his tankard of grog. "You've been hoverin' around yer pretty wife as if you were afraid one of the lobsterbacks was goin' to steal her away from you."

Nolan gnashed his teeth. He wasn't sure what had come over him the past hour. He told himself the reason he kept a close watch on that stunning female was to ensure she didn't charm one of the soldiers into helping her escape or relay a message to Peter Forbes. But that didn't quite explain this fierce need to let every male in the tavern know

Laura belonged to him. 'Twas the damnedest feeling Nolan had ever encountered.

"You know what yer problem is, *Mr. Ives?*" Coon murmured.

"I didn't realize I had one."

"Well, you do," Coon readily confirmed. " 'Tis that age-old male possessiveness at work. It provokes a man to go out of his way to let the rest of his kind know he's staked his claim on his woman."

Nolan muttered foully when one of the soldiers flashed Laura a gallant smile and brushed his shoulder against hers— accidentally on purpose. When Nolan pushed away from the wall, Coon grabbed his arm and yanked him back.

"Cool yer heels, son," Coon advised. "Yer wife seems perfectly capable of dodgin' passes."

Nolan willfully held his ground, watching Laura flit away from the overeager corporal. Damned cocky redcoats, Nolan thought begrudgingly. They all thought they could swagger into the colonies and take whatever they wanted, as if it were theirs by right of English birth. Not bloody damned likely . . . !

By the time another aggressive soldier openly flirted with Laura, Nolan had had all he could stand. He strode over to retrieve the bowl of biscuits and the pitcher of ale from Laura's hands. "You can start cleaning up the kitchen while I serve the men."

Laura's smile faltered when Nolan glared her into retreat. 'Twas obvious he thought she was trying to make contact with the British. Nolan was never going to trust her. Disheartened, Laura ambled off to put the kitchen in proper working order.

Blast it, what was it going to take to convince that obstinate, jackass of a man that she was a patriot, not a Tory. She was having as much success at convincing him of her political loyalties as she was in convincing him of her affection.

Laura inhaled a deep breath, surveyed the impractically arranged kitchen and set to work. If nothing else, she would vent her frustration by setting the kitchen to rights. The place could use some orderliness.

"I suppose you've heard about the fuss the Bostonians put up about the Quartering Act and Stamp Act," Captain Taylor commented as Nolan filled his mug of ale.

"Aye, a few travelers have passed through, keeping us updated."

"Those Sons of Liberty are becoming a real nuisance."

So are the British, Nolan silently replied. It took considerable restraint not to dump the pitcher of ale on the captain's bewigged head when he eased back in his chair and flicked his wrist, indicating Nolan was to remove his plate.

"We'll see how belligerent those bumpkins are when we seal them off and refuse to let them import or export supplies. They'll be crawling to headquarters, begging to be taken back into the Crown's good graces."

Nolan made a mental note to establish relay stations in the backwoods to haul supplies into Boston, should the port be blockaded. These arrogant redcoats were not going to crush rebel resistance, he vowed determinedly.

By the time Nolan made the rounds, serving drinks to all three tables of pompous soldiers, his disposition was sour as curds and whey. Was it any wonder America had such difficulty stomaching their high-handed British cousins? Every bloody one of them behaved as if colonials were second-class citizens— the ignorant, unruly masses who had been shipped to America to keep British bloodlines pure. Nolan would dearly love to tell Captain Taylor and his haughty underlings where they could stash their pedigrees . . .

Nolan halted at the kitchen door, his eyes bulging from their sockets. To his astounded amazement Laura had washed, dried and returned the cooking utensils to the cupboards. She had rearranged shelves and wiped away every speck of dust that had collected— some of which had undoubtedly arrived with Coon. The room was spotless! Nolan was impressed.

Laura wheeled around to see Nolan taking inventory of the room. "I suppose you have an objection to the way I cleaned up, too," she grumbled defensively.

Nolan strolled over to set the empty bowls and pitchers beside the washtub. "Nay, I'm only surprised."

"Why? Because I spent the past few years in the

lap of luxury? Well, I'm here to inform you that I did my time in the streets and back alleys, living in places a rat would turn up its nose at. But I never failed to keep my lowly quarters as clean and orderly as possible, because there simply was not enough living space to be messy!"

Nolan chuckled at her belligerent outburst. "Did I say a word?"

Laura scooped up the bowl and scrubbed it hard. "You hardly need to. Looming behind me every time I so much as answer a soldier's question assures me I'm not trusted. Watching you appraise the kitchen indicates you didn't expect me to be the least bit industrious."

"I'm only trying to protect myself," Nolan assured here. "If the troops discover the Midnight Rider is in their midst, I could find myself in a most vulnerable situation."

Laura set her back teeth and spun around. "How many times do I have to tell you that I'm not one of *them*?" she hissed.

Nolan braced his arms on either side of the counter, pinning her in front of him, his breath stinging her cheek with its harshness. "You'll have to tell me as many times as it takes for me to actually believe it."

The feel of Nolan's powerfully built body pressing against hers triggered sensations too powerful to ignore. Laura stared up into those glittering mercury eyes, willing Nolan to believe her, willing him to trust her with his life as well as his heart.

"There is no other man alive who I desire the

way I desire you, Nolan. I would love you long and well if you would let me, but I can see that I'll have to make some drastic sacrifice to convince you that I didn't betray you then and won't betray you now."

"Laura—" Nolan expelled a frustrated breath when she ducked under his arms and scuttled off.

Hell and damnation, that lovely witch could look a man straight in the eye and almost have him believing every word she said. But Nolan knew better . . . At least he thought he did.

Midnight's lady was Midnight's curse. If he let himself believe those soft words of affection and devotion, if he let his guard down for even a split second, Laura could destroy him.

Peter Forbes glanced up from his desk at headquarters to see a young corporal standing at attention.

"Captain Milbourne said you were the man I should contact, sir."

Peter stared at the poster the frizzy-haired soldier clutched in his hand.

" 'Tis about the reward for information—"

Peter leaped to his feet, causing the corporal to step back apace. "You have seen Laura Chandler?"

The soldier frowned. "Aye, I believe so. The sketch resembles the lady I met. But the name was Laura Ives."

"Where did you meet her? Philadelphia?"

"Nay, sir, she was working as a serving maid at

a ferry crossing southwest of Boston," the corporal reported. "I saw her when my unit came up from New York with Captain Taylor."

"How far south?" Peter snapped back. He had the feeling Laura had changed her name and moved her area of operation south to monitor incoming troops and tamper with supplies— and no telling what else!

"At least eighty miles southwest, sir," the boy-faced soldier replied. "The place is called Tall Oaks Ferry."

"If your information is correct you will be well compensated." Peter wheeled toward his desk to grab his tricorn hat, angrily jerking it down on his head. "Tell Captain Taylor to check his supplies carefully."

The corporal blinked. "Sir?"

"The lady is a spy. She makes it her business to wheedle information from unsuspecting soldiers and she very likely could have tampered with your ammunition and weapons. I wouldn't be surprised to learn the firing pins are mysteriously missing and that your gunpowder is so wet it sets in clumps."

"But there must be some mistake," the corporal objected. "She is a very dignified lady who supports the British army's position in America. She told me so herself."

Peter whirled back around to scoff at the naive soldier, seeing the reflection of his own foolishness mirrored in the man's disbelieving expression. "The lady has been playing a masquerade to make buffoons of you and your unit."

With that, Peter stalked out to gather a company of soldiers to accompany him south. He wasn't wasting even a minute with delays. Laura could be feeding information through the rebel network and destroying all the British provisions she could get her hands on.

'Twas going to be extremely gratifying to tote Laura Chandler back to Boston, Peter thought spitefully. She would pay for making him look the imbecile more times than he cared to count.

Ethan Ryder stared at the reward poster in stunned amazement. Laura Chandler was being charged with treason against the Crown? Sweet mercy, the price on her head equaled the Midnight Rider's. What in the name of heaven was going on here? Could Laura be a double agent who was passing information for both the rebels and the Tories? Had the British grown suspicious when she disappeared?

Frowning ponderously, Ethan strode down the deserted street to pull down another poster hanging beside the street lamp. It looked as though he would have to pay Miriam Peabody another late-night visit to ascertain what she knew about this unexpected twist and tangle of events.

Several hours later, Ethan ascended the back steps of Peabody mansion. This time he was careful to avoid the table he had stumbled over during his first visit. He found Miriam sleeping soundly in her alcove bed and he gently jostled her awake.

Miriam sighed in relief when she spied the darkly clad silhouette hovering over her. "Thank God you're back! I have been worried sick about Laura. I don't have a clue how to get in touch with her to warn her she is wanted for treason."

Ethan eased down on the chair near the bed. "I need some information, madam. Do you know why the posters have been hung all over town?"

" 'Twas all Mercy Reed's fault," Miriam muttered resentfully. "That little snitch saw Laura sneaking in and out of the house in her urchin's garb and tattled to Lieutenant Forbes who—!"

"Sh-sh."

Miriam waved off Ethan's attempt to shush her. "We don't have to fear being overheard. I sold Mercy's indentureship to the baker on Kings Street," she informed him with grand satisfaction. "That chit will have to work for a change. Should be a new experience for her, too, curse her lazy hide."

"What about Lieutenant Forbes?" Ethan wanted to know. "Is he still on duty?"

"Nay, and he isn't here, either. Peter left me a note yesterday, indicating he was on an assignment that would keep him away from Boston for a few days."

"Away from Boston?" Ethan repeated warily. "Did he say exactly where he was going?"

"Nay, only that he was leaving. I was away from

the house, making arrangements for Mercy to become the baker's bondswoman."

Ethan chose his words carefully. "I know you are immensely fond of Laura, but has she done anything that might lead you to believe she is actually working for the Crown rather than for the rebels?"

Miriam puffed up with indignation. "What kind of ridiculous question is that?" she sniffed. "The King's men put a price on her head, didn't they? And if you think Laura harbors some fond affection for Lieutenant Forbes you are sorely mistaken. The man chattered to her like a magpie and she passed along what she learned from him through rebel channels. Mercy Reed betrayed Laura because that spiteful little snip was jealous. The girl wants Peter Forbes all to herself!"

Ethan inwardly groaned. He didn't have a clue how news of the Midnight Rider's rendezvous with the express riders had reached British ears in time to arrange the ambush, but he had the unmistakable feeling that his brother had wrongly accused Laura of serving him up to the Crown. At the moment, Laura was in more danger than the Midnight Rider himself. Yet, the connection between them would evolve into double disaster!

"Is Laura all right? Just where the devil is she?" Miriam wanted to know.

"I'm sorry, madam, I still cannot reveal her whereabouts."

Miriam gave an unladylike snort. "I'm concerned about Laura and I'm beginning to think I'm the only one who is. Is this the way you repay devoted agents when they are found out? Do you make a habit of abandoning them? Well, I am not sure I want to finance a cause that turns its back on loyal crusaders when trouble breaks out. Now tell me where Laura is this instant!"

Ethan smiled faintly at the dowager's spunk. He wondered if Laura's influence had made Miriam so determined, or if the old girl had simply been born that way.

"At last report, Laura was serving as an attendant at an inn near a ferry crossing, monitoring the influx of British troops," he reported.

Miriam flounced back on her pillow. "I pray Peter's mysterious assignment has naught to do with Laura's whereabouts. The man is excessively bitter about being played the fool. Peter found Laura's homespun garb and a cape stashed in the bottom drawer. He suspects the cloak belongs to the Patriot Rider and that Laura is his accomplice. Considering the fierce grudge Peter harbors, I shudder to think what he will do to Laura if he catches her."

Ethan grimaced at the information, but he did his best to reassure the concerned dowager. "Don't worry, madam. We will have Laura removed from the inn immediately."

"Remove her to where?" Miriam grumbled in question. "She is no longer safe in Boston. Society has scorned her and the Crown wants her head on a platter. Hasn't that poor child suffered enough in one lifetime? She was raised on the streets without a family to protect and provide for her. And worse, her dearest friend was— "

Miriam clamped her mouth shut and turned narrowed hazel eyes on Ethan's shadowed profile. "The instant you relocate Laura to a safer location I demand to know where she is. If she needs funds then I will provide them. I only hope there is some place on this continent she can go without having the scarlet dragons breathing down her neck!"

In grim resignation, Ethan made his way out of the darkened house. A sense of impending doom hung over him like a gray fog. Nolan's secret identity might protect him from detection, but Laura was exceptionally vulnerable. If the King's men got hold of her before Ethan could send a courier to warn Nolan, 'twas no telling what kind of complications might develop.

Ethan aimed himself toward Spark McRae's cabin. The crusty frontiersman knew his way around the backwoods as well as Nolan did. If anyone could make tracks to reach Tall Oaks Ferry before disaster struck, Spark could do it.

Ethan prayed for time he wasn't sure he had. If Peter Forbes had already charged off to apprehend Laura . . .

Damnation, Ethan thought as he reversed direction. He didn't have time to tramp out to the secluded cottage. The carrier pigeons would have to deliver the message to Spark— air mail.

'Twas a pity Nolan hadn't taken a few pigeons with him to Tall Oaks Ferry. This was one message that needed to be delivered immediately. Calamity was about to strike and Ethan wasn't sure there was a blessed thing he could do to stop it.

Twenty-three

Nolan leaned back against the bedroom door, an amused smile hovering on his lips. For the third time in two weeks he watched Laura rearrange the furniture in the chamber they shared. One night Nolan had gone to bed facing south. Two evenings later he was facing west. Now he would be facing north. Laura also insisted on having the curtains in the room pulled back to allow sunlight to pour inside. She didn't seem to like confinement any more than Nolan did.

He hadn't realized Laura shared the same penchant for change, until they had begun living in each other's pockets. The woman reminded him so much of himself with her quirks of personality that it astounded him.

For more than two weeks Nolan had wavered back and forth like a clock pendulum, questioning Laura's guilt— and the possibility of her innocence. And all the while that he was trying to sort out his emotions and convictions, he was discovering Laura's amusing idiosyncrasies, feeling oddly content with their masquerade of husband and wife. It felt . . . natural . . . right . . .

Don't let yourself be lured into a false sense of security and become the victim of another deceptive trap, came that suspicious voice from within.

Perhaps she was innocent of treachery and you jumped to the wrong conclusion, the voice of his conscience parried.

And perhaps she wasn't innocent at all . . .

Nolan sighed heavily and peeled off his shirt. He had vowed to enjoy the pleasures this doe-eyed beauty could provide while on this assignment. He had refused to let vulnerable emotion intervene. He had conditioned himself to regard Laura as a spy and he had kept a watchful eye on her each time a unit of soldiers marched to the inn. If Laura had passed along information, she had been incredibly clever and discreet. But then, considering her pickpocketing skills, Nolan couldn't be absolutely certain whether or not she had relayed any messages. He supposed he would only know for sure when he found himself captured and hauled to Boston for a quick trial . . . and an even quicker hanging . . .

"Thinking suspicious thoughts again, Nolan?" Laura questioned when she saw him looming in the doorway. "I dearly would like to climb into bed—just one night—without having you stare at me as if you expected me to bury a dagger in your back while you slept."

Nolan doused the lantern and shed his breeches. He didn't have time for a lengthy debate with Laura, only enough time to catch a cat nap before trotting out to the British encampment to relieve the troops of a portion of their military supplies.

With each unit that passed by, Nolan had managed to swipe several muskets and ammunition to donate to secret militias of minutemen. He had also found time to tamper with firing pins and add sand to kegs of gunpowder. When time and the threat of discovery prevented him from sanding ammunition, Nolan dug into the center of the ammunition kegs and poured in water.

At a glance, the gunpowder appeared untouched. But beneath the top layer was a glob of useless ammunition. By the time the British discovered their provisions had been sabotaged, they wouldn't know how or when the damage had been done. The supplies would be stacked in British storehouses for emergencies. And when the emergency came, the military depots would be filled with useless ammunition and weapons . . .

Nolan's wandering thoughts trailed off while he watched Laura disrobe in a spotlight of moonbeams. He swore she was tormenting him on purpose, drawing him even deeper beneath her spell.

For more than two weeks Nolan had gone to bed wanting Laura like a mindless addiction and had awakened in the same aroused condition. He was honestly beginning to wonder if he was ever going to tire of this lovely sorceress.

By now the newness of their shared passion should have worn off. Nolan should have experienced that familiar sense of restlessness that had followed like his own shadow for as long as he could remember. But the damnable truth was his restlessness came from not having Laura in his arms. Because of her, he had become as content to remain in one spot as a potted plant!

When Laura eased down beside Nolan, treating him to whispering kisses, he felt himself melt in the warm flood of desire she so easily stirred in him. Reaching out to Laura had become an instinctive reflex. These days, she was only a touch away, and she offered no resistance to the passion they aroused in each other. She accepted it, matched him caress for caress, took him with her to blissful oblivion and left him hopelessly satisfied in the silky circle of her arms.

The mere memory was enough to make Nolan groan in anticipated pleasure. He had planned to be away from the inn for at least two full days, maybe more. The last unit of soldiers who tramped past were hauling cannons, not to mention an exceptionally large supply of ammunition. Nolan intended to strike when the soldiers were a day's ride from the inn. This time the wagons themselves would become his targets. When the Crown's men tried to ford the river to the north, the back wheels of the wagons would tumble from their axles, soaking the weapons and ammunition with water.

But before Nolan trotted off into the darkness, he was going to make one more delicious memory to sustain him. He was going to leave his brand of passion on Laura so that she couldn't think of betraying him, of betraying the fragile bond between them. He would hear those soft words she had whispered to him that night in the wilderness, he vowed to himself as he explored her responsive flesh. And this time, she would mean them, every affectionate word she spoke . . .

Nolan became the epitome of gentleness as he returned her caressing touch, giving as tenderly as he was given. He brought Laura to one climactic peak and then another, relishing the pleasure that making love to her aroused in him.

"Nolan, you're tormenting me beyond bearing," Laura gasped.

"Am I?" He watched passion claim her moon-drenched features as he stroked her intimately, feeling her shimmering around his fingertips.

"Come here . . . please," she breathed raggedly. "I need you desperately . . ."

His lithe body glided over hers, his head dipping down to hover scant inches from her parted lips. "How much, Laura? For how long . . . ?"

His voice trailed off when she arched toward him in eager abandon. Nolan felt the heated rush of uncontrollable passion sweep through him like floodwaters. He wanted to hear Laura say she had well and truly fallen in love with him, that her loyalty would be to him— despite the past, despite everything. He wanted to believe in her, to trust her . . . because she mattered— too much.

When he felt the dewy warmth of her body consuming him, Nolan couldn't spare the breath to demand her confession of love. Holding his ravenous needs in check required every ounce of willpower and strength he possessed. He wanted to devour

her, to bury himself so deeply within her that they
would become more than just the same flesh, but
rather the same spirit. He wanted to become so
much a part of her that if she were to betray him
she would be betraying herself.

Desire roiled inside Nolan when Laura met each
driving thrust, clinging to him in a world of tu-
multuous sensations. In this far-flung parallel of
time and space Nolan fought no mental tug-of-war
over Laura's guilt or innocence. 'Twas only the two
of them chasing rainbows and gliding past glittering stars. 'Twas here in this splendorous universe
that Nolan could let go with his heart and respond
without restraint. These intimate moments were all
that kept him from driving himself insane, wanting
to believe her cries of innocence and afraid to trust
what cynical suspicion could not accept.

A long time later, when passion had run its fiery
course, Laura reached up to trace the craggy features of Nolan's face. If there was any doubt about
her affection for him before, there certainly was
none now. She and Nolan had lain side by side
each night, like man and wife. They had worked
together during the days and she had come to admire all he represented, all he was. She had
watched him covetously, fascinated with each man-
nerism, each smile she managed to draw from him.

Laura knew that Nolan refused to accept her
confession of love as truth, but she could no more
refrain from speaking of her love for him than she
could halt the passage of time. Nolan was the exception to her previous theories about men. He

had shown her the difference between brutal force and tender lovemaking and she was hopelessly devoted to him.

Until Nolan came along, Laura believed sex provided no pleasure for a woman, only overwhelming pain and humble submission. Because Martha Winfield had known only a man's savage possession, Laura had lived with false assumptions. But this one remarkable man, this daredevil who risked his life to further the patriot cause, had become essential to Laura's happiness. He had given her life new purpose, new perspective.

"I don't *think* I love you, Nolan," she whispered softly. "I *know* I love you."

Nolan willed himself not to be affected by the words, even though he had longed to hear them. It tormented him to no end to realize how much he wanted to believe her—and still couldn't.

"You're absolutely sure?" he asked in a guarded tone.

"Aye, very sure."

"Sure enough to still be here when I get back?"

Laura lifted her head, sending a tumble of auburn curls cascading over his broad chest. "Get back from where?"

"The soldiers who marched through here yesterday were packing entirely too many supplies. I thought I should relieve them of their excessive load before they turn their cannons on unruly Bostonians."

"Please don't go," Laura pleaded as she nestled

beside him. " 'Tis too dangerous and there are too many of them. Stay here with me."

"I can't."

"Then I'll go with you," Laura insisted.

"Nay, you will stay here with Coon," he ordered sternly. "I plan to set a fast pace, and an even faster retreat."

When Laura fell silent, Nolan dropped a kiss on her petal-soft lips. This was to be the second test of her loyalty, he reminded himself. If she awaited his return with open arms, Nolan could let himself believe 'twas only accidental coincidence that allowed the redcoats to ambush him.

More than two weeks had elapsed since he and Laura had set up housekeeping at the inn. No British patrol had come charging down from the north to apprehend him. As far as he could tell, his identity was still a well-kept secret . . .

"Nolan?" Laura murmured, longing to convince him of her own devotion. "I think 'tis time for you to know why I was following Geoffrey Spradlin."

"What brought that on?" Nolan pried open one eye and glanced down at the tangle of curly hair that splayed across his chest.

"I'm sure you thought he was my secret contact, but 'twas not the case at all."

"Nay?" Nolan felt suspicion rising from the depths of his mind. This could be a deceptive ploy and he had to be cautious about believing whatever Laura had to say. "Then what was your connection with Geoffrey Spradlin?"

Laura traced her fingers across his collarbone

and trailed a caressing hand down the corded tendons of his mended arm. "Do you remember the grave site where I placed flowers?"

"Aye, 'twas Martha Winfield's eternal resting place." Nolan couldn't fathom where this quiet confession was leading, but he waited, wavering among suspicion, curiosity and half-trust.

"Martha Winfield was like my little sister," Laura quietly confided. "We shared a shack on the back streets of Boston, until Miriam rescued me from a near-mauling by a drunken soldier and took me into her home."

"Geoffrey Spradlin tried to molest you?" Nolan muttered in question.

"Aye, but 'twas the night you pulled me from the upturned carriage," she corrected. "I tried to lure him out, hoping to expose him for the brutal savage he was."

Nolan frowned, bemused. "I think you should begin at the beginning. I'm not following you."

Laura inhaled a deep breath and organized her thoughts. "When Miriam took me in and provided me with elegant gowns, the finest tutors and five course meals, Martha decided to turn to . . ." She squeezed back the tormented memories and forced herself to continue. "Martha turned to prostitution to support herself. She worked in the brothel we accidentally burned down . . . 'Twas Geoffrey who beat her to death for refusing to participate in his perverted sexual orgies. 'Twas my intent to see that he didn't repeat his crime with some other unsus-

pecting victim and to see him severely punished
for his brutality."

Now Nolan was beginning to understand why
Laura had kept such close surveillance on that
scoundrel. She had tried to protect others from
Geoffrey's vicious temper and drunken rages. The
thought of Laura using herself as bait to expose
Geoffrey's violent tendencies sent an icy chill down
Nolan's backbone. If he hadn't happened along
that night, Laura could have died trying to seek
revenge on that bastard!

"You should have let the authorities deal with
Geoffrey rather than risking your life," Nolan
chastised her.

Laura lifted her head to meet his disapproving
scowl. "You know how the so-called British authorities handle complaints from colonists. Judge Clover
dismissed the case for supposed lack of evidence.
But the fact was that he considered Martha to be
nothing but a lowly prostitute from colonial streets.
Her passing was of little consequence to him, but
'twas a great tragedy for me."

Laura inhaled a purifying breath and battled
down her resentment. "After Martha was attacked
and beaten, she sent one of the other women from
the brothel with a message for me. When I arrived,
Martha barely had enough strength to speak. I demanded to know who was responsible. She died
with Geoffrey's name on her lips, and I didn't even
have the chance to tell her how much I cared about
her before she collapsed in my arms."

Laura blinked back the mist of tears that clouded

her eyes and forced herself to continue. "I had been granted all the conveniences life could provide and Martha had nothing but poverty and a man's brutality. And 'tis because of Geoffrey that I know I love you."

Nolan frowned at her peculiar logic. "I don't think I appreciate having my name linked to that murdering bastard."

Laura shook her head and sighed. She had jumbled the explanation, because of the turmoil of emotion swirling inside her. She tried again. "Before you came along, I thought all men delighted in using their overpowering strength to take what they wanted from women. My own unpleasant experiences had taught me what Martha's ordeal confirmed."

A rueful smile trailed across her lips as she peered up at Nolan, willing him to believe her. "I learned what love *wasn't* long ago, and I vowed never to let a man dominate my life, never to find myself treated the way Martha had been treated. But then you came along, and even though I believed you to be a Tory, you drew me against my will. I took the risk without judging who you were. And when I discovered you rode for liberty, my admiration for you surpassed all bounds. Because of what you are, because of what you represent, I love you. Please believe that, Nolan, for 'tis true . . ."

When Laura cuddled up beside him, Nolan felt his cynical defenses and firm resolve melt like a snowbank in July. He promised himself that he would give Laura the benefit of the doubt when he returned from his mission. They would make a fresh new start, Nolan decided. Laura had taken him into her confidence, sharing her private feelings and the unpleasant torments of her past. She *did* care, Nolan told himself. 'Twas not an act. She had his best interest at heart.

Nolan drifted off to sleep, cradling Laura in his arms. If she was waiting his return, he would know he had wrongly misjudged her. Nolan wanted to believe the best, not the worst. For the first time in his life, he wanted to open his heart and enjoy the tender emotions Laura had summoned from him. He only hoped that trusting her wouldn't become the most dangerous mistake he ever made . . .

Because 'twould probably be the last mistake Nolan lived to make . . .

Twenty-four

Spark McRae nudged his mare into a canter. The urgency of the message he had received from Ethan—via the homing pigeon—had sent trickles of alarm down Spark's spine. He couldn't imagine what had happened to put Ethan in a state of alert. He supposed he would find out soon enough, he mused, when he saw Ethan scurry from the wayside inn situated on the outskirts of town.

"What took you so long?" Ethan muttered as he watched the stout backwoodsman step from the stirrup.

"I came as soon as I received word," Spark assured him. "What's the problem?"

Ethan motioned for Spark to follow him along the secluded path that led down to the drinking well. He fished the poster from his pocket and handed it to Spark. "Lieutenant Forbes put a reward on Laura's head," he announced abruptly. "She is a fugitive of the Crown."

Spark blinked in disbelief when he saw Laura's likeness sketched on the poster. A hefty reward was being offered for information leading to her arrest. "I thought she was one of them."

"And I kept telling you and Nolan that she was one of us," Ethan muttered. "We have to get word to Nolan immediately. If he decides to bring Laura back to Boston, he'll be serving her up to the British, and his association with her could arouse the kind of suspicion he doesn't need. If the incoming soldiers happen to recognize her and convey the information to Lieutenant Forbes, he could apprehend her. I have received news that Forbes has left town. He could be on his way to Tall Oaks Ferry at this very moment. You've got to warn Nolan before trouble lands on his doorstep."

Nodding grimly, Spark tucked the wanted poster in his pocket.

"I've brought along food, supplies and a bedroll," Ethan said as he gestured toward the saddlebags he had stashed near the well.

Without another word Spark scooped up the supplies and mentally kicked himself for condemning Laura Chandler without solid proof.

Spark piled onto his horse and nodded farewell to Ethan. He trotted away, mulling over the dismal possibilities of what might happen if he didn't reach Tall Oaks Ferry in time to inform Nolan. Spark decided to ride hard and fret later. With any luck, his shortcut through the timbers would allow him to warn Nolan before Forbes showed up.

With that wanted poster hanging all over town, 'twas little wonder Laura had been spotted, Spark thought. Scads of British troops were marching past the ferry by the week. No man with eyes in his head would forget meeting a woman as lovely and vibrant as Laura Chandler.

Spark ducked under the overhanging tree limbs and nudged his mare in the flanks, riding southwest like a house afire. He had to get word to Nolan— and quickly— or else . . .

Spark didn't bother contemplating the consequences. They were too unpleasant to bear thinking about . . .

Nolan grabbed his rifle and knife and then gratefully accepted the sack of food Coon Ashburn provided for him.

"Keep a close eye on my wife," Nolan requested. "I should only be gone two days at the most."

"Good, that will only give the lass time to rearrange the tables in the tavern once," Coon snickered.

Nolan grinned in amusement. "She's as bad about changing things as I am."

"Worse," Coon insisted as he walked Nolan to the door. "But I don't mind. She has this place polished to a shine. You found yerself a woman who suits you well. A perfect match, if you ask me."

Nolan glanced toward the closed bedroom door, remembering the unrivaled passion he and Laura had shared before he slipped away. "Aye, she suits me exceptionally well," he murmured, stepping outside to greet the first rays of dawn.

Inhaling a deep breath, Nolan focused his concentration on his mission. He couldn't afford any distractions, not with two dozen redcoats standing guard over military provisions and weapons. Nolan rode away, forcing himself not to glance at the window, willing Laura to still be there when he got back. She would be, he convinced himself. Laura hadn't wanted him to leave her. Didn't that count for something? She had even volunteered to accompany him, despite the possible dangers. Her confessions of love were honest and sincere. She would be awaiting his return and they would start over again.

No more suspicions, Nolan promised. No more mistrust . . .

Nolan crouched down in the underbrush to survey the British camp situated on the river's floodplain. Darkness had descended and the unsuspecting soldiers were sprawled around the central campfire, taking their leisure over jugs of ale. Nolan took careful inventory of the wagons lined up on the far side of the river. From all indication, the troops had arrived too late in the evening to float the dismantled cannons across the water.

A devilish smile bordered his lips. The ammunition and weapons bound for Boston were not going to arrive in proper working condition, not if he had anything to do with it.

Retracing his steps, Nolan then circled toward the picket line of horses. He inserted stones in the frog of the hooves, giving the impression the mounts had turned up lame—just in case he was discovered and a patrol was sent to apprehend him.

Once the British bedded down for the night, Nolan retrieved his knife and slit the leather straps on the harnesses, bridles and saddles. After he had tampered with the tack, he crawled beneath the unattended wagons to loosen the hubs of the wheels.

Mission accomplished, Nolan buried himself in the underbrush to catch a few hours sleep before the British bugle sounded revelry. From the shelter of the weeds, Nolan watched the redcoats stir like overturned June bugs. After the troops downed their breakfast they strode off to saddle their mounts. The soldiers grumbled and cursed when they noticed several of their mounts were limping.

The comedy of errors had only begun, Nolan mused as he watched the soldiers hitch the teams of mules to the wagons. In midstream, under the strain of pulling heavily laden wagons, the harnesses snapped in two. Wheels wobbled and splashed into the water. Cannon barrels slid from the wagon beds. A raft of curses rose over the river like a black fog. Nolan bit back a chuckle when the redcoats floundered to control their horses with broken reins. Saddle cinches snapped, catapulting the lobsterbacks into the river where Nolan thought they belonged.

By the time the officers had the chaos under control, the troops were several hours behind schedule. A pity, Nolan thought as he left the redcoats to the impossible task of undoing the damage he had done. If the British tried to lay siege to Boston with firepower, they would find themselves battling with rusty cannons and wet ammunition.

In amused satisfaction, Nolan reined his stallion in the direction he had come. Unfortunately, his good mood lasted only half an hour. When he spotted the four-man patrol racing southward, his lips curled in a furious snarl.

Leading the pack of scarlet dragons was none other than Lieutenant Peter Forbes.

Nolan didn't need to be a genius to figure out that Laura had cleverly managed to relay a message to Forbes and summon him to Tall Oaks Ferry. That conniving little witch! While she was plying him with dimpled smiles, empty phrases of love and prefabricated secret confessions about her past, she had been biding her time until Peter arrived to place Nolan under arrest.

No wonder Laura hadn't wanted Nolan to leave the inn. She was expecting Peter and his reinforcements to arrive at any time. Her insistence on traveling with Nolan, when he refused to abort this mission, was undoubtedly her sly attempt to alert Peter to the unexpected change of plans.

Damn her, Nolan silently cursed as he watched Lieutenant Forbes consult with the commander of the convoy. Nolan didn't wait around to watch Peter and his men assist with wagon repairs. He made a beeline for the protection of the dense timber. There was no way in hell he was going to return to the ferry. Laura may damned well have managed to be rescued by her lovesick lieutenant, but she wasn't going to collect the reward on the Midnight Rider's head!

A growl of pure rage rumbled through Nolan's chest. He zigzagged through the trees, hounded by an excruciating emotion that rose from deep inside him and shot through his tormented soul like a piercing arrow. Fury channeled through every taut nerve until he was quivering in outrage. Jaw clenched, silver eyes blazing, his expression hard as stone, Nolan hissed profane curses to Laura's name.

No physical pain could compare to the incredible sense of hurt that ate at Nolan's heart. He had let his guard down and had come to care for Laura. But all along, she had been playing another of her deceptive charades for his benefit. It had been a carefully calculated act, and she had set him up for another perilous fall.

Laura stepped onto the back stoop to call to the critters Coon had taken as pets. She didn't mind the squirrels and the raccoon who scurried from the bushes to feast on the grain she sprinkled on the ground. 'Twas the beady-eyed, mangy possum lumbering forward to retrieve its treat that Laura failed to appreciate. In her opinion, that particular creature was the ugliest animal ever to walk the earth. But Coon was exceptionally fond of all his critters. He spoke to them as if they were human.

Laura supposed 'twas only natural for a man who had spent most of his life roaming the wilderness to take up with animals. She should be thankful Coon didn't have a pet bear that showed up to be fed . . .

The sound of approaching riders prompted Laura to scurry back to the kitchen. Whoever was about to arrive had perfectly timed breakfast. Laura had placed biscuits in the oven before venturing out to feed Coon's pets.

Laura had just removed the biscuits from the oven when footsteps pelted against the stoop. The door crashed against the wall and Laura's welcoming smile evaporated when she was greeted by four bayonets and four loaded muskets. Sizzling blue eyes burned over her with loathing contempt, and Laura instinctively shrank back a step.

"Peter? What are you doing here?" she chirped.

His only response was a menacing growl. Peter had been harboring resentful fury for so long that he wanted to strangle this cunning spy on sight. He nobly restrained himself from doing his worst—but with extreme effort.

"You are under arrest for treason," he gritted out.

"Treason?" Laura looked properly startled.

"Don't pretend you don't know what I'm talking about, damn you," Peter snarled. "I have a credible witness who is ready to testify to your devious activities. Never doubt that you will be tried, convicted and punished—posthaste."

Coon had returned from tending the livestock in the barn and entered the back door in time to see Peter storm across the tavern to clamp his hand around Laura's forearm. "What's goin' on here?"

Peter glared down his aristocratic nose at the whisker-faced backwoodsman. "Your serving maid is under arrest for blasphemous crimes against the Crown. She is a rebel spy who has been wheedling information from soldiers en route to Boston and is also an accomplice to the Midnight Rider."

Coon let loose with a loud snort. "Lieutenant, you've obviously been out in the sun too long. This lass happens to be—"

"He's right," Laura had no choice but to confess before Coon accidentally incriminated Nolan. "I was working as a spy and I have been relaying information about British forces and provisions while working here."

Coon's jaw dangled on its hinges. He knew, of course, that Laura and Nolan were promoting the patriot cause, but he was astounded that she had owned up to the charge of treason. The discreet glances she flashed warned Coon to say no more than necessary. He supposed she was trying to protect him and prevent him from being dragged to Boston with her.

Peter turned his disdainful glower on Laura. "Your housemaid saw a cloaked guest sneaking into the Peabody mansion on two occasions," he took excessive satisfaction in informing her. "I found the black cape, along with your urchin's disguise. Before I'm through with you, I will have the name of the mysterious rabble-rouser and your fellow agents. You and your treasonous nest of rebels will all answer for your crimes!"

Laura stared Peter squarely in the eye and smiled in open defiance. "I am no one's accomplice. *I* am the Midnight Rider."

The other three soldiers gasped in unison.

Peter scowled at her.

Coon sat down before he fell down.

"You can hardly expect me to believe you after you have deceived me— so thoroughly and so often," Peter snorted.

"Nay?" Laura challenged. "And just how many sightings of the Midnight Rider have been reported since I left Boston?"

She had stumped him with that one. Oddly enough, there had been no sightings of the Phantom Rebel since Laura disappeared from town.

"Do you honestly think I am incapable of leading His Majesty's men on a merry chase when I found it simple to deceive you?" she purposely taunted him.

Peter glowered at her. His fingers dug into her arm. "Nay, I suppose— "

"And you of all people know I am adept at handling a variety of weapons," she reminded him. "Haven't you ever wondered why I felt the need to practice my skills with pistols and arrows?"

Peter floundered, mentally counting the number of times he had seen Laura taking target practice with an assortment of weapons. He had simply considered her to be eccentric, adventurous and unconventional. He never dreamed she had a special use for all those weapons!

"I— "

Laura refused to let Peter squeeze more than one word in edgewise. She had to protect Nolan's identity by convincing Peter that she was the Midnight Rider.

"Why do you think 'twas so easy for me to change disguises and escape your patrols?"

Peter's gaze narrowed. "Just how *did* you escape when my men and I followed you into the graveyard?"

Laura smiled mischievously at him. "Fact is that one of your men came very close to discovering my hiding place the night of the ambush. I buried myself in the thick grass a good distance away from the grove of trees. If you hadn't called off the search when you did, I would have been apprehended a month ago."

Peter choked on his breath when Laura accurately described the search he had ordered. Nothing she had said previously had convinced him as thoroughly as that detailed account.

Rekindled fury and indignation bubbled through Peter's veins. Swearing under his breath, he jerked Laura toward him and stuck his scowling face in front of hers. "Don't delude yourself into thinking that just because you are a woman you will escape punishment for high treason. Your rebel friends will watch you be shipped off to England to be hung!"

"And you will invite another riot if you carry out that threat," Laura prophesied. "The destruction of the lieutenant governor's home and his personal property will be nothing in comparison to the forthcoming devastation."

"We shall see about that," Peter sneered.

In dumbstruck bewilderment Coon watched the outraged lieutenant tow Laura out the door. Coon remained glued to his chair, staring out the window, while Peter bound Laura's wrists and confiscated one of his horses for a mount. The backwoodsman was still staring in apprehensive uncertainty when the soldiers rode away, leading their captive behind them.

"Typical British high-handedness," Coon muttered when he recovered his powers of speech. Peter Forbes had stolen one of the horses without so much as a by-your-leave.

And worse, Coon groaned. Laura had confessed to the crimes rather than denying them. Why the devil had she done that? He hadn't realized the lass possessed such self-destructive tendencies!

On wobbly legs, Coon staggered to the counter to pour himself a drink, and then downed it in one swallow. The liquor didn't take off the edge of his frazzled nerves so he poured himself another.

Nolan was going to be beside himself when he returned from his mission to learn that his wife had been arrested and toted off to hang.

Coon's only consolation was knowing that Nolan was due to return that evening. Nolan was adept at handling difficulty, Coon reminded himself. Laura would be rescued before the four-man patrol overtook the last company of troops Coon had ferried across the river.

Nolan would know what to do to save his wife from fatal disaster, Coon thought to himself as he sipped his drink. All Coon had to do was wait until Nolan arrived. Nolan would be back soon.

Coon was still sitting at the table, soothing his jittery nerves with ale and willing Nolan to appear in the doorway— long after the sun hid its head below the horizon.

Twenty-five

Nolan had ridden northeast, pausing only long enough to rest and water his mount. He still hadn't gotten over his anger, even after long hours on the saddle.

The sound of cracking twigs and the flutter of birds rising from their perches in the canopy of trees put Nolan's senses on instant alert. In less than a heartbeat he had dismounted and led his stallion into the underbrush. When the approaching rider descended the hill, Nolan gaped in amazement.

"Spark, what the devil are you doing here?"

Spark expelled a gusty sigh of relief when Nolan emerged from the thicket. "Thank God you've come to no harm."

"No thanks to that conniving little witch," Nolan grumbled acrimoniously.

"Pardon?" Spark dragged his weary body from the saddle and massaged his aching back.

" 'Twas nothing," Nolan said with a dismissing shrug that belied his simmering anger. "Has something happened in Boston?"

Spark glanced around and frowned. "Where's Laura?"

"Don't ever mention that woman's name in front of me again!" Nolan burst out. "I put my trust in her and she betrayed me all over again. She somehow managed to relay a message to her adoring lieutenant, just as you predicted she would, while we were helping Coon at the ferry. If I hadn't left the tavern to destroy incoming provisions and ammunition, I would be in chains by now." Nolan's eyes glittered like molten steel. "I spotted Lieutenant Forbes and his patrol this morning. They were headed toward the ferry."

The color drained from Spark's ruddy cheeks. He hadn't arrived in time to warn Nolan and rescue Laura. "She didn't betray you," he said quietly. " 'Twas a mistake."

Nolan muttered a string of salty curses. "You're beginning to sound like Ethan. You of all people should know better than to put faith in a woman. You tried three times without success!"

Spark fished the wanted poster from his pocket and handed it to Nolan. Nolan unfolded the paper to see a likeness of Laura Chandler staring back at him.

"What new ruse is this?" Nolan scoffed sardonically.

" 'Tis no ruse," Spark said miserably. "Yer brother spoke with Miriam Peabody after he saw the posters tacked up all over town. Accordin' to Miriam, the indentured servant who worked for her saw Laura sneakin' in and out of the house, dressed in her urchin's garb. That snitch handed the information over to Peter Forbes. The maid also claimed to have seen a man dressed in a cloak and dark clothes enterin' the house. 'Twas Ethan sneakin' in to gather Laura's belongin's the night before you left for the ferry. Forbes also found yer cape in Laura's room. He suspects Laura is the Midnight Rider's accomplice."

Nolan groaned aloud. Fate certainly had a nasty way of turning a man's life upside down, didn't it?

"Laura has been accused of bein' a rebel spy, as well as yer accomplice." Spark stared dismally at Nolan who turned even more pale after hearing each bit of information. "Lieutenant Forbes was trackin' Laura down, not you. Nobody knows who you are."

Nolan felt as if because of him, Laura had been removed from Boston, from the comfort and luxuries she deserved. Because of him, she had been left at a jealous maid's mercy. Because of him, Peter Forbes had found the Midnight Rider's cloak among Laura's belongings. And because of him, Laura had been named the ringleader's accomplice and had become a fugitive with a price on her head.

Nolan cursed himself a thousand times over for doubting Laura's loyalty. He had left her to fend off Peter Forbes. Clever though she had proved to be, Nolan wondered how she would fare against a man who knew he had been played for a fool. Peter was probably as furious and vindictive as Nolan had been. If Peter dared to lay a hand on her . . .

The unsettling thought spurred Nolan into action.

"Where are you goin'?" Spark demanded when Nolan wheeled around and stalked off.

"I've got to go back to the ferry to see if I can overtake the patrol."

Spark watched Nolan thunder away and then he glanced back at his mare. After spending endless hours in the saddle, Spark didn't relish the thought of another ride at breakneck speed.

Heaving an exhausted sigh, Spark piled onto his horse to follow Nolan. Spark hoped he didn't fall asleep atop his mare and topple to the ground. At his age, and in his fatigued condition, he wasn't sure he could get back up once he fell down.

Laura was jerked awake when Peter dragged her from the saddle. In swift strides he towed her along behind him by the rope that was bound to her wrists. Peter had set a relentless pace since he had uprooted her from Coon's wayside inn the previous afternoon. Laura was bone-weary, but she was damned if she would plead for mercy. She had done enough begging for handouts in the streets when trying to stave off starvation.

Despite all Peter's snarling and growling, Laura understood his animosity. She had used his affection to acquire valuable information for the rebel cause. Peter was bitter and outraged and he held her personally responsible for his embarrassment.

But no matter what personal sacrifice demanded of her, the Rebel Rider's identity had to be protected at any cost. The torch of liberty must forever burn and the dark specter who rode for freedom must survive. As long as there were wrongs to right, there must be a relentless daredevil like Nolan Ryder to lead the crusade.

Laura mustered her determination when Peter shoved her down and tied her to a tree. He made a production of drinking his fill at the stream, while depriving her from quenching her thirst. She was to be tormented all the way back to Boston, Laura predicted. This was part of the punishment Peter had designed to satisfy his vengeance.

At least some good would come of this, Laura encouraged herself. Nolan Ryder would realize at long last that Laura had offered unselfish, sincere affection. She had volunteered to take his place on the gallows, so that he might live to inspire other freedom-loving patriots. Perhaps Laura couldn't live to see the colonies cast off their British yoke, but she would have been a part of the initial movement that advocated independence. There was that, at least . . .

"Thirsty, little rebel?" Peter taunted, wiping his mouth on his scarlet sleeve. "And hungry, too, I expect."

"Nay, I feed on thoughts of freedom," Laura replied, undaunted.

Peter gave Laura a look of disgust and raised his arm to backhand her for her insolence. But he couldn't bring himself to strike her, much as he despised her for deceiving him. More the pity that Peter had been taught to respect women— even the worst of the lot. His hand dropped limply to his side.

"Why?" Peter whispered in frustration. "Why did you have to be the one to forsake me? I would have offered you my name and my affection. I would have taken you to London after my tour of duty. I would have given you all that was mine to give. Does your hopeless rebel cause mean so much that you would sacrifice your very life for it? You must know these wayward peasants are no match for the King's Army."

Laura felt a knot of regret coil inside her. Although Peter Forbes could be stuffily arrogant and sometimes self-assuming, he had always treated her with kindness and respect. She had repaid him with dishonesty and deceit. Even now, she couldn't tell the truth, because he simply couldn't understand why she was fiercely driven to protect the only man she would ever love and their mutual cause of freedom.

"Do what you must to me, Peter," she said in quiet resignation. " 'Twould never have worked between us. We hail from two different worlds."

"You could make it much easier on yourself if you would divulge the name of the other agents in this secret network of rebel spies."

Laura stared at Peter's moon-drenched features for a long moment. It suddenly occurred to her that Peter knew nothing of dedicated loyalty. His only purpose for assuming a command in His Majesty's Army was to acquire a title and the kind of prestige that second sons of British earls couldn't attain by birth. Peter wanted nothing more than the distinction of his military commission when he returned home to England. He possessed no driving force. His personal ambition centered around improving his position in London society. Peter Forbes didn't stand for much of anything, Laura realized. He simply served his country, just to say that he had.

"The names," Peter prompted. "Give me a list of names to pacify my senior officers and I will do what I can to lessen your sentence."

With unwavering resolution, Laura shook her head and curled up against the tree.

"You're every kind of fool," Peter muttered as he bolted to his feet to tower over her. "No cause is worth dying for, not when there are alternatives."

Laura slowly lifted her tousled head. A rueful smile spread across her chapped lips. "You are wrong, Peter. This cause of liberty is worth the sacrifice. To care so deeply, to believe so strongly is to have a worthwhile purpose. I do not expect you to understand. But if you cared for me, even half as much as you thought you once did, you might be able to comprehend what I feel for every colonist who has struggled against the Crown's decrees."

She stared at him for a long, deliberate moment. "Do you know what 'tis like to care enough about what you believe in to put yourself at risk, in order to protect those who would make the same sacrifice for me if need be?"

Peter opened his mouth to debate the issue, and then decided against it. Muttering, he turned and walked away, leaving Laura tethered to the tree. Curse it, he thought in irritable exasperation. He had vowed to torment that deceitful female and enjoy every minute of it. Instead, her staunch, unfaltering convictions drew his unwilling admiration. Yet, he couldn't release her. She had to be punished for what she had done. Peter couldn't help her if she wouldn't cooperate.

A damned pity and a dreadful waste, Peter mused as he bedded down for the night. Why couldn't Laura see that her cause of liberty stood no chance against Parliament and the Crown. Laura was going to sacrifice her life for a lost cause.

Nolan burst through the back door of Tall Oaks Inn to find Coon Ashburn half-sprawled on the table. Nolan cursed himself to hell and back. He had made matters worse by refusing to return to the wayside inn after he spotted Peter Forbes. Now Laura was God knew where, suffering untold torment because of Nolan. As for Coon Ashburn, he was dead or dying— Nolan wasn't sure which.

"Coon!"

Nolan's trumpeting voice prompted Coon's groggy groan. Coon had dragged himself into an upright position and propped his ruffled red head on his hand by the time Nolan zigzagged around the maze of tables.

Coon stared owlishly at the imposing silhouette. "Nolan? Is that you?" he called into the darkness.

"Where the hell have you been for so long? I thought the British patrol had—"

"Where's Laura?" Nolan interrupted as he checked Coon for bleeding wounds. "Are you all right?"

Coon exhaled a shuddering breath and pushed the empty tankard away. He had consumed enough colonial rum to curb his apprehension— and drown a full-grown horse. "I'll live," Coon mumbled. "I wish I could say the same for yer wife . . ."

"Wife?" came the astounded howl from across the darkened tavern.

Coon half twisted in his chair to see Spark McRae's stout frame filling the moonlit doorway. " 'Pon my word, is that who I think it be?"

Nolan had no time for Spark and Coon to renew old acquaintances. He needed answers and he needed them fast! "Coon," he growled, giving the older man an abrupt shake. "What happened to Laura?"

"You married her?" Spark croaked as he groped his way around the tables and chairs. "You actually married her, even when you thought she was a Tory spy?"

"A Tory spy?" Coon crowed. "Hell and be damned! Nolan's wife is no Tory spy. Those British soldiers arrested her for bein' a rebel spy."

Nolan was growing more exasperated by the second. "Coon, I have to know what happened when the British patrol arrived," he demanded sharply.

Coon shook his fuzzy head to clear the brine

from his pickled brain. Inhaling an enormous breath, Coon assembled his jumbled thoughts.

"Yer wife was preparin' breakfast when four soldiers arrived— "

"When?"

Coon's expression went comically blank. "What day is this?"

"Thursday," Nolan impatiently prompted.

"Yesterday afternoon— I think." Coon massaged his throbbing temples. "Lieutenant Forks— "

"Forbes," Spark corrected.

"Whatever," Coon mumbled with a careless flick of his wrist. "He claimed he was arrestin' yer wife for treason and conspiracy and acting as the Midnight Rider's accomplice. I tried to tell him 'twas all a mistake. I was about to tell Forks— "

"Forbes," Nolan inserted.

"— Forbes that you were her husband, but Laura confessed to treason before I could get the words out. Then she announced that *she* was the Midnight Rider."

Nolan went perfectly still, hardly daring to breathe. Sickening dread seeped into every pore. Nolan suddenly remembered the night Laura had vowed that she would prove she was loyal to the cause and sincere in her affection for him.

Sweet mercy, she wasn't supposed to make the supreme sacrifice to protect his identity! Damnation, she may as well have looped the noose around her own neck while she was at it.

"Of course, Lieutenant Forks— "

"Forbes," Nolan muttered.

Coon scowled. "Who cares what that scarlet dragon's name is. The point is that he didn't believe Laura at first. He thought she was protectin' the mysterious rabble-rouser who's been givin' the British fits. But then Laura described an incident at a cemetery that convinced him that she was tellin' him the truth." Coon glanced somberly at Nolan. "I don't know too many people who would put their life on the line to spare somebody else. She's one of a kind, Nolan."

The words pelted Nolan like a shower of hailstones. Blast it, Laura had proved herself to be every bit the defiant daredevil he was. He wondered if she had devised a scheme to escape the patrol. Nolan remembered her optimistic policy of "thinking of something" when she found it necessary to explain difficult situations. Nolan had the unnerving feeling that Laura had bit off a mite more than she could chew this time around.

Peter Forbes knew he had been deceived and he wouldn't take kindly to having his pride slashed to ribbons by a deceptive female. He also knew the British were desperate to make an example of a rebel— any rebel— especially after the Stamp Act riots. The Crown was trying to exert control over the belligerent colonials. If Nolan didn't catch up with that patrol before they reached Boston, it might become impossible to rescue Laura. By now, there were more scarlet dragons stalking the streets than a man could shake a fist at.

Damnation, Nolan was fighting the clock and all he had was a weary old frontiersman for reinforcement. After his fast-paced ride through the wilderness, Spark was on the verge of dropping in his tracks. Coon couldn't leave the ferry unattended without the risk of incoming troops ransacking the tavern and stealing available supplies.

When Nolan lurched around and surged toward the door, Spark stared after him. "What are we goin' to do, Nolan? I hope you have a plan. And I pray 'tis a damned good one."

"You're going to spend the night here and bring along provisions after you've had the chance to rest," Nolan called over his shoulder.

Spark tried to object. "But— "

"I'll mark a trail for you to follow." Nolan paused in the doorway to glance at the innkeeper. "Coon, send a message to my brother with one of the incoming circuit riders. Tell Ethan I need his assistance, posthaste. He can meet me at the wayside inn south of Roxbury as soon as possible. We have to intercept that patrol before they reach Boston."

When Nolan disappeared from sight, Spark plopped down in the nearest chair. His legs were aching something fierce and he swore he had calluses on his saddle sores. A sense of impending doom settled into his bones. Spark wasn't sure there was a solution to the problem Nolan faced, short of turning himself over to the patrol and taking Laura's place.

If Nolan dared to divulge his identity and the Midnight Rider was taken into custody, all of Boston would be in an uproar. With troops pouring into the city to restrain rebels prone to riot, skirmishes could erupt.

The patriots were unprepared for all-out war, Spark reminded himself. Although 'twas a time of great social and political upheaval, the timing was all wrong for a full-scale tax rebellion. The stockpiles of supplies were just beginning to be collected, and local militias had just begun their secretive drills.

"Do you think Nolan has a prayer of rescuin' his wife?" Coon questioned quietly.

"I don't know." Spark stared through the windows, listening to the pounding hoofbeats recede into silence.

Coon braced his arms on the table and peered at the bulky figure across from him. "Nolan is the Midnight Rider, isn't he? That's why Laura was quick to shoulder the blame. She was protectin' him, wasn't she?"

Spark nodded his gray head. "Aye, and there's no tellin' what Nolan might do to spare her. That boy always was too darin' for his own good. He's been dodgin' bullets so long that it's like a game to him. But this time he's liable to catch more than one with his name on it."

Coon levered out of the chair and steadied himself against the table. "He's goin' to need my help as well as yers," he declared. "Give me a hand stashin' my supplies out of sight so those lobsterbacks don't clean me out while I'm gone. I'll leave a message for the circuit rider who's due in tonight. We don't have much time to spare. Nolan might do somethin' rash if we're not there to run interference for him."

"Aye, that's the truth," Spark agreed as he struggle onto his weary legs. "Nolan looked and sounded damned desperate when he charged out of here."

Spark helped Coon gather the supplies from the kitchen and stash them in the underbrush. All the while, he kept remembering the tone of Nolan's voice when he demanded answers about Laura.

It had finally happened, Spark predicted. Nolan Ryder had finally stumbled upon a woman he didn't want to live without. The way things were going, Nolan might just have to get along without Laura Chandler. She had served herself up to the fire-breathing scarlet dragons like a modern-day version of Joan of Arc.

Twenty-six

Laura tried desperately to swallow, but her throat felt as if it were clogged with sand. As punishment for her crimes, Peter had refused to offer her food and drink during their journey. He had forced her to watch each time the patrol stopped to take a meal. He continually tied her beside the creeks, just out of reach of water.

Laura knew Peter was tormenting her in the hope that she would finally break down and supply the names of the Loyal Nine and active members of the Sons of Liberty in exchange for nourishment. But Laura vowed to die of thirst long before she betrayed the men responsible for keeping the rebel movement alive. And she would starve through eternity before she revealed Nolan Ryder's secret identity.

Although Peter was relying on several methods of torture to loosen her tongue, he hadn't resorted to physical abuse when he wasn't given the answers he wanted. Laura didn't think Peter had it in him to apply such tactics to a woman. He had been raised too much the gentleman to stoop to that.

Her assessments proved correct the following

morning when Peter relented and offered her a sip of water and several nibbles of hardtack. Laura was reasonably certain that Peter's conscience was nagging him. She considered herself fortunate that some other military officer had not taken her captive. Things could have been worse.

Peter sank down on his haunches beside Laura, watching her wolf down the meager rations. "You could make things much easier on yourself if you would cooperate," he told her for the dozenth time. "There are better rations awaiting you when you give me the names I need."

Laura continued to munch on her meager rations, refusing to reply.

"Who are the express riders who are distributing blasphemous propaganda to the Sons of Liberty in other colonies?"

"You are wasting your breath," Laura assured him between bites. "I'm prepared to accept the punishment you think I deserve for standing firm in my belief that these colonies deserve to be free and that our citizens are entitled to their personal rights."

Peter scowled in frustration. "You are going to be very sorry when I am forced to hand you over to my superiors. They won't be as sympathetic as I." Peter vaulted to his feet and glared down at his bedraggled captive. "There are many unpleasant but highly effective methods of prying out information. I promise you that you won't enjoy any of them."

When Peter stalked off to saddle his mount, Laura

mentally prepared herself for the possibility he mentioned. She had felt the flat side of soldiers' swords while she roamed the streets in her misguided youth. She had also seen an occasional hand chopped off when repeat offenders were caught for thievery. She had been knocked down and stepped on plenty of times in the past and she could endure any brand of torture— if it would protect Nolan Ryder and the other patriots from harm. She had to keep silent, even if she was forced to endure agonizing pain . . .

When Peter hauled her to her feet and towed her toward her horse, Laura mustered her determination. No matter what the Crown's torture experts did to her, she would refuse to speak. Too many lives would be at risk if she did!

Nolan erupted with curses when he finally came upon the patrol. Peter Forbes and his men had joined the convoy of troops that were hauling the weapons Nolan had sabotaged several days earlier. If Nolan hadn't wasted a day in the backwoods, Laura might have been spared this ordeal.

When Nolan heard the rustle of underbrush behind him, he instinctively recoiled. To his stunned amazement he saw both Spark and Coon slithering toward him.

"What the blazes are you doing here, Coon?" Nolan hissed.

"I haven't had a good fight since I found myself surrounded by Indians after I accidentally trampled through their sacred buryin' ground." He patted his trusty rifle and smiled, displaying gaps where his teeth were missing at each corner of his mouth. "Thought you could use an extra hand right about now."

"You were supposed to send word to my brother," Nolan reminded him tartly.

"I already did." Coon inched up beside Nolan. "One of the express riders came up from the south an hour after you left. Spark helped me hide my supplies in the woods so the Brits couldn't take whatever they wanted." He tossed Nolan another wide grin before he assessed the encampment of soldiers. "This reminds me of the old days when we had to ward off attacks. Luckily, these uppity Brits aren't as clever as Indians." He counted heads and frowned uneasily. "A bloody lot of them redcoats, aren't there? I hope you have a plan."

"Looks like we'll need one," Spark piped up. He also took inventory of the soldiers who were strung out on the road like a colony of red ants. When he spied Laura tied to her mount, surrounded by armed guards, he sputtered a curse. "Damnation, Nolan, the poor woman looks like she's been dragged through the dirt and is bein' treated like the Crown's most dangerous enemy. Makes me sick to think I rudely insulted her every chance I got. I've got a lot of apologizin' to do when we get her out of the scrape she's in."

Nolan was none too happy about the way Peter Forbes was treating his captive, either. If the way she was slumped on her horse was any indication, she was near exhaustion.

Damn her daring hide, she should have vehemently denied the charges against her. Nolan felt guilty enough about refusing to believe Laura without her accepting tortuous punishment in his stead. Watching her torment was killing him by inches!

When the procession disappeared over the tree-clad hill, Nolan surged to his feet to fetch his stallion. "We had better scout the trail ahead of us," he advised. "The last thing we need is a surprise."

Spark came onto his hands and knees and then clambered to his feet. "I don't want to sound pessimistic— "

"Then don't," Nolan bit off. "Laura is not going to hang for me, and that is all there is to it."

"Aye, we'll all be hangin' together," Coon mumbled. "I never did mind lopsided odds, but three against thirty is a bit much."

"And if we ambush those soldiers, we could invite a war the colonies are ill-prepared to fight," Spark was quick to remind Nolan.

Nay, Nolan told himself as he and the two old frontiersmen circled through the wooded hills. He could not risk a skirmish. He was going to have to rely on cunning and deception to rescue Laura from impending disaster. Problem was, he had yet to devise a workable solution.

Peter Forbes trotted his horse toward the mansion that sat on the spacious estate south of Boston. The acreage was reminiscent of his family's country estate in England. Judge Robert Clover, one of the province's most influential magistrates, was in charge of the Crown's judicial functions. He had migrated to this country home after the Stamp Act riots, having seen what was left of the lieutenant governor's home. Robert Clover had also taken the precaution of protecting himself by quartering Major Isaac Stewart— recently arrived from New York.

Peter had been introduced to the pompous major and his aides when they reported to Boston headquarters. 'Twas his intention to house his prisoner on the magistrate's property rather than in jail.

Peter well remembered how Ebenezer McIntosh had been blackmailed out of jail after he led the riots. The sheriff had received so many life-threatening notes that he agreed to turn McIntosh loose. Peter preferred not to rile the mob. If news that one of the rebel spies had been captured reached Boston more trouble might erupt. Only when a full strike force of British soldiers had arrived to control the city could authorities breathe easy. Until then, precaution was advisable.

Peter was shown into the elegantly furnished dining room to find Judge Clover and Major Stewart leisurely taking their evening meal. Peter's stomach growled enviously when the mouth-watering aromas drifted across the room. After surviving on travel rations for a week, Peter was anxious to sit down to the succulent meals Miriam Peabody's cook served . . .

The thought of delivering displeasing news to the dowager made Peter wince. Miriam was immensely fond of her niece and she had refused to believe the damning accusations. He doubted his amicable relations with Miriam would continue once she learned Peter had handed Laura over to his superiors.

Robert Clover appraised Peter's dusty uniform and gestured for him to approach the table. "Lieutenant Forbes, isn't it?"

"Aye, sir," Peter said politely.

"Are you delivering a message? Not more news of riots from those cantankerous colonials, I hope."

"Nay, I'm returning to Boston with a prisoner who has been accused of spying for the rebels."

Major Stewart bounded out of his chair to take command of the situation. "I should think a good tar and feathering would be in order. Those heathens deserve a taste of their own medicine."

Before the major could strut into the hall, Peter grabbed his arm to detain him. "Sir, the captive is a prestigious member of Boston society. She is also a woman."

That stopped Isaac in his tracks. His pale green eyes widened in surprise. "A female?"

"Aye, and 'tis a rather sensitive situation," Peter confided. "Because of the outbreaks of rebellion in Boston, we cannot give those patriots more fuel to heat the already simmering pot. I was hoping to hold my captive at this estate rather than risk a repetition of the destructive riots."

"A wise suggestion," Robert inserted. He rose from his chair to accompany the officers outside. "We can hold our prisoner in the smokehouse until her trial . . ."

Robert stumbled to a halt when he recognized Laura Chandler standing at the bottom of the steps, bookended by two well-armed guards. "Good God!" he croaked.

Major Stewart surveyed Laura's tattered gown, noting the dark circles under her eyes and the tangle of auburn hair that encircled her wan features. "This is a lady of quality?" he smirked. "She could easily be mistaken for a peasant. And considering the accusations against her, she shall be treated as such."

Laura lifted her head to survey the bulky form of the man perched on the porch like a pompous rooster. Isaac Stewart's arrogant demeanor and the cold glitter in his pale eyes earned him Laura's instant dislike. Dressed in his buff-colored breeches, red jacket and tricorn hat, he reminded Laura of an oversized beetle. Something about him also reminded her of Geoffrey Spradlin— may he rot in hell forever. 'Twas in the eyes, Laura decided. There was a cold, ruthless expression that offered no mercy to anyone, for any reason.

"Has your prisoner given you the names of her conspirators?" Isaac wanted to know as he looked down his broken-branch nose at Laura.

"Nay, sir," Peter replied, shifting uneasily from one foot to the other.

"Then I suggest you begin intense interrogation, first thing in the morning. Singling out other informants from that nest of rebel vipers should put the fear of God in them all."

"Sir, I—"

Isaac waved off the lieutenant with an impatient flick of his wrist. "Take her to the smokehouse and withhold rations. By morning her tongue should be properly loosened."

"I already tried to—"

"Dismissed, Lieutenant!" Isaac snapped brusquely. "I am taking control of this situation. When you are given an order I expect you to carry it out without debate. Place your prisoner in confinement. After you have interrogated her, report directly to me."

Isaac wheeled around and swaggered back to the house to finish his meal. Sighing audibly, Robert pivoted to join his houseguest.

Peter descended the steps and then paused in front of Laura. "I warned you what might happen if you refused to cooperate. Major Stewart isn't known for his compassion or generosity. You should bear that in mind tonight. If you refuse to name names, Major Stewart is likely to lose what little temper he has and employ drastic measures to secure the information he wants."

Laura gulped down her apprehension as Peter led her to the smokehouse situated behind the mansion. She would have to prepare herself for the worst.

Major Stewart didn't appear to be the kind of man who even considered pardons. Now that this cocky rooster had arrived in Boston, he obviously intended to rule the roost and make a name for himself by striking fear among the rebels.

Another power-hungry officer craving promotion, Laura predicted, as Peter secured the loose end of her leash to a concrete vat. Major Stewart was a bitter reminder of why Laura supported the cause of liberty. The colonies had been overrun by pompous materialists who deemed themselves a notch below royalty. Laura had tolerated British hauteur as long as she could stand. No matter how mean and nasty the high and mighty Isaac Stewart became, Laura would tell him nothing. He was not going to further his military career through her.

On that determined note, Laura curled herself into a ball on the flagstone floor. No doubt, the British presumed that being treated like a lowly peasant would break her spirit. They presumed wrong. Laura had slept in worse places and gone days without food. And she'd be damned if even a crowbar would be effective in prying information from her.

Ethan Ryder's shoulders slumped in relief when he saw his brother stride inside the wayside ordinary on the outskirts of Roxbury. "Thank God you're all right."

Nolan didn't feel very all right. Guilt and regret were taking their toll on him. Laura was suffering at his expense, and rescuing her was going to demand clever forethought.

From a concealed location in the underbrush, Nolan had watched Peter and his patrol clatter up the circular drive to Robert Clover's country estate. When Nolan saw the sentinels posted at the front and back of the stone smokehouse, providing round-the-clock surveillance, he had a pretty good idea where Laura was being held captive.

When Nolan dropped into the chair in the corner of the tavern Ethan squirmed restlessly. Nolan noticed his brother's apprehension immediately.

"Now what's wrong?" Nolan demanded after swallowing down his first sip of rum.

"I know where Laura is being held captive."

"That makes two of us," Nolan muttered sarcastically. "Robert Clover is keeping her under close guard, refusing to run the risk of marching her to the courthouse and inciting another riot. That should work to our advantage. Only a small strike force will be needed to effect her release."

"There's a problem," Ethan said grimly.

Nolan felt himself tense. His brother's bleak expression wasn't reassuring. True, Ethan typically fretted and stewed, but tonight he looked exceptionally concerned. "What is this *problem?*"

Ethan gestured his blond head toward the mug in Nolan's hand. "Perhaps you should have a few more drinks before I deliver the news my informants provided."

Nolan downed his rum in two swallows and stared impatiently at his brother. "Out with it, Ethan."

His brother inhaled a deep breath and blurted out, "Major Isaac Stewart has arrived in Boston."

Nolan scowled. Even though Coon had given him the news weeks earlier, another round of tormenting flashbacks from his past leaped to mind. Nolan thought he had learned to cope with the tragedies he had endured. He had sworn that he could be satisfied, never having to see that haughty bastard again. But the mere mention of Stewart's name left Nolan with a compelling sense of unfinished business, a fierce need for revenge.

The cold, hard fact was that Nolan was never going to forget what Stewart had done. He wasn't going to be satisfied until that bastard was dead and buried. A man who would heartlessly sacrifice the lives of infantrymen, simply because of his contemptuous distaste for lowly colonists, deserved to spend eternity in hell.

All the dormant emotion Nolan had tried to suppress throughout the years came bubbling up like volcanic lava. He vowed, there and then, that the Midnight Rider was going to make Major Stewart's life miserable. If Nolan couldn't kill that son of a bitch, for fear of inciting war, he could at least see to it that Stewart did not enjoy his stay in Boston.

Ethan could see the dramatic change come over his brother, almost at once. Nolan's expression turned to stone. Ethan detected a hardness, a deadly menace he hadn't realized existed beneath Nolan's cool, reckless exterior. This, Ethan decided, was the fearless soldier, the seasoned frontiersman that Nolan had become in order to survive. Nolan was like a powerful predator on full alert . . . and Ethan hadn't even given his brother the worst of the news yet.

"Nolan, there's . . . um . . . something else," Ethan began hesitantly. "Stewart is being quartered at Robert Clover's estate. The major has taken it upon himself to deal with the prisoner."

When Nolan's eyes flared like silver torches, Ethan winced uncomfortably. He had never seen Nolan look quite so ruthless or dangerous. Nolan's civilized veneer had buckled, and the lines bracketing Nolan's mouth creased in a wordless scowl.

"My informants have received word that Judge Clover plans to keep Laura at his estate until Stewart acquires the information he wants about the Midnight Rider, Loyal Nine, and Sons of Liberty. The British intend to march her to the Common, only after reinforcements are in place. Then she will be shipped to England to hang for treason."

Nolan gritted his teeth and swore furiously. *He* should be the one in custody, dealing with that unmerciful bastard. He had clashed with Major Stewart over his barbaric military tactics dozens of times. And he wanted to be the one who squared off against that self-important demigod— once and for all.

Without a word, Nolan rose from his chair and strode from the tavern. Ethan was one step behind him.

" 'Tis a ticklish situation," Ethan quietly confided.

"I am aware of that," Nolan said without breaking stride.

"The rebels are not in position to risk war. Shots fired here could be heard all the way to England. If English blood is spilled, we are going to have a battle on our hands that we are not prepared to fight and cannot hope to win."

Nolan kept on walking. "I realize that. Even if I didn't, Spark has harped on the subject on the even hours while Coon mentions it on the odd hours."

"So what are we going to do, Nolan?"

Ethan plowed into his brother when he halted abruptly. Nolan pivoted to stare into Ethan's fretful expression. From out of nowhere a melodic, confident voice whispered to Nolan. The faintest hint of a smile spread across his lips. Laura Chandler had never allowed difficult predicaments to get the best of her, Nolan recalled. She was optimism personified and Nolan— according to his brother— was reckless daring in the flesh.

"I'll think of something . . ." Nolan murmured before he turned and walked away.

Ethan managed a grin as he fell into step. "I could swear I've heard that comment before."

"Aye, you have, and I hope the lady who lives by that philosophy survives to utter these words again. I intend to make damned certain she does."

Twenty-seven

Peter Forbes sighed heavily after exiting the smokehouse. He had threatened, cajoled, pleaded and demanded Laura to furnish the information—but to no avail. Even after hours of intense interrogation and a full day with nothing but a cup of water for nourishment, Laura had refused to divulge the names of other rebel spies and express riders. Neither would she reveal knowledge about upcoming patriot activities. She still maintained that she had posed as the Midnight Rider.

Wearily, Peter trudged up the mansion steps to report to Major Stewart. The stuffy officer was not going to like what he was about to hear.

Major Stewart leaned back in his tuft chair to appraise the handsome young lieutenant who appeared at the parlor door. "Well, did your prisoner finally decide to cooperate?"

Peter shook his blond head. "She insists that she is the masked vigilante and the only rebel spy in Boston."

Isaac snorted disdainfully at that. "Surely you

are not stupid enough to believe a mere woman could accomplish the feats I have heard described since my arrival in town.

"Clashes on horseback with armed guards? Daring chases at breakneck speeds, astride a devil stallion?" Isaac scoffed. "Come now, Lieutenant, you must realize the chit is protecting someone else."

"So one might think. But she accurately described one of the incidents in which I was personally involved with the Midnight Rider," Peter contended. "She couldn't have known what occurred that particular night unless she was—"

"Midnight's *Lady*?" Isaac sarcastically suggested. "Midnight's *accomplice*?" He set his cup of tea aside and rose from the couch. " 'Tis obvious to me that you don't possess the gumption required to pry information from reluctant females."

Isaac looked down his crooked nose at Peter. "You will go nowhere in the Crown's Army if you cannot overlook sentiment and apply effective tactics. We are dealing with underlings here in these backward colonies. The entire population is composed of ignorant misfits and unruly malcontents which British society exiled to these shores. These bumpkins do not deserve an ounce of our respect and they cannot be treated as our intellectual or social equals. Until you learn that, Lieutenant, you will never rise to a position of great authority."

Peter silently scowled as the arrogant officer strutted past. Peter had spent two days with Major Stewart. 'Twas more than enough. "I feel compelled to remind you that our prisoner is well known in Boston. If you employ abusive methods you will definitely incite the riotous masses. Believe me, Major, I have seen the Boston mob in action, you haven't—"

Peter slammed his mouth shut when Isaac wheeled around, his pale green eyes glittering with indignation, his lips twisting in a contemptuous snarl. "Never again presume to lecture me or you will find yourself demoted. Or worse, court-martialed for insubordination. I dealt with a similar case during the Seven Years War. A brash, outspoken captain from the colonial militia never could remember his place." Isaac struck one of his self-assuming poses that left Peter gnashing his teeth in disgust. "The aforementioned officer happens to be dead. Now, would you care to join him?"

Isaac swaggered out the door and Peter cursed under his breath. This past year of service in the colonies had failed to meet Peter's expectations. If dealing with superior officers like Major Stewart was any indication of what a future in the army promised, Peter wasn't so sure he wanted any part of it. He was seriously considering resigning his commission and returning home to manage one of his father's small country estates.

Peter heard Isaac bark orders to his aids and summon the guards. Cold apprehension settled over Peter. He had warned Laura that she might suffer extreme anguish if Isaac decided to utilize his methods of torture. Considering Isaac's low opinion of colonials and his total disregard for their rights and their lives, Laura would be lucky if she survived.

The grim thought prompted Peter to spin around. Despite the threat of a dishonorable discharge, he intended to be on hand— if and when Isaac resorted to cruel and unusual punishment to glean information. Peter had been furious enough with Laura to strangle her for deceiving him, but he could not live with her death on his conscience.

Isaac Stewart strode purposefully around the side of the house, motioning to the off-duty guards. He was bound and determined to train these fainthearted soldiers to deal with these pesky colonials. His staff would all be on hand when Isaac succeeded in dragging information from the reluctant prisoner.

'Twas the trouble with the Crown's policy, Isaac reminded himself as he swaggered toward the smokehouse. These yokels could not be handled with kid gloves. They had to be shown their proper place to ensure they stayed in it. If His Majesty had hopes of keeping the colonies dependent and obedient 'twould be fear of severe consequences that kept them in line. These unruly bumpkins were suffering delusions of grandeur, spouting off about their rights and their freedom.

Bah! Isaac had his fill of coddling these dim-witted miscreants. The sooner they realized that the Crown could— and would— apply force when needed, the sooner these simpletons would accept their fate.

Laura Chandler was the ideal device Isaac needed to restore order and authority. He would prove to every last rebel in Boston that he showed no mercy and no preference to anyone— man, woman or child. Spies would be tortured and hanged, even if the colonies weren't in a true state of rebellion. In Isaac's opinion, they were close enough to apply battle tactics and wartime policies.

"Stoke a fire in the hearth," Isaac demanded of the sentry.

Private Simpson blinked, bemused. "A fire, sir?" But 'tis unseasonably hot— "

"Do not dare question me!" Isaac bellowed. "You are a soldier in His Majesty's Army. When you are given an order by a superior officer you will act at once." He looked down his nose at the corporal. " 'Tis obvious Lieutenant Forbes has been much too lenient with you. Now, do as you are told!"

The private set his musket aside and unlocked the smokehouse door.

"And let that be a lesson to the rest of you lily-livered fools," Isaac announced. " 'Tis not your duty to coddle any of these treasonous rebels. They will never accept submission if you command with a gentle hand. Just because your squeamish lieutenant doesn't have the stomach to do what must be done, see that you don't make the same mistake."

When Isaac made a spectacular display of entering the smokehouse, all eyes turned to the lieutenant who stood a short distance away.

"He's a madman," Peter muttered to his men. "If he intends to disfigure or torture a woman within an inch of her life—"

An all-too familiar torch arched through the air, illuminating the effigy that hung from a tree near the coach house. To Peter's disbelieving eyes, the Midnight Rider appeared out of nowhere, thundering toward the coach house, holding a second torch high above his head. He hurled the glowing missile onto the roof before galloping off in the opposite direction. Flames swept across the wooden shingles like wildfire, lighting up the night like a gigantic torch.

Several of Stewart's aides left their position by the smokehouse to douse the fire. Peter made no attempt to call them back. While the soldiers were fighting the blaze, he intended to gather his patrol and track the Midnight Rider down.

If Major Stewart was hell-bent on practicing inhumane torture, better to let him do it on the rebel's ringleader, Peter decided. 'Twas obvious now that Laura had indeed been protecting the real culprit. The only way to spare her was for Peter to apprehend the Phantom Patriot . . . and Peter had better do it quickly!

Nolan bounded from the saddle and handed the stallion's reins to his brother, who was identically dressed in a hood, cloak and dark clothes. The flames that consumed the roof of the coach house made it easy to count British heads. Four soldiers, toting water buckets, were trying to extinguish the fire before the landau and buggies inside the building were no more than kindling for a bonfire.

When Peter Forbes and his patrol appeared on horseback, Nolan urged Ethan onto the stallion. "Lead them to the creek and keep them occupied for at least a quarter of an hour," Nolan instructed. "That should give me time enough to pay my last *dis*respects to Major High and Mighty Stewart and whisk Laura off to safety."

"Be careful," Ethan cautioned. "No daring heroics. I— "

Ethan wasn't allowed to finish his brotherly lecture. Nolan whacked the stallion on the rump. The spirited steed grabbed the bit between his teeth and bolted off, forcing Ethan to hang on for dear life. The muscular stallion leaped the picket fence and thundered across the lawn, remaining just out of the pursuing soldiers' musket range.

When Peter's patrol spotted the fleeing rider, the chase was on. Nolan monitored Ethan's hasty departure long enough to ensure that his brother could handle the spirited animal. Then he glanced toward the shadowed spot beside the storehouse where Coon and Spark waited with a bucket of tar and a sack of feathers.

With a slight inclination of his head, Nolan sent the two old frontiersmen off on their crusade. The haughty Judge Robert Clover was about to suffer the same fate as the Crown's stamp distributors.

And the next time His Majesty's magistrate sentenced a colonial citizen to a public flogging, he would be able to sympathize with the painful ordeal, after having his skin peeled off by hot tar.

Nolan turned his attention to the smokehouse. He had hoped the commotion outside would distract Major Stewart. But then, Nolan reminded himself, Isaac possessed single-minded obsession when it came to doling out unmerciful punishment.

Nolan still bore the scars on his back to prove it.

Stifling the tormenting memories, Nolan concentrated on his purpose. With the silence of a stalking cat, he crept toward the smokehouse. If Isaac had been granted time to scar Laura for life, the bastard was doomed to suffer the same disfiguring fate himself. Nolan didn't want to incite a war over this incident, but the taste of revenge was so thick he nearly strangled on it. He was stung by the fiendish desire to carve Isaac into so many pieces that even the devil wouldn't recognize him. 'Tis what that ruthless bastard deserved as retaliation for his past and present sins.

Laura bit back a whimper when another lock of her hair fell to the floor. When she had refused to give Isaac the information he demanded, he had backhanded her so hard that her head slammed against the stone wall. Fuzzy stars were still orbiting around her line of vision when Isaac grabbed a handful of her hair and snipped off a clump with sheep shears.

Even the shouts of alarm and the glowing flames seen through the window hadn't distracted the fanatical lunatic Laura had encountered. Indeed, Isaac seemed intent on doing his worst while the guards were preoccupied. But Laura swore to herself she would not utter a single name, especially not Nolan's. His identity would remain a solemn secret, even if her life was the price she had to pay.

"Give me the name of the man you're whoring for," Isaac snarled as he sheered off another handful of auburn hair. "Who is the Midnight Rider?"

When Isaac yanked her head back, Laura spit in his puckered face. Her hostile defiance earned her another stinging blow to the cheek. Tears misted her eyes, but Laura refused to give this fire-breathing scarlet dragon the satisfaction of sobbing aloud.

"You're every kind of fool," Isaac sneered maliciously as he wiped his face with his sleeve. "I will have the names I demand . . . one way or the other."

Laura choked back a gasp of terror when Isaac stalked toward the hearth and lifted the glowing branding iron. Her blood turned to ice when Isaac's pale green eyes sparkled with fiendish glee. She had considered Geoffrey Spradlin a menace to all women everywhere, after he had fatally beaten Martha Winfield for refusing to cater to his perverted sexual practices. But Isaac Stewart was frighteningly worse! 'Twas not uncontrollable temper that provoked his demented violence. This crazed brute looked as if he actually derived satisfaction from inflicting pain and torment.

When Isaac took the first step toward her, his green eyes glowing with satanic menace, Laura strained against the confining rope. However she was too weak from lack of nourishment to pose a serious physical threat. She resigned herself to feeling the searing poker against her flesh, but she vowed to make a battle royal of it. She would not faint, giving Isaac the chance to do his worst. She would fight him to the bitter end!

" 'Tis such a pity to mar feminine beauty, simply to acquire the Midnight Rider's name," Isaac chuckled wickedly as he neared Laura with the poker, holding it close enough to her face for her to feel its radiating heat.

Laura shivered uncontrollably when Isaac inched the branding iron ever closer.

"But of course, no one will see the ugly scars while you're standing on the gallows, prepared to hang for treason. You will have a mask over your face, from this day forward. Your rebel friends won't see the damage a branding iron can do, so don't think you will become a martyr who incites riot. You won't be marched through Boston. The bumpkins you are trying to protect will never know what became of you."

Isaac smiled nastily. "Perhaps we should start with the soles of your feet and work our way up.

You may decide to divulge a few names before I disfigure your face."

Laura gritted her teeth when Isaac lowered the poker to her battered, mismatched shoes. The smell of burning leather and a curl of smoke filled the air. When Isaac glanced up at her, smiling in devilish amusement, Laura thrust her foot upward, causing the glowing poker to slam against his shin. Isaac let out a howl of pain and instinctively recoiled. Laura didn't wait for him to recover, she struck out with both legs, forcing the poker against Isaac's thigh.

"You little bitch!" Isaac snarled furiously.

When he lifted the branding iron, as if it were a saber, and lunged toward her, Laura waited until the last possible second to roll sideways. The restraining rope prevented her from wrenching the poker from his clenched fist before it seared her arm.

Laura cried out in pain when Isaac swung wildly again, catching her on the hand. Before she could scoot away, Isaac grabbed another handful of her hair and jerked her head back to an awkward angle.

"Give me his name, damn you," Isaac growled. "If you don't, I swear you won't even recognize yourself in a mirror!"

Laura prepared herself for the inevitable. Nolan's name would whisper through her soul and his darkly handsome image would float above her pained gaze, but she would never divulge his identity to this demented fiend! Despite what Nolan believed about her, and probably still did to this day, she would never betray him.

She loved him more than life itself . . . and this crazed maniac intended to see that she proved it . . .

Twenty-eight

Laura's muffled scream went through Nolan like a sword lodging between his ribs. The calm, deliberate control he maintained when he inched toward the smokehouse crumbled in less than a heartbeat. He wasn't sure just when and how he had become so aware, so sensitive to Laura's needs, to her pain, but 'twas as if the agony she was enduring at Isaac's hands was his own.

Murdering fury consumed Nolan. Snarling, he lowered his shoulder and plowed through the door. Laura lay there like a lamb prepared for slaughter. Her glorious head of auburn hair had been unevenly chopped off. Clumps of tangled curls were strewn across the flagstone floor. The seared fabric on the sleeve of her dress revealed the burn wound above her elbow. Another red welt inflamed her wrist.

Everything civilized and refined inside Nolan rebelled against Isaac's brutality. He remembered the pain he had suffered beneath Isaac's biting whip, but the anguishing memories were overshadowed by the roiling hatred he experienced now. When Nolan saw the demented bastard holding the glowing poker within inches of Laura's bruised cheek, he wanted to tear Isaac apart with his bare hands.

Isaac shifted sideways, dragging Laura up in front of him, holding the poker dangerously close to her throat. A triumphant smile trickled across his froglike lips as he appraised the masked vigilante who had been giving the Crown's men fits.

"Are you afraid I'll scar your dirty little whore?" Isaac smirked as he pinned Laura before him like a protective shield.

A loud squawk erupted in the distance. Nolan never took his eyes off Isaac, but he was reasonably certain Coon and Spark had caught up with Robert Clover and had applied the first coat of tar to the insensitive magistrate's shirt. Before long, Robert would become a great deal more sensitive to the brands of punishment he was known to dole out.

"Take off that mask," Isaac demanded. "I'd like to see the coward who is afraid to show his sniveling face, while he trots around Boston waving his torch of liberty."

"Nay!" Laura railed. "Do not reveal yourself to him!"

With extreme satisfaction, Nolan lifted the black hood and watched recognition dawn on Isaac's harsh features. "A ghost from battles past, Major," Nolan announced. "Is it any wonder all the King's horses and all the King's men couldn't capture a phantom?"

Laura frowned, puzzled by the comment and the tautness she felt seize Isaac's bulky body. She had the unshakable feeling Nolan and this fiendish officer were old enemies.

"I see your fascination for leaving your mark hasn't changed the past few years," Nolan added. "Is that your attempt to prove that all colonials are less perfect than you, Isaac? A pity that my manacles landed a blow across your face during our fiasco in the stockade. 'Tis difficult, no doubt, to look down your broken nose on all of us underlings."

Laura was certain now that Isaac was the one who left his mark on Nolan's back. She also knew how Isaac had come to have a broken nose.

"I thought you were dead," Isaac muttered as he clutched Laura ever closer for his own protection.

"I am," Nolan said with growling menace. "Just like all the men under my command, the ones you sent into the valley of doom, knowing full well they couldn't battle those nests of snipers." Nolan took an ominous step forward. His dark cloak went swirling like a hissing snake. "Let the woman go. Hiding behind her skirts won't save you from me. We have an old score to settle."

Isaac put a stranglehold on Laura and tilted his chin in defiance. "If you try to lay a hand on me, I'll kill her, I swear I will!"

Nolan stalked closer, defying the snarled threat. "And if you lay another hand on her, I'll do worse than kill you."

Laura took advantage of Isaac's preoccupation. She gouged her elbow into Isaac's soft underbelly and dropped to her knees before the poker grazed her cheek. The smell of singed hair followed her to the floor.

Isaac suddenly had no shield of defense, save the poker clutched in his whitened fist. He instinctively stepped back apace when he heard the enraged growl and saw the vicious sparkle in those silver eyes. Isaac panicked, swinging wildly with the poker, but Nolan agilely dodged the attack. He answered with a doubled fist that packed enough wallop to send Isaac stumbling against the wall.

"Bloody damned colonial bastard!" Isaac sneered as he groped for his flintlock. "I'll send you back to the grave where you belong! And you can take your whore with you—"

Isaac managed to draw his pistol, but he didn't have time to fire before Nolan's booted foot slammed into his wrist, sending the weapon cartwheeling across the floor. Laura watched in amazement as Nolan launched himself at Isaac. Both men rolled across the flagstones, exchanging punishing blows, but Isaac—she was happy to see—was no match for Nolan Ryder. He had become fury personified, venting years of frustrated vengeance. The repetitive blows Nolan delivered had Isaac squealing like a stuck pig, and left his crooked nose hanging on the right side of his face.

Laura was certain Nolan meant to beat the fiendish scoundrel to a bloody pulp, and he would have if Coon and Spark hadn't appeared in the doorway.

"Lieutenant Forbes is circlin' back," Spark reported hurriedly. "If we're goin' to get while the gettin' is good, it has to be now."

The murderous haze that clouded Nolan's thoughts evaporated at the sound of Spark's voice. He still wanted Isaac dead. But the repeated warnings of not starting all-out war kept ringing in Nolan's ears. Perhaps he couldn't send this heartless bastard to his grave, but he could damned well prepare Isaac for what frying in hell was going to be like!

Pinning Isaac's flailing arms to the floor with his knees, Nolan reached toward the hearth to retrieve the second poker that set ready and waiting. Nolan laid the glowing iron against Isaac's cheek, branding him for life. Isaac's bellow of pained rage reverberated around the stone walls. When Nolan released him and bounded to his feet to retrieve his mask, Isaac was in too much agony to retaliate.

"I'll hunt you down like the bastard you are!" Isaac railed as he covered the burn on his cheek with a shaky hand. "There is no place on this continent you can hide that I won't find you!"

The sound of an approaching rider put Coon and Spark on alert. They hauled Laura to her feet and severed the rope that bound her to the concrete vat.

"Curse your black soul," Isaac snarled as he came upon his hands and knees. "When I find you, I'll crucify you for this! And your whore right along with you!"

Nolan turned his back on the contemptuous threats. His gaze dropped to the tangle of chopped hair that framed Laura's bruised face. When the pathetic sight of her refueled his fury, Nolan lurched around to brand Isaac once more.

"Nay!" Coon hooted, grabbing Nolan's arm. "He doesn't deserve to live, but you can't afford to kill him, even if he knows who you are. Every rebel in every colony will suffer because of it! Let it go, Nolan. Just let it go!"

Nolan cursed under his breath and wheeled to lift Laura into his arms. He wanted Isaac to pay for what he had done to this spirited beauty, what he had done to an entire company of volunteer militia. But more than that, Nolan wanted to take Laura away to safety, to compensate for the untold suffering she endured in an effort to protect him.

When Coon and Spark scuttled out the door, Nolan cast one last glance at his mortal enemy. Isaac had scrambled to his feet, the red welt clearly visible on his puckered features. Before Isaac could scurry across the room to retrieve the flintlock that lay beneath the concrete vat, Nolan carried Laura away.

Coon and Spark had already managed to reach the concealment of the trees when Nolan stepped outside with Laura clutched protectively in his arms. Nolan was only halfway across the lawn when Peter Forbes thundered toward him, with pistol drawn.

"Halt!" Peter ordered as he drew down on the Midnight Rider's broad back.

Nolan slowly pivoted to see Peter's handsome face illuminated by the flames that consumed the coach house. He set Laura on her feet, nudging her toward the safety of the trees, but she refused to take a step.

Peter gasped in shock when he noticed Laura's singed gown, battered cheeks and mangled hair. "Dear God, what has that maniac done to you?"

A furious growl erupted from the doorway of the smokehouse. Nolan half twisted to see Isaac bracing himself against the doorjamb, his pistol barrel aimed at Laura's back. Nolan grabbed Laura's arm and hauled her behind him, keeping her out of Isaac's line of fire.

Despite the constant warnings of possible repercussions, Nolan drew his pistol and fired. Isaac stumbled forward, clutching his chest, determined to get off at least one shot before he crumbled to the ground. With a curse and a sneer, he squeezed the trigger. The shot danced in the dirt at Nolan's feet. Expelling one last oath, Isaac collapsed, his life's blood spilling out of him.

The crack of Peter's pistol caused Nolan to wheel back around, frantically clutching at Laura, fearing she had been shot. To Nolan's amazement, he saw Peter sitting astride his wild-eyed mount, his smoking flintlock pointing skyward.

Peter stared deliberately at the masked vigilante. "The report I deliver to British headquarters will state Major Stewart was killed in friendly crossfire, while we were trying to apprehend the Midnight Rider . . . and failed . . ."

When Peter holstered his pistol, Laura peered up at him. "Why are you letting us go free?"

"Because Major Stewart was a madman. What he did to you was unforgivable and barbaric." A remorseful smile traced Peter's lips. "And because I admire your special kind of loyalty. You were prepared to die for what you believe in, and to protect your mysterious patriot."

Peter glanced at the ominous silhouette who had not shown fear since the moment he found himself at Peter's mercy. The man simply defied death, as if it were an insignificant probability. Indeed, he hadn't even flinched when Major Stewart's discharging gunfire scattered dirt at his feet!

"I don't have the heart to destroy the rare, unfaltering commitment the two of you have made to your cause." Peter focused his sympathetic gaze on the bedraggled beauty. "You were wrong about me, Laura. I do stand for something, believe in something. I admire remarkable courage, and I have seen it in both of you."

Peter reined his horse around, pausing to glance over his shoulder one last time. "Because my pride was smarting, and I thought I deserved a measure of revenge, I have made it impossible for Laura to return to Boston without risking arrest. For that I'm sorry. It has taken me awhile, but I have come to realize that petty revenge is a dim shadow compared to your unselfish devotion to the rebel cause."

When Nolan and Laura stood there, staring up at him, Peter flicked his wrist. "Be on your way before my patrol returns to discover I let the two most sought-after rebels in the province walk away unscathed."

When Peter galloped off, Nolan lifted Laura into his arms and strode toward the grove of trees. Nolan had considered the young lieutenant to be cocky and shallow. But Nolan couldn't help admiring Peter's noble generosity.

Of course, Nolan gave full credit to Laura for changing Peter's perspectives on life. 'Twas her bravery and devotion that impressed Peter. The man, of course, was still very much in love with Laura, Nolan realized.

Impulsively, Nolan held Laura close and ducked beneath the branches. For a man who was hailed as daring and fearless, Nolan felt himself shaking in the aftermath of what had come unnervingly close to disaster. The thought of losing Laura had rattled him in ways he never dreamed possible. This mere wisp of a woman had gotten to him. Nolan wasn't quite sure what to do about it, either. He had made a dedicated commitment to the rebels in Boston. But Laura couldn't risk showing her face in town again, without being hauled to jail.

Blast it, Nolan had adjusted to leading a double life, but he hadn't figured out how to split himself in half, so he could be two places at once.

Twenty-nine

Nolan set Laura to her feet in the shelter of the trees. To his surprise and amusement she rolled out the heavy artillery and let loose with barrels blazing.

"Damn you, Nolan Ryder, don't you ever do that again!"

Nolan did a double take. "Do what?"

Laura glared at him. "Do what?" she parroted incredulously. "Has it not occurred to you that I have gone to considerable trouble, not to mention enduring several methods of torture, in order to protect your identity and your life? You could be a mite more careful about thrusting yourself in harm's way when bullets start flying!"

Nolan glanced over Laura's head to see Coon, Spark and Ethan creeping closer. He had the feeling he was being lured into one of those one-sided conversations Laura Chandler was famous for— the kind in which she posed leading questions to bring other folks around to her way of thinking.

"Believe me, my lady, I am vividly aware— "

"Are you indeed?" she sniffed. "Then why didn't you do me the simple courtesy of accepting the protection I was offering when Major Stewart tried to shoot you down?"

"I was only trying to— "

"To get yourself killed on my account," Laura cut in crossly. "Don't you realize that would have defeated my whole purpose?"

"Perhaps, but— " Nolan watched his friends prop themselves against the trees, grinning widely when Laura interrupted him again. He had considered her technique amusing . . . unless he found himself on the receiving end of it— as he was now.

"Has it also not occurred to you that you have become the symbol of invincibility that inspires patriots everywhere? Don't you realize your capture and demise would be a severe blow to rebel morale?"

"I suppose— "

"You *suppose?*" Laura persisted, her voice quavering with the effects of sheer exhaustion. "There is no supposition about it. And you should never have revealed yourself to Isaac. Had he lived, you would have become a marked man. You are entirely too reckless and daring . . ."

When darkness spun furiously around her, and her head became light as air, Laura staggered, struggling to draw breath. "I hope I have driven home my point . . . because I fear I'm about to fa— "

When Laura folded at the knees, Nolan caught her up in his arms.

"I second what she said," Ethan added. "And don't forget it, little brother."

"Don't start with me," Nolan warned as he carried Laura toward the tethered horses.

"I didn't start it, she did," Ethan didn't hesitate to point out. "I keep telling you that you take too many unnecessary chances—"

"This conversation is officially over," Nolan decreed, handing Laura's unconscious body over to Ethan. After he had mounted his stallion, he leaned out to hoist Laura onto his lap. "All I want is to return to the cabin and tend to our brave but exhausted little patriot. You will have to make the necessary arrangements, Ethan. Boston is off limits to her. Since she has been forced into exile, accommodations will have to be made— and quickly."

While Ethan mounted his steed, Coon clasped Nolan's hand and grinned. "Take care of that courageous lady of yers," he murmured. "And bring her around for a visit every chance you get. I've grown immensely fond of the lass, and so have my critters."

"You and everyone else around here," Spark said as he stepped into the stirrup. "If I'd had at least one fiancée who could measure up to Laura, things might've turned out differently." His meaningful gaze shifted to Nolan. "She's a rare treasure— one of a kind, in fact."

Nolan stared into Laura's pale face, marveling at the tender emotion and feelings of proud possession that bubbled inside him. For weeks he had wavered back and forth between suspicions about her guilt and hopes of her innocence. This ebony-eyed beauty had proved herself more than worthy of his admiration and respect. To him, she had become the symbol of rebel spirit, the human torch of liberty. The sentimental flame she ignited in Nolan wasn't likely to burn itself out for a long time to come.

Nolan bent to press a kiss to her soft lips and felt the now-familiar stirring of his body, the uncontrollable tug on his heartstrings. Letting Laura go was going to be the most difficult task he had ever undertaken. What would become of this lovely firebrand who could never return to the life she had known in Boston?

Knowing Laura, she would think of something, Nolan told himself as he rode off into the night. Question was: How was he going to be able to think of anything . . . except her . . . ?

Laura awoke to the sound of trickling water and the feel of gentle hands gliding over her. She moaned softly, drifting somewhere beyond the shores of reality. She was so incredibly tired. Her arms and legs felt as if lead weights had been strapped to them, making it impossible to move without exerting tremendous effort. She simply wanted to remain suspended between wakefulness and sleep, savoring the sweeping caresses that soothed her aches and pains.

Nolan smiled tenderly as he bathed Laura in the stream below his secluded cabin. During their journey home, she had slept in his arms, curled up against him with an instinctive trust and contentment that humbled Nolan to the very soul. He was aware of the sacrifices she had made for him, because of him. Considering the disgraceful way he had treated her, he didn't deserve a single kindness.

For years Nolan had sworn up and down that women knew nothing of loyalty and dedication. Laura had proved him wrong a dozen different ways. There was at least one female on the continent who placed honor and patriotism above personal whims. There was one woman who proved her devotion and affection for him with words and deeds. This exceptional female had scattered his cynicism to kingdom come.

When Nolan had completed his ministrations, he carried Laura ashore and wrapped her in a quilt. She was still groggy from exhaustion and hunger when he tucked her in his bed. After pressing a kiss to her forehead, Nolan strode away, leaving Laura to rest.

When Nolan entered the parlor, Spark was sprawled in his favorite chair, puffing on his pipe. The old frontiersman studied Nolan with silent scrutiny.

"I was wrong about the lady," Spark murmured.

"So was I," Nolan agreed.

"Remember what I said about it bein' a damned sight better to eat crow in yer porridge rather than someplace else?"

"Aye, I remember," Nolan mumbled.

"We both got a full helpin', with humble pie served for dessert." Spark sighed audibly. "They don't come better than Laura Chandler."

"Nay, I don't suppose they do."

"What will become of her, do you think?"

Nolan sank down at the table to pour himself a mug of rum. "She's a survivor. I expect she'll succeed at whatever she decides to do with the rest of her life."

"Did you really marry her?" Spark asked after a moment.

"Nay, 'twas a charade for Coon's benefit."

"And to keep the redcoats at bay when they passed by the ferry?" Spark added curiously. When Nolan looked the other way, Spark's amber eyes twinkled with sly amusement. "You could have accomplished the same purpose by pretendin' to be her overprotective brother or a devoted cousin, you know. Funny that you should choose marriage as yer masquerade."

Nolan slanted the gray-haired backwoodsman a glance before sipping his drink. "It seemed the most practical and believable explanation."

"And most natural?" Spark prodded, before blowing smoky halos in the air. "I may be old, boy, but my eyesight hasn't failed me quite yet. When we pack that girl off for safe keepin', she'll be takin' a piece of yer heart with her, even if you'd rather not admit it. But a man can't function properly when part of him is somewhere else. And like I told you once before, 'tis not the deception that's so hard to fight, 'tis the truth. One of these days ye'r goin' to figure out what I'm talking about."

Nolan muttered under his breath, "I have a commitment to Boston, and to every colony that is working toward unification. Until every stamp agent in every community has resigned his commission, Parliament won't repeal this cursed legislation that will stifle our economy worse than it already is."

He stared long and hard at Spark. "What would you have me do? Turn my back on a cause I've risked life and limb to promote? As far as I know, patriotism isn't something you practice at your convenience."

"Aye, 'tis true," Spark agreed.

"Ezra Beecham must make his usual appearance in Boston or he might be linked to Laura's long absence. Peter Forbes might also make the connection if Ezra never shows his face again. And there is still the matter of a hired informant feeding information to British patrols," Nolan reminded him. "If Laura didn't betray me, the traitor is still running loose—"

The coo of a returning pigeon caught Nolan's attention. Before he could rise from his chair, Spark surged to his feet. Within a few minutes, Spark returned with a seemingly blank strip of paper and held it up to the lantern.

"Yer presence is requested tomorrow night in Concord," Spark reported. "The patriots are plannin' a protest to force their stamp distributor out of office."

Nolan plucked the paper from Spark's hand and held it above the lantern, watching it catch flame, curl and crumble into ashes.

Heaving a tired sigh, he bid Spark a good night

and made his way to his room. As he eased into bed beside Laura he found himself torn between a fierce sense of duty and the overwhelming desire to hold onto the woman who had been prepared to sacrifice her very life to protect him.

Hell and damnation, Nolan thought as he instinctively gravitated toward Laura's soft warmth. Spark was right. Nolan was only going to be half a man when Laura went away. He wondered if seeing another stamp agent ousted from his commission, or running interference for revenue cutters would be enough to satisfy him in the weeks and months to come.

It had to, Nolan told himself. 'Twas physically impossible to split himself in half. He could lead a double life, but in order to follow one dream he had to let the other one go. Nolan had a commitment to honor. Laura had made it crystal clear that she expected him to continue working for the cause. She had lectured him on the subject earlier that evening. She had asked nothing in return, even when she deserved a wealth of compensation for the torment he had put her through.

Compensation? Nolan mused before he slumped into deep sleep. Ah, if only that was all he felt compelled to give Laura . . .

Laura came awake with a start and stared up into the darkness. It took a moment for her to orient herself to her surroundings. The last thing she remembered was yelling at Nolan. Then the world tilted on its axis and then turned pitch black.

When she realized she was in Nolan's cabin, she levered up on an elbow to rake the choppy auburn strands away from her face. Her jaw was still sore from the blows Isaac Stewart had delivered. The burns on her arm were still tender, but the wounds had been packed with soothing poultices and sleep had regenerated her strength.

She was, however, so hungry she considered chewing on her fingernails to stave off starvation.

Laura swung her legs over the side of the bed and rummaged through the drawer to locate her shabby, homespun clothes. As soon as she found something to appease her hunger pangs, she needed to tend to an important errand. It couldn't wait a moment longer.

Before Nolan had whisked her away from Boston, believing she had betrayed him and the cause, Laura had not been permitted to conduct her own investigation. However she had had the unmistakable feeling she knew who had been selling information to the British. She didn't want to believe her suspicions. But the time had come to find out for certain— before another trap was baited to apprehend Boston's mysterious Midnight Rider.

Dressed in her urchin's garb, Laura tiptoed to the door and inched it open. The lantern on the table illuminated the vacant parlor. No doubt, Nolan was out doing what he did best— running interference and overseeing rallies. Spark was either tucked in bed or waiting in the shadow of the trees with Nolan's spare mount.

Good, Laura thought as she strode toward the table to rub lantern soot on her cheeks. She didn't want to have to conjure up a reasonable explanation for her jaunt to town. Spark and Nolan would probably ply her with a thousand and one reasons why she shouldn't take the risk of traveling into town.

Laura grabbed a few slices of bread and a chunk of cheese before slipping off into the night. Her destination was the complicated maze of byways in Boston. If her suspicions proved correct— and she was afraid they would— she had been sold out for the want of gold coins.

'Twould not happen again, Laura vowed determinedly. She wanted answers and she wanted the promise that the Midnight Rider would not find his life in jeopardy again!

Thirty

Nolan swung down from his lathered stallion and glanced toward the dimly lit cabin, wondering if Laura had finally roused after sleeping a full day away. If she hadn't, Nolan intended to shake her awake and force her to eat. She had gone too long without nourishment.

"Well, that's one more stamp distributor who won't be slappin' taxes on every deck of cards, newspaper and legal document in this colony," Spark said with satisfaction.

He dismounted and worked the kinks from his back. "Accordin' to the information Ethan sent me this afternoon, the patriots in Charleston organized the largest demonstration the town has ever seen. They carried a British flag with the word LIBERTY written across it. Needless to say, the stamp collector resigned before the crowd degenerated into a mob. 'Tis another example of the influence we've had on our fellow colonists. Folks are speakin' up everywhere to gain Parliament's attention."

Well pleased with the efforts he and other Bostonians had contributed to colonial unification,

Nolan strode toward the cabin. Although he experienced satisfaction in forcing another of the Crown's agents into resignation, Nolan was anxious to check on Laura. These days, his restlessness stemmed from being away from that unconventional female. He had grown accustomed to having her underfoot while they posed as man and wife at Tall Oaks Ferry. The very thought of sending her away, even for her own protection, provoked another brand of restlessness within him. Damnation, the woman had become a habit that was going to be difficult to break . . .

Nolan swore sourly when he eased open his bedroom door to find Laura gone. When he whirled around, Spark blinked owlishly at him.

"What's wrong?"

"She's not here," Nolan muttered. "I swear, I'm going to nail that woman's mismatched shoes to the floor to ensure she stays put!"

"Where would she go?" Spark questioned. "She knows Boston isn't safe for her these days. She's a fugitive of justice."

Nolan expelled a sarcastic snort. "As if a minor inconvenience like that would slow her down. She thumbs her nose at danger."

Spark chuckled as he watched Nolan stalk out the door. "She reminds me of somebody else I know."

Nolan pulled up short, his black cape swirling as he spun toward the gray-haired frontiersman who was grinning from ear to ear. "You find this amusing, do you? Well, 'twas not so long ago that

Laura was lambasting me for being inconsiderate enough to put myself at risk. Now she is the one flirting with danger. How bloody damned funny is that?"

"I would say the lady is head over heels in love with you, hence her self-sacrificin' attempt to protect you from discovery and harm." Spark lifted bushy gray brows and stared quizzically at Nolan. "What's yer excuse for frettin' over her, Nolan?"

Nolan grumbled something inarticulate and stamped to the shed to retrieve his stallion. Damn fool female. If she got herself arrested in Boston, 'twould take a full-scale riot to effect her release. Nolan was contemplating wringing her reckless neck before the magistrate could do his worst.

Now, how in heaven's name was he going to send that woman off, knowing she never gave a second thought to courting catastrophe? She was too independent for her own good . . . and for Nolan's peace of mind.

Scowling irritably, Nolan thundered off. He hoped he could overtake Laura before she reached Boston. If not, he wasn't sure he could find her, because he didn't have the slightest idea where in the hell she was going!

Nolan had ridden only three miles when he noticed the silhouette of "his" urchin scuttling across the bridge. When he spotted the British patrol passing beneath the streetlamp he forgot to breathe. To his anger or amazement— he couldn't decide which— the street-wise waif vanished into a darkened alley.

Dismounting, Nolan tethered his steed and used the same tactic Laura had employed to dodge the British guardsmen. He paused at regular intervals, listening to the footfalls echoing off the cobbled streets ahead of him. Nolan considered tearing off pieces of his cloak to leave a trail he could follow— in case he got lost. Boston's narrow alleys and byways were worse than blazing a path through the wilderness. Here, Nolan was the one who was out of his element, while Laura was scampering through the familiar haunts she had known as a child.

Where the blazes was she going? Nolan asked himself irritably. He followed the muffled footsteps down another dark maze that left him hopelessly disoriented and completely lost . . .

Laura didn't bother knocking on the door of the clapboard shack tucked in the deepest reaches of Boston's honeycombed byways. She surged inside, causing Daniel Goreman to stumble out of his chair in stunned surprise.

"Ya nearly scared ten years off my life, muffin!" Daniel wheezed. "What are ya doin' here?"

Laura surveyed the fine set of clothes that lent testimony to the fact that Daniel was living beyond his meager means. She didn't have to be a genius to guess where he had acquired the funds to purchase his fashionable garments and the stockpile of food that lined the cupboard.

Disappointment etched Laura's battered features when she stared at her long-time friend. "Why, Danny?" Her voice quivered with hurt and frustration. "Why?"

Daniel glanced in every direction except Laura's. "Why what, muffin?"

"Why did you deceive me? I thought you were my dearest, most dependable friend. We grew up fending for each other, providing for each other—you, Martha and I. How could you turn against me like that? What did I do to make you betray my trust in you?"

Daniel scowled and pivoted away, but Laura had come for answers and she wasn't leaving without them. "Although the other agents promote the cause, out of love of country, I paid you from my own allowance for delivering messages through the patriot network— "

"*Yer* allowance," Daniel grumbled, wheeling to face her. " 'Twas the worst part o' it. How do ya think I felt when I saw Miriam Peabody pick ya up off the street and tote ya to her fine mansion on Beacon Hill, treatin' ya like some fairy princess? You've enjoyed every luxury to be had the past five years and I've had more of the same slop.

"And what of poor Martha? She had to make her livin' by whorin', until that British bastard beat the very life outa her. I wanted more than yer handouts! I wanted some respectability!" Daniel all but shouted.

"So you took handouts from the Crown instead," Laura quietly accused. "You nearly served the living symbol of liberty up to the British. The Midnight Rider was wounded because of you, just so you could shrug on a fine set of clothes. Don't you know that clothes don't make the man, Danny?"

"Aye, but—"

"Haven't you learned by now that what's in your heart, the noble ideals you believe in count most?"

When Daniel stared over her head, Laura stalked a step closer, demanding his full attention. "Did it even occur to you that I would have to accept the blame for being a traitor in order to protect you?"

"Well—"

"Do you realize, I have been banned from Boston for life?"

"I'm sorry—"

"You were like the little brother I never had," Laura cut in again. "And Martha was like my sister. I have done all I could to make your life more tolerable, even to the point of asking Miriam to take you in. Even though she was reluctant to take another urchin from the street, she has been funding you. She has always known where most of my allowance has gone and she has never objected to providing for you."

She stamped in annoyance when Daniel continued to stare past her. "Will you kindly pay attention to me! I came here to resolve this matter, once and for all. I will not have you leaking information to the Crown, and I expect no less than your solemn promise, 'twill never happen again."

When Daniel gulped audibly, Laura spun around to determine what was so bloody distracting that he couldn't give her his full attention. To her disbelieving eyes, she saw the Midnight Rider looming in the doorway like a dark, avenging spirit.

"Oh . . . dear . . ." Laura chirped uneasily.

The ominous figure in swirling black cloak pushed away from the doorjamb and strode deliberately inside. "Well, muffin, aren't you going to introduce me to your friend— or whatever you call a half-grown pup who values gold coins more than the sole survivor of his adopted family?"

The Midnight Rider's dominating presence and the threatening growl in his baritone voice sent apprehensive tingles down Laura's spine. It obviously had the same unsettling effect on Daniel, for his thin face turned the color of whipped cream.

"I'm sure Danny is dreadfully sorry and sorely regrets what he has done. Don't you, Danny?" Laura hurriedly prompted.

"Sorely," he warbled, while the masked vigilante towered over him like a black thundercloud.

"And you would never think of threatening the cause of liberty again, would you?"

"Nay, I— "

"And you would never divulge a single name of the contacts you have made in our secretive clan, would you? Not for all the jewels in King George's crown."

Daniel wasn't allowed to respond. Nolan snaked an arm past Laura's shoulder to jerk the lad clean off the floor, leaving him hanging in midair.

"Do you have the slightest idea how much an-

guish Laura has suffered because of you?" Nolan
snarled into Daniel's blanched face.

"N-nay, s-sir," he stuttered, goggle-eyed.

Nolan reached out with his free hand to yank
the cap off Laura's head. "She had sheep shears
taken to her, not to mention the brands burned
on her arm and wrist, not the bruises disguised by
that layer of soot on her face," Nolan snarled.

Daniel hung there, turning another shade paler,
quivering like a tuning fork.

"And let's not forget the way I treated this devoted little rebel because I thought she was the one
who set a trap for me. I put her through hell myself, and all because of a scrawny, disloyal, envious
little brat!"

"I-I'm s-sorry . . ." Daniel whimpered.

"Do you know what happened to the last informant we found in our midst, brat?" Nolan sneered
through his black hood.

"Aye," Daniel croaked. "Tarred and feathered— "

"And left looking like a molting chicken. I ought
to dip you in a vat of boiling tar and hang you
out to dry!"

"He's only a boy," Laura hurriedly defended.

"He's a traitor of the worst sort!" Nolan boomed.

"I'm sorry," Daniel blubbered, slumping in Nolan's fierce grasp. "I only wanted out of this hell-
hole— "

"At Laura's expense," Nolan growled venomously. "She paid the supreme price and she de-
fends you even now. You aren't worthy of her
affection and her friendship."

Nolan set the scrawny lad to the floor— and none too gently, either. "If I even suspect you are leaking information, if you ever break your vow never to repeat your offenses, tar and feathering will be the least of your woes. Do I make myself clear, Daniel?"

"A-aye, s-sir, p-perfectly," Daniel squeaked.

With his black cape whirling around him like a cloud of smoke, Nolan wheeled away. He clasped Laura's hand and towed her along behind him. When Nolan slammed the door behind him, the clapboard shack rattled like chattering teeth.

"You had no right to follow me," Laura grumbled as Nolan half dragged her down the alley.

"No right?" Nolan snorted. "I was afraid you were going to get yourself into trouble— again. You've done that a lot of late."

"And 'tis no skin off your back if I do." Laura pulled up short, causing Nolan to break stride. "You're going the wrong way."

"Then you lead," Nolan scowled. "Honest to God, I don't know how you find your way around this cursed maze."

Laura veered down another dark alley, with Nolan following in her wake. "I made it clear that you do not have to feel responsible for me. 'Tis quite enough that you are the living symbol of freedom— with a good and noble cause to defend."

Nolan screeched to a halt. "I have had quite enough of this noble martyrdom business, thank you very much." He inhaled a deep breath and blurted out, "I owe you an apology for refusing to trust you. I also owe you compensation for the torment you endured."

Laura sighed heavily and turned to face the towering shadow among shadows. "I am trying to make an important point here. You have plenty to do without fretting over me. I am well aware that you feel responsible because I ran amuck."

"Amuck?" Nolan choked incredulously. "Starved, sheared and branded do not qualify as 'running amuck.' You were tortured because I wasn't there when you needed me."

Laura stared up into eyes that glistened like stars through the holes in his black hood. She loved Nolan Ryder more than life itself and had been prepared to prove it. Now he was feeling sorry for her because of Major Stewart's abusive tactics. But Laura didn't want his pity, she wanted his love. Yet that was something Nolan obviously wasn't prepared to give. She had to let go—for his sake, for the sake of every citizen who followed his lead in promoting the rebel cause.

"You seem to have forgotten that I was taking care of myself long before we crossed paths," Laura reminded the fuming vigilante. "I can take care of myself now, too."

"Oh? And what do you intend to do? Take up residence in some other maze of streets in some other city? Picking a few pockets when times are lean?" Nolan smirked at the independent-minded urchin.

"I will only pick British pockets," Laura promised him. "Does that make you feel better."

"Nay, it does not. I will see to arrangements," he insisted.

"Why? Because you know I love you and you feel guilty because you don't love me back? Because you believed I betrayed you and yet I still protected your identity?" Laura stalked closer to poke him in the chest with her index finger. "Well, let me tell you something, masked avenger, I do not want or need your pity. You no longer have to worry about me. As of this minute, I am walking out of your life . . ."

Nolan was still standing there like a thunderstruck imbecile when Laura darted sideways, evaporating in the dark, twisted maze of alleys Boston was famous for.

"Blast it, woman, come back here!" Nolan demanded as he charged after her. "Where will you go? How will you live?"

An echo ricocheted through the darkness, as if it were winding through an endless tunnel. "I'll think of something . . ."

Nolan sputtered several curses and glanced around to find himself alone and totally disoriented. "Bloody damned, bullheaded woman!"

His words rumbled down the abandoned byways and whispered back to him through the confusing maze. Scowling, Nolan stamped down the cobbled streets. After getting himself thoroughly lost, he finally spotted a familiar landmark. The Green Dragon Tavern was just ahead. Once Nolan got his bearings, he aimed himself toward his waiting stallion.

Confound that woman! She had freely offered him love and asked nothing in return. She had risked her own neck to save him and she had come away looking like a half-sheered, branded lamb. She had taken the blame to protect that lanky, half grown brat named Daniel. Now she had spirited away, leaving him with her confident assurance that she would get by—somehow, somewhere.

He should be relieved.

He wasn't.

Nolan bounded onto the saddle and thundered back to the cabin, trying to outrun every memory he and Laura had made together.

Now he could concentrate on setting a smoke screen for every revenue cutter in Boston Harbor. He could intimidate every stamp agent—in every nearby community, in every nearby colony into re-signing from office. He had no other obligations, except to the cause of freedom.

In a day—or four—her memory wouldn't haunt him the way it did now. He would be fine, he tried to reassure himself, and so would she. Laura Chandler was a survivalist.

Nolan repeated every consoling platitude that came to mind at least a half dozen times during his ride to the cabin.

He half believed them.

'Twas a start.

'Twas the best he could manage at the moment, because the only truth that rang clear and true was that . . .

She was gone . . .

Thirty-one

Twilight sprayed across the horizon like the bold slash of an artist's paintbrush, casting slanting shadows through the trees that surrounded the concealed cabin. Ethan Ryder, with his hands stuffed deep in his pockets, stood on the stoop beside Spark. He listened to the scrape of furniture being dragged across the planked floor.

" 'Tis the tenth time in four months," Ethan murmured.

"Eleventh, and I have the bruises to prove it," Spark grumbled before lighting his corncob pipe. "And you haven't seen restlessness until you've seen Nolan when he returns from a raid, demonstration, or one of them fancy Tory parties. The man can't sit still for five minutes before he's up and pacin' like a caged bear. He's worn ruts in the floor. If I dare get within snappin' distance of him, he bites my head off."

Ethan inhaled a courageous breath. "I should go talk to him."

"Take a whip and a chair with you," Spark advised. "He'll chew you up and spit you out if you even look at him the wrong way."

"He simply cannot keep this up!" Ethan insisted. "He has been living on raw nerves and frustration too long. Sooner or later something has got to give."

"Somethin' already has," Spark reported. "He keeps cuttin' the gap so close while the British patrols are on his heels that 'tis a wonder he's still alive. He dares those lobsterbacks to give him their best shot, just to see if he can dodge it. I thought he was a dead man last night." Spark shook his gray head, pausing to listen to the scrape of more furniture. "He won't sleep and he doesn't eat enough to keep a gnat alive. I tried to feed him owl meat so he would wizen up, but as you can tell, it hasn't helped. And he won't listen to reason, either."

Ethan drew himself up to full stature and strode toward the door. "I'm his older brother. He will listen to me."

"Don't bet on it," Spark grumbled before he ambled off to feed the horses.

Ethan forged into the cottage and stopped in his tracks. The parlor now occupied the space where the dining area had once been. The kitchen cupboard was now set against the north wall. Nolan was in the process of organizing the food supplies— by size. Last week Nolan had arranged them by color. Ethan couldn't even remember if the supplies had been in alphabetical order two or three weeks before. Things changed so often around here that 'twas impossible to keep up.

"Nolan, I think we should talk," Ethan declared with firm resolution.

"I'm busy."

"How many times do you plan to change everything around?"

"As many times as it takes," came the gruff reply.

"As many times as it takes to what?" Ethan prodded relentlessly.

Nolan lurched around, a permanent scowl stamped on his rugged features. "Go away, Ethan, you're annoying me. And take that old chatterbox with you. He's driving me crazy."

"You don't have far to go," Ethan said half under his breath.

Nolan bared his teeth and glared at his brother. "I heard that. Unless you came here with news of another assignment, kindly take you're leave. You're bothering me."

"I know where Laura is," Ethan burst out. "I have seen her, in fact. I think 'tis time you did, too."

Nolan raised his ruffled raven head, his dull gray eyes testifying to the dramatic effect the mere mention of Laura's name had on him. "It doesn't matter," he whispered hoarsely. "I'm needed here."

Ethan strode across the room. He confiscated the jar of fruit from Nolan's hand and placed it on the cupboard shelf. " 'Tis over, Nolan."

" 'Twill never be over," Nolan muttered.

"Some things won't be perhaps, but I was referring to our purpose here in Boston. Every stamp collector in every community in every colony has resigned. The protests that began in Boston and spread like wildfire left Parliament with no choice but to back down before a tax rebellion breaks out. We have received word that the Stamp Act has been repealed."

Nolan shook his head slowly. " 'Tis only one skirmish won. Parliament will find new ways to keep these colonies under its thumb. Our English cousins have only retreated to reorganize and regroup. The battle has only begun and you know it, Ethan."

"I realize that. But you will be in no condition for all-out war, if and when it comes, because you are too busy fighting an impossible enemy— yourself." He waited for Nolan to meet his level gaze before continuing. "You're in love with Laura and you haven't been the same since she left. Why don't you simply admit it? You're killing yourself trying not to care."

"Since when did you become an authority on love?" Nolan snorted sarcastically.

Ethan flashed his brother a disparaging frown. "You are being deliberately stubborn."

"Nay, I am being deliberately sensible."

Spark poked his head in the open door to add his tuppence worth. "You're the only one around here who thinks so."

Nolan flung up his arms in frustration. "This from the man who has had three fiancées, none of which he cared to keep?"

Ethan calmly retrieved a letter from his pocket, unfolded it and laid it on the table. "Considering the Crown upped the reward on your head another £100, it might be advisable for you to take an extended vacation. There is a small, out-of-the-way inn on the back roads near the Blue Hills. We have established the ordinary as a relay station for circuit riders. We have a very capable agent managing the inn, but she is extremely overworked. According to her latest letter, she requests assistance. She hasn't complained, mind you, but cooking for travelers and express riders, cleaning the rooms and tending the livestock has become more than she can handle."

Ethan smiled wryly when his brother's dark brows rose like exclamation marks. "We can serve our cause in a variety of ways, Nolan. The inn isn't all that far from Boston. Spark and I could pay regular visits." He turned away, still grinning. "But I wouldn't think of telling you what to do. You are entirely too stubborn for that."

When Spark and Ethan ambled outside, Nolan pivoted to finish stacking the supplies in the cupboard. After a moment, his shoulders slumped and he braced the heels of his hands on the cabinet. He inhaled deeply and felt what was left of his soul shrivel in his chest like a roasted chestnut.

Nolan was well and truly at the end of his tether. He had worked himself into exhaustion. He had ignored what had been missing from his life. He had tried to cure the restlessness that ate at him, by riding down the nights to further the cause. He couldn't eat and he couldn't sleep. He was simply existing in an emotionless vacuum.

And to prove what? he asked himself sourly. That he could survive without the only woman who meant something to him? The only woman who would ever mean anything to him? Aye, he had survived without her . . . and just look at him!

Wheeling around, Nolan stared at the paper Ethan had left on the table. Perhaps . . .

"Oh, to hell with it," Nolan growled as he stalked to his bedroom.

He was tired of trying to get through one day at a time, plodding through the paces of living, as if he were keeping himself on a restrained leash. He hadn't been the same since he met that unusual female and he certainly hadn't been the same since she left. Living without Laura had been hell—pure, simple and endless. And furthermore, the only change Nolan had experienced lately had been from bad to worse.

When Nolan strode outside with his satchels slung over his shoulder, Spark and Ethan were grinning like two fools. "What are you two bumpkins staring at?"

"We're starin' at a man who's finally come to his senses," Spark replied before he puffed on his pipe. "Keep in touch," he insisted. "Ethan has already delivered pigeons to the relay station so you can keep abreast of the goings-on in Boston."

When Nolan passed by, Ethan slapped a marriage license in his hand. "You'll need this. Posing as man and wife on this new assignment simply won't do, Nolan. I want my niece— or nephew— to have a proper name and a proper family."

Nolan spun around so fast he nearly screwed himself into the ground. His jaw dropped like a trap door. He tried to formulate words, but his vocal cords had collapsed in his throat.

"Laura made me promise not to tell you where she was, but prospective uncles have a devil of a time keeping secrets." Ethan's evergreen eyes twinkled. "Congratulations, little brother. Soon, there will be one more Ryder riding for liberty."

Without a word— he still couldn't find his tongue— Nolan lurched around and dashed off to fetch his steed. Hell and be damned! Laura was managing the inn all by herself? Tending to strenuous chores in her fragile condition?

He was going to strangle that woman the first chance she got! She should be taking better care of herself . . . and of their future child!

Daniel Goreman was sprawled on the cot in his crude shack on Boston's back streets when the door crashed against the wall, causing dust to dribble from the woodwork. The Midnight Rider's ominous form appeared like the dark, avenging angel of doom. Daniel squawked in terror and clambered to his feet, preparing to fend off the inevitable attack.

"I didn't tell nobody nothin'!" he insisted before the formidable phantom could land a brain-scrambling blow. "I swear it!"

"Pack your belongings, brat," Nolan growled impatiently. "You're coming with me."

"But I didn't— "

Nolan stalked a threatening step closer. Daniel scrambled away to do as he was told. When his belongings were crammed in his tattered knapsack, Nolan grabbed him by the nape of his shirt and propelled him toward the door.

Without so much as one word of explanation, Nolan propelled the boy through the dark byways. Nolan was proud to say that he only lost his way twice before he found a recognizable landmark.

Thirty-Two

Laura brushed a recalcitrant strand of hair away from her face and massaged the dull ache in her back. After the travelers had departed from the tavern there was so much rum spilled on all the tables that shirtsleeves stuck to it. If she could manage to clean the ordinary before feeding the relay horses for the express riders she might have enough spare time to catch a nap, before preparing supper for incoming guests.

Sweet mercy, she was so unbelievably tired these days. Rising from bed in the morning had become an effort. And as optimistic as she had always been, her spirits kept scraping rock bottom.

Thoughts of Nolan constantly preoccupied Laura. She wondered if she crossed Nolan's mind half as often as his memory flitted through hers. Probably not, Laura told herself realistically. Nolan Ryder was a man dedicated to a noble mission. She had provided temporary appeasement for him while she was underfoot— or rather while Nolan was keeping an eye on her to ensure she didn't betray him. Even if he had never come to love her, he had finally been convinced that she was loyal to their mutual cause.

There was that, at least, Laura consoled herself. And anyway, she was the one who had always spouted off about enjoying her freedom without a man dominating her life. She would manage as she always had— somehow.

Ethan paid regular visits and had kept in constant contact through the carrier pigeons he had left in her care. His latest message was of Peter Forbes's resignation from the army when his tour of duty ended. Peter had returned to England to manage one of his father's country estates. Mercy Reed had not been invited along.

Laura could also anticipate visits from Aunt Miriam. 'Twas enough to see Miriam and Ethan from time to time and catch up on the latest news from Boston.

It had to be enough, because that was all there was. But soon, Laura would have a family of her own to enrich her life.

On that satisfying thought, Laura braced her feet to hoist the water bucket onto a sticky tabletop.

"Put that down before you hurt yourself!"

When the deep baritone voice boomed across the tavern Laura froze to her spot. She swiveled her head around to see Nolan, garbed in buckskins, looming in the doorway. Daniel Goreman was behind him, partially eclipsed by Nolan's powerful frame.

"What are you two doing here?" she asked, astounded.

Nolan didn't respond to the question, he simply grabbed Daniel by the ear and led him into the ordinary. "Clean up this mess and then mop the floors," he ordered. "And when you've finished in here, shovel out the stalls and toss hay to the horses."

"Aye, sir," Daniel mumbled, massaging his ear.

"Then see what you can round up for supper. I'll be back to help you when I've tended to Laura."

Laura found herself scooped off the floor and carried down the hall.

"Which room is yours?" Nolan demanded.

Laura indicated the chamber on the left and found herself deposited on the bed in the time it took to blink. A wary frown knitted her brow as Nolan knelt to fluff her pillow and then removed her shoes.

"He told you, didn't he? Why did he do that? I specifically told your brother to keep silent. Some secret agent he turned out to be," Laura scowled. "That's why you're here, isn't it?"

"I'm needed here," Nolan insisted.

"I told you the first time we— " Laura blushed and glanced away. "I told you that you would not be responsible for consequences. I am managing perfectly fine."

"Really? You look like hell," Nolan observed.

Laura bristled indignantly. "And you think you look a blessed sight better, do you?"

"Nay, and I don't feel any better than I look, either."

Nolan brandished his finger in her bewitching face, noting the evenly clipped auburn curls that now skimmed her shoulders. Each time thoughts of Isaac Stewart's brutality came to mind, Nolan felt the insane urge to dig the bastard up and shoot him again.

"Now you listen to me, woman. I am here to manage this ordinary and see to it that you don't overwork yourself."

"Is that so?"

"Aye, 'tis so," he was quick to confirm.

"Then why is Danny doing all the work?"

"Because someone has to teach that skinny brat to become a responsible, hard-working man. He claims he wants to better himself and I fully intend to be here to ensure he does."

Laura braced upon her elbows and tilted a determined chin, refusing to be intimidated by the towering figure at the foot of the bed. "I will see to Danny, just as I always have. 'Tis no need for you to tarry longer than the time required to feed and rest your horse. You have other obligations to tend to."

"I'm staying," Nolan declared in a tone that brooked no argument. He wasted his breath.

Her delicate chin elevated a notch higher. "I don't want you here."

Nolan peered into her enchanting face and hypnotic obsidian eyes and felt his heart crumble in his chest. Even now, this self-sacrificing beauty was prepared to send him on his way, because she was convinced that was what he wanted, what was best.

She asked for no strings, no commitments— other than his crusade for personal rights and colonial liberty. She didn't realize he hadn't been a free man since the first time he had met her. It had taken a while, but Nolan had finally accepted what he had known all along.

He was hopelessly, completely in love with this vibrant, energetic female.

Nolan had felt it happening the night he watched Laura try to hold back the rowdy mob during the riot. Even when he believed she supported the opposing cause, he had admired her courage. And when she had tried to protect him from harm, by confessing to crimes of treason, Nolan had felt unbearably guilty, humbled by her unshakable devotion.

Laura Chandler was a woman of generous heart and spirited soul. She unselfishly gave everything of herself to serve and protect those she loved . . . And Nolan had given her nothing but heartache, suspicion and mistrust. He knew he didn't deserve Laura's love. That knowledge had prevented him from tracking her down when she left him lost in the honeycomb maze of cobbled streets. He still didn't deserve a woman like Laura, but living without her had driven him to the breaking edge. Just standing there staring at her was enough to rejuvenate his flagging spirits.

"Nolan . . . please . . ." Laura's dark eyes misted with tears, but she was determined to memorize each bronze feature of his face, to emblazon his beloved image on her heart and soul. "I know you are an honorable man who believes he has an obligation to fulfill. But I accepted the possible consequences that first night we spent together, and every night thereafter. I ask nothing and expect nothing from you. 'Tis best that you leave. You must leave. I want you to leave."

She didn't mean it. He knew she didn't. "Why, Laura?"

She muffled a sniff and struggled for hard-won composure. "Blast it, I just explained why."

"Nay, you offered an excuse." Nolan eased down on the side of the bed to catch the betraying tear-drops that tumbled down her cheek. "Now, tell me the real reason you want me to go away."

When Laura's gaze dropped, Nolan cupped her chin in his hand, forcing her to meet his probing silver gaze. "The honest truth, Laura," he demanded softly. "Not the excuses."

More tears welled up in her eyes and rolled down her cheeks. A knot of torment coiled in her stomach when she stared at his cloudy image. She had held all the hurt inside, determined to be strong, to pretend she could cope with every trial and disappointment fate tossed in her path. But having him here, having him so close and yet so unbearably far away shattered her emotions.

"Because you don't love me!" she blurted out miserably. "I can't bear to have you here, knowing the only reason you care to touch me is to satisfy an elemental need that any other woman could appease, knowing you're staying because you feel a responsibility for a child you hadn't planned to have."

Her breath sawed in and out. Laura battled to get herself in hand and failed miserably. "And damn it, I don't know why I suddenly feel the urge to bawl my head off all the bloody time!"

Nolan felt every ounce of tension and restlessness dissolve when he peered down at Laura's flushed face. He could no longer deny what was in his heart and his soul, not if he had any plans of retaining his sanity. He had reached the point where crusading for freedom meant nothing unless his incentive was battling to make a better life for himself and Laura— together. She had become his purpose, his inspiration. Without her, liberty and freedom were words without meaning. As for life, it could get no worse— or better. 'Twas merely an isolated state of existence without hopes and dreams.

As if he were starving to death for a taste of her— and he was— Nolan bent his raven head to take her trembling lips beneath his. 'Twas like sipping from a refreshing mountain spring, appeasing a thirst that had remained unquenched for months. After just one magical kiss, Nolan felt his soul burgeon with revived spirit. He knew beyond all doubt that he couldn't walk away from Laura again— not without leaving the most vital part of himself behind.

After thirty years of restless wandering, searching for that elusive "something" he needed and decided didn't really exist, Nolan had discovered the essence of his world wrapped up in this delightful, free-spirited female. She had become as necessary to him as breathing, as essential as nourishment. She had taught him the true meaning of loyalty, devotion and dedication.

"I can't leave you," Nolan whispered as he raised his head, losing himself in the depths of those dark, thick-lashed eyes.

"Why not?" Laura cried, despite her attempt to regain some measure of dignified control.

"Because, even when I believed the worst about you, I couldn't keep my distance. And when I discovered the truth, I tried to maintain an emotional distance, because I thought you deserved better than I had given you." His hands tenderly framed her face and his silver eyes glittered with feelings he couldn't disguise— and no longer cared to try. "I can't leave . . . because I love you."

Laura burst into another round of sobs. "You're just saying that to make me feel better. But it isn't working. I don't want your pity . . ." She hiccuped, sniffled and blotted her weepy eyes with her sleeve. "Now see what you've done? I'm leaking tears like a bloody sieve!"

Nolan chuckled at the endless streams of teardrops and gathered her in his arms.

" 'Tis not the least bit funny," Laura blustered, swatting at his broad shoulders that shook with silent laughter. "And furthermore, you will never convince me that you're sincere, especially when you are amusing yourself at my expense!"

"Don't underestimate me or my love, imp." Nolan eased away and got down on bended knee. "I'm more sorry than you'll ever know for doubting you. I swear I will never do so again, as long as I live."

Laura marshaled her faltering defenses, touched by his apology, but refusing to believe 'twas more than guilt and pity that brought him here. "You have been forgiven."

"Thank you."

"Now you can leave."

"I'm not going anywhere," he assured her. "I am here to convince you that I'm sincere and hopelessly devoted to you."

"Oh? And how do you propose to do that?" she asked, blinking back another infuriating dribble of tears.

Nolan sank down beside her, deftly unfastening the buttons of her muslin gown. "Somehow, some way . . . I'll think of something . . ."

When he lifted his head and smiled the most tender, most adoring smile she had ever seen etched on his craggy features, Laura's breath caught in her throat. She peered up into those dancing mercury eyes, marveling at the emotion glistening there.

Hands as gentle as a tide whispered over her, cherishing her as if she were a precious gift. Laura felt herself melt beneath his seductive touch, as she always had, as she always would.

"I love you with every beat of my heart . . ."

Nolan whispered the words he had kept locked inside and, when Laura smiled that dimpled smile, he felt a refreshing new breath of life consume him. He touched her and discovered a permanent cure for the restlessness that once plagued him. He wanted to make love to her as softly as the darkness consuming the night, as tenderly as dewdrops touching leaves in spring sunshine.

"Never again doubt that what I feel for you is less important to me than our crusade for freedom," he murmured as he came to her, giving himself up to the wondrous sensations he had found only with her, because of her. "I need you like the day needs light. Without you I'm half, not whole . . . because you have become the very best part of my soul . . ."

When she surrendered to him as sweetly and generously as she always had, Nolan welcomed her into his heart. At long last he found that deep sense of inner peace that had eluded him.

For the first time in years, Nolan felt as if he had come home, as if he belonged.

Laura stared up at him, her heart in her eyes— in his hands. "I love you, Nolan, I will always love you," she softly assured him.

Nolan reveled in the all-encompassing passion that forged their bodies and souls into one. 'Twas a time, not so long ago, when total loss of control was what Nolan feared most. Now 'twas what he loved dearest and best. He needed Laura in ways he had never dreamed possible, wanted her with him from now until long past forever.

She was *Midnight's Lady* . . . the best part of his life . . . his greatest love . . .

Letter to Readers

"Whatever happened to Colonel Jared Daulton Whitaker?"

A full year after the end of the Mexican War, the mystery surrounding the revered colonel's sudden disappearance remains unsolved. Was he killed? Captured and locked away in some remote Mexican prison? Most people agree that it must have been one or the other, or why does the coveted Medal of Valor bestowed upon him remain unclaimed?

Only one man knows the answers to these questions. That man is Jared Daulton Whitaker.

Haunted by his tortured past, Jared Whitaker has assumed a new identity— one he hopes will help him forget the tragedy that sent him running.

And so, he becomes Hunter, the dark and mysterious owner of an expeditionary company which guides pioneers to the rugged Oregon wilderness. It is the perfect existence for the world weary man— an existence which allows no time to build relationships, no opportunities to fall in love. No chance to *feel* . . .

. . . until Tess Caldwell joins his wagon train.

Despite his vow to never again involve himself with any woman, Hunter finds himself unable to ignore this one— especially after he discovers that, like him, Tess has a tragic secret of her own.

Now, he has no choice but to resurrect feelings he thought had died, to confront the very emotions from which he fled, and to face the exquisite agony of love reborn.

"Whatever happened to Colonel Jared Daulton Whitaker?"

The real answer lies within the pages of HUNTER'S KISS.

HISTORICAL ROMANCE FROM PINNACLE BOOKS

LOVE'S RAGING TIDE   (381, $4.50)
by Patricia Matthews

Melissa stood on the veranda and looked over the sweeping acres of Great Oaks that had been her family's home for two generations, and her eyes burned with anger and humiliation. Today her home would go beneath the auctioneer's hammer and be lost to her forever. Two men eagerly awaited the auction: Simon Crouse and Luke Devereaux. Both would try to have her, but they would have to contend with the anger and pride of girl turned woman . . .

CASTLE OF DREAMS   (334, $4.50)
by Flora M. Speer

Meredith would never forget the moment she first saw the baron of Afoncaer, with his armor glistening and blue eyes shining honest and true. Though she knew she should hate this Norman intruder, she could only admire the lean strength of his body, the golden hue of his face. And the innocent Welsh maiden realized that she had lost her heart to one she could only call enemy.

LOVE'S DARING DREAM   (372, $4.50)
by Patricia Matthews

Maggie's escape from the poverty of her family's bleak existence gives fire to her dream of happiness in the arms of a true, loving man. But the men she encounters on her tempestuous journey are men of wealth, greed, and lust. To survive in their world she must control her newly awakened desires, as her beautiful body threatens to betray her at every turn.

Available wherever paperbacks are sold, or order direct from the Publisher. Send cover price plus 50¢ per copy for mailing and handling to Penguin USA, P.O. Box 999, c/o Dept. 17109, Bergenfield, NJ 07621. Residents of New York and Tennessee must include sales tax. DO NOT SEND CASH.